# 1022 EVERGREEN PLACE

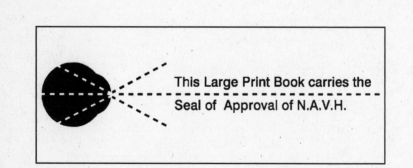

This Large Print Book carries the Seal of Approval of N.A.V.H.

# 1022 EVERGREEN PLACE

## DEBBIE MACOMBER

**WHEELER PUBLISHING**
*A part of Gale, Cengage Learning*

GALE
CENGAGE Learning·

Detroit • New York • San Francisco • New Haven, Conn • Waterville, Maine • London

# GALE
## CENGAGE Learning

Copyright © 2010 by Debbie Macomber.
Cedar Cove Series.
Wheeler Publishing, a part of Gale, Cengage Learning.

Wheeler Publishing Large Print Hardcover.
The text of this Large Print edition is unabridged.
Other aspects of the book may vary from the original edition.
Set in 16 pt. Plantin.

**LIBRARY OF CONGRESS CATALOGING-IN-PUBLICATION DATA**

Macomber, Debbie.
    1022 Evergreen Place / by Debbie Macomber. — Large print ed.
        p. cm. — (Cedar Cove series)
    Originally published: Don Mills, Ont. : Mira Books, 2010.
    ISBN-13: 978-1-4104-2833-2
    ISBN-10: 1-4104-2833-8
    1. Washington (State)—Fiction. 2. Large type books. I. Title.
PS3563.A2364A619 2010
813'.54—dc22                                                    2010030214

Published in 2010 by arrangement with Harlequin Books S.A.

Printed in the United States of America
1 2 3 4 5 6 7  14 13 12 11 10

To Marcia Hestead,
a woman of grace and charm who has
blessed me with her friendship and
many talents

# CAST OF CHARACTERS

**Some of the Residents of Cedar Cove, Washington**

**Olivia Lockhart Griffin:** Family Court judge in Cedar Cove. Mother of **Justine** and **James.** Married to **Jack Griffin,** editor of the *Cedar Cove Chronicle.* They live at 16 Lighthouse Road.

**Charlotte Jefferson Rhodes:** Mother of **Olivia** and of **Will Jefferson.** Now married to widower **Ben Rhodes,** who has two sons, **David** and **Steven,** neither of whom lives in Cedar Cove.

**Justine (Lockhart) Gunderson:** Daughter of Olivia. Mother of **Leif.** Married to **Seth Gunderson.** The Gundersons owned The Lighthouse restaurant, which was destroyed by fire. Justine has recently opened

The Victorian Tea Room. The Gundersons live at 6 Rainier Drive.

**James Lockhart:** Olivia's son and Justine's younger brother. Lives in San Diego with his family.

**Will Jefferson:** Olivia's brother, Charlotte's son. Formerly of Atlanta. Divorced, retired and back in Cedar Cove, where he has bought the local gallery.

**Grace Sherman Harding:** Olivia's best friend. Librarian. Widow of **Dan Sherman.** Mother of **Maryellen Bowman** and **Kelly Jordan.** Married to **Cliff Harding,** a retired engineer who is now a horse breeder living in Olalla, near Cedar Cove. Grace's previous address is 204 Rosewood Lane (now a rental property).

**Maryellen Bowman:** Oldest daughter of Grace and Dan Sherman. Mother of **Katie** and **Drake.** Married to **Jon Bowman,** photographer.

**Zachary Cox:** Accountant, married to **Rosie.** Father of **Allison** and **Eddie Cox.** The family lives at 311 Pelican Court. Allison is attending university in Seattle, while her boyfriend, **Anson Butler,** has joined the military.

**Rachel Peyton (formerly Pendergast):** Works at the Get Nailed salon. Recently married to widower **Bruce Peyton,** who has a daughter, **Jolene.**

**Bob and Peggy Beldon:** Retired. They own the Thyme and Tide B & B at 44 Cranberry Point.

**Roy McAfee:** Private investigator, retired from Seattle police force. Two adult children, **Mack** and **Linnette.** Married to **Corrie.** They live at 50 Harbor Street.

**Linnette McAfee:** Daughter of Roy and Corrie. Lived in Cedar Cove and worked as a physician assistant in the new medical clinic. Now living in North Dakota.

**Mack McAfee:** A fireman and paramedic, who moved to Cedar Cove.

**Gloria Ashton:** Sheriff's deputy in Cedar Cove. Natural child of Roy and Corrie McAfee.

**Troy Davis:** Cedar Cove sheriff. Widower. Father of **Megan.**

**Faith Beckwith:** High school girlfriend of Troy Davis, now a widow. Has moved back to Cedar Cove, where she is renting 204 Rosewood Lane. Recently engaged to Troy.

**Bobby Polgar and Teri Miller Polgar:** He is an international chess champion; she was a hair stylist at Get Nailed. Their home is at 74 Seaside Avenue.

**Christie Levitt:** Sister of Teri Polgar, living in Cedar Cove.

**James Wilbur:** Bobby Polgar's friend and driver. Has been romantically involved with Christie.

**Pastor Dave Flemming:** Local Methodist minister. Married to **Emily.** They live at 8 Sandpiper Way and have two sons.

**Shirley Bliss:** Widow and fabric artist, mother of Tannith (Tanni) Bliss.

**Miranda Sullivan:** Friend of Shirley's. Also a widow.

**Shaw Wilson:** Friend of Anson Butler, Allison Cox and Tanni Bliss. Now at art school in California.

**Mary Jo Wyse:** Young woman who had her baby, Noelle, in Cedar Cove on the previous Christmas Eve, assisted by Mack McAfee.

**Linc Wyse:** Brother of Mary Jo, formerly of Seattle. Opens a car repair business in Cedar Cove. Married to **Lori.**

**Lori Wyse (formerly Bellamy):** From a wealthy area family. Recently eloped with Linc Wyse.

# ONE

Almost home. Grateful for the end of his shift, Mack McAfee turned the corner onto Evergreen Place and approached his house, the duplex at 1022. He felt an instant sense of peace when he saw Mary Jo Wyse working in the garden, taking advantage of the longer days and the perfection of a Pacific Northwest spring. At six, the sun was still bright and the sky had the clean-washed look of early May. Mack had to smile as he watched Mary Jo. The young single mother was his tenant, his friend — and the woman he'd fallen for. Hard. Lovely as ever, she wore jeans and a pink, long-sleeved top that clung in all the right places. Noelle was asleep in a stroller a few feet away.

Mack had delivered the baby last Christmas — or assisted in her delivery; that was probably a better way to put it. He'd just joined the Cedar Cove Fire Department and as the most recent hire, he'd pulled duty on Christmas Eve. It'd been a quiet night until the call from the Harding ranch. A woman said she was about to give birth. Mack had taken a medical course and received his emergency medical technician certificate, but nothing he'd learned had prepared him for the exhilaration of being at a delivery. The moment little Noelle drew her first breath she'd completely won him over.

Noelle *and* her mother had laid claim to Mack's heart.

Mack parked on his side of the driveway and climbed out of the truck. He was outwardly calm, but his thoughts were in chaos. He hadn't seen either of them in two days.

With his help, Mary Jo had planted a small garden, which she tended daily. "Hi," she said, getting up from her knees. She brushed the dirt from her pant legs and glanced at him with a shy smile.

"Hi," he responded. Afraid that Mary Jo would be able to interpret his feelings, he studied the neat row of green seedlings that had begun to poke through the earth. Mary Jo was still suspicious of men, thanks to her experience with David Rhodes, although Mack was making a serious effort to gain her trust. "The garden's starting to take

14

shape, I see."

He crouched down and peeked at Noelle, who slept contentedly with one small clenched fist raised above her head. The baby mesmerized him. For that matter, so did Mary Jo. . . .

"I . . . missed seeing you the past couple of days," she said in a low voice.

That was encouraging. "You did?" He hated to sound too eager since he was treading carefully in this relationship. He'd made a big mistake with her and was almost afraid of what would happen next.

"Well, yes. The last time we talked, well . . . you know."

Mack straightened and nervously shoved his hands in his back pockets.

"You told me it wasn't a good idea for us to continue with the engagement," she said, although he didn't need any reminder.

"That seemed for the best," he muttered. "But —"

Before he could qualify his remark, she broke in. "And you're right, it *is* for the best, especially if you don't love me."

Mack couldn't believe he'd actually said that. "No, I just thought —"

"I understand," she said, cutting him off again. "You proposed because you were trying to protect me."

Mack studied her through narrowed eyes. "You didn't hear from David Rhodes again, did you?"

"No." She shook her head emphatically.

Noelle's biological father had threatened, more than once, to take the baby from Mary Jo, which Mack felt was nothing more than a bluff. But it had frightened her so badly that she'd panicked and decided to move back to Seattle. Back to her brothers, who'd look after her and the baby.

Afraid he was about to lose them both, Mack had suggested marriage. Mary Jo had accepted, with the stipulation that they have a six-month engagement.

That wasn't the *only* stipulation. She'd insisted there be no physical contact. That was when Mack had realized his mistake. Mary Jo's sole reason for moving to Cedar Cove had been to escape her domineering older brothers. In offering to marry her, Mack was doing exactly what they'd done. His motive had been to keep a close watch over her, to protect her. Because he loved her, yes, but without recognizing it, he'd assumed the role her brothers had played in her life. No wonder Mary Jo had stalled their relationship.

A few days after they became engaged, he noticed the shift in her attitude. No longer did she treat him as her friend. No longer could they tease and joke and affectionately kiss. He'd taken control of a situation in *her* life, squelching Mary Jo's first tentative efforts toward independence. She'd said yes to his proposal, but it wasn't because she loved him.

A month passed before Mack figured out what was wrong and why he had to break off the engagement. In his eagerness to be with her, to marry her, he'd nearly ruined everything.

At least neither of them had mentioned the engagement to their families. For his part Mack knew his parents would've seen through his reasons immediately. They would've said it was too soon, pointing out that Mack and Mary Jo didn't know each other well enough to make that kind of commitment.

They would've been right.

Mack had acted on impulse, his desire to protect her overcoming his better judgment. He needed to bide his time and let the relationship progress naturally.

One problem was his lack of finesse with women. Not that he was totally naive, but none of his relationships prior to meeting Mary Jo had been serious or long-lasting.

He did have a sister — two sisters, actually. Only he hadn't known about the second one until a few years ago. He'd always been close to Linnette and had now begun to develop a friendship with Gloria.

Linnette had often advised him on relationships, but she'd moved to some Podunk town in North Dakota. They managed regular phone conversations; despite that, Mack hadn't been smart enough to seek her opinion before he proposed to Mary Jo.

In trying to undo his mistake, Mack had committed another one. He'd broken off the engagement by telling Mary Jo that although he was fond of her, his real love was for Noelle.

It'd seemed like a reasonable approach at the time. He'd hoped to back out of the engagement and save face as he did — let her save face, too. Instead, he'd further complicated an already complex relationship. If there'd been a worse way to handle the situation, he couldn't imagine it.

What he should've done was simply be honest. Whoever said honesty was the best policy — Ben Franklin? Mother Teresa? Bill Clinton? Oprah? — was absolutely correct.

Then the following morning, Mack had been on duty at the fire station. He'd felt uncomfortable and anxious about seeing Mary Jo ever since. This was their first encounter since that day.

"I don't expect to hear from David again," Mary Jo was saying. "Like you said, I think it was an empty threat. He only wants Noelle so he can manipulate his father into giving him money."

Mack nodded. "If you do see him, call me and I'll deal with him." As soon as the words were out, Mack wished he could take them back. The whole point of breaking off the engagement was to let Mary Jo solve her own problems.

Instead of responding, she occupied herself with rearranging Noelle's blanket.

Mack rocked back on his heels and removed his hands from his pockets. He wanted to groan. Why couldn't he keep his mouth shut? "I guess I should check the mail," he said with a sigh. He'd just headed over to the mailbox when Mary Jo called him back.

"I learned something about those letters."

"Letters?" Mack asked in confusion.

"The ones I found under the floorboards in the closet."

That box of World War II letters had completely slipped his mind. "Tell me," he said quickly.

"I'd rather show you."

"Okay."

"Would you like to come by for dinner?" she asked. She bit her lip, as if she wasn't confident that inviting him was such a good plan, after all. "I don't want you to feel any obligation. . . ."

"No, I want to," he said with more enthusiasm than he'd intended. "I mean, if you're sure about having me over."

"I am."

Mack checked his watch. "It's quarter after six now. Shall we say in an hour?"

"An hour," she agreed.

His spirits lifted. Maybe he *hadn't* ruined everything the way he'd feared. "See you then," he said with a relieved smile.

"Okay." She smiled back, and he felt a sudden hopefulness.

Not until he was on his porch steps did it occur to him to ask if there was anything he could contribute. A salad? No, wine was probably better. He turned and, to his surprise, found Mary Jo watching him. Looking guilty, she glanced away.

"What can I bring?" he asked. "For dinner."

She gave a half shrug. "I've got chicken-and-vegetable stew in the Crock-Pot and I'm making biscuits. I can't think of anything else."

"How about a bottle of wine?" When she

nodded, he said, "See you around seven."

After collecting the mail, Mack let himself into his side of the duplex, closed the door and breathed deeply. His sense of excitement was nearly overwhelming. In less than an hour he'd have a chance to make up for the foolish, clumsy way he'd ended the engagement — with a lie. He'd have a chance to start again, to reestablish their relationship on a more equal footing.

Fifteen minutes later, Mack had showered, shaved and changed clothes. He threw a load in the washing machine and set the dials. With another half hour to kill, he walked restlessly from room to room. This evening was important, and it could set the tone for many evenings to come.

In the past he'd often visited Mary Jo and Noelle. She'd regularly invited him over but not, he now suspected, out of any great desire for his company. Mary Jo was simply accustomed to having people around. Until recently she'd lived with her three older brothers.

She'd cooked for her family, although Mack knew they did their share of household chores. She was used to preparing meals for three hungry men; no wonder she always made enough to feed a family. So it was easy to invite an additional person,

Mack told himself. She didn't make extra with him in mind.

Not that he was complaining. Far from it. He liked spending time with her, being part of her life. Entertaining Noelle — that was his job most nights. He held and played with the baby while Mary Jo finished dinner preparations, and then later, they sat together and watched television or played cards. She had card sense, as his father would've put it. They talked, too, but not about anything deep or too personal. They'd talk about what they'd read or seen on TV, or mutual friends and acquaintances in Cedar Cove. Both were careful to avoid religion and politics, although he guessed they held similar views.

At the end of the evening, he'd kiss her good-night. After their so-called engagement, those kisses had become more brotherly than playful or passionate. That was what had initially convinced him the engagement was all wrong.

Considering the way David Rhodes had treated her, he understood that Mary Jo would be wary of entering a new relationship. Her trust in men — and in her own ability to judge them — had been badly shaken. But surely she'd come to recognize that Mack was a man of his word. That he genuinely cared for her and the baby and would never do anything to bring them harm.

He worried that he wasn't as good-looking as Rhodes. He wasn't as smooth, either, but that probably didn't attract Mary Jo anymore, not after being involved with a player like David. Unlike Rhodes, Mack wasn't tall, dark and handsome. He was just under six feet and his brown hair had a hint of auburn in it, which accounted for the sprinkling of freckles across the bridge of his nose. He was an average guy, he supposed. He might work for the fire department, but he doubted anyone would select him for one of those hunk calendars.

Mary Jo, however, was beautiful. He wasn't surprised that someone like David Rhodes would notice her. Mack had long decided that her beauty was part of the problem; it put her out of his league. He was sure she could have her pick of any man she wanted. All Mack could hope for was that, given enough time, she'd want *him.*

When he knocked at her front door, Mary Jo immediately opened it, almost as if she'd been waiting for him, although that was unlikely to be the case. Noelle cooed from her seat and waved her arms, and he chose to see that as a greeting just for him.

"How's my girl?" he asked. He handed Mary Jo the bottle of chilled pinot grigio he'd taken from his fridge, then walked into the living room and reached for the baby. As he lifted her in his arms he grinned at Mary Jo. "I've only been away a couple of days and I swear she's grown two inches."

"She changes every single day," Mary Jo said. "I see it, too."

He tickled Noelle's chin and she gurgled back, which made him laugh.

"There are those World War II letters," Mary Jo said, pointing at the coffee table.

Mack looked away from Noelle long enough to glance at the cigar box sitting there. He could tell it was faded and a little shabby. "How many letters were inside?"

"Dozens. It didn't seem like that many when I found them, but the paper is really thin."

She'd been enthralled by her discovery. Mack was interested, too — who wouldn't be? These letters were a direct link to history, a personal connection to some of the most momentous events of the previous century.

"The article I read on the internet called this paper onionskin and it said the letters were referred to as V-mail." She smiled at that. "I think the *V* stands for *victory*." She sat on the sofa and Mack joined her, still holding the baby. He divided his attention between Mary Jo and Noelle.

"I've read them twice. They're addressed to Miss Joan Manry."

"I remember." Mack recalled the recipient's name, now that she mentioned it, although not the sender's. He cocked his head but couldn't read the return address. "Who are they from?"

"His name is Jacob Dennison and he was a major stationed in Europe during the war. Some of his letters have black marks on them, but a lot of them don't have any at all. I assume those marks were put there by censors. You know, I read that there were over two hundred censorship offices. Their job was to ensure that military personnel didn't reveal anything sensitive in their letters." She paused. "Of course, that doesn't explain why these letters were hidden."

"I'm sure that had more to do with Joan's circumstances than Jacob's," Mack said wryly.

"Well, even with the black marks, I've been able to follow quite a bit. They're fascinating. I can hardly wait for you to read them."

Mack nodded, caught up in her excitement.

"Joan worked at the Bremerton shipyard," Mary Jo went on, "and she lived with her older sister. Elaine — that's her sister — was married and her husband was somewhere in the South Pacific. I gather Joan met the major at a USO dance and they started writing after he shipped out to England."

Mack gently bounced the baby, to Noelle's evident approval. "I'd like to take a look at the letters," he said.

"Here's the first one. I put them in chronological order." She unfolded the letter carefully and handed it to him.

Maj. Jacob Dennison
36354187 Hgs. Co.
Hgs. Cond. 1st
Service Platoon.
U.K. Base APO 413%P>M> N.Y., N.Y.
January 15, 1944

Dear Joan,
How's my best gal? My only gal! I just got another letter from you. When I was given the envelope and saw the return address it gave me the biggest smile. I read it three times because it made me feel even closer to you. I'm awfully homesick, but I close my eyes and see

your face and everything seems better. I think about you a lot; it helps me when I can remember familiar places and people I care about.

Until I joined the Army I'd never left the state of Washington. My mom and dad write me, too. My brother's in the South Pacific and is seeing a lot of action. Sometimes I wish I'd joined the Marines instead of the Army because I'm eager to do my part to end this war. No one knows when the invasion's going to happen. Soon, I hope. They have us training day and night. I'm getting to where I'm almost used to leaping out of an airplane. That sounds nuts, doesn't it? My mother always said I was a daredevil. I guess she was right.

I'm glad you got the Christmas gift I mailed you. Sorry it arrived late. I hope that when Christmas rolls around this year I'll be with you. I thought about that a lot when I heard Bing Crosby on the radio singing "I'll Be Home for Christmas."

I don't know what to say about Elaine. I feel bad that she's causing you problems. I wish I could figure out what she objects to about me. Would it help if I wrote her a letter? I'll do whatever you say — anything other than not have you as my girl.

I'll write more when I can.

Hugs and kisses,<br>Jacob

Mack finished the letter and set it aside. He read the next two in quick succession.

"Aren't these letters *wonderful?*" Mary Jo was watching his reaction avidly.

Mack had to agree. "Yeah, they are." He reached for another.

Maj. Jacob Dennison
36354187 Hgs. Co.
Hgs. Cond. 1st
Service Platoon.
U.K. Base APO 413%P>M> N.Y., N.Y.
March 3, 1944

Dear Joan,
How's my best gal? I got a day pass earlier in the week and went to London and ate fish and chips. They were the most delicious I ever tasted, and that's saying something, since I was born and raised near Puget Sound. My dad loved to fish and my mom fried up the best trout you can imagine. This fish was different and they served it wrapped up in

newspaper. I even took the train to Stratford and got to see one of Shakespeare's plays. Did you ever see *King Lear?* I'm not much for that fancy language, but it was a good story and it broke up the monotony. Some of the guys got drunk and didn't get back to base on time. Don't get me wrong — I drank my share of brew, but I was smart enough not to overdo it.

Thank you for writing. I can't tell you how much your letters mean to me. The instant I see 1022 Evergreen Place on the corner of the envelope, my spirits rise. Meeting you was the best thing that ever happened to me. I love you, Joan. You said it's too soon for me to tell you that, but I know what I feel. It isn't just being away from home like you suggested, either. This is real. You said you can't really get to know a person through letters. I think you can. I feel as though I know you, and can you honestly say you don't know me? When I get home, God willing, I'll ask you properly, down on one knee, to be my wife.

I'll write again tomorrow. Write me again, too. I'll keep in touch as much as

I can. It's lights-out so I'll sign off for now.

Hugs and kisses,
Jacob

Mary Jo leaned forward slightly. "Were you able to find out anything about the previous house owner?" she asked. "I want to learn whatever I can about Joan and Jacob."

Mack had forgotten that he'd volunteered to check with "the landlord" — although it was hardly necessary, since he owned the duplex. He regretted now that he'd lied to Mary Jo about that. He knew she'd be upset at the low rent he was charging her if she realized *he* was her landlord. She'd feel he was patronizing her or maybe that he expected something in return. Mack suppressed a despairing sigh. He just kept digging himself a deeper hole. One of these days he'd have to tell her the truth — and he would, when the time felt right. Although he wasn't quite sure how he'd recognize that moment of clarity . . .

"I did say I'd look into that, didn't I? I apologize, but I haven't got to it yet."

"That's okay," she said, accepting his answer easily enough. "Ready to eat?"

He saw that the table was set, with the

pot of stew and a plate of biscuits placed in the middle of the table, wine and water glasses by each plate.

"I fed Noelle before you got here," she told him.

That was his cue to put the baby back in her seat and sit down at the table, which he did. Mary Jo was an excellent cook — as good as his mother, and *that* was a real compliment. Her own parents died when she was still in high school, and she'd taken over kitchen duties, more out of necessity than desire. Still, she seemed to enjoy cooking and took pride in putting together meals that were nutritious as well as appealing.

He was no slouch in the kitchen, if he did say so himself, but until she'd moved in next door, his meals had been haphazard affairs. Other than when it was his turn at the firehouse, he never really bothered with cooking. He usually relied on frozen microwave dinners or the various fast-food choices available in Cedar Cove. He didn't make a habit of dropping by unannounced at his parents', but whenever he did, his mother always insisted he stay for dinner. Mack didn't often refuse.

"Hey, this is *great*," he told Mary Jo after the first bite. And it was. Tender chunks of chicken, fresh vegetables that weren't cooked to mush, lots of flavorful broth. The biscuits that accompanied it melted in his mouth. "A guy could get used to eating like this," he said jovially.

Mary Jo didn't comment.

Oh, boy, he'd done it again. Would he never learn? "I, uh, didn't mean that the way it sounded. I just wanted you to know the meal's delicious. . . . I'm not suggesting anything else."

Mary Jo carefully set her fork next to her plate. "I was afraid of this."

"Afraid of what?" He swallowed before he'd finished chewing, and the biscuit nearly stuck in his throat.

"It's still awkward between us, don't you think?"

He nodded, grabbing his wineglass and gulping down a mouthful.

"You don't need to work so hard, Mack."

He frowned, unsure what she meant.

"We're friends, right?"

"Friends," he repeated.

"Good," she said. She seemed satisfied. "Friends are comfortable with each other. We shouldn't worry that what we say is going to be taken wrong or out of context."

He coughed and nodded again.

"Then relax and enjoy yourself. Stop worrying that I'll be offended, okay?" She sent him a dazzling smile.

"Okay," he said. This comment was supposed to put him at ease, and yet her words had the opposite effect. Yes, they were friends, but Mack had hoped they would be so much more.

# TWO

It still felt strange, yet, oh, so wonderful, to wake up every morning with his wife beside him. Linc Wyse had grown accustomed to married life with a speed that astonished him. He'd been caught up in a whirlwind from the moment he met Lori Bellamy.

Less than two months ago, her car had broken down on the highway. Linc had been in Cedar Cove checking up on his stubborn little sister, who'd moved out of the family home and into a duplex next door to Mc-Afee. The firefighter had delivered Noelle, and next thing Linc knew, the guy was her neighbor. He seemed to be over at Mary Jo's far too often, and Linc considered it his responsibility — his *duty* — to make sure nothing untoward was going on. He wasn't entirely comfortable with the situation his sister had gotten herself into now. One man had already taken advantage of her, and Linc wasn't letting *that* happen again. He didn't care how many times Mary Jo told him to butt out and to stop interfering.

Lori made a faint, waking sound, then yawned and arched her back before snuggling into Linc's arms. "Is it morning?" she asked, still groggy with sleep.

Linc kissed the top of her head. Mornings with Lori were the very best of his life. "So it seems."

"I'll make coffee." She leaned over to turn off the clock radio, cutting off a traffic report in midsentence.

When she started to toss aside the covers, Linc stopped her. "No need to get up so soon, is there?" He nuzzled her neck and slipped his arm around her, bringing her closer. She was warm and soft and infinitely lovely.

"I didn't think you were the sort of man who liked to linger in bed," Lori teased as she slid her arms around his neck. Her breasts grazed his chest and he briefly closed his eyes at the sensation.

"I never used to be," he murmured. "Until now." She had no idea how true that was. As the oldest, Linc had held the family together after his parents died — the family and the business.

He was the first one at the car repair shop every morning and the last one to leave at night. All he'd done was work and worry. He worried about his family, about the business, about the economy. If there was something to lose sleep over, Linc was ready to take it on.

Then he'd met Lori.

His relationships with women had always soured and he'd never been able to figure out where he'd gone wrong. But it was definitely a pattern; he'd meet someone, things would be great for a while and then it was over. He didn't understand it. Mary Jo claimed he was too "bossy" and "controlling" but she wasn't exactly a relationship expert, so he ignored her opinion — and the cycle of ever-shorter romances had continued. But all of that changed the night he'd stopped to help when Lori's car had broken down.

He'd nearly driven past. He'd already put in a long day and he was still annoyed by the heated argument he'd had with his sister. But he'd stopped, because if it was Mary Jo stranded there on the highway Linc would want someone like him to help. So he'd pulled over. Lori's car had run out of gas and he'd taken her to a service station. They'd ended up having dinner together, and then spent hours talking during the next few days.

Linc had learned that Lori had recently come out of a broken engagement — to a man who'd gone to prison for theft. Not surprisingly, it had left her disillusioned. Linc knew the feeling well. She was an old-fashioned kind of woman who expected a man to behave honorably. He was an old-fashioned kind of guy who demanded honor from himself and others. On impulse, before they could talk themselves out of it, they decided to get married.

It was crazy. It was wonderful. Linc had never in his life felt this happy and carefree.

"Why are you smiling?" Lori asked, rising up on one elbow to study his face.

Just looking at his wife made his chest tighten. "I never in a million years thought I'd sleep in a canopy bed under pink sheets and be okay with it." He paused. "*More* than okay."

Now it was Lori's turn to smile. "I told you it wouldn't be so bad, didn't I?"

"Not that I remember. What I recall is the promise you made when you lured me to your bed."

"Lured you?" She raised her eyebrows. "As *I* recall, you hauled me into your arms, slammed my bedroom door and carried me across the room caveman-style."

"Caveman? Please."

"He-man, then."

He-man, he could live with. "After that, I didn't even notice the canopy, which was what you intended all along."

"Do you mind it now?" she asked.

Linc shrugged. He'd lived with his brothers for so many years, he didn't pay attention to all the froufrou stuff women had. Mary Jo probably had it, too, but she was his baby sister, so that was different.

*Everything* about Lori had his attention from the moment she'd stepped out of her car that first evening. And when she'd emerged from the bedroom in that black silk piece-of-nothing on their wedding night . . . The memory still excited him.

"I'll make coffee," she volunteered again when he didn't respond.

"Not so soon," he said, kissing her until they were both breathless. He watched as her eyes widened and she realized what he wanted. "Linc! I have to get ready for work!"

"You won't be late," he promised as he urged her onto her back and brought his mouth to hers.

Ah, yes, marriage had a lot to recommend it, and Linc was going to enjoy every minute.

A half hour later, having forgone coffee, Lori was rushing to get dressed when Linc stepped out of the shower. Her makeup — not that he felt she needed it — was done. She wore a business skirt and was pulling on a soft blue sweater. "What are you doing today?" she asked as she adjusted the neckline.

"I'm signing the closing papers on the garage."

She looked surprised. "The deal went through already?"

Linc stood in the doorway to the tiny bathroom, a towel wrapped around his waist. "It sat empty for two years and the owner really wanted to sell." Linc planned to open a branch of the family business, Wyse Men Auto and Body Shop — formerly *Three* Wyse Men — in Cedar Cove. His brothers were competent enough to handle everything in Seattle. By starting a second shop, he was giving them an opportunity to succeed on their own. Besides, one of the three needed to be close at hand to keep an eye on Mary Jo, although he had to admit that was more of an excuse than a reason. Linc liked living in Cedar Cove.

Okay, to be honest, he liked living with Lori.

"I only work until three this afternoon," Lori said, moving about the room. She slipped her arms into a black jacket that didn't match the skirt but looked good with it, then pinned a cameo to the lapel. Even Linc, most comfortable in a T-shirt and jeans, recognized that Lori had a real sense of style. He supposed it was why she worked in a high-end dress shop in Silverdale. She dabbled in designing, too, and knew how to sew.

"I'll get groceries on the way home." She brushed her hair, slung her purse over her shoulder and was about to leave.

Linc grabbed her hand. "Aren't you going to kiss me goodbye?"

A smile made her eyes sparkle mischievously. "No, kissing leads to other things and I'm already late."

"One kiss," he begged. "Please?"

"Linc," she groaned, but then complied.

Her kiss left him weak in the knees. He had to clear his throat before he could speak again. "I'll be back from the title company around four."

"Great. I'll pick up a bottle of wine so we can celebrate."

"Good idea."

"See you later," she said, and kissed him again, letting her mouth linger over his. She was well aware of what she was doing to him, and he nearly staggered backward when she abruptly broke away.

"You're an evil woman, Lori Wyse," he called after her.

Linc headed out fifteen minutes after Lori. He had several stops to make, plus he needed to drive into Seattle and meet with his brothers about the business there. By the time he returned to Cedar Cove, he had to sign the papers for the garage. That all took longer than he'd expected and it was almost five when he'd finished.

Linc collected the keys to the garage and went home, hoping to pick up Lori and take her down to see the garage. He had a notebook filled with ideas on how to build the business. He wanted to tell her about them, and above all, he wanted to share this moment with her. They'd take the wine over to the property and toast there.

When Linc arrived home, he saw a black Town Car parked in the very spot where he normally left his truck. Even before he reached their apartment, he heard raised voices.

"Don't say that, Daddy!" Lori cried. She sounded close to tears.

Oh, boy. Lori hadn't told her family yet that they were married. Linc didn't understand why she'd delayed, but the decision was hers. When he'd asked her about it, Linc could see how uncomfortable the subject made her, so he'd dropped it.

Now her father was upset, and frankly, Linc didn't blame him. He'd do his best to set things straight.

Squaring his shoulders, Linc opened the door and walked into the living room. Lori stood next to the fireplace, her father — a balding, heavyset man — no more than a foot away. One of his hands was raised, as if he'd been wagging his finger at her. The other was clenched at his side. At Linc's entrance, they both turned to stare at him.

"Hello," Linc said, hoping he sounded calm and composed. "You must be Lori's father. A pleasure to meet you, Mr. Bellamy." He thrust out his hand, which the older man ignored.

Instead, Leonard Bellamy turned back to his daughter. "Is that the man?"

"Daddy, this is my husband, Lincoln Wyse. Linc . . . this is my father."

Linc walked over to Lori's side and placed his arm protectively around her shoulders.

Bellamy continued to ignore him. "You've pulled some stupid stunts in your life, but *this* takes the cake."

"Mr. Bellamy, I realize —"

"If I want to hear from you, I'll say so," the older man shouted. "Don't you have any sense, Lori Marie? You married this man and you don't even *know* him? What about his family? Who are his people?"

"If you'd allow me —"

"You," Leonard said, pointing an accusing finger at Linc, "mind your own business. This is between me and my daughter."

Lori squeezed his arm, indicating that Linc should do as her father said. He didn't like it, but he clenched his jaw and waited impatiently for the other man to get to the end of his rant.

"First, you were engaged to that . . . that felon."

"Geoff was a mistake."

"A mistake!" Leonard shouted. "So that's what you're calling him. He was a major embarrassment to the whole family. How do you think your mother and I felt when we had to cancel the wedding? We couldn't even say it was wedding-day jitters or make up a decent excuse. Oh, no. Geoff's name was plastered across the front page of every newspaper on the Kitsap Peninsula. Everyone in the entire county knew why the wedding was canceled."

"I . . . I didn't know what kind of man Geoff was," Lori said, defending herself. Her voice quavered with mortification. "I agree I misjudged Geoff, but you liked him, too, remember?"

43

Her father brushed off her comment. "What makes you think you have better judgment this time?" he demanded. "How long did you two know each other, anyway?"

"Long enough," Linc said, unable to remain silent.

"I asked you to stay out of this," Bellamy shouted. He started pacing, then stopped and glared at Lori. "What were you thinking?" Briefly he closed his eyes. "What on earth possessed you to marry a *stranger?*"

"Daddy . . ."

"Can you imagine how your mother felt to have a friend — mind you, a *friend* — announce that you'd recently married?"

"Daddy, please . . ."

"You couldn't have told us yourself?" he bellowed, refusing to let Lori explain.

"Mr. Bellamy," Linc said, trying again.

Lori covered her face with both hands and began to sob.

"You've really done it this time," Leonard said. "You've consistently shown poor judgment, and worse, you never seem to learn from your mistakes."

Frowning, Linc took a step forward. He understood why Lori's father was upset, but the man was crossing the line now.

"No one in the family has ever done

anything like this. Your mother's beside herself."

"I'm sorry," Lori sobbed.

"As you should be. You made one stupid mistake and then you immediately followed that up with another." He whirled around and studied Linc through narrowed eyes. "A mechanic, Lori? For heaven's sake, why would you marry a mechanic? It isn't embarrassing enough that our daughter elopes without a word to her family, but then you have to marry a man with oil under his fingernails, an uncouth, uneducated . . . mechanic? What's the matter with you, girl? Don't you have a brain in your head?"

"Mr. Bellamy," Linc said, his voice hard. It was one thing to belittle him, but Linc wasn't going to stand idly by while Lori's father chastised her as if she were a child. "I can see why you're upset. I'll be the first to admit that we rushed into this marriage, but that doesn't give you the right to come to our home and ridicule my wife."

"*Your* home?" The other man's face reddened.

Lori's hand tightened around Linc's forearm and she squeezed hard. "This building belongs to my parents," she whispered. "I don't pay rent."

45

Linc hadn't known that — and wished she'd told him. "If you want us to move, we'll be out by the end of the month," he offered.

"I want you out, all right," Bellamy raged, jerking one thumb at the door. "Out of my daughter's life."

That wasn't going to happen. Rather than argue, Linc shook his head. "Lori and I are married."

Her father snorted contemptuously. "You saw a good thing, didn't you? Lori was easy prey. She was at a low point in her life and you decided to take advantage of her because of her name."

The name meant nothing to Linc. "Bellamy?"

"Lori comes from a wealthy family and you were trying to —"

"Now, just a minute here!" Despite his efforts, Linc was fast losing his temper. "I don't need your money *or* your name."

Bellamy scowled back at him, his expression filled with disbelief and disdain. "We'll see about that." His threat hung heavy in the air.

Linc wouldn't allow Bellamy to intimidate him. "You might own this building, but you don't own your daughter. I suggest you leave now, before we both say or do something we'll regret."

Bellamy jabbed his index finger at Linc several times, then whirled around and stormed out the door. He slammed it so hard the windows rattled.

The room seemed to vibrate with tension. Lori burst into tears, and Linc put his arms around her. He held her tight against him, his shirt absorbing her tears as he gently stroked her hair.

"My mother's friend Brenda owns the dress shop and . . . she must've told Mom. She promised she wouldn't say anything until I'd spoken to my parents but . . ."

"It's okay, Lori," Linc whispered into her hair. "We should've told them sooner."

"I know . . . I know — but I was afraid of what my father would say, what he might do. . . ."

"He'll get used to the idea soon enough." Linc said, hoping that was true.

"You don't know my father."

"We'll give him time," Linc said. "I'll do everything I can to prove to your family that I'm going to be a good husband."

"It won't matter," she whispered. "Daddy will never forgive me. . . . He was still angry about Geoff and — and then I married you."

"Do you want to end the marriage?" he

felt obliged to ask.

"No, never," she said, her arms tightening around him.

"Me, neither," Linc murmured, and he thought he felt her smile against his shoulder. "Come on," he said, easing her out of his arms. "We have some celebrating to do."

She looked up at him blankly.

"I signed the final papers for the garage this afternoon, remember?"

Lori smiled weakly, then slipped her arms around him again. "I don't care what my family thinks. I'm grateful I married you."

Linc was grateful, too. Swinging her into his arms, he moved toward the bedroom.

"Will it always be like this?" she asked, sighing as she kissed his jaw.

"I hope not," he said with a chuckle. "This much happiness just might kill me."

# THREE

Staring at the phone on his desk, Will Jefferson mentally prepared to call Shirley Bliss — again. Twice now she'd come up with a convenient excuse to turn down his invitations. Either the woman had an incredibly active social life or she wasn't interested. Without being vain, he found that difficult to believe. Okay, he was a *little* vain. He knew he was a good-looking charmer — smooth but not too smooth. Smart, successful and sexy, the latter according to more than one woman.

He was also persistent. He hadn't come this far in life without a healthy dose of good old-fashioned grit. He'd returned to his hometown, purchased a failing art gallery and was determined to make a fresh start.

Admittedly he'd made his share of mistakes. If he had it to do over again, he would've done certain things differently. For one, he would've paid a lot more attention to his kid sister's best friend, Grace.

Years later Grace did attract his notice, but by then it was too late. They'd reconnected shortly after Will learned of Dan Sherman's death. He'd sent her a sympathy card and, on a whim, added his email address. Not long after that, they'd begun a friendly correspondence.

Will hadn't known about the crush Grace had on him while they were in high school. That information had soothed his ego. His marriage was deteriorating; he and Georgia were just going through the motions. About five years into the marriage he'd stumbled into an affair with one of the women from his office. Naturally he regretted it and begged Georgia to forgive him. She did, and he was grateful. Yet his indiscretion had always been there between them, like a bad break that had never totally healed. A broken limb could remain weak forever after, unable to tolerate pressure or stress.

Her forgiveness hadn't been complete, he realized now. It was as if she'd been waiting for him to do it again.

And he had.

But Will didn't blame Georgia. After all, *he* was the one who'd strayed. Still, his wife had given him the cold shoulder for so long that when a friendly young waitress flirted with him, he'd been flattered and receptive. Sally was young, attractive and impressionable, and he'd responded.

Georgia knew about it. She had to have known, but she didn't say a word and neither did he. Sally wanted him to leave Georgia and he might have if not for the fact that Georgia was diagnosed with breast cancer. He couldn't walk out on his wife when she needed him most. After two years Sally ended the relationship.

Thankfully Georgia recovered and for a while he thought they might be able to have a successful marriage. He'd tried to make her happy, to recapture what they'd shared in the early days. Each week he brought home flowers and gifts; he'd suggested date nights and made a genuine effort to win back his wife. Yet nothing he did seemed to bring the light of love and affection to her eyes. Apparently it was too late; he'd cheated not once but twice, and she never trusted him again.

At that point, he was only in his late forties and, except for convenience and companionship, his marriage was dead. In the years that followed he had several other affairs. Georgia no longer seemed to mind and after a while these little flings didn't bother his conscience, either. As it was, he and Georgia lived more like siblings than husband and wife. And yet they stayed together. He supposed it was easier for both of them than not staying together, particularly since their business and social lives were intertwined.

He'd misled Grace into thinking he was divorcing Georgia. He didn't want to lose her the same way he had Sally. He'd fully intended to explain his situation . . . when the time felt right. Grace was everything he wanted, but Will had blown it. Before he could explain the whole complicated mess, she was out of his life. Nothing he said or did afterward changed her resolve. What she never knew, what he'd never had a chance to tell her, was that if she'd asked he would've left Georgia. Not right away but soon. As soon as he'd made the necessary arrangements.

Will had done more harm than good in his efforts to get her back. By this time Grace had met and fallen in love with Cliff Harding. She wanted nothing more to do with Will. Desperate to prove he cared, Will had acted like a total fool at the farmers' market and started a fistfight with Cliff. He must've been out of his mind. The incident still made him cringe with embarrassment.

It was at this stage that Will's life began to fall apart. Georgia found out about Grace, although they hadn't done anything more than email and talk on the phone. Still, his online relationship was the crack that broke his marriage wide-open. After all the years, all the extramarital affairs Georgia had purposely ignored, she left him because he'd sent a few emails to an old friend. Ironic, to say the least.

In retrospect, Will was relieved. His marriage had been over for years. Although he'd never expected to reach retirement age alone, that was his life now. Hard as it was to accept at the time, he and Georgia were better off apart.

Once the divorce was final, Will had moved home, back to Cedar Cove and the only family he had. Returning to town after all these years hadn't been easy, especially since he'd arrived with nothing but a rental truck and a few suitcases. He'd sublet an apartment while he searched for some way to fill his time.

Olivia was the one who suggested he consider buying the art gallery. Leave it to his sister to steer him toward a worthy purpose. The gallery had been about to close, and he'd bought the business, any remaining stock and the building itself, which was one of the oldest in town and in need of repair. To this day Will wasn't sure why he'd thought he could make a success of this. But then, he'd always enjoyed a challenge.

Drawing a deep breath, he picked up the phone. He knew Shirley Bliss's number by heart. He'd called so often that his fingers hit the numbers automatically.

Shirley, a widowed artist whose work he'd displayed, interested him in a way no woman had since Grace Sherman — Grace Harding now. He'd fallen for Grace and come so close to making her part of his life; the fact that it hadn't happened still depressed him.

"Hello." Shirley's teenage daughter, Tanni, answered his call.

"Hello, Tanni," Will said cheerfully. "How's it going?"

"Okay, I guess."

"You heard from Shaw lately?" he asked. By pulling a few strings he'd been instrumental in getting Tanni's boyfriend into the San Francisco Art Institute. He wanted Shirley to be in his debt, although so far she'd shown little appreciation.

"Not really."

The girl's voice tensed. Clearly this was a delicate subject and one he should avoid.

54

"Is your mother home?" he asked next. Not having had children, Will felt at a distinct disadvantage while talking to teenagers.

"She's in the dungeon."

"The dungeon?"

"The basement," Tanni said. "Where she works."

Oh, her studio. "Would you mind letting her know I'm on the phone?"

The girl hesitated. "Mom doesn't like to be disturbed when she's working."

Evidently Tanni was prepared to stand guard over the moat leading to the castle — and the dungeon. "Just tell her I'm on the phone, if you would."

"All right." She didn't seem pleased about it.

Will heard Tanni set the phone down and walk away, her shoes tapping against the floor. Then he could hear her shout into the basement. After a few minutes she returned and picked up the receiver. "Mom says if you sold another piece, would you please put the check in the mail."

"I didn't. Tell her I have a question for her."

"Okay."

Once again Will heard her set the phone down, trot across the room and shout. He didn't hear anything for another minute or so.

Then . . . "This is Shirley."

If he'd recognized the lack of welcome in Tanni's voice, it came through even more clearly in her mother's.

"I hope I'm not interrupting you." Will forced himself to sound his most charming.

"It's fine." Some of the irritation left her voice. "I was in the middle of something but I needed a break, anyway."

He relaxed a bit. "I called to see if you were available this Saturday night. I have tickets for the Playhouse." He didn't give her a chance to reject yet another invitation. Instead, he continued in a conversational tone. "Peggy Beldon stopped by earlier in the week. She's redecorating the master bedroom and bought an original piece — a collage. She mentioned that Bob's starring in the production of *Fiddler on the Roof.* That's a favorite of mine and I like to support our local theater."

"This Saturday?"

"Yes."

"Oh, Will, I'm sorry but I promised Miranda I'd attend the fundraiser at the library this Saturday."

Okay, he'd half expected this kind of response. "I might be able to trade in the tickets for another night." He wasn't giving up that easily.

"Unlikely," Shirley said, and he heard a hint of regret in her voice — or thought he did. "I read in the *Chronicle* this morning that the tickets have completely sold out. The theater might add extra shows."

"Well, maybe we can go to one of those."

"Maybe," Shirley said.

"What about Sunday?" he blurted out, not sure what to suggest. A stroll along the waterfront? A movie? Coffee? He'd tried all those before and gotten nowhere.

"That won't work, either. Miranda and I —"

"Just who is Miranda?" Will asked, gritting his teeth. He'd never heard the other woman's name before and all of a sudden it was Miranda this and Miranda that. He hadn't even met the woman and already he had the distinct feeling she was a trouble-maker.

"Miranda's a good friend. We've known each other for years. We drifted apart but after my husband died we reconnected. Miranda lost Hugh, her husband, about five years ago. You might've heard of him — Hugh Sullivan, a landscape painter. Anyway, she's been helping me navigate widow-hood."

Will wanted to be the one to guide Shirley to new love and a new life. He'd hoped they could find this path to happiness together.

"I think it might be best if we tried to get together another time," she said with finality.

Before he could propose another potential outing, Shirley ended the conversation. "Thanks for calling, Will. Bye now."

He couldn't come up with anything fast enough to stop her from disconnecting. When he started to sputter something, the telephone droned in his ear. Shaking his head, he hung up.

Perhaps he was losing his touch. It wasn't his looks. Even now that he'd grown older, his brown hair with its silver accents gave him the distinguished appearance of a man who was confident and comfortable with himself.

He routinely worked out; he wasn't fanatical about exercise but he kept in shape. Although he'd recently purchased the gallery, he'd managed his finances effectively. He wasn't rich, but he was well off.

Georgia, being Georgia, had been more than fair in their divorce settlement. Apparently she felt guilty for filing. Another irony, since he was the one who'd cheated on her. He knew his mother and sister kept in touch with his ex. He didn't. Contact between them would be just too . . . awkward.

Will didn't know what it was about him that scared Shirley Bliss away. So many women fawned over him, and attracting the opposite sex had never been a problem until he met Shirley.

Despite her skittishness, Will sensed that she was attracted to him, that she wanted to know him better. For whatever reason, Shirley couldn't or wouldn't let him get close.

Then he understood.

The answer should've been obvious. Shirley *did* want to date him. She felt, just as he did, that they'd be terrific together. She felt the same sparks Will did.

But Shirley was afraid.

That was understandable. He should've recognized it long ago. After years of being married to the same man, Shirley was terrified of what would happen if she allowed herself to have strong feelings for someone else.

Now that he'd figured it out, Will decided he could afford to take some time to work on a strategy to convince her. . . .

Saturday night, after closing, he looked through the gallery windows and caught a glimpse of the flickering lights of the shipyard across the cove. Down at the marina, sailboats bobbed on the gentle swell of the wake created by the Bremerton ferry. From there, his gaze moved toward the library. He'd read about the fundraiser but hadn't thought much about it until Shirley said she had plans to go with her friend.

Doubt flickered in his mind. He couldn't help wondering if what she'd said was true — if she really was at the fundraiser. The only way of confirming it was to show up there himself. He didn't have any other plans, since he wasn't willing to attend the theater on his own. So Will made the sudden decision to become a library supporter. He still found it uncomfortable to see Grace, but she needed to know he'd moved on, too, and there was no better way to prove it.

He shaved and splashed on a light dose of citrusy cologne, then put on a gray vest his mother had knit him on impossibly small needles. He couldn't begin to imagine how many hours this had taken Charlotte. Will tended to wear it on special occasions and this evening, he felt, *was* special — an opportunity to make a real connection with Shirley.

With his hands in his pants pockets, Will walked casually down the hill to the library.

Even before he reached the end of the block he could hear the music drifting up from the open library doors. Grace had brought in a chamber music group; this event was more formal and elegant than he'd assumed.

As he entered the library, the first person he saw was his sister, Olivia. Her husband, Jack Griffin, stood attentively by her side, and Will recognized the concern on his face. His sister was recovering from cancer. Just before Christmas they'd nearly lost her to a massive infection with temperatures high enough to make her delirious. The episode had shaken the entire family, as well as her many friends. Like Grace.

Will had viewed Olivia with fresh eyes after seeing her so ill. The surge of love and protectiveness he'd felt had taken him by surprise. He hadn't realized how deeply he loved his little sister.

Will wasn't aware that he was blocking the doorway until someone politely asked to step past.

"Sorry," he mumbled as he went farther into the room.

Waiters moved among the throng hoisting trays with champagne flutes and tiny hors d'oeuvres. It occurred to Will that he might need a ticket. He saw a woman at a table collecting money and hurried toward her. While he waited in line, he glanced around, hoping to find Shirley. A moment later he did. She stood talking to Grace; the woman beside her must be Miranda.

As if Shirley's friend felt his gaze she turned in his direction. Her eyes locked on him and then ever so slowly narrowed. Will stared back.

Miranda said something to Shirley, who instantly looked at him. Then she nodded.

So Miranda had asked about him. That was interesting, he thought, as he surreptitiously observed Shirley's friend. She stood nearly a head taller than Shirley. Will suspected Miranda was close to six feet; he was six-one. By contrast, Shirley was petite, delicate, fine-boned. Miranda was none of those things.

He paid for his ticket and decided to approach Shirley. Perhaps they could mingle for a while and then ditch her friend and go to dinner. He didn't see any need to waste a beautiful evening. On his way over to Shirley, he grabbed a flute and took a sip. Not real champagne, but a decent sparkling wine, probably a California label.

Shirley gave a small wave and started toward him. Miranda came with her. Both women held half-full flutes that they balanced carefully as they walked.

"Will," Shirley said, smiling up at him warmly. "I didn't expect to see you here. Weren't you going to the theater?"

"Last-minute change of plans," he said, returning her smile. He flicked a glance at her friend.

As if suddenly realizing she needed to make introductions, Shirley said, "This is the friend I mentioned. Miranda Sullivan, Will Jefferson."

"Pleased to meet you," Miranda said, sounding anything but.

Her attitude annoyed him. "Same here," he responded, matching her tone. What was this woman's problem, anyway? She seemed to disapprove of him for some reason, even though she knew next to nothing about him.

Shirley appeared to notice because she looked quickly from one to the other.

"I was just telling Miranda how grateful I am for all your help with Tanni and Shaw."

He bowed his head. "I was happy to be of assistance. Shaw is a talented young artist who deserved a hand up."

Miranda smiled cynically but didn't comment.

"Speaking of Tanni, I see she came, after all," Shirley said breathlessly. "If you'll both excuse me for a moment, I think I should check on her." She headed toward the door, leaving Will alone with Miranda.

He didn't usually take an immediate dislike to anyone, especially a woman. He supposed he was reacting, at least partially, to *her* dislike of him. He couldn't understand it, unless she'd heard rumors. . . . Perhaps his reputation had preceded him. However, he wasn't particularly worried. Instead, he made up his mind to treat her as a challenge. She was Shirley's friend, and if he could make her an ally, his chances with Shirley might improve.

"So you're a good friend of Shirley's?" he asked.

"A very good friend," she told him, and brought the flute to her lips. "What makes you ask?"

She was direct and, as he'd guessed, didn't seem too fond of him. Switching tactics, Will decided to be equally direct. "The look you gave me."

Her dark eyebrows arched slightly. "I gave you a look?"

"Didn't you?" he asked.

"No."

He smiled softly and had to admit he was rather amused by this silly game. "Liar."

She laughed. "The fact is, Mr. Jefferson, I don't think I like you."

He should've asked why, but the truth was, he didn't really care. He met her eyes. "Actually, the feeling is mutual, but we do have one thing in common — our high regard for Shirley."

Miranda answered with a short nod.

"So that gives us common ground, agreed?"

She studied the bubbly liquid in her glass. "Agreed," she finally said.

"Don't you feel it would be easier on Shirley if we made an effort to get along?"

This required more consideration on her part. "Perhaps."

"On a different but related matter, I'm looking for someone who's knowledgeable about the local art community to pitch in at the gallery when I need it." He remembered what Shirley had told him about Miranda's husband. "I gather from Shirley that you're eminently qualified," he said. A stretch, perhaps, but whatever worked . . . "Would you be willing to consider doing that?" He really could use the help, she could probably handle the work and, with her at the gallery, he might be able to gain information about Shirley. In fact, this idea might be impetuous but it was a stroke of genius.

"My husband was an artist," she murmured.

"Hugh Sullivan, the landscape painter." He made a mental note to do some quick research on Hugh.

She smiled, a smile he found a trifle condescending. "I'll think about it, Mr. Jefferson."

"Good." He seemed to be winning her over and that pleased him. Now he had the larger task of working his way into Shirley Bliss's affections.

With — he hoped — the blessing of her friend Miranda.

# FOUR

Sunday afternoon — more glorious weather. As Mack worked in the yard, Mary Jo diligently washed the outside windows. She'd gone to church earlier that morning while Mack was finishing his overnight shift at the fire station. He got home at about the time she returned from services and they'd decided to spend this beautiful afternoon outdoors.

Mack reveled in the sense of peace and companionship he felt as they both worked quietly; he seeded bare portions of the lawn and she cleaned every window and wiped down every sill. Since Noelle was asleep inside the house, Mary Jo kept her front and back doors ajar so she could hear the baby. When they were done, she and Mack made small talk, complimenting each other's work, then put away their supplies. The windows gleamed from their washing, the lawn was greening and the garden — vegetables and flowers — now *looked* like a real garden. The lettuce leaves had started to sprout and Mary Jo had planted pole beans, corn and peas earlier in the week. The bulb flowers had sprung up in vivid color.

"I need to go to Wal-Mart," Mary Jo announced at about four o'clock.

"Do you want company?" There was nothing he needed himself, but he couldn't think of anything he'd rather do than spend time with Mary Jo.

"Sure, if you want. I have to get diapers and a few other things. I won't be long."

"I can take you out to eat afterward, if you'd like." He spoke casually, but his heart pounded with anticipation. It seemed that whenever he was making headway in this relationship, something would set the whole thing back. He knew he had to tread lightly with Mary Jo.

"You don't have to take me out, Mack, but thanks."

"It's the least I can do," he argued. "To pay you back for all the dinners you've made me."

"No, really, I'm happy to have your company. Besides, I'm used to cooking for my brothers. I always make far more than one person could eat, anyway. You're actually doing *me* a favor."

That was exactly what he'd told himself earlier in the week, but he didn't like hearing it now.

He shrugged, smiling, as if her comment amused him, although what he felt was frustration. How was it that he could fall in love with the one woman in the world who was determined not to venture into romance again? He could only hope she'd eventually start to trust him, eventually return his feelings. . . .

Noelle was awake and cheerful when Mack, having showered and changed, joined them in the driveway. He picked up the baby seat and made silly noises that delighted Noelle as he fastened the carrier in Mary Jo's car. She'd suggested they take her vehicle; he offered to drive and she accepted.

On the way to Wal-Mart, they said very little.

"Have you found out any more about the letters?" she asked after a while.

"I thought of something that might help us," he said.

"What?" Her interest was immediate.

"In one of the letters, the one where Jacob mentions eating fish and chips, he wrote about being raised in the Pacific Northwest."

"Yes, I remember," Mary Jo murmured. "So he wasn't just at a base in this area, it was also his home."

"Right. So, it should be easy enough to check local high school records from that time — say, the mid-thirties through early forties. Her surname might have changed, but not his."

"Maybe we can learn his family's address that way," she said excitedly. "I'll start checking them out tomorrow. Also, could you talk to your friend?"

"My friend?"

"Yes, our landlord. Maybe he can tell us about the previous owners, or at least the most recent ones."

"Ah . . ." Mack quickly recognized that this was a troubled path, one he didn't want to follow. Lying didn't come naturally to him but he was afraid to tell her the truth, afraid that if she knew, she'd pack up and move out, angry about being manipulated.

"Yeah, I will," he promised.

"Soon?"

"Soon," he agreed, trying to change the subject.

"It's just that I'm so curious about those letters," she burbled on. "Oh, Mack, I wish you'd read more of them. They're *so* beautiful.

70

"I was thinking," Mary Jo continued, "that if anyone could tell us about the previous owner it would be Charlotte Rhodes. Maybe she even knew the Manrys."

"Yeah, good idea." He'd ask her, but he'd do it when Mary Jo wasn't around. He was worried that his mother might have told her friend that he'd bought the duplex.

"She knows everyone in town," Mary Jo was saying.

"Right," he said curtly.

Mary Jo sent him an odd look, which he chose to ignore. He pulled into the Wal-Mart parking lot and heaved a sigh of relief, grateful for an opportunity to direct the conversation away from the duplex, the letters and talking to Charlotte Rhodes. He found an empty space not far from the entrance and turned off the engine.

When Mary Jo had retrieved Noelle from the backseat, the three of them went into the store. Mack grabbed a cart and Mary Jo set Noelle safely inside.

"Do you want me to push?" he asked.

"Please."

This felt good to Mack, almost as if they were a young married couple. Maybe it was foolish, but he liked to pretend they were and hoped to make that vision a reality one day.

71

Mary Jo walked toward the baby department with Mack and the cart behind her. He was making *vroom-vroom* noises, his attention on Noelle, when he suddenly heard Mary Jo say, "Look! There's Charlotte and Ben." She pointed at the book and magazine section.

Mack's head snapped up. Great. Just his luck. He wondered what Charlotte might know regarding the letters, but he was worried she'd reveal more than he was ready to divulge.

"Maybe she's in a hurry. . . ."

"Don't be silly." Mary Jo bustled after Charlotte, and Mack had no choice but to follow, pushing Noelle in the cart.

"Charlotte!" Mary Jo called loudly, and the older woman turned around.

Charlotte was with her husband, Ben Rhodes, Noelle's grandfather. Her eyes brightened as soon as she saw Mary Jo, Mack and Noelle. "Oh, my, this is a pleasant surprise," she said, moving toward them with her hands extended. After hugging Mary Jo and Mack, she smiled down at Noelle. "I can't believe how much she's changed since we last saw her."

"It wasn't that long ago," Ben said mildly. He was leaning forward, chucking Noelle under the chin.

Ben was still distinguished-looking, and Mack had no difficulty picturing him as an admiral. He knew Ben Rhodes was an honorable man who took his responsibilities seriously. His son David had deeply hurt him by his actions.

"If you like, I could bring Noelle by once a week for a short visit," Mary Jo offered. "You're the only grandparents she has."

Charlotte and Ben exchanged a glance. "We'd love that," Charlotte said enthusiastically. "Thank you, Mary Jo. That would mean so much to us."

"Wednesdays would be best for me if that's okay with you? I can come by when I've picked her up from Kelly's."

Kelly Jordan was Noelle's day-care provider.

Again, the older couple conferred with a single glance. "That would be perfect," Ben assured her.

"I'll stop by after work, then. I won't stay long, I promise."

"You stay as long as you like. Ben and I will look forward to seeing our granddaughter — and you, too, of course."

"Actually, Mack and I were just talking about you," Mary Jo told Charlotte.

"Oh?"

"We discovered the oddest thing in the

duplex. I found a box of old letters under the floorboards of my bedroom closet."

Mack moved closer to Mary Jo.

"They've been there for years," Mary Jo said. "The letters were written in the early 1940s to a woman named Joan Manry, who lived in the house."

"Joan Manry." Charlotte slowly repeated the name.

"Does that sound the least bit familiar?" she asked hopefully.

Charlotte's forehead wrinkled. "I can't say it does. I was a young bride myself back then. Clyde and I had just married, against the wishes of my parents, mind you. I was far too young, but these were desperate times and Clyde was about to go off to war."

"From what I've been able to decipher, Joan lived at 1022 Evergreen with her sister and worked in the shipyard."

"As I did," Charlotte said. "I'm sorry, but the name doesn't ring a bell. Let me think about it, though."

"Who wrote the letters?" Ben asked. "A soldier?"

"Yes. His name was Dennison," Mack supplied. "Jacob Dennison."

"Jacob Dennison." Charlotte frowned thoughtfully. "His name does sound familiar but I can't recall why."

"I'd love to find out what happened to those two," Mary Jo said, her voice full of enthusiasm. "I want to know if Dennison survived the war and if he and Joan ever got married. If so, I'll bet their children and grandchildren would treasure these letters. They're beautifully written and very moving."

"Hidden away like that, too," Charlotte commented.

"Yes, I can't imagine why she'd do that. The only thing I've come up with is that, for some reason, Joan's sister didn't like Jacob."

"Maybe," Charlotte murmured. "I'll see what I can learn about those names for you," she said.

"That would be great." Mack felt some of the tension ease from between his shoulder blades.

Mary Jo turned to Charlotte again. "You don't happen to know who lived in the duplex in the forties, do you?"

Charlotte shook her head. "No, sorry, but I do know it wasn't originally a duplex."

"When did it become one?"

"Oh, heavens, I'm not sure. It must've been twenty years ago. The previous owner hadn't kept up the place, but that all changed when Mack bought it. He's made such a difference."

Mack's heart sank all the way to his feet. He glanced covertly at Mary Jo and was surprised she didn't react to the news.

"Mack's made improvements, then?" she asked without letting anything slip.

"The difference is like night and day," Charlotte said.

Mack stayed quiet, for fear that any remark he made would damn him all the more in Mary Jo's eyes.

"I've kept you long enough," Mary Jo said after a moment. "I'll come by on Wednesday with Noelle."

"Ben and I will see you then." Ben started to push the cart away when Charlotte turned back. "I'll find out whatever I can about Joan Manry and Jacob Dennison in the next couple of days and tell you what I learn on Wednesday."

"Oh, thank you. I can't wait."

Mary Jo yanked the cart away from him and steered it back to the diaper aisle at a clipped pace. Mack had to hurry to keep up with her. The anger and betrayal she felt seemed to radiate from her rigid back and stiff shoulders. Unsure how best to proceed, Mack trailed silently behind her.

Not a word passed between them as Mary Jo finished her shopping. He stood, still silent, as she paid for her purchases and exchanged pleasantries with the friendly cashier. The woman's name tag said Christie Levitt. He thought he'd seen her before, but troubled as he was, Mack couldn't remember where.

Mary Jo seemed quite cheerful — until he caught her eye. Her gaze narrowed and Mack knew there'd be no reprieve for him. She was upset and she wasn't going to forgive his deception easily.

Once she'd paid and collected her bags, Mack dashed ahead of her and unlocked the car, opening Mary Jo's door. Usually he put Noelle in her infant seat but this time Mary Jo did it, not giving him a chance. With nothing more to do, Mack slid into the driver's seat, and simply waited until Mary Jo got in. His hand on the ignition key, he looked at her.

"Can we talk about this?"

"No."

Her voice was stark.

"Uh, can you let me know when we *can* talk about it?"

She didn't answer.

"I guess that means it won't be anytime soon?" he asked, attempting a bit of levity.

"Probably not." She stared out the passenger-side window.

Mack exhaled slowly, then backed out of the parking space. He drove in silence.

"Just when I thought I'd met a man I could actually trust," Mary Jo blurted out five minutes later, "I discover that not only did you outright *lie* to me but you continued with the fabrication when you had every opportunity to set the record straight. Were we not discussing this very matter no more than thirty minutes ago?"

"Well, yes, but —"

"Can I trust *anything* you have to say?"

"Yes," he insisted.

"I doubt it." She looked pointedly out the passenger window again, her arms crossed.

"Would it help to say I'm sorry?" he asked. And he was. But once he'd told her someone else owned the duplex, he couldn't ever find a way to introduce the truth. He wished now that he'd tried harder.

"No."

"That's pretty harsh, don't you think? Okay, I screwed up. I admit it."

"Fine, apology accepted."

Despite what she said, it certainly didn't sound as if she meant it. "Thank you."

"Why did you lie?" she demanded.

"Okay, good question. I was afraid —"

"Of what?"

"Afraid you wouldn't agree to the lower

78

rent payment if you knew I owned the duplex."

She threw him an angry look. "You're right, I wouldn't have. What I want to know is why you felt it was so important for me to move next door to you."

"Because." He didn't have an answer that would satisfy her. He couldn't very well say he'd fallen completely and totally in love with her and that he couldn't stand the thought of losing Noelle. Not that she was really his to lose . . .

" 'Because'? Oh, *that* explains everything."

"I wanted to be nearby in order to protect both of you," he returned, losing his own patience. "What's so underhanded about that? If David showed up, I wanted him to deal with me, and leave you and Noelle alone."

"I can take care of my own problems," she snapped. "I don't need a knight in shining armor riding to my rescue."

More like tarnished armor, he reflected, but didn't say anything.

"Besides, David did show up," she added.

"And you panicked," he reminded her.

"Yes, I did panic, and then you jumped into hero mode again, asking me to marry you."

That hadn't been one of his finer moments.

"Of all the ridiculous solutions to come up with," Mary Jo muttered. "And I was frightened enough and foolish enough to say yes."

"We came to our senses," he said.

"Yes, thankfully."

He sighed. "I'm sorry, Mary Jo. I was wrong to mislead you."

"You did more than *mislead* me. You lied."

"Okay, I lied."

"I don't appreciate it."

"That I get," he said drily. "I just want you to know I regret the lie — and the, uh, misguided proposal."

No response.

They arrived at the duplex, but neither seemed ready to get out of the car.

"Where do we go from here?" Mack finally asked.

Mary Jo didn't answer for the longest time. When she did, she turned sideways and looked at him, her eyes wide and imploring. "Can I trust you, Mack?"

"Yes." He said it without hesitation. "I'd do anything for you and Noelle."

"Why?"

His shoulders rose as he took a deep breath. He was afraid of Mary Jo's reaction

80

if he confessed his feelings. She'd probably leave, go back to Seattle, uproot the life she'd created here.

"You don't know?" he asked instead.

"No," she said. "I don't."

"You need someone. You don't want to admit it but you do, and I want to be that someone." He'd toned down his feelings and hoped she'd understand — and not take offense.

"Of all the people I've met since Noelle was born, you were the one I felt I could trust the most. I'm devastated to learn otherwise."

"Will you give me another chance?" he asked. He wouldn't plead with her, wouldn't state his case. The decision was hers; this was make-it-or-break-it time. He'd faltered badly but, God willing, Mary Jo would look past his error in judgment and agree to move forward.

"I'm not making any promises," she said.

"I'm not asking for any."

She nodded. "Just don't ever lie to me again."

"You have my word." The second he spoke, he realized that expression was a poor choice.

"Your word," she repeated. "For what *that's* worth."

Mack would need to show her that his word was good and his lie of omission was the wrong thing done for the right reasons.

"From this point forward I'll pay fair market rent," she insisted.

Mack didn't feel he could argue, so he let it go. But he had to acknowledge, if only to himself, that he was relieved the truth had come out.

# FIVE

Christie walked out of her sister's house and slumped against the closed front door. She didn't know how Teri managed with three tiny infants. Identical triplet sons.

After a single afternoon of helping Teri with the babies, Christie was completely exhausted. Thankfully Teri's husband, Bobby, had insisted on a live-in nanny; otherwise, Christie had no idea how the family would've coped.

Nikki, the nanny, was off on Wednesdays, and Christie had arranged to have her afternoons free on the same day so she could come over and assist Teri. To her surprise, she'd discovered that when she focused her attention on others, she was a happier person. She'd learned that lesson over Christmas, which had otherwise been a miserable time for her. James, Bobby's closest friend and chauffeur, had vanished. In an effort to divert herself from her unhappiness without him, Christie had helped distribute food and gifts to the needy. It turned out to be the best thing she could've done. Christmas Day was another matter, but she didn't want to think about that. And then weeks later, he'd returned, without apology or explanation.

The apartment door above the garage opened, and James stepped onto the small porch. While he didn't invite her into his apartment, he made it clear that he'd welcome her company. The fact that he stood there quietly, waiting, told her as much.

Tired though she was, Christie couldn't walk away. She loved James. He'd hurt her badly when he'd disappeared without a word — and then seemed to think all should be forgiven once he came back. Eventually she *had* forgiven him, although she still didn't understand exactly why he'd left. For good measure she'd tossed in a threat or two. If he ever walked out on her again, it would be over.

She had legitimate reasons for being upset with him. She'd believed he was different from her various exes. Christie had a bad track record with men, starting in high school. The only thing her ex-husband had ever given her — besides trouble — was his name. And every man she'd loved, before and since, had left her high and dry. She'd had a pattern of finding losers she felt she could rescue with enough love and sympathy. Generally they moved in together and for a while all would go well. Then, invariably, there'd be a fight or a betrayal or some kind of disastrous revelation, and the affair would be over, leaving Christie sick at heart, crying her eyes out and desperately alone.

Yes, she'd believed James was unlike any other man she'd ever known. Certainly in the obvious ways, such as the fact that he wasn't nearly as handsome as the guys she usually went for. Tall, skinny, with facial features that were sharp and slightly irregular, he resembled the caricature of a butler in some English comedies she'd seen. But that was superficial and irrelevant. He was compassionate, caring and kind, and that made him more appealing than all the good-looking men she'd been attracted to in the past.

Furthermore, James had inspired her to become a different woman, to look beyond herself. She'd laid out her past, ugly as it was, so there'd be no secrets between them. Then *poof!* Like every other man she'd ever loved, he'd disappeared from her life.

When he'd come back a few weeks later,

Teri and Bobby had championed his case, but Christie was having none of it. Then Teri went into labor and they'd met at the hospital. After that, Christie decided to give their relationship a second chance. However, things were still tentative. She was bruised, weary, uncertain; experience had been a brutal taskmaster and she'd already given too many second chances.

"You look tired," James said. He met her halfway down the stairs and slipped his arm around her waist. Walking beside her, he guided her up the rest of the steps.

"You would, too, if you'd held a fussy infant for the past three hours."

"Jimmy?"

"No, Christopher." Her sister had named the three little boys after Bobby, James and Christie. Naturally, Christie couldn't help being partial to Christopher, the smallest of the three and — of course — the one who demanded the most attention.

"What did you do to your hair?" James asked as he kissed the top of her head.

Christie had recently had the front bleached blond and then added streaks of auburn. She never could wear her hair just plain. That was far too boring. Good thing Teri was a hairdresser by trade, or had been until her difficult pregnancy, which had put a temporary end to her career. Her friend Rachel Peyton had done a terrific job with this new style.

"Do you like it?"

"I like *you*," he said, drawing her inside his small apartment. He led her to the sofa and urged her to sit down. Christie didn't object as he went into the kitchen and put water on for tea.

"I like you, too," she told him.

James brought her a cup of tea, sweetened with honey and with a fresh slice of lemon on the side. No other man had ever waited on her. None had loved her in quite the way James did, either. It would be easy to let down her guard yet again, but she couldn't. She needed time to feel confident in his love. Everything she knew about James said she could trust him; however, she'd believed that before, and he'd abandoned her. No, for her own peace of mind, her own emotional well-being, she had to play it safe.

"How's school?" he asked.

Christie had signed up for photography and accounting classes, and another business course, intent on starting a company that specialized in documenting personal property for insurance purposes.

"Okay." Having a reliable vehicle was a huge benefit. Getting to school by bus could be a daunting task, especially since she still worked at Wal-Mart. James had been instrumental in getting her that car, although she hadn't known it at the time. She would never have accepted his assistance had she been aware that Bobby and Teri had involved him.

"I'm helping one of the girls in my accounting class." Christie was proud of that. "I'm actually pretty good with numbers."

"Me, too."

"I guess that means we'll have smart babies one day," she said, laughing. She couldn't resist teasing him a little.

James's face flushed at the mention of children. He was worlds behind her when it came to sex and relationships. Christie knew he'd had some brief and not very successful liaisons, but had never been in a serious relationship before now. He'd been a chess prodigy — like Bobby — until he'd suffered a nervous collapse. Bobby was a good friend to James, and had eventually hired him as his driver. To the best of Christie's knowledge, James hadn't played chess since he was a teenager.

James sat close to her and slid one arm around her shoulders. Christie relaxed against him, shutting her eyes and sighing contentedly.

"I want us to get married soon," he said.

She savored his words, wanting to believe they'd spend the rest of their lives blissfully together. But her experience shouted otherwise.

Several of the men in her past had offered to marry her; the marriage proposal typically came just before certain awkward matters arose.

Yeah, right. Awkward didn't begin to describe them.

With Jason, they'd had to wait until his divorce was final — and then she'd learned he hadn't even bothered to file.

With the next guy, it was problems with the IRS. Big problems. . . . He'd expected her to pay off his debt.

And with Danny . . . He'd had trouble with the law. In fact, she'd found out just in time that he was only interested in marriage so she would make conjugal visits while he served a twenty-year prison sentence for fraud. Plus, her role as his wife meant supplying him with money for the entire length of his term.

"Christie?"

She knew James was waiting for her response.

"I . . . I don't think I'm ready for marriage yet," she murmured, and felt him tense. She didn't expect him to be pleased but she couldn't say anything different.

James didn't respond right away. "I thought marriage was what you wanted," he finally said. "What we both want."

"I do . . . but not yet."

He removed his arm and straightened. Leaning forward, he stared down at the floor, then asked, "When do you suppose you will?"

"I don't know. Why? Are you planning to walk out on me again?" If so, she wanted to know that now.

"No. I plan to spend the rest of my life loving you."

She'd heard that before. Her suspicions rose again; it sounded so promising, but then it always did . . . until she learned the truth.

"Why do you want to get married so quickly? Do we really know each other, James? I trusted you and look what happened." She didn't mean to keep throwing that one transgression in his face, but she was genuinely worried about it.

He stood and walked to the other side of the room. "I'd hoped we could let it go."

Christie wished their situation was that simple. "Do we really know each other?" she repeated. "Sure, we're attracted and it would be easy to become physically in-volved . . ."

"Okay." He perked up at that.

How predictable men were. This was usually when other men she'd dated would suggest they "test" their relationship by setting up house together. Naturally they always moved in with her — because they could no longer afford rent. Granted, that wasn't the case with James, but she realized he was growing frustrated, although *he* was the one who'd initially wanted to wait. He'd resisted jumping into bed a few months ago, when she'd been willing. Apparently their views on this subject had been reversed. Imitating a game-show host, she blared, "Wrong answer."

The vehemence in her voice made his head jerk back. "You aren't interested in sex?"

She laughed spontaneously. "I didn't say that."

"Okay," he said with reluctance. "Then what's the problem? You were certainly ready to do it with other men. Why not me?"

Christie blinked at the physical pain that struck her at his words. She pressed her hand against her heart until it passed. Then she drew in a deep breath and slowly expelled it before she stood.

"I think it's time I left. Thank you for the tea." She carried her mug to the sink. Her hand shook as she set it down and she tried to swallow the constriction in her throat. She turned to leave and found James blocking the door.

"I didn't mean that," he said, sounding utterly miserable.

He wasn't the only one feeling bad. "Sure you did," she said, putting on a bright face. "And why shouldn't you? It's true. I was all too willing to give myself to other men. There were a lot of them, too. And then I was stupid enough to tell you everything, thinking — oh, I don't know, thinking that if you knew, we could put it behind us. Thinking you'd understand how important a clean slate was to me. And let me remind you, James, you turned *me* down a few months ago."

"Yes, but . . ." He sighed. "You can trust me, Christie. You know I'd never intentionally hurt you."

"I used to think so," she muttered. "Now . . ."

He closed his eyes. "Maybe you're right. Maybe it's best to hold off on marriage. I'll tell you what — you let me know when you're ready to forgive and forget, and we'll talk again."

"Good idea," she said cheerfully. "And you do the same."

His brows shot up, and he stepped aside so she could exit the apartment.

Christie walked past him and was halfway down the stairs when he said, "I don't suppose this is a good time to mention that I'm going away for a few days."

She paused, her foot midway between two steps. The only reason he'd told her this now was to get her attention. For all she knew, it might not even be true. "When did this come up?" she asked without turning around.

"An hour ago. It's business. Bobby and I have some meetings in L.A."

Which explained why Teri hadn't said anything earlier. Questions buzzed in her brain, demanding answers. She wanted to know exactly how long he'd be away. What kind of business? And why did he leave it until now to tell her? But making an issue of this would've been too much like the old Christie, the insecure Christie, the woman who required constant reassurance.

"Okay," she murmured, although she clenched the railing so tightly that her fingers ached.

"Should I call you when I'm back?"

She gave a quick shrug. "Up to you. Have

a good trip."

He sighed loudly enough for her to hear. "I don't think I can."

She turned to face him with a tentative smile. "No, I mean it, James. I want you to have a good trip." She felt his gaze follow her as she descended the steps and walked to her car. She didn't look back.

As she pulled out of Teri's driveway, she couldn't help wondering if she'd just rejected a marriage proposal from the only decent man who'd ever asked her.

# SIX

On Thursday, Grace hurried into the Pot Belly Deli five minutes late. She'd arranged to meet Olivia for lunch at noon, but she'd had to deal with a patron's inquiry. She didn't like to keep her friend waiting.

Now that Olivia had finished her chemo, she was on the way to remission. She'd given herself the summer off to regain her strength before returning to the courthouse, where she was a family-court judge.

"Sorry I'm late," Grace said, sliding into the chair across from her best friend.

"I took the liberty of ordering for you."

Grace smiled. "Oh, good. What am I having for lunch?"

"Cream of potato soup and a green salad with ranch dressing on the side. No scone."

Olivia knew her likes and dislikes, which stood to reason after forty-some years of friendship. "And you?" Grace asked.

"A salad and scone."

Grace threw her friend an accusing look. Olivia was still far too thin; she needed more than just a salad.

Olivia grinned. "And a slice of double chocolate cake."

"Excellent."

"With two forks."

"Even better."

"So, are you ready for Rover?" Olivia asked.

Grace leaned back in her chair. After months of preparation, the Reading with Rover program was about to launch at the library. She'd worked hard to get it set up. Children with below-grade-level reading abilities could come to the library, where they'd be paired with a dog. The dogs made the reading environment nonthreatening; kids could read simply for enjoyment. With a dog — and a silent companion — as their audience, they didn't risk being embarrassed in front of their teachers or peers. Children loved dogs, and the dogs loved them back. She'd learned about the program in a professional journal and been intrigued.

"Am I ready?" Grace said, repeating the question. "I think so. I won't know until this afternoon. So far, I have two teenage volunteers and two adults from the community."

"How many dogs?"

"We're starting with six dogs and six children between the ages of seven and eleven. They're all at risk schoolwise."

"The superintendent's on board?"

"Oh, yes. The superintendent herself told me she's impressed with the idea."

Olivia reached for her tea. "I'm absolutely enthralled with the whole thing."

"Me, too, and I'm so glad they all came from the animal shelter."

Olivia glanced up. "Aren't they trained? I thought you told me they were."

"Well, yes, they are. Beth Morehouse chose the dogs from the shelter and then trained them as therapy dogs. She does wonders with these animals. She's been taking them into nursing homes and hospitals for the past couple of years."

"Beth Morehouse? You've mentioned her, but we've never met. She wasn't at the fundraiser, was she?"

"No, she was out of town, working with a dog owner in Seattle."

"Tell me about her." Olivia grimaced. "You've probably told me before but, you know — chemo brain."

Grace was well aware that chemotherapy often resulted in a mental fog that could take months or even years to lift.

Grace nodded sympathetically. "She moved into the area a few years back. She's a divorced mother of two and a dog trainer by profession. She already had three dogs of her own and then adopted the others . . . and it sort of grew from there."

Grace had met Beth while working as a volunteer at the animal shelter. When she discovered Beth had therapy dogs, it seemed natural to use them in the Reading with Rover program. Grace had first spoken to Beth in early winter, and the other woman had immediately caught her vision and agreed to help.

"I'm excited about it," Grace said. Not only did she love bringing new programs into the library, but this one had felt right from the moment she'd heard of it. Now, after months of planning, she was about to see it come to fruition.

"I know it's going to go well," Olivia said with unwavering confidence.

"I hope you're right."

"Do I detect a note of hesitation?" Olivia asked.

Having been friends all these years, Olivia knew her better than anyone, even Cliff. "Not hesitation, exactly. I'm a bit concerned about the two high school volunteers."

The waitress brought their meals and they both started to eat.

"One is Tanni Bliss and the other is Kristen Jamey," Grace said after a spoonful of soup. "Those two are about as different as any two teenagers can be. Kristen is a cheerleader and I understand she's well liked. Tanni, on the other hand, goes out of her way to avoid hanging out with the popular crowd. I know from her mother that she's had a rough time of it since her father died and pretty much isolates herself. I just hope Tanni and Kristen can work together."

"What makes you suspect they can't?"

Grace wasn't sure how to explain it. "At the first volunteer meeting, I saw how Tanni looked at Kristen, like she thought the time I spent training Kristen was a complete waste. She as much as said so — she hinted that after a couple of weeks, Kristen would be gone. Kristen pretended not to hear, but she did and I could tell she was offended."

Olivia paused with her fork next to her plate. "Why would Tanni take such a strong dislike to Kristen?"

"She seems to view Kristen as an airhead who's gotten involved because she needs a volunteer project on her college application. Tanni implied Kristen wasn't going to get into college on her grades alone. She's a cheerleader, very cute and bubbly, and Tanni isn't that type. Like I said, the two are total opposites."

"She's recently lost her father, so my guess is that Tanni's dealing with depression."

"I think so, too." Grace hoped the program would provide Tanni with some encouragement — and that the girls would keep their mutual dislike out of the library.

At three-thirty that same afternoon, Grace was surrounded by dogs and kids and mild chaos as the children were matched up with their new canine friends.

"Kristen," Grace said, "I want you to work with Mimi and Aubrey." Mimi was a mixed breed, part Pomeranian and part something else she couldn't identify. Aubrey was a first-grader who clung to her mother's hand until she was introduced to Mimi. Grace found it gratifying to see how quickly the youngster responded to the dog.

Kristen led the girl to a fairly secluded area by the window, where the lighting was good. Together Aubrey and Kristen sat down on the carpet. Mimi snuggled up next to Aubrey and placed her chin on the little girl's knee.

"Tanni, I'm going to assign you to Boomer and Tyler."

"You got it." The girl nodded and led

seven-year-old Tyler and Boomer to the opposite end of the area reserved for the program. Boomer was a golden retriever who reminded Grace of Buttercup, her own dog.

Grace couldn't help noticing that Tanni moved as far away from Kristen as she could, which didn't surprise her.

She paired the two adults with two children and two dogs each, but those children were older — ten and eleven, eight and ten, respectively.

Grace stood back and waited. Her research indicated that the children felt more comfortable reading aloud to the dogs than to adults and achieved higher reading levels with practice, which of course made sense. Research showed that being with dogs enhanced their social skills and helped overcome shyness. Watching the children interact with the animals, she witnessed a startling — and very rapid — transformation in each child. She smiled as Boomer, the golden retriever, looked up at Tyler with his big brown eyes and actually held the book open with his paw pressed across the top of the page.

Grace had learned that various bookstores as well as libraries across the continent participated in programs very similar to this.

In fact, one large Seattle bookstore brought therapy dogs into the children's section twice a month. Apparently other bookstores were starting to do the same thing.

Grace only hoped that the reading program at the Cedar Cove library would prove to be as popular and as rewarding.

The thirty minutes seemed to flash by. She moved silently from one reading group to another. It was important that the children feel relaxed and at ease; the volunteers were there to oversee the kids and dogs, but once the children were set up with books, they were to quietly extract themselves and watch from a distance, letting the children read to "their" dogs alone.

Grace joined Kristen after she'd left Aubrey. "What do you think?" she asked.

Kristen's pretty face lit up with a smile. "Aubrey took to Mimi right away. It was amazing. Did you notice how Mimi cuddled up to Aubrey? It was so sweet."

From the corner of her eye, Grace noticed as Tanni made a face. Kristen saw it, too. Grace saw a flicker of pain in the girl's eyes. She didn't say anything but Grace knew Tanni's look of contempt had hurt.

When the children were finished, Beth Morehouse collected the dogs and walked them out of the library, with Kristen and

Tanni's help.

Tanni returned to retrieve her backpack. "Do you have a minute?" Grace asked, stopping her.

"Yeah, sure."

Grace led the way into her small office. "How did you feel the first session went?" she asked, gesturing for Tanni to take the seat across from her.

The teenager slouched down in the chair. "All right, I think. Tyler and Boomer seem to be a good match. I was surprised by how easily Tyler felt comfortable with such a big dog. He's small for his age and I was afraid a golden retriever might intimidate him, but that wasn't the case."

"Beth suggested the pairings."

"A couple of times I wanted to jump in and correct Tyler, but I knew that's not what I'm supposed to do."

"Great." The children needed to gain self-confidence and self-esteem. That wouldn't happen if the volunteers intervened and corrected their pronunciation.

Tanni reached for her backpack, which she'd dropped at her feet when she sat down.

"I had another reason for asking to speak to you," Grace said, broaching the subject carefully. "It's about Kristen."

103

Tanni frowned. "What about her?"

"Do you dislike her?"

The girl shrugged. "Not really."

"Do the two of you have a history I should know about?"

Tanni stared down at the floor and shook her head. "No."

"But you don't like her, do you?" Grace asked, pressing the point.

"No," Tanni was honest enough to admit.

Grace leaned forward. "Do you mind telling me why?"

Tanni didn't answer right away. When she did respond, the words seemed to spew out. "Kristen isn't doing this because she wants to help these kids. You realize that, don't you?"

Grace raised her eyebrows. "She told you this?"

"Well, no, but it's obvious. She's volunteering because she's hoping for this Citizen Award that's given out at graduation."

Olivia had gotten the award the year they'd graduated. The Rotary Club gave it to a graduating senior with good marks who'd shown leadership skills and had a history of volunteering in the community.

"She'd never get it with her grades," Tanni said scornfully.

"You know this for a fact?" Grace asked.

Tanni hesitated. "Not for sure, but like I said, it's obvious."

It didn't appear all that obvious to Grace. "I think you're making an assumption about Kristen that might be way off base."

"It isn't," Tanni said without a hint of doubt. "She's a cheerleader." This was added in the most contemptuous tone.

"You don't like cheerleaders?" Grace asked mildly.

"Hardly."

"I was a cheerleader in high school," Grace told her.

Tanni chanced a look in her direction. "But things were a whole lot different back then."

She made it sound like the days of the Wild West, when covered wagons roamed the prairie. "Oh? How's that?"

"You know," Tanni said with another shrug.

"Sorry, I don't."

"Cheerleaders these days are real airheads. Kristen is, anyway. She's got this laugh that makes me want to puke every time I hear it."

Grace wondered what *that* was about. "Does she have a boyfriend?" she asked.

Tanni lifted one shoulder. "I suppose so. They all do in that crowd."

"Oh."

"If you think I'm jealous, you're wrong! I have a boyfriend, too. Shaw Wilson."

"Shaw who works at Mocha Mama's?"

"He isn't there anymore. He's at art school in San Francisco. A friend of Will Jefferson's helped him get in. It's a really big deal that he was accepted."

"I didn't know Shaw wanted to be an artist." Grace was well aware that Tanni's mother, Shirley Bliss, was both gifted and successful.

"He's really talented," Tanni said, her voice fervent with conviction.

"How wonderful that he has this opportunity."

She nodded, but Grace could see that the girl missed her boyfriend. "I'll bet you're at loose ends without him around," she said.

Tanni gave the same careless shrug, which wasn't really a response. "I am. It's one of the reasons I volunteered here."

"I'm glad you did."

Tanni raised her eyes to meet Grace's. "You mean you want me to stay?"

"Of course."

"Even if I don't get along with Kristen?"

"Well, I'm hoping you'd be willing to cut her a little slack."

Tanni frowned. "How?" she asked.

"Drop the dirty looks and the sarcastic comments."

Tanni shuffled her feet back and forth. "I'll try. The thing is," she said wryly, "it comes sort of instinctively."

"I'm not saying you have to be friends, Tanni. All I'm asking is that you respect her and stop judging her motivations. So what if she volunteered because she's going after the Rotary award? Her being here isn't taking anything away from you, is it?"

"Not really," she reluctantly agreed.

"That's what I thought."

Tanni bent to grab her backpack. "Can I go now?"

"Of course. Thanks for hearing me out."

"Sure thing."

"You'll be back next week?" Grace asked, following her to the office door.

Tanni nodded. "I might not like Kristen, but I think Tyler and Boomer are cool."

# SEVEN

Rachel Peyton stopped at the dry cleaners to pick up her good jacket on the way home from Get Nailed. As she waited, a wave of dizziness nearly overwhelmed her and she quickly found a chair.

"You okay?" Duck-Hwan Hyo asked, his eyes dark with concern.

Rachel tried to reassure him. "Yes, yes, I'm fine," she said, but her voice sounded shaky.

"You have baby?"

Rachel nodded. Funny, the man at the dry cleaners had figured it out, but not her own husband. There were times Bruce could be so dense that she wanted to hit him over the head with her shoe. She longed to tell her husband; despite the fact that this pregnancy wasn't planned, Rachel was excited about the baby.

Duck called something in Korean to his wife. The petite woman came out from the back of the shop and joined her husband at the front counter. They had a brief conversation that involved several sympathetic glances at Rachel.

"You want tea?" his wife, Su Jin, asked softly. "I make you cup of green tea."

"No, I'm okay, really."

"You sure?" her husband asked.

"I'm sure, Duck," Rachel told him. "Thank you. I just got light-headed for a moment."

"I change my name," Duck said with a polite bow of his head. "I not Duck anymore. I pick American name." His face beamed with pride.

"I choose American name, too," Su Jin announced.

"My American name," Duck said, squaring his shoulders, "is José."

"José," Rachel repeated, and struggled not to laugh.

"My American name," his wife said next, "is Serenity."

"I'll remember both," Rachel promised them. She collected her dry cleaning and went out to her car. Going to the cleaners had been a delaying tactic. Jolene would be home and there'd be the usual tension between them once Rachel entered the house. If anything, that tension had been escalating.

Jolene and Rachel used to be close; Rachel had been friend as well as surrogate mother to the girl. That changed when Rachel married her father. Then they'd gone from friends to adversaries. Jolene appeared to see Rachel as competition for her father's affection. The groundwork of friendship Rachel had laid had given way like quicksand as soon as Bruce slid the wedding ring on her finger.

Rachel was still shocked that her relationship with Jolene had disintegrated so fast. She'd done her utmost to be patient and understanding. At first, she'd tried to keep Bruce out of it; she didn't want her husband caught in an impossible situation, forced to side with either his wife or his daughter. That hadn't worked. Jolene's antagonism had grown to the point of near-belligerence, and Rachel no longer knew what to do.

The pregnancy complicated everything. She'd warned Bruce that they needed to be more careful about protection when making love. She'd gone on the pill right away, but had a rare adverse reaction to it. So Bruce had said he'd take responsibility for birth control and he had — most of the time.

She blamed Bruce; she blamed herself. When she'd realized that their occasional slips had resulted in pregnancy, Rachel had been stunned. She'd needed to adjust to it before she told Bruce, knowing he wouldn't be able to keep the secret from Jolene for long. Based on recent experience, Rachel recognized that the situation, which was barely tolerable now, would only get worse.

She should be heading home and getting dinner started, but the thought of facing Jolene was more than she could bear, especially when she felt queasy, as she seemed to every afternoon. She suspected it was a combination of nausea caused by the pregnancy, worrying about Jolene's reaction and the constant stress at home.

She couldn't do it. Instead of driving home, she went to Teri's place on Seaside Avenue. Rachel hadn't been to see her friend in nearly a week. She turned into the long driveway and parked in front of the house with a feeling of reprieve — however temporary that reprieve might be.

Rather than ring the doorbell for fear of waking the triplets, she tapped on the door.

To her surprise Bobby answered, a baby tucked in the crook of his arm. "Teri will be glad to see you," he said, bouncing the baby as he spoke. This was a sight Rachel had never expected to see. Bobby, who was a world chess champion, holding an infant in his arms. It warmed her heart and helped her believe that the power of love could change things for the better.

"Is this a bad time?" she asked, afraid she might've walked into the middle of a feeding. Those were always hectic.

"Are you kidding?" Teri asked, sweeping into the foyer. "I'm dying for company. Come on in and make yourself comfortable. Let me bring Jimmy here over to Nikki. I'll be back in a minute." Teri took the baby from her husband's arms and briefly disappeared. When she returned, without little Jimmy, she flopped down on the sofa next to Rachel. Bobby, who'd been awkwardly trying to entertain Rachel with an account of some chess game or other, hurried off, his relief all too evident.

"You look exhausted," Rachel told Teri.

"I am," Teri admitted. "We haven't got the boys into a routine yet. Nikki's helping me with it." She sighed gustily. "I have no idea what I'd do without such a wonderful nanny."

"You were lucky to find her."

"I know." Teri smiled, clasping her hands prayerfully. "I'm so grateful. Now . . . what about some tea?"

"I'd love it," Rachel said. Ever since she'd declined the cup of tea Su Jin — or Serenity — had offered her, she'd been craving one.

"Me, too. I haven't had a chance to sit down all afternoon." Despite looking worn out, Teri leaped back up and hurried into the kitchen, Rachel trailing behind her. "I hope you're here to tell me Bruce knows you're pregnant," Teri said.

Rachel shook her head. "Not yet."

"Rach, you *have* to tell your husband."

Rachel shrugged. "I agree. I just want to preserve what peace there is for as long as I can."

"You can't allow Jolene to run your life — which is exactly what's happening now."

"Then tell me how to change that and I'll be happy to do it."

Teri sat down at the kitchen table, and Rachel took the chair across from her. "Have you tried taking Jolene out, just the two of you?" Teri asked.

Rachel nodded. "But she isn't interested in going anywhere if I'm along."

"I thought she liked to shop?"

"She does, but not if I'm with her." Part of the problem was that Jolene preferred to be with kids her own age rather than an adult. Like almost every young teenager, she was far more influenced by her friends and their opinions than by her parents.

Granted, she idolized her dad, but Rachel had become the evil stepmother.

"That's too bad."

"I've also tried to get her interested in taking a class with me."

Teri's eyes shone with approval. "Great idea!"

"I signed us up for cake decorating. You know how much Jolene loves to bake. Bruce thought it was a good idea, too, but it backfired. The night of the first class she pretended to be sick and stayed home. Bruce said the minute I was out the door Jolene experienced a miraculous recovery." She sighed. "So it's not like he hasn't seen some of her bad behavior, but he doesn't see the whole picture. Anyway, I finished the classes without Jolene attending a single one."

"Why? Did she get 'sick' every week?"

"No, she flat-out refused to go. She said she missed too much the first week and would always be behind. Besides that, she said she wasn't interested in decorating cakes. That was for retards like me — her word, by the way."

Jolene was free with her insults but smart enough not to say them in front of her father. And so far, Rachel hadn't been able to bring herself to tattle.

"How are things between you and Bruce?" Teri asked.

The kettle whistled then and Teri got up to make the tea — decaffeinated, in deference to Rachel's pregnancy — and assemble a plate of crackers and various cheeses. They carried everything back into the family room and sat down on the sofa again.

"Bruce is . . . Bruce," she murmured.

"Oblivious, right?"

Rachel nodded, making a wry face to hide her unhappiness. The pregnancy was playing havoc with her emotions. In the past, she'd never dissolved easily into tears but they sprang to her eyes now. She fought to hold them back, blinking furiously. "He's got a one-track mind," she whispered, dabbing at her eyes with a napkin.

"And that one track leads directly to the bedroom."

Rachel nodded again.

"The fact that he wants to go to bed at eight o'clock every night infuriates Jolene, too. The girl isn't stupid. She knows why her father's suddenly so *tired.*" Rachel had tried to explain to him that his sexual appetite wasn't helping the situation between her and Jolene, but Bruce said his love life was none of his daughter's business. He was right; nevertheless, it made Rachel's relationship with Jolene even more difficult.

Rachel loved the way her husband desired her. The hours they spent locked in their bedroom were the only peaceful times she had. Whenever they made love she had the urge to tell him about the baby . . . but she hadn't. She simply couldn't. And she hadn't told him he could dispense with using protection. Even Bruce might've been able to figure *that* one out.

It didn't help, either, that Jolene was often still up, slamming things around, making sure they knew that *she* knew what they were doing. And Bruce himself often went right to sleep afterward. So . . . she hadn't found a natural opportunity to tell him.

Rachel tentatively chose a sliver of cheese from the platter Teri had set on the table. "I dread going home at the end of the day," she said.

"That's not good."

"No, it isn't, and I feel helpless to change anything. I don't know what to do, Teri."

"Well, you could try family counseling." Her friend pulled up her knees, resting her feet on the edge of the sofa. "Or . . . do you want Bobby to talk to Bruce?" she asked.

Rachel was grateful Teri had offered, but she couldn't see how it would improve matters. "Thanks, but no."

Teri actually looked relieved. "I can't imagine that Bobby would know what to say, anyway," she confessed. "I adore that man, but this is not the sort of thing he's comfortable with. Did I tell you he was away for a few days? The boys and I missed him like crazy."

"Bobby was away? Where?"

Teri took a sip of her tea. "Bobby and James went to L.A. They had some business they needed to attend to — I don't know the details." She frowned as she said it.

"Nothing's wrong, is there?"

"No, no," Teri was quick to assure her. "Not with Bobby. It's my sister again. Christie and James have had another falling-out. James can be as stubborn as my little sister. I don't think they're speaking."

"Oh, no." Hearing that saddened Rachel. Everything had been going so well between them.

"I'm sure they'll work it out," Teri said. "James loves her and my sister feels the same way about him. My guess is that this will blow over in a few days."

"I hope so. The next time I talk to you, I want to hear that they've set a wedding date."

Rachel finished her tea and left soon afterward, driving straight to Yakima Street.

She hadn't come up with any solutions but felt better for having discussed the problem with her best friend.

When she finally got home, Bruce was already there. She pulled her car into the garage beside his and grabbed her dry cleaning from the backseat. Bruce had the garage door open before she'd even reached the house.

"You're late," he said in aggrieved tones.

"I went to see Teri."

"You didn't let Jolene know where you were. She was worried." The accusation in his voice stung, although Rachel didn't believe for a minute that her stepdaughter was worried.

Jolene stood behind her father, looking far too pleased with herself. "You told me I have to let *you* know if I'm going to be home late," she said smugly.

"Well, yes, but I'm the adult here. I don't report to you." Perhaps that was too blunt, but she couldn't restrain herself. Rachel was barely inside the house and the attacks had already begun. "If it'll make you happy, I'll call the next time I'm going to be late."

"I have to abide by the rules, but you don't?" Jolene said as Rachel stepped past her and into the kitchen.

Rachel ignored the comment, hung her

dry cleaning in the hall closet and then walked back to the kitchen, past both Jolene and Bruce. "I'll start dinner now."

"What are we having?" Jolene asked, following her.

Rachel had put ground chicken in the refrigerator to thaw. "What would you like?"

The girl shrugged. "Nothing you cook," she said under her breath.

Rachel pretended not to hear. "Bruce, do you have any preference for dinner?"

"How about tacos?" he called out from the living room, where he sat at the computer desk he'd placed in one corner. He was, as usual, unconscious of the tension between Rachel and Jolene.

"Sounds good to me," Rachel said, not looking at Jolene as she brought the thawed chicken out of the refrigerator.

"I hate tacos," her stepdaughter said.

"Since when?"

"Since you started cooking them. My dad used to make them better. We made tacos together and had a lot of fun."

In other words, Rachel's advent into their lives had ruined everything.

"I'd love your help," Rachel said, striving to speak pleasantly and disregard Jolene's insults. "If you showed me how, then maybe I could make them the way you like them."

"Not a chance," Jolene said, and disappeared down the hallway to her bedroom.

Trying to salvage the evening, Rachel went to work; she seasoned the chicken with taco seasoning, grated the cheese, diced fresh tomatoes and shredded lettuce. Then she put the meal on the table, which, to her pleasure, Bruce had set without being reminded. He summoned Jolene and the three of them sat down.

"How was school?" Bruce asked his daughter.

"Great. I got an A on my history test."

"Congratulations," Rachel said.

Jolene glanced away as if to discount any praise from Rachel. "Misty asked me to spend the night on Friday. I can, can't I, Dad?"

Bruce looked at Rachel. "I don't have any objection if you don't."

"I thought Misty's parents worked swing shift."

"So?" he asked.

"So, who else will be there until her parents get home?"

"No one," Jolene said irritably. "Her parents let her take care of herself. We're not babies, you know."

"Jolene's spent the night at Misty's before," Bruce added, siding with his daughter.

"But that was a Saturday and her parents *were* home," Rachel pointed out.

"Oh, right."

"Why don't you have Misty spend the night at our place?" Rachel suggested.

Jolene glared across the table at her. "Not with you here."

"Jolene," Bruce snapped, reprimanding her.

"I wish you'd never married Rachel," she shouted at her father. "I hate having her in our house. I want it to be like it was before."

"Jolene, please . . ." Rachel began but her stepdaughter wasn't willing to listen. Instead, she jumped up from the table and ran down the hallway to her room. Rachel flinched as the door slammed shut.

After a moment of silence, she met her husband's eyes across the table. Bruce released a pent-up sigh. "I'm sorry. That was . . . unfortunate."

"I shouldn't have said anything." Hard as Rachel tried, it never seemed to do any good.

"No, you brought up a valid point. If Jolene spends the night with one of her girlfriends, I want there to be adult supervision. I know Misty's grandmother stays with her some of the nights her parents are gone, but apparently she's alone the rest of the time. Those two girls together, without any supervision, could get into trouble."

Rachel stood and started to clear the table. She considered bringing up the possibility of counseling, then decided to wait until she didn't feel quite so tired.

"Do you want me to get Jolene to help with the dishes?" he asked.

If he did, Jolene would sulk and argue, and that would only increase Rachel's stress. "No, thanks. I'll do them."

Bruce frowned. "She should be doing chores."

"Yes, but . . . not tonight. She's upset with us both. She can do the dishes tomorrow."

"You're sure?" he asked.

Rachel nodded wearily. A few minutes later, as she stood at the sink, rinsing off the plates and setting them in the bottom rack of the dishwasher, Bruce moved in behind her. He'd finished clearing the table and had put the leftovers in the refrigerator. Now he slipped his arms around her waist and nuzzled her neck, dropping warm, moist kisses beside her ear. Shivers of awareness raced down her spine.

"Bruce . . ." she whispered, but then she let him continue. She closed her eyes and leaned back, her weight resting against his strength. She was vaguely aware of a noise behind her, but it didn't register at first. When she realized Jolene had come into the room, she instantly stiffened.

"You two are *disgusting!*" the girl screamed. "I can't have friends over because you embarrass me. It would help if you could keep your hands off each other for five minutes, you know." With that, she stormed down the hallway and banged her bedroom door shut for the second time that night.

Bruce released Rachel and sighed. "I guess that means Misty won't be spending Friday night with us."

Rachel didn't know if he was joking or simply unobservant. Either way, the only response she could manage was to roll her eyes.

# EIGHT

Mary Jo Wyse woke, startled out of a deep sleep. She wasn't sure if that was because of a dream she'd been having or because Noelle had made some small noise as she slept. At almost five months, the baby was sleeping through the night — well, *practically* every night. Mary Jo was grateful for that. Noelle slept in a crib in her room; Mary Jo wasn't ready to move her to the nursery yet.

As she lay in bed, staring up at the dark ceiling, Mary Jo mulled over what she'd discovered the previous weekend. Mack owned the duplex. He'd wanted her living close by and, in order to make that happen, he'd misled her into thinking a distant friend of his was the owner.

His lie disappointed her deeply. She liked Mack; in fact, she liked him a great deal. Nevertheless, she was wary of embarking on another relationship. David Rhodes had taught her several painful lessons and she'd be a fool if she didn't take those lessons to heart.

The problem was that she *wanted* to trust Mack. But she'd yearned to believe in David, too. She'd clung for much too long to the fiction that her baby's father loved her and welcomed their child, refusing to accept what was obvious to everyone else . . . and should've been to her.

Even her brothers knew what kind of man David was without ever meeting him. When she'd finally recognized the truth, Mary Jo had been devastated. Yet, despite everything, she'd never regret having Noelle. The baby gave her life purpose. And hope.

Because of Noelle, there was more to think about than herself. Any decision she made, any action she took, would have an impact on her daughter, too.

To his credit Mack had tried to make amends. Monday afternoon Mary Jo arrived home from her job at Allan Harris's law firm to find a large bouquet of flowers on her doorstep. The card that accompanied it said simply, "I'm sorry," and was signed by Mack.

Tuesday and Wednesday nights he was at the fire station, but on Thursday there was another gift. A set of cake pans.

Cake pans! Of all the silly things to

remember she needed. She wanted to bake a coconut cake using a recipe Charlotte Rhodes had generously shared. Mary Jo had purchased the ingredients, but when she reached home, she realized she didn't have circular cake pans. By then she didn't feel like returning to the store. She'd bake it another time.

Mack was working so hard to convince her to forgive him. Again, every instinct told her she should. She'd always be grateful for his help in finding a home for her and Noelle — even though she firmly disagreed with his deception, regardless of how well-intentioned it was. Without him, she might still be living with her three overbearing brothers. She loved them — they were her family — but they were suffocating her.

When she'd lost her job with the insurance company, she'd flown into a panic, although it was a blessing in disguise if ever there was one. Her fear was that once she returned from maternity leave she'd be forced to see David Rhodes again, since he worked for the same company. But her employer had taken that worry off her hands and presented her with another — no job at all. A friend had recently told her that David was no longer employed by the company, either.

The opportunity to move to Cedar Cove had come at the perfect time. Mack had been instrumental in that decision. Grace Harding and Olivia Griffin, who'd also befriended her, had made the transition as effortless as possible. The two women had helped her find a new job, and Grace's younger daughter, Kelly, provided day care for Noelle.

Once she'd secured employment and child care, all Mary Jo needed was an affordable place to live. She knew housing costs would be significantly lower than Seattle prices, and she'd been delighted that rent on a refurbished duplex was so reasonable. No wonder. Mack could've rented it for twice what he charged her. Well, she'd taken care of that, although it put a serious strain on her budget. She'd checked with a real-estate agent Grace recommended and come up with an appropriate amount. Mack obviously saw that she wasn't changing her mind on this, since he hadn't argued when she'd insisted on paying full rent. She also planned to repay him the balance for the months she'd already lived there.

At one point after she'd been confronted by David, Mack had offered to marry her, which had felt . . . weird, but she'd said yes, anyway. Fortunately, they'd both recognized

127

what a mistake that was and called it off before they'd made any family announcements. She could only imagine how Linc would react if he'd learned about *that.*

Linc.

Thinking about her brother, Mary Jo smiled as she rolled onto her side and punched her feather pillow to reshape it. She couldn't remember ever seeing her brother this happy. She wouldn't have guessed it, but marriage suited him. He and Lori hadn't known each other long — a shorter time, even, than she'd known Mack — but they seemed to complement each other well.

Linc wasn't an impulsive man, but in the past couple of months he'd made two drastic changes to his life. The first was marrying Lori Bellamy. The second was moving to Cedar Cove and starting a branch of the auto body and repair business their father had established more than forty years earlier. Mel and Ned, the two younger brothers, were now in charge of the Seattle shop.

The fact that Linc had handed over the business to his siblings said he believed they were capable of handling it without him. Apparently he, too, had felt the restraints imposed by family and was ready to move

128

ahead with his life. Good for him!

At first Mary Jo had suspected that Linc's reason for coming to Cedar Cove was to stand guard over her. That, however, didn't appear to be the case. The truth was, she rarely saw him. He was busy setting up his business, equipping and renovating the commercial garage he'd purchased, and enjoying married life.

Mary Jo must have fallen asleep again because the alarm woke her abruptly at seven. Immediately Noelle woke up, too, hungry and badly in need of a diaper change. Mary Jo gave her a bath, fed and dressed her and took her to Kelly's house on her way to the office.

Mary Jo was tired all day, no doubt because of the hours she'd lain awake, thinking about Mack and David Rhodes and Linc. . . . "Well, at least it's Friday," she muttered to herself as she corrected a document for the third time.

When she finally got home that afternoon, she saw Mack's truck in their shared driveway. He must've been waiting for her because he came onto the porch as soon as she climbed out of the car. She gave him a cursory wave, then lifted Noelle from her carrier in the backseat.

"Hi," he said, looking unsettled and yet

eager to talk. He'd slid his hands in his hip pockets, a habit that signaled he was ill at ease.

"Hello, Mack."

"Are you still angry?" he asked.

"I don't think *angry* is the right word. I think *disappointed* says it better."

He took a moment to consider her reply. "I really am sorry."

"I know." Mary Jo had sensed his guilt and regret the minute he'd confessed. "I just wish you'd been honest with me from the beginning."

"I will from now on."

Mary Jo nodded. She really didn't have anything more to say. She figured everyone was entitled to one mistake; if anything else happened, she'd know it was time to move on.

"Can we let bygones be bygones, then?"

She nodded again. "Yes, let's do that."

"Thank you." His relief was obvious. He stepped down from the porch and started toward her. "I wanted to tell you — I went to the library this afternoon."

"Oh?"

"I don't remember that much about World War II from my high school history class, so I took out a couple of books on the war. I'd like to familiarize myself with some of the details."

Mary Jo smiled. "I talked to Charlotte this Wednesday and also last week, when I took Noelle over there," she told him. "And I did an online search of every high school in the area, but I didn't find a single Jacob Dennison in the 1930s or early forties. I'll expand my search the next chance I get." She shifted Noelle from her right arm to her left.

"Did Charlotte have any information?" Mack asked, reaching inside her car for the baby seat and diaper bag.

"Oh, yeah. She thought Joan Manry might have attended Cedar Cove High School, so I went online and checked out the names of everyone who graduated during the war years. She wasn't there."

"That's too bad."

"I want to look online for telephone directories from that era, too, but I haven't had time."

"Is that even possible?"

"We won't know until we try."

Mack's face broke into a bright smile.

Mary Jo frowned, wondering what he found so amusing.

"I love that you said 'we,' " Mack explained, clearly understanding her question. "I want us to work together to track down those two. I don't understand why Joan would hide the letters. I'm grateful she did, but it makes me wonder."

"All I can think is that her family objected to her soldier boy and this was the only way to keep his letters to herself."

"Hmm. Jacob did say something about her sister not liking him, didn't he?"

"Yes, and I have no idea why. Although I gather the two of them — Joan and Elaine — didn't get along that well."

"You said she lived with her sister here in Cedar Cove? What about their parents?"

"Not sure. What I've picked up from the letters is that she and Elaine did live here, but I haven't seen anything about their parents. It's difficult to follow everything just reading his half of the correspondence." Mary Jo held her door open for Mack. "Do you want to come in? Stay for dinner?" She could tell right away that the invitation pleased him.

"How about if I order pizza? That way we can look at the letters and check the dates against the books I got from the library."

"Pizza sounds fabulous." Mary Jo had planned to make clam chowder, but she was exhausted at even the prospect of cooking. A broken night and a long week took their toll, and the strain between her and Mack hadn't helped. "Just make sure none of those anchovies you like so much end up on my half of the pizza," she warned laughingly.

"I'll try," Mack said with a grin.

An hour later, they sat at her kitchen table, the pizza box open on the counter. Noelle lay on her stomach in the playpen nearby, gurgling and chewing on her toys. Both history books were on the table, along with the cigar box of letters. Mack and Mary Jo had finished eating and were prepared to start their research.

"Okay, check this date," Mary Jo said, unfolding a letter. "June 3, 1944. That's the last one in the box. Listen to what he has to say." She began to read.

Hi Honey,
How's my best gal? I don't know what's happening but there's been a lot of talk lately. If I say any more it'll probably get cut out of this letter, so I won't. Whatever it is, I know I'm going and soon. I feel it in my gut.

At a time like this, I want you to understand that no matter what's ahead of me, I'm ready. If the invasion comes to pass — although I have no idea where or when — you should know there's a strong likelihood that I won't make it back. Don't get me wrong. I don't want to die. None of us do. But this is war, Joan, and if I have breath left in me, I will fight. I'm no hero, but I am willing to do what's required of me so that you, my parents, my brother and sisters — and everyone in Europe and America and the rest of the world — can live in freedom.

If I had a choice, I'd be with you, making those babies we talked about. Instead, I'm all the way over on the other side of the world, ready to do whatever it takes to send Hitler straight to hell where he belongs.

Remember I love you. I can't say it any plainer than that. If I lose my life, then please remember that nothing here on earth or in heaven will stand in the way of my love. Pray for me, my darling. Pray for us all.

Hugs and kisses,
Jacob

Mary Jo's voice broke as she read the last few lines.

Mack couldn't help responding to her emotion. Focusing on his task, he reached for one of the library books, flipping through it. "Oh, my goodness," he whispered.

"What?" Mary Jo set aside the letter and walked over to his side of the table, looking over his shoulder.

"June 6 of that year was D-day. When the Allies invaded Europe on the beaches of Normandy."

"That was his last letter," Mary Jo repeated. She returned to her chair and slumped down. She realized what must have happened.

"Remind me what some of the previous letters say."

"Well, he said the men were in constant drills. I know Jacob was a paratrooper with the 101st. He talked about what it was like when he made his first jump. He was scared out of his wits, but he said it got easier the more often he did it."

"He must've been practicing for the landing," Mack said. "That makes sense."

"At the end of the letter, when he said that if anything happened to him —" Mary Jo couldn't continue.

"What?" Mack asked, glancing up.

Mary Jo blinked back tears. "He was killed, wasn't he? He didn't survive the invasion."

"We don't know that. He might have been wounded."

"Maybe," she agreed with some hesitation. "But don't you think she would've kept the letter notifying her of that?"

"They weren't married, right?"

"No." They were engaged; Jacob had left for Europe with the promise that if he made it back they'd be married.

"But if they weren't husband and wife, the army wouldn't have notified Joan that Jacob had been wounded," Mack explained. "The only way she'd learn that was if someone in Jacob's family told her."

"There's nothing here from his family."

"We still can't rule out the possibility that he might've been wounded. I don't think we should leap to the conclusion that he was killed in the invasion."

"What does the book say about D-day?" Mary Jo asked, feeling she was sadly lacking in her knowledge of Second World War history.

"Okay," Mack said, scanning the information. "The Normandy landings by the Allied forces were the largest amphibious invasion ever undertaken. Wow, listen to this! There were one hundred and seventy-five thousand troops and over five thousand ships. I can't even imagine what that must've looked like."

"They came from England, didn't they?"

She remembered that much, anyway.

He nodded. "The landings took place along a fifty-mile stretch of the Normandy coast and were divided into five sectors." He listed them. "I remember something about Omaha Beach and Utah Beach in history class — and from that movie, *Saving Private Ryan.* That's where the Americans landed."

"Oh, yes . . . Of course." Mary Jo had watched the movie with her brothers on DVD. The battle-scene action had upset her — and now she knew of someone who'd actually been there, part of the battle. Someone who might have died there. Someone whose handwriting she'd become familiar with, whose thoughts she was privy to.

"I believe the English and Canadians were on Juno Beach and Sword Beach," Mack went on. "Omaha and Utah were definitely where the Americans landed."

"Jacob —"

"Jacob wouldn't have been on the beaches," Mack said.

"He wouldn't?"

"He was a paratrooper, wasn't he?"

"Yeah. He was." She wasn't entirely sure what that meant, other than that he jumped out of planes.

"Then he must've parachuted in behind

enemy lines."

" 'Behind enemy lines,' " she echoed in a hushed voice, hardly aware she'd spoken the words aloud.

Mack glanced over at her. "That doesn't automatically mean Jacob was killed," he said again.

"I know, but without another letter after the invasion, it doesn't bode well."

Mack didn't say anything for a minute or two. "Are you sure there wasn't more than the cigar box hidden under the floor-boards?" he eventually asked.

At the time, Mary Jo had been so excited about finding the letters that she hadn't searched further.

"Maybe we should go and look," she said. "Want to do it now?"

"Why not."

She led the way into her bedroom. The more she thought about it, the more convinced she was that Jacob Dennison had been killed. Perhaps that was why Joan had hidden his letters. She couldn't bear to part with them, but couldn't bear to look at them, either.

Mack opened the closet door and got down on all fours to remove the loose planks. Mary Jo doubted that anything else could've been hidden inside that small space.

"Do you have a flashlight?" Mack asked.

"Yes, hold on." She hurried into the kitchen, opening the utility drawer and pulling out the flashlight. Linc had bought it for her and she was grateful because she'd already used it once during a power outage.

When she returned to the bedroom, Mary Jo found Mack lying on his stomach.

"Here," she said, handing him the light.

Mack stretched out his arm and took it from her.

"Do you see anything?" she asked.

"I think so."

"You *do?*" She couldn't keep the excitement out of her voice.

"Wait," he said in a half grunt. Whatever he'd uncovered was in his hands now. He scrambled into a kneeling position and gave Mary Jo what appeared to be a small square with a piece of oilcloth wrapped around it.

"What is it?" she asked, hardly able to believe her eyes.

"Open it and see," Mack said.

Mary Jo knelt on the floor next to him and reverently peeled off the protective rag to discover a small brown book, closed with a tiny hinged lock. Across the top *Five Year Diary* was written in faded gold lettering.

"It's Joan's diary," Mary Jo exclaimed. She pressed it to her heart. At last they'd have their answer. At last they'd learn the fate of the man who had become so real to them.

If Mack hadn't thought to look in the hiding space again, she might never have seen this diary. "Thank you, Mack," she said, and spontaneously leaned forward to kiss him. It was a simple kiss, but it instantly stirred Mary Jo's emotions.

Neither of them moved for a long moment and then, as if drawn together by some outside force, they simultaneously reached for each other. . . .

The diary was forgotten as Mary Jo threw her arms around Mack and gave herself over to his kiss.

# NINE

Will Jefferson was certain he'd made some headway with Shirley Bliss. After several disappointing conversations, she'd finally accepted a date. This was no small achievement on his end; Shirley had agreed to attend a Seattle art show featuring the work of Larry Knight.

When the invitation arrived Will knew right away that this event would interest Shirley. She'd always been impressed by his connection with a major art-world star like Knight. Will had asked her out on several other occasions in the past month and she'd had excuses every time. He'd prefer to believe she would've been eager to accompany him if not for her "prior engagements."

He knew at least one of those engagements was real, the one with her friend Melinda, Matilda . . . *M* something-or-other Sullivan. *Miranda.* That was it. He and

Miranda had chatted briefly on the phone and she'd said she'd assist him when necessary. So far, he hadn't needed her. She hadn't sounded any friendlier during that conversation than she had the night of the library event. However, Will was confident he'd win her over without a lot of effort.

Despite his offer to pick her up at home, Shirley had insisted on meeting him at the Bremerton ferry. He wasn't happy about it, but at this stage he was willing to let her set the parameters of their relationship. If she wanted to go slow, that was fine; he was a patient man.

When he got to Bremerton, Will found Shirley waiting in the ferry terminal.

"It's good to see you." He held out his hands as he walked toward her and leaned forward to kiss her cheek.

"Good to see you, too." She stepped back quickly. He knew she wasn't physically demonstrative, especially in public, so he wasn't offended.

She looked lovely, dressed in a bold black-and-teal outfit. Will felt fortunate to have her at his side. He'd taken care with his appearance, too. He recognized the importance of dressing well and didn't mind splurging on suits that fit him properly. In his experience, money spent on a man's wardrobe produced dividends. Clothes made the man; that might be a cliché but Will was in full agreement.

"I'm so glad you invited me," she said as they walked onto the ferry. "I'm a big fan of Larry Knight's."

They made their way to the front, getting to the choice seats before those who'd driven on could reach them. They sat on the comfortable padded benches across from each other.

"Larry Knight is a friend of mine," Will reminded her. He didn't want to point out that if it weren't for him, Tanni's boyfriend would never have gotten into that San Francisco art school. Thanks to him and his connections, Shaw was doing what he wanted — and at a considerable distance from Shirley's daughter. Fortunately, Larry felt Shaw had talent and was willing to help him.

"I really admire his work, especially some of the recent pieces. You know, the ones that were influenced by sixties pop art."

"Yes, he's very talented." Will knew he sounded a bit cursory.

"He's more than talented," Shirley said. "The man is a genius."

Will frowned. Saying Larry was a genius was going overboard in his opinion. Maybe

Shirley thought too highly of the man. Nevertheless, Will was determined to make this an evening she'd long remember. The dinner he'd arranged for afterward was guaranteed to impress her.

"He's worked in almost every medium," she said, and seemed unable to keep her admiration at bay. "I don't think I've ever met anyone as versatile as Larry. Well, actually, we *haven't* met, not officially, but I'm familiar with his work and I almost feel I know him through you. It's such a privilege to finally meet him."

Will was growing tired of this. "I've known Larry for years. We met in Atlanta in '96, at the unveiling of a painting he did for the Olympics," Will said, bringing the conversation back to himself. He'd been involved in organizing the cocktail party and subsequent press. Truthfully, Georgia had done much of the work, but she preferred to remain in the background, whereas Will enjoyed the limelight.

Shirley nodded. "Were you aware Larry used to do cover art?"

"Cover art?"

"For novels."

Will hadn't known about that part of Larry's portfolio. "Really?"

"At one time he illustrated children's

books, too."

He arched his eyebrows in a show of surprise. "He doesn't anymore, does he?"

"No. He's priced himself out of that market and probably the commercial art market, as well."

Will murmured something noncommittal.

"I'm so thrilled to have this opportunity to meet him," Shirley said, sounding more animated than he'd ever heard her.

Will crossed his legs and suspected now might be a good time to reinforce the fact that her entrée to the great Larry Knight was due to him. "Like I said earlier, we're old friends." He didn't mention that the artist had lost his wife five years before, because it gave Larry and Shirley a common bond, which didn't do anything to set his mind at ease.

"Oh, I know," she said reverently.

He nodded, basking in her appreciation.

"If it wasn't for you and Larry, Shaw would probably still be working at Mocha Mama's."

Some of his tension ebbed. Shirley understood; he hadn't invited her so she could fawn over Larry Knight. She was *his* date.

The Seattle Art Museum was already crowded when they arrived. The walk from the ferry dock up to First Avenue had been exhilarating. It was a beautiful spring night, and the "glitterati" were out in force. Will felt he and Shirley blended perfectly with the rich and cultured art lovers making their way to the event. The tickets hadn't been cheap, and Will hoped Shirley appreciated that he'd put down serious money for this opportunity. He'd also made dinner reservations at an expensive restaurant.

When they entered the gallery, Larry was standing with a group of people, all chatting and drinking a variety of high-end wines, if the bottles on display were any indication. Larry was a tall man, two or three inches over six feet. He wasn't big or muscular but he had a commanding presence. These days he sported a neatly trimmed salt-and-pepper beard and tonight he wore a Western-style jacket. His hair, a bit too long by Will's standards, was combed back from his forehead.

"Come on. I'll introduce you," he said, steering Shirley in Larry's direction. Knowing how many people Larry met, Will hoped there wouldn't be an awkward moment before he recognized him.

He waited politely until Larry was free, then stepped forward. "Larry, I'd like to introduce my friend, Shirley Bliss."

"Will Jefferson." Larry shook hands with

him. "Wonderful to see you again."

"You, too," Will told the other man, hoping his relief wasn't evident.

Next, Larry turned to Shirley and extended his hand. "Shirley Bliss," he repeated slowly. "I recognize the name. You're an artist?"

Shirley blushed profusely and seemed too tongue-tied to answer.

"Shirley is a fabric artist from Cedar Cove," Will said.

"Shirley Bliss," Larry said, as if the name had suddenly clicked in his mind. "Of course. I've seen your work."

"You have?" Shirley seemed stunned by this revelation.

"Yes. Will here sent me a photograph of his gallery, and I had an excellent view of the dragon, which he said is currently on display. An incredible piece."

"Why . . . thank you. That's one of the biggest compliments of my career."

"Red wine or white?" Will asked brusquely.

Shirley glanced at him. "Red, please."

"While Will's getting your wine, allow me to show you one of my own pieces."

"I'd be honored."

Will scowled as Larry led Shirley away, one hand under her elbow. He didn't quite

147

know how things had gotten so quickly out of control. He sensed an instant rapport between Larry and Shirley, and it worried him.

Will located a waiter and obtained two glasses of red wine. When he rejoined Shirley and Larry and handed her the cabernet, she regarded it blankly for a second, then thanked him.

"We've dominated too much of your time," Will said abruptly, prepared to usher Shirley to the opposite side of the room.

"We have," Shirley agreed with obvious reluctance. "I can't tell you how much I enjoyed speaking with you, Larry. Thank you again."

"No, thank *you.*" Larry bowed his head slightly and held her gaze a moment longer than necessary.

"Shall we look around?" Will suggested.

"That would be lovely," she said breathlessly.

Will drew her away from Larry but saw how Shirley's eyes followed the other man as he strolled about the room, greeting his guests and chatting with them.

As they surveyed the paintings, Will had to appreciate Larry Knight's talent — although he wasn't the least bit inclined to appreciate the attention Larry had paid to *his* date.

Each canvas seemed to mesmerize Shirley. "His use of color and shadow is awe-inspiring," she said at least a dozen times.

Will knew Larry's work sold for six figures and up. At those prices they *should* inspire awe.

An hour later, the room started to clear. Will was about to suggest they leave when Larry unexpectedly sought them out.

Shirley's eyes lit up as he approached. "Do you two have dinner plans?" he asked.

"We do," Will said, not giving Shirley an opportunity to answer.

"That's a shame," Larry said. "I'd like it if you could join me at a private supper this evening. I fly out early in the morning. It'll be my agent, the exhibit's curator, a few other people and me. We're getting together at a club not far from here."

"Unfortunately, we can't," Will said, trying to sound genuinely sorry.

Shirley shot him a pleading glance. "Can't we change our plans?"

"Unfortunately, no. I've made dinner reservations."

"Oh." She was obviously none too happy.

Will locked eyes with the other man, warning him to butt out. Shirley was *his* date and Larry was treading on *his* territory.

"Another time, then," Larry said smoothly.

"Another time," Will echoed. He clasped Shirley's elbow as he led her toward the exit.

Once outside, he half expected Shirley to argue, but she accepted his unwillingness to share her company. Her attitude soothed his ruffled ego. It was bad enough that Shirley had hung on every word Larry Knight uttered.

Will had made reservations at the best steak house in Seattle and preordered a bottle of expensive wine. He was surprised to learn that Shirley wasn't fond of red meat. Maybe he didn't know her as well as he'd thought. . . .

She was subdued on the ride back to Bremerton. When the ferry docked he insisted on walking her to the parking garage, where she'd left her car.

"Thank you," she said as they reached her vehicle. "I had such a nice time."

"I enjoyed myself, too," he said, hoping to emphasize that the evening wouldn't have been half as pleasurable without her.

"Meeting Larry was definitely a highlight."

"I'm glad I could make that happen for you." Will hated to be so blatant; still, he wanted Shirley to acknowledge his role in presenting her with that "highlight."

"He lost his wife, you know."

"Yes, I know." So Larry had told her he was a widower. Too bad, since Will had made a point of not mentioning it. . . .

"Five years ago. She had a heart ailment. Apparently she'd been born with it but they didn't find out until it was too late."

"Tragic," he said. Those were details he hadn't known. Obviously the two of them hadn't been discussing artistic techniques in the few minutes it had taken him to get the wine. Shirley had probably revealed that she was a widow, too.

"Yes," she murmured, searching inside her purse for her car keys.

"How about a nightcap?"

Shirley smiled and shook her head. "No, thanks."

Will hadn't thought she'd agree, but he'd felt he should ask.

She'd started to open her car door when Will gently placed his hand on her shoulder. After everything he'd invested in making this evening a success, he'd appreciate a kiss.

But Shirley turned her face and pressed her lips to his cheek. "Thank you again for a lovely, lovely evening."

He stepped aside as she climbed into her

car, backed out of the space and drove away.

Will felt an odd mixture of emotions as he walked toward the lot where he'd left his own car. For the past year he'd lived a restrained and modest life. Practically like a saint, if he said so himself. Or a monk. It hadn't been easy, either. There'd been more than one opportunity to connect with a beautiful woman, to spend a night or a week with her, no questions asked.

But the whole point of moving to Cedar Cove was to make positive changes in his life, to break old patterns. He wanted a lasting relationship and he wanted it with Shirley Bliss. Not only was she talented, intelligent, classy, but he found her extremely attractive.

What he hadn't considered was the fact that she might not find *him* attractive. That thought did more than sting; it was a hard blow to his ego. He recognized that Shirley was strongly attracted to Larry Knight, although he doubted a romance between them would go anywhere. Larry's travel and engagement schedule would make maintaining a relationship next to impossible.

That left room for Will. . . .

As he drove back to Cedar Cove, his mind was whirring with ideas on how to pursue the reluctant Shirley Bliss. So far, he'd failed; that was because he'd been too eager, he decided. A bit of circumspection would go a long way. Playing hard to get was a classic strategy, as every high school kid knew.

He'd wait at least a week before contacting Shirley again. If another one of her pieces happened to sell, great, but he'd mail her a check at the end of the month, like he did for everyone else. No more personal phone calls or special deliveries.

That would work. He should probably date someone else, too. He considered the options — and then in a flash it came to him. Grinning broadly he slapped his hand on the steering wheel. If anyone would get Shirley's attention, it would be her best friend.

Oh, yeah, Will liked a challenge and this was a two-for-one. Miranda Sullivan *and* Shirley Bliss. Tomorrow he'd call Miranda and ask her out.

# TEN

Waiting for Peggy Beldon the morning after Memorial Day weekend, Corrie McAfee glanced out her living room window. Peggy, who was picking her up for their shopping expedition, had taken a break from the renovations she and her husband, Bob, were doing at their Thyme and Tide Bed and Breakfast on Cranberry Point. The place was deservedly popular; Peggy possessed the gift of making guests feel welcome in their home. She was a multitalented cook, as well. Her breakfasts — *all* her meals — were feasts to behold. And to enjoy.

Corrie moved away from the window and grabbed her purse when Peggy pulled up.

"She's here," Corrie called out to her husband. Roy would be leaving for his office in half an hour or so, while Corrie, who worked as his assistant, had taken the day off. That was definitely one of the benefits of keeping employment in the family.

"Have fun," Roy said without lowering the paper.

"Aren't you going to warn me about spending too much money?" she teased.

Roy laid the newspaper on his knee. "Would it do any good?"

"Probably not," she said.

"Just one small reminder," Roy said. "You don't save money by spending money."

"Yes, dear."

He scowled in her direction but his eyes shone with barely disguised amusement. "That's what I thought you'd say."

Hiding her own smile, she blew him a kiss and was out the door.

Peggy was on her cell phone when Corrie slid onto the passenger seat. Finishing the call, Peggy closed her cell and smiled over at her friend.

"I was talking to Bob. He's painting the bedrooms this week and I wanted to confirm that I had the right color for each room." The goal for this excursion was to purchase bedspreads and sheets for the guest rooms at the B and B.

"I thought we'd go to the outlet mall in Chehalis."

"Great. I haven't been there since last Christmas."

The drive would take more than an hour

but that gave them a chance to catch up. Corrie wasn't looking for anything in particular at the stores. True, a bargain was a bargain, but even though Roy had implied otherwise, she was sensible.

"How's Mack?" Peggy asked.

"Very well," Corrie replied. She was happy to have her son living so close. His relationship with his father was better than it'd been since he was a child. They'd been at odds for years, which had made family gatherings uncomfortable. For her sake, Roy had tried not to goad Mack but his resolve never seemed to last long. She wasn't sure how or why things had improved. Nothing had really changed other than the fact that Gloria had come into their lives.

Sadness settled over Corrie as she thought about her oldest daughter. She'd given birth to Gloria as a college student and surrendered her for adoption. She and Roy had broken up; he was involved with another girl by the time Corrie discovered she was pregnant. Without telling him about the baby, she'd returned home to her family and quietly waited out the pregnancy. Not until they'd reunited a couple of years later did Roy learn they'd had a child.

Then, as an adult, Gloria had tracked them down. Corrie was overjoyed at this opportunity to know the infant she'd relinquished to another family. After Gloria's adoptive parents were killed in a private plane crash, she'd gone in search of her birth family. Gloria had been shocked to learn that her birth parents had married each other and that she had two full siblings — a younger sister and brother.

All in all, their reunion had gone well. Everyone had made an effort, although a certain hesitation remained. Linnette and Mack didn't share a family history with Gloria, who'd been raised as an only child. They had no memories or experiences in common.

Everyone had worked hard, and continued to work hard, to make Gloria feel loved and wanted. And yet, at times, Corrie sensed a dissatisfaction in her oldest daughter, a feeling that she didn't belong. In some ways they were still strangers.

"How's it working out with Mack and Mary Jo living next door to each other?" Peggy asked next.

"So far so good." Corrie held up one hand, fingers crossed.

"She's a lovely girl."

"Did I tell you Mary Jo found a box full of letters from World War II? Mack mentioned that they've been doing research on

157

the war," Corrie said.

"Do you remember who wrote the letters? Or who received them?"

"They were written to a Joan Manry, and they're from her soldier boyfriend. She worked in the shipyard during the war years, but Mack doesn't seem to think her family was originally from Cedar Cove."

"I don't recognize the name," Peggy said. She'd been born and raised in Cedar Cove and had married Bob Beldon, her high school sweetheart. They'd lived in the Spokane area for a number of years and then returned to Cedar Cove to retire, buying the bed-and-breakfast.

"Mack said there was an influx of families during the war years."

"Yes." Peggy nodded. "They came to work in the shipyard."

"The young soldier who wrote the letters is called Jacob Dennison. Does that name sound familiar?" Corrie asked hopefully.

"Sorry, no."

"I was afraid of that." Corrie sighed. "It's such an intriguing mystery."

"What are Mack and Mary Jo doing with the letters? I wonder if either party is still alive." Peggy checked her rearview mirror as she merged with the freeway traffic heading toward Olympia, the state capital.

"Mary Jo wants to give them to the heirs if they can be located. Mack and Mary Jo have told us quite a lot about those letters. They really are a treasure."

"I'd like to see them sometime."

When Corrie murmured, "Oh, I would, too," Peggy added, "I occasionally look at Bob's letters from Vietnam and . . . well, they really bring back that whole time."

They were silent for a while after that.

"The baby's growing so fast," Corrie eventually commented. "Mack asked if I'd watch Noelle for a couple of hours this past Sunday so he could take Mary Jo to the movies. I loved every minute of it."

"Are you ready to be a grandma?" Peggy asked with a smile.

"More than ready." Corrie looked forward to it, but she suspected it would take a few years. Unless, as she hoped, she inherited baby Noelle as her granddaughter. That would thrill her, and Mack, too. A marriage between Mack and Mary Jo seemed increasingly likely.

She was sure Linnette would eventually marry, as well, although Corrie had the feeling it wouldn't be for some time. Her daughter wasn't over losing Cal Washburn, who'd broken her heart. As a result, Linnette had quit her job, packed up her car and set out with no destination in mind. She'd ended up in a small town in North Dakota called Buffalo Valley.

As a physician assistant she had a lot to offer the community, which had welcomed her with open arms. Last Christmas, Buffalo Valley had remodeled an old house to use as a medical clinic and hired her to run it.

Linnette was dating a farmer but Corrie doubted the relationship was serious. At least, that was the impression she had, based on meeting the young man briefly and on what Linnette had to say. In their previous conversation, Corrie had asked about Pete Mason, and her daughter had quickly changed the subject. She surmised that the relationship hadn't developed and Linnette was easing her way out.

"Gloria's doing well . . . I think," Corrie said.

"How does she like working with the sheriff's office here?"

"Fine, as far as I know."

Gloria had made the transfer from the Bremerton police to Cedar Cove as soon as an opening became available. She had only praise for Sheriff Troy Davis and his department. Corrie was delighted that their oldest daughter had gone into police work. Roy's career had been with the Seattle police until he was forced into early retirement because of a back injury.

They arrived at the outlet center just before ten, and stopped for coffee and a muffin before tackling any serious shopping. Peggy described the rehearsals for the community theater's new production. Bob had won the role of Jacob in the Andrew Lloyd Webber musical, *Joseph and the Amazing Technicolor Dreamcoat*. Peggy, as usual, had volunteered to work on costumes.

"I ran into Olivia the other day," Peggy said between bites of her bran-and-cranberry muffin. "She's looking more like herself these days."

"I'm glad to hear it." Corrie had ordered the same muffin and felt it was nowhere near as good as the ones Peggy baked.

"Olivia said she plans to return to work in September."

Corrie smiled on hearing that. The last time she'd talked to Olivia, the family-court judge was weighing her options and considering early retirement. Apparently Olivia had made her decision.

"Oh, and I had lunch with Faith Beckwith last week," Peggy said. "She's busy making plans for the wedding. You'll never guess where Troy wants to go for a honeymoon."

"Hawaii?"

"No — Alaska. Some lodge up near the Arctic Circle. To *fish*."

Corrie wrinkled her nose and laughed.

Peggy dug the paint samples from the bottom of her purse and sorted them out. Then they went in search of bedspreads.

For some reason Corrie didn't really understand, she found herself wandering through the baby section while Peggy visited the bedding department. Maybe it was because of Peggy's earlier question about being a grandmother, but Corrie couldn't make herself leave.

Holding up a tiny yellow sleeper, she felt a stirring deep inside. "I'm buying this," she said to no one in particular. Then, almost immediately, she muttered, "That's ridiculous!" She put it down again. Roy would think she'd gone crazy, buying baby clothes when she didn't have the slightest idea when, or even if, she'd become a grandmother.

She rejoined Peggy and they discussed bedspread choices for the different rooms. They went to three other stores, and Peggy made purchases at each. Corrie helped carry the bulky packages to the car.

"I think that about does it for me," Peggy said. "What about you?"

"Ah, I'm finished." Corrie glanced over at the outlet where she'd stumbled on the infant jumper.

"You don't look like you're ready to go."

"Okay, this won't take long." Corrie rushed back to the store while Peggy waited in the car. She grabbed the yellow sleeper and two others, along with a set of receiving blankets. Before she could stop herself, she added more and more clothes, and blankets and toys to her load. All the while she told herself this was crazy. Roy would laugh his head off, but she didn't care.

They managed to squash the bags in the backseat. Corrie didn't tell Peggy what she'd bought. They resumed their easy camaraderie, discussing movies they'd recently seen and books they'd read and exchanging gossip of the unmalicious but still enjoyable variety.

"Thanks for coming with me. I appreciated the company," Peggy said, parking in front of 50 Harbor to let Corrie out.

"Anytime," Corrie said. "It was fun." She started to walk away when Peggy called her back.

"Don't forget your bags."

"Oh, yes!" Corrie had nearly left them behind.

Roy, of course, was at the office, which

was just as well. She dreaded telling him the only purchase she'd made was baby clothes — for a nonexistent baby. Even now, she wasn't sure why she'd done it. Guiltily, she shoved the packages in the spare-bedroom closet.

The phone rang as she entered the kitchen, and a quick glance at caller ID told her it was Linnette's cell. Hearing from her daughter in the middle of the week, let alone the middle of the day, was highly unusual. Linnette was often so busy at the clinic that she didn't get home until six or seven at night. Thankfully Buffalo Valley had provided housing close by, so her daughter didn't have far to go when she finished at the end of the day.

"Hello, sweetheart," Corrie greeted her cheerfully. "Is the weather in North Dakota as nice as it is here?"

"Where were you?" Linnette asked. "I tried earlier and no one was home."

"Shopping with Peggy. Is everything all right? Did you try your father at the office?"

"I didn't want to talk to Dad. I wanted you."

Corrie sat on the kitchen stool she kept near the phone. "I'm here now. What's wrong, Linnette?"

Her question was met with silence. "I

guess there isn't any easy way to say this."

"Say *what?*" Corrie tried to control the stomach-churning anxiety she immediately felt.

"I should've told you before and I didn't, and then the longer I put it off, the harder it got, and now . . . now it's going to come as a shock and I apologize. Please, please, don't be mad at me."

Inhaling deeply, Corrie said, "Linnette, of course I won't be angry with you. *Just tell me what's wrong.*"

"Nothing's wrong, Mom. In fact, this is really good. At least, I think it is."

A tingling sensation went down Corrie's spine. "You're pregnant, aren't you?"

"Yes." The response was half laugh and half sob.

"Oh, my goodness . . ." Corrie slid off the stool and stood upright. Excitement bolted through her — excitement followed by anxiety. Who was the father? Would Linnette, single and self-supporting, keep the baby? Somehow Corrie felt sure she would. "I must've known. Somehow I must've suspected. I was shopping with Peggy Beldon and I had this irrepressible urge to buy baby clothes."

"Um, there's more," Linnette said.

"You're having twins," Corrie blurted out.

"No. I'm married."

"Married." For some reason, this second shock hit her harder than the first. "To whom?"

"Pete, of course."

"Pete Mason? The guy we met at Christmas?"

"Yes."

Pete had driven Linnette home so she could visit her family for the holidays. Corrie had liked him, but hadn't sensed that he and Linnette were anywhere close to marriage.

"Do you love him?" Corrie's biggest fear was that her daughter had married on the rebound.

"Oh, yes . . . . We got married when we were driving home. We stopped in Vegas on December twenty-ninth. We didn't *plan* to get married. I know it sounds insane, but we could only find one hotel room, and then Pete said we should take it even if it just had one bed. I joked that I wasn't that kind of girl and he said, Well, why don't we get married, and I said, Let's do it, and we did." Linnette hadn't paused for breath, and this all came out in a rush. "I think I must've gotten pregnant that night."

Corrie needed to sit down again. Looking at the calendar, although it hardly seemed necessary, she realized her daughter was five months along. "You mean you've known all this time and didn't tell me?"

"Yes. Mom, I'm sorry. I wanted to say something but I was afraid you and Dad would be upset with us, so like I said, I kept putting it off."

"I'm not upset. I'm thrilled!"

"Will you tell Daddy for me?"

"Of course."

Linnette hesitated. "Do you think *he'll* be mad?"

"No, sweetheart, I think he'll be overjoyed. Can I tell Mack and Gloria?"

"Oh, of course. Except . . . Mack already knows."

"Mack knows." Corrie found it hard to believe her children had been able to keep this secret — hard to believe and a little hurtful.

Swallowing her disappointment, she asked, "What about Gloria?"

"I haven't told her yet. Do you want to do it or should I?"

"I will," Corrie said. It would be a good — and legitimate — reason to visit her.

Linnette expelled her breath loudly. "I feel so much better, Mom. I can't tell you what a relief it is finally to let you know about Pete . . . and the baby."

They spoke for another ten or fifteen minutes, and by the time Corrie hung up, any hurt or disappointment had disappeared. She felt . . . ecstatic. Okay, so she'd hoped to arrange the perfect wedding for her daughter someday, but she reminded herself that the marriage was more important than the wedding. She wondered if this baby would be a boy or a girl; Linnette had chosen not to know. So . . . yellow was the right color, at least for now.

Caught up in her musings, she did some housework and prepared a special dinner of pork tenderloin and sautéed spinach, Roy's favorite meal.

"Hello, darling," she said when he walked into the house shortly after six. She met him in the living room, and slipped her arms around his waist.

Roy eyed her suspiciously. "Okay, what did you buy? How much is it going to set us back?"

"Roy," she chided. "I spent less than two hundred dollars."

"On what?"

"Baby clothes."

"Baby clothes?" he repeated, his forehead creased.

"Yes, Grandpa. We're going to have a baby in . . . oh, late September."

"We are?" He looked as if he needed to sit down. "Who's having the baby?"

Corrie started to laugh. "You'll never guess. Linnette and Pete, and before you say anything, they're married."

# ELEVEN

Gloria Ashton paced the small living room of her apartment as she waited for her dinner date. She'd gone out with the doctor only once before, nearly three years ago. From her point of view, the evening had been a disaster. Afterward, Chad had made numerous attempts to ask her out a second time, but Gloria had declined repeatedly.

Just thinking about that long-ago date made her cheeks burn with mortification. She'd spent the night with him. One date, and she'd fallen into bed without a single thought to the consequences. She'd never done that before or since and would never do it again. Such irrational, impulsive behavior went against everything Gloria believed. In her opinion, lovemaking should be reserved for committed couples. All she could attribute her conduct to was the fact that she was lost, lonely and unsettled. She'd moved to Washington State in search of her birth parents shortly after the death of the two people who'd adopted, raised and loved her. She was alone and vulnerable, and for reasons she still couldn't fathom, she'd lowered her natural reserve with this stranger. Afterward she'd felt embarrassed and frankly humiliated by her own behavior, so she'd refused to see him again.

Then she'd learned that Chad intended to move away from Cedar Cove and she realized she didn't want him to go. Overwhelmed by unfamiliar emotions, she recognized that she didn't want to lose him but equally disturbing was her fear of what might happen if she allowed him back in her life. Before she could properly assess her feelings, she'd accepted this date. Their second in three years.

In retrospect, she thought she understood why she'd reacted to him the way she had that first night. Chad had been wonderful, listening to her, offering encouragement and support. That time with him had been like finding a lifeboat after losing the safety of the ship. She'd told him everything, about the death of her parents, the search for her birth family, her doubt and anguish. She'd bared her soul to this man who was virtually a stranger.

The doorbell chimed. Gloria closed her

eyes, took a deep breath and let Chad into her apartment.

"Hi," he said with an easy grin. He was casually but smartly dressed in a well-fitting beige sports jacket and a blue shirt that reflected the color of his eyes — deep blue with dark lashes. Gloria knew other women found him attractive, too. But his appeal went far beyond his all-American good looks. He exuded confidence and genuine charisma.

Gloria managed a return smile. "Hi. Would you like to come in for a few minutes?"

"Sure." He stepped inside the apartment and shrugged off his jacket, draping it over the sofa arm. "I'm glad you agreed to dinner."

A thousand times since, she'd wondered what had possessed her to say yes. He frightened her, intrigued her and mystified her, all at once. She'd never wanted to see him again and yet she was convinced to the very marrow of her bones that if he walked out of her life, she'd always regret letting him go.

Her hands felt moist and she rubbed her palms against her thighs.

"I'm not going to bite, you know," Chad said, grinning again.

She blinked. "Do I look that tense?"

"Yes," he said with a chuckle. "Sit down."

Being a good hostess demanded that she ask him if he'd like a drink first. "Wine? I have both red and white. The white's from New Zealand. Roy recommended it." She couldn't quite think of him — or refer to him — as her father.

"That sounds nice."

Gloria was grateful for something to do. She made a beeline for the kitchen and got the bottle of sauvignon blanc from the fridge. Taking two glasses from the cupboard next to her sink, she deftly filled them and carried them into the living room.

Chad, watching the view from her front window, turned as she approached.

Gloria handed him a glass and squared her shoulders. "I'd like to start over, if we could."

"Start over? You mean you want to forget our first date?"

She didn't blush often, but she did now. Lowering her gaze to the carpet, she nodded. "Please."

Holding his wineglass, Chad turned back to the window that overlooked Sinclair Inlet. "I don't know if I can. I treasure that night. I always will."

"It won't be repeated, if that's what you're

thinking."

He faced her again. "I don't think it could be," he said softly. "I met the most incredibly warm, beautiful woman that night."

She was embarrassed by what he'd said. "I've never done anything like that in my life."

"And I have?" he countered.

"I . . . I wouldn't know. I don't know you. We don't know each other."

"Ah, but we do," he insisted. "You're Gloria Ashton and you're generous, loving, courageous —"

"If I'm so courageous, then why am I shaking like a leaf?" She held out her hand so he could see how just being close to him made her tremble.

"But you agreed to see me again."

"I didn't feel I had a choice," she blurted out.

"No, you didn't," he said. "And I had no choice but to keep asking you. I fell in love with you that night, Gloria. Why else would I stand up to the kind of rejection you constantly threw at me?"

"You can't love me," she told him sharply. These were the very words she'd been afraid he'd say. "You don't even know me."

"Why are you fighting me so hard?" He set his wineglass on the coffee table and

174

moved to her side. Placing his hands on her shoulders, he stared down at her.

Although it was difficult, she met his eyes.

"Okay," he finally said. "If you want to start again, we will." He dropped his arms. "Hello, my name is Chad Timmons." He held out one hand in a gesture of mock solemnity.

"Gloria," she said. Her voice was breathless and quavery. "Gloria Ashton." She briefly touched her hand to his, suppressing a shiver at the contact.

"Pleased to meet you."

"Likewise. So . . . we're going out to dinner this evening," she murmured.

"Yes."

It all seemed a bit ridiculous, but she'd asked for this. "Good," she said in response. She was able to offer him a small grateful smile.

"Are you ready to leave now?" he asked.

"Okay." She took a quick sip of her wine, then brought both glasses back to the kitchen. Standing by the counter she closed her eyes, praying she could get through the evening without making an idiot of herself.

"I made reservations at D.D.'s on the Cove," Chad said as he retrieved his jacket.

"Sounds good," she said, joining him again.

Chad helped her on with her sweater. Gloria had fretted over what to wear; she didn't want to appear too casual, nor did she want to overdress. In the end she chose white linen pants, a sleeveless white top and a pink sweater with a rose pattern.

She locked her apartment and they walked to the restaurant. "I parked my car there earlier," he explained. "I thought after dinner we could go for a ride, if you'd like."

"Sure. That would be nice."

He reached for her hand and she let him take it. His hold was gentle; she could feel herself beginning to relax. If they *could* start over, they might actually become friends — and then they could see if friendship led to anything else.

The dinner was everything she'd hoped it would be — and feared. Once the awkwardness left her, they talked for two hours over succulent crab cakes and the same wine she'd served at the apartment. Chad told her about his experiences at the clinic and she responded with stories from her years of police work.

"I'd accepted a position in the E.R. in Tacoma," he said at one point.

"Were they upset when you changed your mind?" If so, Gloria would have to take the blame.

"Not too much. They said if I ever wanted a job to let them know."

She looked into her wineglass and whispered, "I'm glad you stayed in Cedar Cove."

"I am, too."

He added something Gloria couldn't quite make out. It sounded like "More than ever." But she couldn't be sure.

They finished their meal, ending with coffee, and strolled along the waterfront for a while. Warm from the bottle of wine they'd shared and feeling more at ease than she'd thought possible, Gloria smiled over at Chad. "I'm really enjoying myself."

"Don't act so surprised."

"But I *am* surprised. I didn't expect it to be like this."

Chad rested one hand lightly on her shoulder. "I always knew it would be," he said.

Gloria decided not to respond.

They walked in silence for another ten minutes, and then Chad led her to his car, a sporty convertible. He put the top down. "Don't worry," he said, "I only had a glass and a half of wine."

She nodded. "Where are we going?" she asked once they were both seated inside.

"Where would you like to go?"

The answer that came automatically to

mind was "home." She wanted her life to go back to the way it was when her parents were alive. She wanted to go home to California, where she'd been raised and everything felt familiar. But that wasn't possible. Her life there was over. Her parents were buried, her home sold. Everything she knew and loved was gone.

"Wherever you'd like," she said, since he was waiting for an answer.

"Okay." He put the car in gear and they headed down Harbor Street, then around the cove toward Bremerton. Chad turned on a golden-oldies station and they sang along to classics from Elvis to the Rolling Stones. The car took the corners smoothly and soon Gloria was laughing, closing her eyes in exhilaration and letting the wind tangle her hair.

"I love the sound of your laughter," Chad said as he pulled into a parking lot near the shipyard and shut off the engine.

Gloria smiled when he reached for her hand.

"I feel good," she whispered. "I don't know why, either — unless it's the wine. And the music."

"Well, those things help, and so does my charming company, but I know what the big reason is."

Curious, she looked at him.

"You found your family," Chad said.

"My birth parents," she said. The McAfees had made every effort to welcome her into their lives but it hadn't really worked. Not for her. She didn't fit. Much as she wanted to belong, she simply didn't. It felt forced, like trying to break into a closed circle. The desire was there on both sides, but it would take more than blood to create this bond.

"You have a new family now," he added.

Gloria didn't doubt that Roy and Corrie loved her. She felt their love — and their regret. She'd been excited to learn she had a full sister and brother, but try as they might they hadn't truly connected. Not like real siblings. Yes, they'd become friends, but these weren't intimate friendships.

"Gloria?"

"*Do* I have a family?" she asked, and was shocked when her voice cracked. She so badly wanted to fit in with the McAfees and didn't. Couldn't. Linnette tried to keep in touch but they weren't close, not the way Gloria wanted. Only yesterday she'd found out from Corrie, who'd come over to her apartment with the news, that Linnette was married and having a baby. Gloria was the last one in this so-called family to hear of her sister's marriage. Okay, so Linnette had kept her wedding and pregnancy a secret from her parents, too, but Mack knew. Linnette hadn't told Gloria, though.

To her acute embarrassment, tears gathered in her eyes.

"Gloria?"

"Linnette's married," she whispered, and blinked furiously, embarrassed beyond words by this unexpected display of emotion.

Chad frowned.

"She married P-Pete Mason." Somehow Gloria managed to choke out the words. "I'm going to be . . ." She was about to say *an aunt,* when Chad slipped his finger beneath her chin and turned her face toward him.

He was going to kiss her. She started to tell him she didn't want his kiss when his mouth settled lightly on hers. Awareness ripped through her, and even as her brain screamed in protest she willingly surrendered her mouth to his. Winding her arms around his neck, Gloria yielded to the comfort of his embrace.

She wasn't sure how long they kissed. They couldn't seem to get enough of each other. When Chad broke away, he released a shuddering breath, then immediately started the car and drove out of the darkened lot.

Gloria didn't know where they were going. She didn't care. Closing her eyes, she leaned her head against the back of the seat and tried to understand what had just happened. Or, more accurately, what was *about* to happen.

They arrived at Chad's apartment near the medical facility. He turned off the engine and looked straight ahead. "Tell me to take you home, Gloria."

"Why?" she asked. Her voice shook.

"Because if we go inside, we both know what'll happen."

She didn't speak.

"Tell me," he insisted.

"Chad, I —" She couldn't do it. With Chad, every defense she'd ever erected tumbled down as soon as he kissed her. Her resolve, her determination that this wouldn't be a repeat of their first date, flew out the proverbial window.

Reaching over, she slipped her hand around his neck and brought his lips back to hers. That kiss was like setting a match to a keg of dynamite. Chad pulled away from her and got out of the car.

Gloria didn't wait for him to come around and open her door. She climbed out and was in his arms again within seconds. They kissed continually on the way to his apartment.

He fumbled with the keys. She didn't make it any easier, nibbling on his ear as he attempted to unlock his door.

Once inside he didn't turn on the lights. Gloria was glad. She removed her sweater, hardly able to get it off fast enough; her top and her bra followed. With the same sense of urgency, Chad threw off his clothes and led her into the bedroom.

Entwined, they fell onto the bed without bothering to pull back the sheets. They made love once, drifted off to sleep, and then again when they woke in the middle of the night. Afterward, he cuddled her spoon-fashion, wrapping the sheet and blanket around her shoulders, placing his arm around her waist.

Gloria woke up at five that morning, feeling sick to her stomach. They'd done it again. She'd spilled her guts to a man she barely knew, revealed her disappointment after finding her family. Even now, she couldn't figure out what it was about this man that made her forget every scrap of common sense she'd ever possessed.

Chad snored softly close to her ear. Taking care not to wake him, Gloria slid out of bed. Her clothes were scattered across three rooms. She collected everything in the dark and quietly dressed.

She left Chad a note and propped it against his coffeepot, then tiptoed silently out of his apartment and walked back to her own. The early-morning chill seeped into her bones.

This wouldn't happen again. It *couldn't*. They'd been in such a hurry, so hot for each other, they hadn't even taken time to use birth control. They'd behaved with complete irresponsibility. Not once, but twice. They were a doctor and a cop — two people who certainly knew better. Her face burned.

Chad had some mystifying, incomprehensible hold on her that stripped away all logic, all reason. It was this quality of his that frightened her — his ability to leave her powerless, vulnerable. She'd never experienced anything like it with another man.

Not that she didn't blame herself just as much for ceding control to him. When she talked to high school girls, didn't she tell them that was exactly what they *shouldn't* do? Some role model she was! She'd put herself in a situation she couldn't handle, one she *knew* she couldn't handle.

The only option, the only way to make

sure this wouldn't be repeated, was to tell Chad she never wanted to see him again. She'd written a note that made it clear once and for all.

# TWELVE

Mary Jo had dinner in the oven when she heard Mack's truck pull into their shared driveway. Despite everything, her heart beat a little faster but she tried to ignore the way he made her feel. Falling in love could be dangerous, as she well knew, and she refused to put Noelle and herself at risk again. As much as possible, she ruthlessly shoved aside every bit of tenderness she felt for Mack. He made that difficult, however, and she'd started to weaken. . . .

As he climbed out, she opened her front door and stood on the small porch.

"Hi," she called. She couldn't forget the kiss they'd exchanged when he'd found Joan's diary. She tried not to think about it and yet it popped into her mind at the most inopportune times. Like now . . .

"Hi." Mack walked over to where she stood. "Something smells good," he said, attempting to look around her and into the kitchen.

"Is that a hint?" she asked, raising her eyebrows.

"Could be. What's cookin'?"

"I call it Reuben casserole. Linc had me make it at least every other week."

"What's in it?"

"Sauerkraut and corned beef."

"Sauerkraut." Mack wrinkled his nose in distaste.

"You don't like sauerkraut?"

"Not particularly, but if this is Linc's favorite, then I'd be willing to give it a try." His gaze held hers, and Mary Jo had the impression that even if she'd baked rocks he would've been happy to come for dinner. The thought made her feel light-headed. They'd kissed before, plenty of times. But the night he'd discovered the diary it'd been different, more intense . . . deeper. It was as though the barriers between them had vanished. Together they'd found a missing piece of the puzzle that intrigued them both. And perhaps a missing part of *their* puzzle, as well, a connecting piece that brought them together.

"You're welcome to join us," Mary Jo said, and had to admit she hoped he would.

"I'll go clean up and be back in ten minutes," he said.

186

Mary Jo watched him walk into his own place and then turned to look at her daughter, who sat in her baby seat, chewing on her tiny fist. Noelle was teething, which made her irritable and a bit feverish. "Mack's coming for dinner," she announced giddily. She'd fed Noelle earlier and the baby had fussed, not really interested. Mary Jo didn't blame her.

The previous Sunday, Mack and Mary Jo had gone to the movies. It'd felt more like a real date than the other times they'd gone places together, perhaps because they were on their own, without Noelle to consider. Their relationship still seemed casual but was quickly gaining momentum. Noelle had stayed with Roy and Corrie; Corrie said she'd loved having her and seemed to mean it.

Mary Jo had set the table and placed the casserole in the middle, together with a green salad and fresh bread, by the time Mack returned.

"Dinner looks great," he said, eyeing it appreciatively as they sat down.

She dished up the casserole and passed him the salad. "I've been reading Joan's diary whenever I have a chance," she said. Actually, she'd done little else during her free time since they'd found the book. She'd started with January 1, 1944, getting to know the intimate thoughts of this woman who'd become so important to her.

"Anything interesting so far?"

"It's *all* interesting. She refers a lot to how she didn't get along with her sister. Apparently Elaine wanted her to date Marvin's brother Earl."

"And Marvin is?"

"Oh, that's Elaine's husband."

"Was Earl in the service?"

Mary Jo shrugged. "She doesn't say. It's sort of hard to follow because each entry is only three or four lines. Joan writes in this shorthand way. 'Busy today,' 'no letter from Jacob,' that kind of thing."

"Can I see the diary when we're finished eating?"

"Oh, sure." They continued their meal, with Noelle — finally content — in her baby seat. Mack had obviously changed his views on sauerkraut, since he had two helpings. They cleared the table and Mary Jo made coffee, then retrieved the journal from her room. The night before, she'd read until the words had started to blur.

"Did you get to June 6, 1944?" he asked.

"No, just to the first part of May." Perhaps because she was afraid of what she might learn or because she was so involved in

Joan's day-to-day life, Mary Jo hadn't skipped ahead.

"I wonder if she mentions D-day," he said, opening the clasp and flipping through the pages. " 'June 6, 1944. Did my washing. No mail from Jacob. Worked hard all day on troop transports.' "

"Troop transports? What does that mean?" Mary Jo asked.

Mack shook his head. "I don't know."

"What about June 7?" she asked, resisting the urge to read over his shoulder.

Mack turned the page. " 'No mail from Jacob. My heart is broken. Had to tack on 3. Got some 200 w lightbulbs. Wrote letters and emb.' " He looked up. "I see what you mean about the shorthand. I wonder why she's talking about lightbulbs."

"They were probably being rationed." Mary Jo had only recently learned about ration books. "Did you know it was because of rations that the recipe for red velvet cake was developed?"

Mack looked up from the diary and stared at her blankly. "Red velvet cake? What's that?"

"It's my brother Ned's favorite. I bake it for his birthday every year with cream-cheese frosting."

"What makes it red? Strawberries?"

"No." She took a sip of her coffee. "I've been reading about domestic life during the war. You're not the only one with a library card," she told him primly. "I checked out a couple of history books, but they weren't about battles." She set down her cup. "Like I said, they focused more on the home front and how families coped with their men being away, women working in large numbers, rationing. Stuff like that." She paused. "Cocoa's one thing that was rationed."

"Cocoa," Mack repeated. "So?"

"So there was a scarcity of cocoa, and women couldn't make chocolate cakes. Oh, and sugar was rationed, too."

"Which means . . ." He gestured with his hand, urging her to continue.

"Which means," she said, thinking it should be obvious, "that women came up with the idea of substituting red food coloring for chocolate. You mean to say you've never had red velvet cake?"

"Can't say I have."

"I'll bake you one."

"Will I have to share it with your brother?" he teased.

"Probably."

He smiled and she smiled back, and for a moment they seemed to be lost in each other. Mary Jo looked away first, but her entire body remained aware of the man sitting across from her.

Mack returned to the diary. "June 8, 1944, says, 'Jacob, oh, Jacob, why don't you write. I'm losing my mind.' "

A sick feeling assailed Mary Jo's stomach. "What about June 9?"

Mack turned the page, silently read the entry, then glanced up. " 'I scrubbed the house. No letter from Jacob. I'm so afraid. . . .' "

"Keep reading," Mary Jo whispered. She had to know, and yet, at the same time, she didn't think she could bear it if this man had died.

"For June 10 and 11, 1944, all it says is, 'No letter.' " He flipped over the page.

"What about June 12?" she asked.

"Nothing."

"Where does it pick up again?"

Mack started flipping pages again and then set the diary aside. "The rest of the book is blank," he said.

"She wrote nothing more?" Mary Jo murmured. "He died, then. Jacob must've been killed on D-day."

"We don't know that for sure. Maybe we can access military records."

"Maybe. Or what about looking for Elaine Manry?" she suggested. They might not find

191

Joan, but they might be able to locate her sister.

"Did she mention Elaine's married name?" Mack asked.

Mary Jo exhaled in frustration. "No, but then there wouldn't be any reason to in her journal, would there?"

She knew she was overreacting, but she couldn't help it. After reading Jacob's beautiful love letters and Joan's diary so full of longing and angst, she'd come to care deeply about these people. They weren't just names on a page; they were real people who'd lived through a hellish time.

"I . . . I have to believe Jacob was killed," she murmured, hardly able to say the words aloud. "It makes sense that if Joan didn't hear anything after June 6, 1944, something happened to him. Why else would she leave the pages blank?"

"I still don't think we should make that assumption," Mack said.

"Jacob was a paratrooper," she went on.

Mack nodded.

"The airborne units suffered tremendous losses." She'd read about troops who parachuted behind enemy lines. One entire unit was mowed down when they landed in a town swarming with German troops. The thought of Jacob's death felt like a personal loss.

"True, but —"

"I think I made the right assumption," she said, close to tears. That was why she hadn't read ahead in the diary. Because she knew. Deep down, she knew. This must be why Joan had hidden his love letters. It was too painful for her to see them.

"We're just guessing here," Mack reminded her.

"But how can we find out?" she asked.

Mack looked perplexed. "I don't know, but I'll work on it."

"Maybe there's a record of all the men buried in France." Mary Jo had seen pictures of acre upon acre of white crosses on the rolling hills of Normandy. If Jacob had died in France, there was a good chance he'd been buried there.

"I'll try to get that information," Mack said. "We might also discover he's *not* there."

He seemed so optimistic, so eager to believe Jacob had survived the invasion.

"He might've been wounded," Mary Jo said.

"Yeah. We wondered about that earlier, remember?"

She nodded. "Communication took a long

time, so it could've been weeks before Joan learned what had happened to him."

"Exactly," Mack said.

She nodded, but the possibility that Jacob had never come back from the war was still very real to her.

Noelle began to cry, and before Mary Jo could reach for her, Mack stood and took her out of the infant seat.

"She's teething," Mary Jo said. "That's why she's been fussing lately. Plus it's seven-thirty — time for bed."

Mack rocked Noelle in his arms and soon the baby girl was smiling, drool dripping off her chin and onto her pink sleeper. "I should get her into her crib," she said, feeling slightly guilty that she'd ignored her daughter this long, caught up in the drama of World War II.

"I'll take care of the dishes," he told her. They'd piled everything in the sink and on the counters.

Getting her brothers to help in the kitchen had always been a struggle, although they paid lip service to the concept of doing their share. Mack's volunteering was a pleasant surprise.

"You don't need to do that," she said.

"Sure I do. My mom said if she cooked, she shouldn't have to do the dishes. Dad agreed, so Linnette and I had kitchen duty every night." He grinned wickedly. "Then Linnette and I left home, and Mom pointed out that the dishes had now become my dad's responsibility."

"Does he do them?"

"Every night," Mack said. "In fact, I think he and Mom have fun doing them together. I've caught them more than once dancing to old rock 'n' roll tunes."

Mary Jo smiled. "Do you want me to put on some music?"

Mack smiled back. "Maybe later."

By the time she'd finished getting Noelle changed and ready for bed, Mack had cleaned up the kitchen. He turned on the television to the nightly news, keeping the volume low, while she fed Noelle. Then he sat down next to her and, after a moment, put his arm around her shoulders. Mary Jo felt the warmth of his affection and she was convinced Noelle did, as well.

Her daughter fell asleep in her arms and Mary Jo was far too comfortable to move. She rested her head against Mack and sighed deeply. "I so badly want Jacob to have survived the war," she whispered.

Mack kissed the top of her head. "Me, too."

They sat there, quietly watching television

for the next hour. When he left, Mary Jo settled Noelle carefully in her crib. She almost didn't hear the gentle tap on her front door ten minutes later. When she opened it, Mack stood on the other side, the look on his face exultant.

"I went online as soon as I got home."

Mary Jo's heart leaped. "Jacob Dennison made it?"

"I can't say for sure, but I do know he didn't die in France. His name isn't on the list of Americans buried there."

"Then maybe he was injured, after all, and sent stateside," Mary Jo said. That, too, might explain why Joan had ceased writing immediately after the Normandy invasion. Somehow, Mary Jo conjectured, she'd made her way to the hospital where Jacob was sent. She'd left everything behind and didn't want her sister finding her diary. Then, after Jacob had healed, they'd gotten married and Joan had never gone back to retrieve her diary and the letters.

Mary Jo felt giddy with relief.

"There," Mack said. "Aren't you happy?"

"I'm ecstatic!"

"The last time you were this happy it was because I found the diary — and you kissed me."

Mary Jo laughed at his broad hint, then

leaned forward and threw her arms around his neck.

"That's more like it," Mack said just before he lowered his mouth to hers.

# THIRTEEN

Roy McAfee glanced up from his computer screen as Corrie let herself into his office, closing the door behind her.

"Leonard Bellamy is here to see you," she said, frowning.

Roy looked at his desk calendar.

"He doesn't have an appointment," Corrie said, confirming Roy's assumption. "He asked to see you *right away*." The last two words were stated with more than a hint of disapproval.

Roy already knew his wife wasn't impressed with Bellamy. His family, probably the wealthiest in the area, owned half of downtown Bremerton and several large properties on Bainbridge Island. Roy knew they had several holdings in Cedar Cove, as well. He'd done work for the man before, mostly background checks on potential hires.

"I can see him." Roy was admittedly curious — it wasn't every day Leonard Bellamy stopped by for a chat.

"He didn't make an appointment," Corrie reminded him.

"That's okay. I'm available," Roy said. Corrie was well aware that not everyone scheduled appointments with him; he always had a certain number of walk-ins. He wasn't going to hold that against Bellamy, even if his wife did. Leonard Bellamy paid his bills promptly.

The last case Roy had worked on for Bellamy had concerned an employee who'd filed for workers' compensation, claiming that due to a serious back injury, he was unable to continue in his current position. Having suffered from back ailments himself, Roy was in full sympathy with the employee — until he caught him training to climb Mount Rainier hefting a fifty-pound knapsack. Leonard had paid Roy a handsome bonus at the end of that investigation.

"He comes in without an appointment and just assumes you'll see him because he's the great and mighty Leonard Bellamy," Corrie muttered. "In my opinion, he's arrogant and demanding and a jerk."

"Show him in, Corrie," Roy said pointedly.

"I will, but I don't like him taking advantage of you."

He didn't bother to defend Bellamy, since Corrie's dislike of him made her unwilling to listen.

A minute later she escorted Leonard Bellamy into Roy's office. Roy stood and the two men exchanged perfunctory handshakes.

"Good morning," Roy said, and waited until the other man had taken the upholstered chair across from him before sitting down again. "What can I do for you?" he asked. He was a busy man and so was Bellamy. They didn't need to waste time with further chitchat.

"I believe you've met my daughter, Lori."

Roy wasn't sure he had. "I'm afraid I don't recall."

"But you know I have two daughters, correct?"

"Yes." And a son. Older than the girls. Both Robert and Denise worked with their father.

"You may remember that Lori was engaged to . . . to that felon Geoff Duncan."

Roy knew the Duncan case well. Geoff had worked for attorney Allan Harris as his legal assistant. Harris had been handling Martha Evans's estate when several pieces of expensive jewelry went missing. All the

200

evidence suggested that Dave Flemming, a local pastor, had been responsible for the theft. Sheriff Troy Davis and Roy had solved the case together. In a systematic search of pawnshops, Roy had come across one where Geoff had left a piece of the jewelry.

Geoff had accepted a plea bargain and was now serving a prison sentence.

"I do remember that Duncan was engaged at the time," Roy said.

Bellamy sighed loudly. "I swear that girl doesn't have the sense God gave a duck. You'd think she'd have better judgment, but Geoff managed to convince her that he was madly in love with her and the two of them were meant to be together. I had my suspicions the minute we met. The man was a con artist of the first order. He didn't love Lori. It was blatantly obvious he was after her money." He shook his head. "I have to admit he grew on me after a while — that con-artist-charmer type, you know. But I should've gone with my gut instinct."

Roy didn't respond, although he had his own opinion on the matter. He'd seen Geoff Duncan as an unfortunate case. The young man had gotten in over his head financially, trying to impress the Bellamys, and when his money situation became precarious, he'd stolen the jewelry. Roy didn't believe Geoff

Duncan was a career criminal — just irresponsible and desperate to make a good impression on his fiancée and future in-laws. His plan had backfired, and the man seemed genuinely repentant when confronted with the truth.

"I hate to say this, but my daughter isn't the brightest girl you could hope to meet." Bellamy sat back in the chair and crossed his legs. "I'm afraid she's jumped directly from the frying pan into the fire with this latest stunt of hers."

Roy had perfected his poker face years ago and was able to conceal his aversion to the way Bellamy spoke about his daughter.

"How do you mean?" he asked in a mild voice.

The question was ignored. "Did I mention she works at a dress shop? *My* daughter in a dress shop. Three years of college and she drops out because she's got some fantasy about becoming a designer. This friend of my wife's owns a dress shop and hired her. If Lori wanted to quit school and find a job, I could've given her one. When I offered, you know what she said?"

Roy wasn't allowed to answer.

" 'No, thank you, Daddy,' " he said in a falsetto voice. " 'I'd rather work with Brenda.' " He closed his eyes, apparently overcome with frustration.

"You want me to check out her employer?" Roy asked, figuring this must be what he had in mind.

"No," he barked, then cast Roy an apologetic look. "I'm afraid Lori's done something to top all the other foolish decisions she's made in the past few years."

"And what is that?" Roy asked.

Bellamy clenched his hands until his knuckles went white. "She married a man she barely knows."

"I see," Roy said thoughtfully.

"From what I understand, she met this man and married him within a month. Perhaps less. I don't know if my wife got the story straight. As you can imagine, Kate was more than a little upset." He blew out a sigh, and his shoulders slumped. "Naturally Lori tried to keep it a secret from us. If it hadn't been for the fact that Kate's friend Brenda — the one who owns the shop — let it slip, heaven knows how long it would've taken us to find out. When I talked to Lori after Kate told me, the girl didn't bother to deny it. She admitted she'd married this man — as if getting married is something you do on a whim. My wife was mortified that a friend had to be the one to tell her our daughter has a husband."

Roy could empathize with their shock. Knowing what he did about the family, Roy suspected the Bellamys would have expected to throw a huge wedding. Not only had she eloped, but she'd deprived them of putting on the event of the year.

"You can imagine how upset Kate is about this," he said again.

"You obviously are, too," Roy murmured.

"Can you blame me?"

"Not really." Roy did understand his feelings — to a degree — because he'd experienced something similar. Linnette had recently surprised him and Corrie with her news. Marrying Pete Mason without a word to family until the deed was done had been a shock to them, too. However, they'd met and liked Pete. Roy considered himself a good judge of character, and he trusted the man. Pete was a decent, hardworking farmer, and their daughter loved him. The fact that Linnette was about to make them grandparents only sweetened the deal.

"It gives me no pleasure to come to you with this," Leonard continued. "I want you to find out whatever you can about this man who manipulated my daughter into marriage."

"I can do a background search for you."

"Dig up everything there is," he said, his

face growing red. "This man is a parasite. I can feel it."

"Do you have his name?"

"Oh, yes, and that's another thing. Lori's taken his name. She's no longer Lori Bellamy but Lori Wyse. Not even Bellamy-Wyse."

"Wyse?" Roy repeated slowly.

"Yes, like wise guy." Bellamy smirked as he said it.

"Any relation to Mary Jo Wyse?"

Bellamy stared across the desk at him. "Don't know who that is. Why?"

Roy picked up his pen and rolled it between his palms. "My son, Mack, is dating Mary Jo Wyse. She lives on the other side of his duplex. I seem to remember Mack mentioning that her brother's moved into town."

"You've met this Linc Wyse?"

Roy shook his head. "No, but I've met Mary Jo a number of times."

"Well, Lori married Lincoln Wyse. Linc, for short." He seemed to wait for Roy to respond.

"They might be related, which means it could be a conflict of interest for me to take this case."

"Are you saying you can't be objective?"

"No, I'm saying I know a relative or

someone who might be a relative. I'd want you to be aware of that up front. Not telling you would be a breach of ethics."

"Okay, I know it. Now find the dirt on this man."

"Dirt?"

"He's a money-grubbing thief, hoping to swindle my idiot daughter out of every penny she's due to inherit." He scowled. "Fact is, I'm tempted to cut her out of my will. Then we'll see how long this so-called marriage lasts. It would serve her right, too. When can you start?"

Roy hesitated.

"Will you take the case or not?" Bellamy demanded.

"I'll be happy to investigate Lincoln Wyse," Roy said after a moment, "but with your full understanding that this man could very well be related to the woman my son is dating."

"I already said I don't care." Bellamy waved off his concern. "How soon could you get me the information?"

"How soon do you want it?" Roy asked.

"Yesterday. I want this man out of my daughter's life before she does something even more foolish and gets pregnant. I swear she's determined to age her mother and me before our time. If it isn't one thing with

Lori, it's another. The girl seems to do nothing but embarrass us. First it was Duncan and now she marries a stranger."

"She does seem to have an impulsive nature," Roy said carefully, still somewhat perturbed by the man's contempt for his daughter.

Bellamy stood and again they exchanged handshakes. "I'll wait to hear from you, then."

"I'll be in touch in a few weeks."

The other man held his look. "Don't spare the truth. I want it all, understand?"

"I'll make sure I do a thorough search," Roy promised.

"Good."

With that, Bellamy was out the door, seemingly eager to escape. No sooner had he left the office than Corrie got up from her desk.

"What did he want *this* time?" she asked, her eyes narrow with suspicion. She stood in his doorway, her arms folded.

Okay, the guy was arrogant and demanding, but he wasn't the first client who'd behaved that way. Roy didn't know why his wife found Bellamy so objectionable. "He wants me to do a background check on someone."

Corrie made a snorting sound.

"I realize you don't like him."

"I have a bad feeling about him," she said. "A bad vibe, as we used to say." She looked at him earnestly. "You've always been particular about the cases you accept. Even when I don't like one of our clients, I've never expressed my opinion."

Roy cocked his eyebrows.

"Fine. Maybe I have . . . occasionally. Bellamy pays his bills on time, which is good, but if it were up to me — and I know it isn't — I'd steer clear of him."

"Apparently his daughter eloped a few weeks ago and he's afraid the young man married Lori for her money." Roy stood and walked over to his wife's side. "Lori married Lincoln Wyse. I think he might be Mary Jo's brother."

Frowning, Corrie met his eyes. "He is."

"I told Bellamy that was possible and I said it might cause a conflict of interest, but he didn't care. He wants me for the job."

"I've met Lori and Linc," she said, her frown deepening. "They're a sweet couple. I refuse to believe Linc married her because she's related to Leonard Bellamy."

"I'll find out soon enough," Roy said.

Corrie returned to the front office and Roy sat down at his desk again. He was logging on to his computer to begin the search when Corrie came back. "I still don't think you should take this case."

"Really?" he said, leaning back in his chair. He linked his fingers behind his head and regarded his wife. "And why is that?"

Corrie seemed flustered. "He . . . he wants you to dig up something damaging. If you don't, he'll believe you didn't do your job."

"What makes you say that?"

"Isn't it obvious?" she snapped.

Actually, it was. Roy suspected Bellamy was hoping Roy would come up with a divorce or two or perhaps a bankruptcy, just to prove to his daughter how wrong she was.

"I told him I'd take the job," Roy said, and he was a man of his word.

"Then untell him."

"I can't do that." If he accepted a job, then he intended to follow through — and he'd conduct his investigation with integrity. At the same time, he'd never seen his wife this adamant about a case.

"I had a feeling you were going to say that," Corrie said with a deep sigh of resignation. "I hope you don't regret this."

Roy waited until she'd left the office and closed the door. When he was fairly sure she wasn't listening, he reached for his phone and dialed his son's cell.

"Hi, Dad." Call display was a marvelous

thing, Roy mused.

"Hi, Mack."

"What can I do for you?" Mack asked.

Roy got right to the point. "What do you know about Linc Wyse?"

"Linc Wyse," Mack repeated. "Mary Jo's brother?"

"Yeah."

"Salt of the earth. Honest as the day is long. And other assorted clichés. He's a good guy."

"He's married to Lori Bellamy?"

"Yeah."

"Does he love her?"

"He married her, didn't he?"

Roy smiled. "Men marry for reasons other than love."

"Not Linc. He's not like that." Mack spoke with certainty. "You didn't say why you're asking."

"You're right, I didn't." He rarely approached family with business matters but he felt Mack's judgment about people was reliable. "Thanks. You told me what I needed to know."

"That's all you wanted?"

"That's it," Roy answered. "Thanks for your help."

"No problem."

As Roy disconnected, he grinned. He'd

look into Linc Wyse's background, but he doubted he'd find anything that would satisfy Leonard Bellamy's hunger for negative information. Roy acknowledged he'd derive some pleasure from that when he made his report.

# FOURTEEN

After three straight days of rain, the sun broke out shortly after noon on Saturday.

Mary Jo was more than ready to leave the duplex for a while. Noelle had been irritable all morning and a distraction would be good for both of them.

Despite the overcast skies and drizzle earlier in the day, Mack had been working outside, wearing rubber boots. He'd weeded the garden and was now erecting a fence around the backyard. He'd also promised to put up a swing for Noelle, which he planned to do.

There was a chance of rain, so Mack had suggested they drive down to the farmer's market and include a stop at the library. Immediately after lunchtime, she bundled up Noelle and they set off, again taking her car.

When they'd parked in the free lot next to the library, Mary Jo got Noelle from the backseat while Mack set up the stroller. The baby gurgled happily when Mary Jo fastened her inside. Her little girl was growing so quickly. Already Noelle was sitting up on her own, and it wouldn't be long before she started crawling.

They returned their library books, then walked over to the market, chatting about Joan and Jacob and the letters.

"There's Grace and Olivia. At that booth with all the soap." Mary Jo caught their attention and waved.

The two women immediately came toward them. Grace carried a small bag from the Soap People and as they drew closer Mary Jo could smell the distinctive scent of lavender.

"Don't tell me that's Noelle," Olivia said, leaning over to get a better look at the baby. "Oh, my, she has two little teeth."

After the months of chemo, Olivia's hair had grown back in short, bouncy curls all over her head. Mary Jo wasn't sure what the color or texture had been before but it was silver now, and Mary Jo thought it was beautiful. She hadn't met Olivia until last December, when she was in the middle of her fight with cancer. She'd been so thin and pale. So fragile. She was a different woman now, still thin but healthy and vibrant.

"We're off to shop," Grace told them after they'd visited for a few minutes.

"Have fun, you two," Mack said as he steered Mary Jo toward the market.

Mary Jo purchased two pounds of fresh clams and invited Mack to share in her feast that night. He bought a crusty loaf of French bread from the local bakery and salad makings, plus a bottle of white wine to complement their meal. She told him that soon they'd have produce from their garden — lettuce and peppers and beans.

"*Our* garden," Mary Jo said again. Mack had done all the hard work, tilling the ground and preparing the soil. True, she'd done the planting, but they'd both contributed to the weeding and watering. From the beginning they'd agreed to share the bounty.

"Well, sure, it's *our* garden," Mack said, sounding surprised. "And I've enjoyed working in it as much as I'm going to enjoy eating all that good stuff."

A man who liked gardening. That seemed to her a very positive thing. It showed how nurturing and patient he was, how generous. She didn't want to fall in love with him and yet it was almost impossible not to. . . .

214

Out of the corner of her eye, Mary Jo noticed her brother and his wife. She was about to mention it when she saw Linc place his arm around Lori. Marriage had changed her oldest brother. Mary Jo became aware of the subtleties it had brought into his life — or, perhaps, revealed in his personality — every time she saw him.

For years Linc had been on his guard, looking after his family. He'd taken on the responsibilities of a parent, constantly worrying about his siblings, trying to protect them. He hadn't liked it when Mary Jo had moved to Cedar Cove, but her decision had been a turning point for him, as well.

She'd made a mess of things by trusting David Rhodes. Naively, she'd believed he loved her, because it was what he'd said and what she *wanted* to believe. All his lies and false promises had left her pregnant and alone.

In giving herself to David, she'd rebelled against the control Linc had over her. Her pregnancy had complicated everything — and yet it was the beginning of a new order in the Wyse family. She'd moved to Cedar Cove and, as an indirect result of that, Linc had met Lori. Over the past few months Mary Jo's relationship with her brother had begun to change. He became her brother for the first time since they'd lost their parents. Her *brother* and not a surrogate father.

"Isn't that Linc and Lori?" Mack asked.

Mary Jo nodded. The differences in Linc were apparent in more than just his attitude. He seemed at ease with himself and the world. He behaved like a carefree young man, and she realized how much he'd been robbed of after their loss. Selfishly, all Mary Jo had thought about were her own feelings, not his. She regretted her adolescent rebelliousness, recognizing that, without ever intending to, she'd made his life harder.

They met and chatted for a few minutes, making tentative dinner plans for later in the week. Then Mack and Mary Jo resumed walking through the market. Mack purchased a couple of quilted bibs for Noelle, who seemed to constantly drool now that her teeth were coming in. Mary Jo tied a pink one around her neck right away.

Around three o'clock, the market started to wind down. Mack suggested they continue their stroll along the waterfront. The afternoon was so bright and sunny that Mary Jo eagerly agreed. Noelle had fallen asleep, and Mary Jo felt relaxed, contented in the sunshine and Mack's presence.

The Seattle ferry had just pulled into the

Bremerton dock and seagulls circled over-head. The scent of the tide going out filled her nostrils.

Pushing the stroller with one hand, Mack clasped her hand with the other. They didn't speak. The simple pleasure of walking by the water, all her senses engaged — being with *Mack* — made her happier than she'd been in a long time. She was about to tell Mack exactly that when a familiar voice spoke behind them.

"Well, isn't *this* a cozy picture."

Mary Jo's blood turned to ice. David Rhodes.

At the sound of David's voice, Mack whirled around. Instinctively Mary Jo moved closer to him.

"What do you want?" Mack demanded.

"That's none of your business," David answered defiantly.

Seeing her baby's father so unexpectedly was almost more than she could tolerate. Her entire body started to shake.

"I see it didn't take you long to find my replacement," David said, staring at Mack. He smiled then, that easy, confident smile she knew so well. "Actually, he's welcome to you. All I care about is my daughter."

"What are you doing here?" Mary Jo asked, then regretted the question. The answer was obvious. He'd come to see his father and stepmother. Or worse, he'd come in search of her and Noelle.

While he claimed all he cared about was Noelle, she noticed that he hadn't glanced once at the stroller or their daughter, as if Noelle didn't even exist.

"I came to find you," David said, looking directly at Mary Jo.

"Why?" She hated the way her voice trembled.

"You know why."

But she didn't. Nor did she want to.

"Stay out of Mary Jo's life," Mack said from between clenched teeth.

Mary Jo placed a calming hand on his forearm. She didn't want this to turn into a sparring match, although she was fairly sure that if it did, Mack would easily overtake David. Seeing him now, with his puffy face and bloodshot eyes, she wondered why she'd ever been attracted to the man.

Even as she asked herself that question, her mind provided an immediate response. In David she'd seen freedom, a way out from under her brother's thumb. David Rhodes had offered her an escape, and she'd been both foolish and blind enough to take it.

David returned his attention to Mary Jo.

"I'm here to warn you that if you file for child support with the state, you'll be sorry."

"You threaten Mary Jo and you'll deal with me," Mack growled. He brushed her hand from his forearm and stood directly in front of David.

David didn't back down. "As I mentioned earlier," he said in a congenial voice, "this really isn't any of your business. The matter of our child — and who gets to keep her — is between Mary Jo and me." He looked at Mary Jo again, his eyebrows raised. "My father said he advised you to file for child support."

Mary Jo swallowed uncomfortably. Ben had brought up the subject this past Wednesday, when she'd stopped by for her weekly visit. He'd felt David should be held financially accountable for his daughter. The fact that David had denied any responsibility disturbed Ben, and he'd urged Mary Jo to file for support. She'd promised to consider it. She hadn't discussed any of this with Mack, but had been quietly contemplating a course of action. Her biggest fear was that if she did file, David would insist on visitation rights, and he seemed to be implying that he would. She couldn't bear the thought of handing Noelle over to David, since she didn't trust him.

"I won't," she blurted out.

A slow smile appeared on David's face. "That's a wise decision."

Mack took a menacing step forward.

David held up one hand. "Mary Jo can make her own decisions," he said calmly. "She doesn't need any help from you."

"I plan on marrying her," Mack told him.

David shrugged. "Well, good for you, but don't forget I had her first."

For an instant Mary Jo felt as if she was going to be sick. "Stop it!" she shouted. "Just stop it."

Noelle woke with a piercing cry. Mary Jo and Mack reached for her at the same time, bumping heads in the process. Mary Jo grabbed her daughter, turning her back on both Mack and David. She was shaking so badly it was almost impossible to walk.

This confrontation was horrible. Every fear she'd ever had regarding David seemed to be staring her in the face. For the second time since leaving Seattle she had the strongest desire to move back to her family home.

Mack caught up to her a moment later, touching her shoulders. "David's gone," he said quietly.

She nodded, unable to speak.

"Are you all right?" he asked, his face

concerned.

Mary Jo wasn't sure how to answer him. Every part of her trembled with shock and reaction. She never wanted to see David again as long as she lived. As for turning Noelle over to him — she'd rather die. His threat was all too real, and Mary Jo refused to take chances with her daughter. The less Noelle had to do with her biological father, the better.

"Mary Jo?" Mack's hands tightened on her shoulders. "Answer me. Are you all right?"

"I . . . I don't know."

"You're shivering."

Perhaps because she sensed her mother's tension, Noelle began to cry. Mary Jo bounced her baby gently in her arms and whispered words of reassurance.

Mack took control then, getting Mary Jo and Noelle back to the car, then dealing with the stroller. Once inside, he started the engine.

"I want to go home," she whispered.

"That's where I'm taking you," Mack said soothingly.

"I mean Seattle." She gazed straight ahead.

"Mary Jo —"

"Noelle and I will be safe there."

221

"You're safe with me," Mack countered.

"David's never been to the house in Seattle. He . . . he doesn't even know where my family lives."

"You're not thinking clearly," Mack said urgently. "He could get their address, no problem."

Although she knew he was right, Mary Jo didn't care. Every instinct she possessed told her to run and hide. She didn't want to risk running into David ever again and if she remained in Cedar Cove that would always be a possibility.

"I'm calling Troy Davis," Mack told her.

"The sheriff? Why?"

"I want you to file a restraining order against David Rhodes."

"On what grounds?" she asked.

"There must be something," he said stubbornly. "We can look into it."

Still, she didn't know if that was the best way to handle the situation.

In what seemed like only a minute, they were back at the duplex. But when Mack pulled into the driveway, he made no move to leave her car.

"Will you get a restraining order?"

"That won't stop him."

"Maybe not, but it gives the sheriff the authority to arrest him. I refuse to allow this man to threaten you and Noelle."

"I . . . I —"

"We've come too far to let him stand between us now," Mack said.

Wiping her face, Mary Jo felt torn by indecision. Her afternoon had begun with such promise, meeting special friends, seeing her brother and Lori — and now this.

She looked at Mack. "Hold me. Please, just hold me."

He wrapped his arms around her, and Mary Jo buried her face in his chest. Closing her eyes, she took in his warmth and his love. Soon the trembling subsided.

"Okay now?" Mack whispered.

She nodded.

"No more talk of moving back to Seattle?"

"Not my smartest idea," she admitted.

"Good."

She straightened. "You heard what David said. Ben wants me to file for child support. He believes David needs to be held responsible for Noelle."

"Is that something you want to do?"

"I . . . I don't know." Ben had made a good case, but although she'd listened intently to everything the older man had said, Mary Jo wasn't convinced.

"I don't like the idea of David talking to you like that." Mack's voice was steely. "I don't like his threats or his insinuations."

"He's afraid." She realized that he dreaded facing eighteen years of child support and wanted out. If that involved making her life miserable, then he'd do it.

Mack opened the door. "I meant what I said."

Mary Jo looked at him, confused by his comment. "About what?"

"Marrying you."

Not that again. "Mack, thank you, but no."

He stared at her, and for an instant she saw hurt and disappointment in his eyes before he could disguise his feelings.

"Haven't we been through this before?" she asked, hoping to make light of his proposal. "The last time, your proposal was prompted by another one of David's threats." If he really wanted to marry her, Mary Jo wanted to be loved for *herself* and not because Mack was afraid of losing her or Noelle to David Rhodes.

"I guess I forgot," he muttered, striding toward his side of the duplex.

"Mack!" she called.

Abruptly he turned to face her. "What?"

"You're still coming for dinner, aren't you?"

He shook his head. "No, thanks. I've lost my appetite."

# FIFTEEN

Shirley Bliss was curled up on her living room sofa, feet tucked beneath her and a cup of tea in her hand. Her friend Miranda sat across from her, holding an identical mug, also filled with steaming tea. Miranda had recently accepted a part-time job with Will Jefferson, which in Shirley's opinion was good for Will *and* for Miranda. Her friend didn't need the money, but she was at loose ends and Will could use the help. Besides, Miranda had connections that could benefit the gallery.

Her husband had been a well-known landscape artist. Miranda dabbled in art, too, although she lacked the discipline to capitalize on her talent. However, she had an excellent eye and her criticism was incisive.

"I've been dying to hear about your hot date with Will Jefferson," Miranda said.

"I wouldn't exactly call it a hot date,"

Shirley said, not meeting her eyes. Shirley felt mildly guilty for accepting Will's invitation. In all likelihood, she would've found yet another excuse to refuse if not for the fact that he'd asked her to the gallery event, where she'd met Larry Knight. Shirley couldn't turn down the opportunity of a lifetime.

When they did meet, Larry was everything she'd imagined and more. They hadn't spoken long. He'd told her he'd lost his wife five years earlier, and an instant rapport had developed between them. Those minutes alone with him — despite being in a room full of people — had been magical.

"Will took you to Canlis, didn't he?" This was one of the most exclusive and expensive restaurants in Seattle.

"Uh, yes."

Miranda gave a short laugh. "Apparently he didn't get the message that you don't eat red meat." Shirley wasn't a full vegetarian and did on occasion eat beef, but not often and never steak.

"He got it by the end of the night." The message about her food preferences wasn't the only one. She couldn't have been any clearer — she wasn't interested in pursuing a relationship with Will Jefferson. While she appreciated everything he'd done for Tanni

226

and Shaw, that appreciation didn't imply any kind of romantic relationship.

"He talked you into letting him display your dragon piece."

That, too, had been prompted by the guilt Shirley felt over using Will, primarily in the situation with Tanni and Shaw. The dragon was a deeply personal work of art that she'd never allowed in public before and wouldn't again. He wanted it up for the summer and she'd reluctantly consented, after initially agreeing to only one month.

To her, the dragon symbolized the fiery grief the death of her husband had brought into her life. Shirley had made the fabric collage shortly after her husband, Jim, was killed in a motorcycle accident. Will had taken one look at it and practically begged her to let him display it. After weeks of turning him down she'd finally acquiesced, with the proviso that specific measures be taken to protect it. Will had accepted her conditions.

"Have you talked to Will since last Sunday?" Miranda asked.

Shirley shook her head. His reticence was mildly surprising. He'd been finding one reason or another to contact her every other day and then . . . silence. Not that Shirley was complaining.

"Does the fact he hasn't called concern you?" Miranda asked.

Sipping her tea, Shirley watched her friend over the rim of her mug. "Why all these questions about me and Will Jefferson?"

Miranda shifted uncomfortably. "No reason. I was just wondering."

"I enjoyed talking to Larry Knight for five minutes far more than I enjoyed that expensive dinner with Will."

"But you would never have met Larry if it hadn't been for Will."

That was true enough. "I know."

"And you feel guilty about that, right?"

Shirley sighed. "Right."

"I did," Miranda mumbled, looking decidedly uncomfortable.

"You did what?" Shirley asked in confusion.

"I heard from Will."

"Will Jefferson? He called you about work, you mean?"

Miranda shrugged. "At first I thought he wanted me for the gallery. I've already worked a couple of afternoons. However, this time he called and . . . asked me out to dinner."

That was encouraging news. "And?" Shirley asked, excited for her friend.

"Absolutely not." Her reply was forceful.

"I wouldn't go out with the man my best friend's dating if you paid me a million bucks." She grinned. "Well, maybe I would for that kind of money."

Shirley smiled, too. "I get your drift, but you don't have to turn him down."

Miranda looked in every direction except Shirley's.

"In other words, it wouldn't bother me in the least if you wanted to go out with Will," Shirley said, hoping to reassure her.

"But it would bother me." Miranda spoke just as adamantly as she had earlier. "He's interested in you. The only reason Will asked *me* is to get a reaction out of you."

"Why would you think that?"

Miranda rolled her eyes. "Oh, please."

"Okay, you could be right." Shirley laughed. "So call him back and tell him you've had a change of heart."

"Why?"

"Why?" Shirley repeated. "Because I have a feeling you might actually be interested."

"You've got to be kidding! That man's used to women falling all over themselves to make him happy. He's had his way for far too long." Amusement glimmered in her eyes. "You were the exception, the woman he couldn't get."

"Well, rumor has it there were others,"

Shirley said, thinking of Grace.

"He needs a woman who'll tell him what's what."

"The woman he needs, Miranda, is you," Shirley said.

"Sorry, not interested."

Shirley wasn't convinced that was even close to the truth. "Whatever you decide is fine with me. I don't want him, so he's all yours."

"I don't want him, either," Miranda said stubbornly. "It would take far too much time and effort to whip him into shape. I don't have the inclination or the patience to take on that project."

"Uh-huh."

"I'm serious," Miranda insisted.

"If you say so." Shirley had seen the spark in Miranda's eyes whenever Will's name was mentioned.

"Don't you start with me, Shirley Bliss."

"Fine. I won't," she returned, smiling. Oh, her friend was interested, but at the same time she was afraid. Miranda's marriage hadn't been nearly as happy as Shirley's. For all his talent, Hugh Sullivan had been a difficult and demanding personality.

A half hour later, Shirley was in the kitchen preparing a chicken-and-rice casserole dish when Tanni came home.

Her relationship with her teenage daughter was rocky and hadn't improved much. Shirley tended to tread lightly, always unsure of Tanni's mood. It was usually best to wait for her to speak first.

"What's that?" her daughter asked, wrinkling her nose as she watched Shirley work.

"Dinner," Shirley said without elaborating.

"You aren't putting mushrooms in it, are you?"

"No." She *had* planned to add mushrooms but wouldn't now. "This is chicken with cheese and rice. Does that meet with your approval?"

"Sounds okay, I guess."

Evidently Shirley had deflated her daughter's indignation. She chanced a look in Tanni's direction and took a leap of faith. "Is everything all right?" she asked tentatively.

Tanni whirled around, and Shirley was shocked to see tears in her eyes. In the past she would've pretended she hadn't noticed, but she couldn't do that anymore. She reached out her arms and hugged Tanni.

Tanni released a sob as she slid her arms around her mother's waist. "He won't even answer my text messages anymore," she wailed.

"Shaw?"

Tanni nodded jerkily.

The two of them — Tanni and Shaw — had been together constantly for about eight months. Shirley had been nearly frantic with worry that they might become physically involved. Her fear was that they'd already crossed that line. Will Jefferson had thrown her a life preserver when — with Larry's assistance — he'd arranged for Shaw to attend the San Francisco Art Institute.

At first Shaw and Tanni were in frequent communication, but then as the weeks passed, Tanni heard from him less and less often. In the beginning she'd made excuses for Shaw. "He's busy," she'd say, keeping her cell phone close at hand.

"I thought he loved me," Tanni blurted now. Shirley could feel her daughter struggling to control her emotions.

She had no words of advice to offer. It didn't matter. What Tanni needed was comfort and love, and Shirley had both in abundance.

"I volunteered at the library because I thought it would help take my mind off Shaw, but that's no good, either."

The Reading with Rover program was going well, and Shirley assumed Tanni enjoyed being part of it. Every indication from

Grace Harding suggested that Tanni was doing a terrific job.

"You seemed to like working with the kids."

"I do, but I hate having to deal with Kristen." She twisted her lip as she pronounced the other girl's name. "She's such a goody-goody," Tanni spat out. "And Grace wants me to make nice. Give me a break."

"I'm sure you'll work it out." Shirley couldn't think of anything else to tell Tanni.

"I want to quit, but I can see how much the little kids love reading to the dogs. And if I left, Grace would have to remove someone from the program. That'd be wrong. Besides, I'd just go back to worrying about Shaw."

"You can't quit without a good reason."

Her daughter glared up at her as if Shirley had uttered the stupidest words ever spoken by a parent. "Thanks, Mom, but I already figured that out on my own."

"Oops, sorry." They rarely had a conversation without Shirley making at least one critical error in judgment, saying either too much or too little.

Tanni broke out of her arms. "I'm not calling or texting Shaw ever again."

That was no doubt for the best, although hard to pull off, especially since these kids seemed to have cell phones permanently attached to their hands.

Tanni hesitated. "Not today, anyway."

"Do you want me to hold on to your cell phone for you?" Shirley asked, thinking it might help if she kept temptation out of the way.

"No." Tanni sent her a scornful look and went into her bedroom, closing the door.

"Okay, sorry I asked," Shirley muttered.

The phone rang and caller ID said it was a private number. As usual, Tanni answered after a solitary ring. Two or three seconds later her daughter shrilled down the hallway, "It's for you!"

"Who is it?" Shirley asked. If she didn't get this casserole in the oven, dinner wouldn't be ready until eight.

"I don't know. Some man."

"Some man" probably translated into Will Jefferson, but if that was the case Tanni should have recognized his voice. He certainly phoned often enough.

Sighing, she reached for the phone. "This is Shirley."

"Shirley, it's Larry Knight. Am I calling at a bad time?"

Shock and delight rippled through her. "No, not at all. This is perfect." Any time he called would be perfect as far as she was concerned. She hadn't dared to hope she'd hear from him.

"I wanted to tell you what a pleasure it was to meet you last week."

"The pleasure was mine." The expression was commonplace, but she meant it sincerely.

"I'm going to be in the Seattle area again soon."

"That's . . . wonderful." She wished her voice wasn't so breathless.

"It's another show."

"Of your work?"

"No, a friend of mine."

Shirley waited for him to continue.

"I'm calling to ask if you'd be free to join me."

"I would," she said, regardless of the details.

"It's on Sunday the twenty-seventh."

"That's perfect." She bit her lip, embarrassed that she no longer seemed to know any other words.

"I can get a third invitation if you'd like to include Will."

"No. No, that isn't necessary."

"You're sure?" Larry asked.

"Oh, yes."

"I arrive early Saturday and fly out Monday morning."

"Would you like to come to Cedar Cove?" she asked, and immediately regretted it. She imagined how awkward it would be if they ran into Will Jefferson.

"Perhaps," he said, "but I have commitments in Seattle on Saturday."

Of course he would. Shirley felt gauche for having made the suggestion. Larry was an important artist, a celebrity, and he had better things to do than visit Cedar Cove.

"Would it be possible to see you on Sunday? Have dinner after the show?"

"No . . . I mean, yes, it would be possible." Every time she opened her mouth she seemed to say something stupid. She had to wonder why Larry wanted to see her at all.

"Great." He sounded pleased, which only added to Shirley's delight.

"I'm so glad you called," she said. "I didn't expect to hear from you, and, well, I'm . . . more than a little flattered." It was probably all wrong to tell him that, to be so effusive, but she didn't care.

They talked for another five minutes while they made arrangements. He'd send a car for her and, if he could manage it, he'd come with the car, although at this point that looked doubtful. As he spoke, Shirley got a pen and pad from the kitchen junk drawer and wrote it all down, certain that if she didn't she'd forget every word.

As soon as she was off the phone, Shirley rushed down the hallway to her daughter's bedroom and threw open the door. Tanni lay on her bed, cell phone in hand, text messaging.

"You'll never guess who that was!" Shirley cried.

Tanni looked up with a bored expression. "Hugh Jackman."

"No, silly. Larry Knight."

Tanni gaped at her. "*The* Larry Knight. The artist?"

Shirley nodded.

"Did he say anything about Shaw?"

It hadn't even occurred to Shirley to ask. "No, he didn't," she said, feeling a little guilty.

The hope that had flared in Tanni's eyes was quickly extinguished.

"He asked me on a date," Shirley told her.

"A date with *you?*"

Shirley knew it probably sounded as inconceivable to her daughter as it did to her that Larry Knight had asked her out.

"You're going?"

Shirley nodded, trying not to act too happy when her daughter was so miserable over Shaw. Still, she couldn't quite contain her joy as she hurried back to the kitchen.

She could hardly wait to tell Miranda
about this.

# Sixteen

Charlotte sat in her favorite chair, doing her favorite thing — knitting. Her fingers were as busy as her mind and although she'd knit this same sweater a number of times she kept making small mistakes that she had to rip out, kept needing to refer to the pattern. She'd been so distracted and forgetful. She blamed it on this stress caused by her husband's son, David.

Ben had turned on the television and sat staring at it, apparently engrossed, although she doubted either of them was concentrating on the evening news.

"Ben," Charlotte finally said.

He glanced away from the TV and looked at her. "Yes?"

"Let's ask Olivia. She knows about the law in situations like this." She didn't elaborate; there was no need to. Ben knew very well that she was talking about David's daughter, Noelle.

Ben's mouth thinned. "Let me think about it."

Charlotte had no intention of pressuring him. Ben loved his little granddaughter and had already taken financial measures to secure her future. His son's actions had devastated him — and this wasn't the first time. David had a history of hurtful and irresponsible behavior, which included "borrowing" money from Ben. Money that was rarely ever repaid. A "sponger," her own son had called him. Maybe Will's behavior hadn't always been exemplary, either, but compared to David he was a paragon.

Charlotte knew Ben had been hoping David would do the right thing, the responsible thing, and support his child. That hadn't happened and probably wouldn't. Instead, David had obstinately insisted Noelle wasn't his child, even after admitting it earlier. But he could no longer deny his paternity, since a DNA test had proven it conclusively.

They'd spoken with David on Saturday. Now he'd started claiming that DNA testing wasn't infallible and that Mary Jo was some kind of fraud. Or — and he'd also claimed this — she was promiscuous, although he'd put it more crudely.

Ben wasn't having any of that and neither was Charlotte. He'd urged Mary Jo to file a paternity suit. For David to acknowledge his responsibility and accept it would be the honorable course of action, but as Charlotte had learned, David Rhodes was not an honorable man.

"Maybe it *would* be a good idea to discuss this with Olivia," Ben said after several minutes.

"She deals with similar cases every day in court, or she did," Charlotte amended, "when she was working."

"The problem is . . ." Ben let the rest of his thought fade.

Charlotte knew better than to prompt him. Ben often broke off in the middle of a sentence while he considered a dilemma or mulled over a solution.

"The problem is," he began a second time, "I don't know if Mary Jo is willing to take our advice."

Charlotte was knitting at a frantic pace, ignoring any errors she might be making. The poor girl had arrived at the house late Saturday afternoon, so upset she'd hardly been able to speak; they got the story out of her in bits and pieces. From what Charlotte recalled of the conversation, David had confronted Mary Jo and more or less threatened her if she pursued child support.

Charlotte was outraged whenever she

thought about it. She didn't say anything because it would only upset Ben, and he'd already endured about all he could from his youngest son.

"I was thinking I'd make up a batch of that soup you like. The one with the meatballs and fresh spinach." For the life of her, she couldn't remember the name of it.

"Italian wedding soup," Ben said.

"Yes, that's the one. I bet Olivia would enjoy it, too. I'll make a big pot and we'll bring it over tomorrow afternoon for lunch." She'd spend the morning baking a loaf of oatmeal molasses bread and would add that to her basket.

Ben reached across the space between their two chairs and took her hand. "Thank you," he whispered.

"Why are you thanking me, Ben Rhodes?"

He answered her with the sweetest of smiles. "For your love and patience."

"I vowed to love you, and I do, and as for the patience part, you don't need to thank me for that. You're a good man, and a good father, too."

He shook his head. "I don't feel like one."

"Nonsense. We can't take on the faults of our children. As adults, we all make our own decisions and live our own lives."

"That's true," Ben agreed. "But it's still

hard to see our children acting badly."

Charlotte couldn't argue with that.

The following afternoon, Ben drove Charlotte out to Lighthouse Road. As they walked to the back door, she studied the small vegetable garden and the strawberry patch, dotted with succulent red berries. She'd pick some later and make Olivia that freezer jam she liked.

"Anyone home?" Charlotte called out as they entered the house.

"Mom?" Olivia's voice came from the spare bedroom. "Oh, is it lunchtime already?" She hurried into the kitchen with a measuring tape around her neck and a pair of scissors in one hand. She must be working on a quilt. Ever since Olivia had started to recover, she'd been designing and sewing quilts for her grandchildren. They were lovely, too. It was an activity that occupied her time and gave her a creative outlet.

Ben set the Crock-Pot filled with soup on the kitchen counter and plugged it in.

"As promised, we brought lunch," Charlotte announced. She opened the kitchen cupboard, taking down three soup bowls and three bread plates. "Is Jack going to be joining us?"

Olivia nodded. "Have you ever known my husband to miss one of your meals?" She got another bowl and plate, while Ben efficiently collected the silverware. "He's been taking time off every day to drive home and check on me. Oh, he makes it sound like he's just home for lunch, but I know that man and he's watching over me."

"As well he should," Charlotte said. She approved of Jack's less-than-subtle approach to caring for her daughter. She was grateful he kept a close eye on Olivia; the cancer was bad enough, but they'd very nearly lost her last fall, and the scare had put them all on edge. The memory of those weeks always sent a chill down Charlotte's spine.

As if he'd been able to smell the fresh-baked bread, Jack pulled into the space behind Ben's car. He bounded out of his vehicle and came through the kitchen door, clutching a copy of the latest *Cedar Cove Chronicle.* "You've got your very own delivery boy," he said cheerfully, handing it to Olivia. "Hi, everyone."

They all greeted him and Charlotte smiled at him fondly.

"Do I smell lunch?" he asked, glancing expectantly around. He kissed Olivia's cheek and walked straight past her to the Crock-Pot on the counter. Lifting the lid, he closed his eyes. "Mmm. Homemade soup?"

"Italian wedding," Ben said.

"As usual, you're right on time," Charlotte told him. "Everything's ready."

Within a few minutes, the four of them were sitting at the kitchen table; the bread was still warm enough to melt the butter, and the soup was delicious, if Charlotte did say so herself.

"Actually, Olivia, we're not just here for lunch —" he inclined his head at Charlotte "— delectable though it is. We have a few questions for you, if you don't mind," Ben said.

"Of course." Olivia looked somewhat surprised.

"This has to do with Noelle," Charlotte supplied, eager to help.

"It has more to do with my son than Noelle," Ben inserted.

Charlotte saw that he'd set his spoon aside and didn't reach for it again. The subject of David had obviously ruined Ben's appetite. "I urged Mary Jo to file for child support," he said.

"She should do it," Jack seconded vigorously, an opinion Charlotte strongly agreed with.

"Mary Jo knows David's unemployed. She thinks there's no point in filing when he isn't making any money." Ben turned to

245

Olivia with a questioning look.

"Whether he's currently employed or not doesn't matter," Olivia said.

"Good." Ben's expression was one of relief.

Charlotte felt they should review the facts. "Mary Jo's been taking care of Noelle on her own and it isn't right. Ben wanted to help her financially, but Mary Jo wouldn't accept money." She had to admire the young woman, although her situation must be difficult.

"I did include Noelle in my will," Ben explained. "But I feel it's David's responsibility to support his daughter even if he wasn't married to the child's mother. As it is, he's not supporting the child he had with his ex-wife, either."

"Ben told his son how he felt and I'm afraid their talk didn't go well. Unfortunately, David ran into Mary Jo shortly after meeting with his father." Charlotte glanced at Ben, wanting his permission before she continued. He nodded.

She paused a moment to butter some bread. "It turns out that David saw Mary Jo and Mack McAfee with Noelle down by the waterfront on Saturday afternoon. You remember how lovely the day was, don't you? Well, Mary Jo said David threatened her again."

"Threatened?" Olivia asked, frowning. "How, exactly?"

Ben took over then. "From what Mary Jo could tell us, it seems David implied that if she went after child support, he'd fight her for custody of Noelle. By the way," he added, "I've recently learned that he's moved to Seattle."

Charlotte noticed that he didn't say anything about the woman David was living with, the woman who was supporting him. She knew it was a source of great shame to Ben.

"I suppose being in Seattle gives him greater access — and makes him more of a threat," he went on to say.

"In these situations, the state virtually always keeps the infant with the mother," Olivia assured them.

"My son has no intention of raising that child. He has another daughter from his marriage that he rarely sees. He has no interest in being a father to either of his children, painful as that is for me to admit."

Charlotte placed her hand over Ben's, offering him what comfort she could.

"In my opinion, Mary Jo should call his bluff." Olivia spoke in a no-nonsense voice. "The courts don't take kindly to these types of threats."

"According to Mary Jo, David didn't even look at the baby once," Ben said. "In Noelle's whole life, he's never held her, never touched her, and to claim now that he'll fight for custody is just plain ludicrous."

"Especially when he denied even fathering the child," Charlotte said.

"The judge will ask about his involvement with Noelle to this point," Olivia told them. "That is, if the case ever comes before the court, which I doubt will happen."

Jack didn't look convinced. "You never know. He might get himself some crackerjack lawyer with a bee in his bonnet about father's rights."

"True." Olivia sighed. "My guess is that David's using intimidation, hoping Mary Jo won't ask for money from him, especially now that he's unemployed."

"Well, if she does, I'm afraid David will refuse to pay," Ben murmured. "Even if he finds another job."

"Since paternity is verified, the state will garnishee David's unemployment check, presuming that he's receiving one. He won't have any choice but to pay child support."

Charlotte knew he wouldn't like *that,* and his current girlfriend wouldn't, either.

"What's the situation between Mack and

Mary Jo?" Olivia asked thoughtfully.

"You've probably heard that they're sharing a duplex," Ben answered. "Each living in one half."

"He loves that little baby. Why, Mack's far more of a father to her than David," Charlotte put in.

"That's what I figured," Olivia said. "I saw the three of them at the market on Saturday and they looked just like any young family on an outing."

"I'm sure Mack's sweet on Mary Jo," Ben told them.

*Sweet* was such a lovely word, Charlotte mused. Old-fashioned and charming. Anyone could see that Mack and Mary Jo were falling in love.

"If I was a betting man, I'd say they'll end up married." Jack reached for his third slice of bread.

Charlotte passed him the butter, which he took gratefully until Olivia placed a hand on his forearm. Without saying a word, Jack pushed the butter aside and patted his wife's hand.

This exchange took only a few seconds and it made Charlotte smile despite the seriousness of their conversation. A couple of years ago, Jack had suffered a heart attack, and ever since, Olivia had stood guard over his diet. The way she and Jack looked after each other was inspiring.

"Has Mary Jo given you any indication that she'll eventually marry Mack?" Olivia asked her mother and Ben.

"Well, no, but like Ben said earlier," Charlotte replied, "it's obvious that they're close."

"If they *were* to marry, do you believe Mack would want to legally adopt Noelle?"

Charlotte didn't need to think about her response. "I believe he would. He's crazy about that baby. Noelle and Mary Jo are all he talks about." To be fair, she hadn't had a *lot* of conversations with Mack, but whenever she did, he was full of stories about them. And his mother said the same thing.

Ben raised a cautious hand. "I suspect —" He hesitated, then started again. "I suspect that Mack and Mary Jo had some sort of disagreement after seeing David."

"Now, Ben . . ."

He raised his hand again, stopping her. "I know Mary Jo was flustered and upset when she came to see us, but I'm sure it was over more than what happened with David."

Thinking about it, Charlotte had to agree. Mary Jo had been in a real state. She'd needed to get away, she said. She needed to talk to someone. With Mack living right next door, wouldn't she go to him? Unless she couldn't. . . .

Of course, he might've been at the firehouse, but then Charlotte remembered Olivia mentioning that she'd seen Mack and Mary Jo together that same afternoon. So Mary Jo could easily have discussed the matter with him. Instead, she'd come to Ben and her.

Charlotte turned to her daughter. "Why are you asking about Mack?" He wasn't part of the equation. This had to do with David, Mary Jo and Noelle.

"The reason I asked about Mack's feelings toward Mary Jo," Olivia said, "is because he might want to adopt Noelle if and when he marries Mary Jo. You told me you thought that would be the case."

Oh, yes. She *had* said that. And it was true.

"I just want everyone to be aware of the potential complications."

Ben shrugged. "If I know David, I'd say he'll do everything within his power to make the adoption as hard as possible. He doesn't want Noelle himself, but he won't want anyone else to become her father. It's unfortunate, but that's how my son's mind works." Ben lowered his head. "Much as I hate to admit this about my own flesh and blood, if David feels he has the upper hand, he'll use it to his advantage."

"Then I suggest," Olivia said, "that you take that power away from him now."

"What do we need to do?" Ben asked.

"Have Mary Jo file for child support."

"If she will," Charlotte felt obliged to insert. The girl had been so terrified that David would try to take Noelle away from her.

"David will put up a fight, so warn her in advance to be prepared for that. Really, it's what we want because the next move will be Mary Jo's. She can then approach him with relinquishment papers."

"What does that entail?" Ben asked. "Is it as straightforward as it sounds?"

"Pretty much. If David signs those papers, he relinquishes his rights as Noelle's father. Then Mack would be free to adopt Noelle," Olivia explained.

Charlotte clasped her hands together. "That would be wonderful!"

"And if not Mack, some other man in the future," Olivia added. "If David wants out of paying child support, this is the way to do it. I can almost guarantee it'll save Mary Jo untold heartache later on."

Charlotte was more than satisfied. "We need to discuss this with Mary Jo," she said.

"At our earliest opportunity," Ben concurred.

For the first time since David's last visit, Charlotte noticed that the frown he'd constantly worn had disappeared.

## Seventeen

"You know what Mack's going to tell us, don't you?" Corrie said confidently as she finished setting the table for dinner. Mack had asked if he could bring Mary Jo and Noelle over on Friday evening. That was unusual, so Corrie was convinced she knew the purpose of this visit. Their son was going to announce that he'd asked Mary Jo to marry him. They'd planned to drop by for coffee or a drink, but Corrie had invited them all to dinner. After checking with Mary Jo, Mack had confirmed that they'd be available.

Roy was in the living room, watching the news, and didn't answer.

"Roy!" Corrie said, so excited she could barely contain herself. "Mack is going to tell us he's asked Mary Jo to be his wife."

"You're sure of that?" he asked, glancing briefly away from the screen.

"Not one hundred percent. Call it a

mother's intuition, but I know my son, and he's head over heels about Mary Jo and that baby girl."

Roy shrugged. "Time will tell. Don't plan the wedding yet."

Corrie set the casserole dish on the table to cool. She'd made one of Mack's favorite recipes, shepherd's pie with a mashed-potato base.

Mack had asked for this dish on every birthday for as long as Corrie could remember. It seemed fitting to prepare it for him the night he told them he was engaged. She wondered what kind of ring he'd bought Mary Jo. . . .

"They're here." Roy was looking out the front window, which provided a good view of the driveway.

"Perfect timing," she said, rubbing her hands together. And she meant it in more ways than one. Linnette and Pete were married and now their son, too, was ready to start his family.

Corrie removed her apron and tossed it on a kitchen chair. She'd take the salad out of the refrigerator just before they sat down at the table. They'd visit first, with some hors d'oeuvres and a congratulatory glass of wine.

Roy opened the door for Mary Jo and

their son, who held Noelle's baby carrier.

"Welcome, welcome." Corrie rushed forward to hug Mary Jo and her son. Her eyes instantly went to the baby who would soon be her granddaughter. She looked forward to becoming a grandmother — twice in one year — and already adored Noelle. She envisioned cooking with her one day and teaching her how to make shepherd's pie. They'd have tea parties and would fill coloring books together.

"I was hoping you'd make that," Mack said, gesturing at the table. "Smells fantastic." He kissed his mother on the cheek as Mary Jo dealt with Noelle.

Corrie noticed that Mary Jo wasn't wearing an engagement ring, but maybe Mack hadn't bought it yet. All through their drinks and carefully chosen appetizers — cheese, crackers, stuffed mushrooms and tiny sausage rolls — she waited for an announcement that didn't come.

"Everything's ready," Corrie finally said, and stood to bring the salad to the table.

They sat down together, and after a short grace, Roy refilled their glasses. Corrie handed the serving spoon to her son.

"This is my favorite dinner," he told Mary Jo. "Mom makes it every year on my birthday."

"I'll give you the recipe if you like," Corrie was quick to tell Mary Jo.

"Why, thank you. I'd enjoy that."

"My mother's a great cook."

Corrie blushed at the praise. She took her first bite and was pleased with how well the shepherd's pie had turned out — every bit as good as last year's. She didn't make it often, since Roy had his own favorites.

Halfway through the meal Corrie couldn't stand the suspense anymore. "I believe I know why you and Mary Jo wanted to stop by," she said coyly, glancing at her husband.

"You do?" Mack's gaze shot to Mary Jo.

"You know we came about the letters?" Mary Jo asked Corrie.

Corrie frowned. "Letters? What letters?" She turned to her husband, hoping for an explanation.

"Mary Jo found a box filled with letters from World War II," Mack said. "Remember?"

Corrie nodded. "Of course I do," she replied. In fact she'd had a long conversation with Peggy about them.

"Then Mack found a diary, hidden in the same space," Mary Jo added.

"You came here because you wanted to talk about the letters?" Corrie was fascinated by them, too, but couldn't let go of her hope that they'd come to share the news of their engagement.

"They're incredible, Mom." Mack's voice rose with enthusiasm. "Did I tell you Mary Jo and I have been doing research on D-day? The Normandy invasion."

"June 6, 1944," Roy said, apparently in case she'd forgotten the date.

"Joan Manry and Jacob Dennison were so much in love, and then after the invasion . . . there's nothing." Mary Jo looked at Corrie and then Roy. "No more letters, no more diary entries. It's a mystery."

"Mary Jo and I keep wondering what happened to them."

"We're dying to find out," she told Corrie. "The letters —"

"You asked to have dinner with us because of the letters?" Corrie broke in. She couldn't conceal her disappointment.

Mack stared at her blankly. "Actually, you asked *us* to dinner, remember?"

"Yes . . . no. I apologize." Corrie placed her hands in her lap. "I thought . . . I hoped you'd come for another reason."

"Corrie . . ." Roy warned, his voice low.

"What?" Mary Jo asked.

"Well, I'd hoped . . ." Corrie managed a half smile as she turned to her son. "I just assumed, you know, with the two of you spending so much time together, that you might've decided to . . . get married." She looked from her son to Mary Jo and then at Noelle. She'd swear the baby wasn't pleased, either, making a sad face and kicking out her legs as if struggling to break free of her carrier.

"Mack and I —" Mary Jo's eyes widened. "No, that isn't it at all."

"So I see."

"Tell me more about the letters," Roy said, changing the subject and not being subtle about it.

Mack seemed as eager as his father to talk about something other than marriage. "Seeing how abruptly the letters stopped after the invasion, Mary Jo and I thought Jacob must've been killed."

"We don't think so now," Mary Jo said, "because we can't find his name on the list of soldiers laid to rest in France following D-day. Nor is he among those recorded as missing in action."

"He might have been wounded," Roy suggested.

"We thought so, too, but getting that kind of information is much more difficult."

"I see," Roy said, casting Corrie one of his I-told-you-so looks. "So you want me to help you with the research?"

259

"Not yet," Mack responded. "For now, we'd just like any ideas you might have. Any new directions you could point us in."

Mary Jo smiled. "We're actually having a lot of fun reading about the war and looking for information on Jacob's role. We found some maps of Normandy — of the beaches — on the internet with the battle plans marked on them. We know approximately where his division landed."

Mack gave a slight nod of his head. "I was never that interested in history, but these letters have opened my eyes to how exciting it can be. These were real people who put their lives on the line. Jacob didn't want to die — I mean, no one does. He said in one of his letters that he didn't see himself as any sort of hero."

"But he was. They all were," Mary Jo said. "And I'm sure Joan must have told him that. Unfortunately, we only have the letters Jacob wrote, not hers."

"But we have Joan's diary, which is filled with little details about everyday life during that time period," Mack went on to say. "I think they're fascinating. She has just a few lines for each day and agonizes when she hasn't heard from Jacob."

"She talks about saving her sugar coupons to make a cake and walking for miles to save on gas."

"Nearly everything was rationed during the war years," Roy said. "I remember my parents talking about that."

Mary Jo nodded. "And there are abbreviations for things, but we can't always figure them out."

Corrie felt their enthusiasm and, despite herself, was becoming intrigued.

"If and when you decide you need help," Roy said, "you let me know and I'll see what I can find."

"Thanks, Dad," Mack said.

"Yes, thank you so much, Mr. McAfee."

"Call me Roy."

*Or Dad,* Corrie wanted to say, but didn't; she'd annoy Mack, not to mention Roy, and embarrass Mary Jo, if she did. But she knew her son and every indication she saw said that Mack was in love with this girl.

The baby began to whimper, and Mary Jo immediately pushed back her chair. "Noelle's teething. She's had a difficult week."

"I'll take her," Mack offered, getting up.

While they discussed who should comfort the baby, Corrie leaned toward her husband. "Look at them," she whispered. "They act just like a married couple."

"Corrie," Roy said in a warning voice. "Keep out of this."

"I think they need help. You know, to re-alize how they feel about each other."

"If so, it shouldn't come from us."

Corrie didn't agree, but there wasn't much she could do. Roy obviously felt she'd interfered enough.

When Mack and Mary Jo returned to the table, he held Noelle in his arms while Mary Jo rubbed a numbing gel over the baby's gums.

"She's usually a happy baby," Mary Jo said apologetically.

"Of course she is," Corrie said. "Listen, would you two like me to watch her so you could go out for the rest of the evening?" Perhaps if she gave them some time alone, they'd reach the same conclusion she had. Roy might not think the young couple needed her assistance, but in Corrie's view they did.

Mack glanced at Mary Jo. "What do you think?"

Mary Jo thanked Corrie with a smile. "I don't want to leave Noelle when she's this fussy, but I appreciate the offer."

Corrie's spirits sank.

Mack got to his feet and started to clear the table. "Any dessert?" he asked, peering into the kitchen.

"Ah . . ."

"I thought you baked a cake," Roy said. "Didn't you tell me that earlier?"

"Yes, well — it didn't turn out."

"It's inedible?" Roy asked, looking disappointed. Thanks to his sweet tooth, he didn't understand what she was trying to hint.

"I didn't say that."

"Corrie, just bring out the cake," Roy said.

"Mom, who cares what it looks like? It's what it tastes like that matters."

"It tastes fabulous," she told them. Fine. They'd asked for this, so she wasn't going to deny them dessert.

She left the table and returned with the dessert plates and silverware, then went back into the kitchen to carry out the four-layer coconut cake. Charlotte had given her the recipe and it had become a family favorite. Corrie set the cake in the center of the table for all to admire.

Roy stared at it and his eyes veered back to her. The lettering on the cake, written in bright red frosting, said, *Congratulations, Mack and Mary Jo.*

"Shall I cut the first slice?" she asked.

Mack nodded politely. "Please."

"I'll cut through the part that says *congratulations,*" she teased. "I guess this is what I get for being such a know-it-all."

"Oh, Corrie, it was such a sweet thing to do," Mary Jo told her.

"I wish we were at the point that we *could* tell you we had wedding plans," Mack said. He looked at Mary Jo, who stared uncomfortably down at the table. "But we, uh, have a few things we need to work through."

"I . . . I —" Mary Jo started, then stopped, as if she felt she needed to say something but wasn't sure what.

"You don't owe us any explanations," Roy assured Mary Jo. "If you decide to become part of our family, we want you to know we'll welcome you with open arms."

"And Noelle, too," Corrie said.

Mary Jo looked up, and Corrie was surprised to see the glint of tears in her eyes. "Thank you both," Mary Jo whispered. "It means a great deal to me."

"Can we drop the subject now?" Mack asked pointedly.

Corrie nodded. She'd been so positive this dinner had one specific purpose, only to discover she'd been way off base. Instead of celebrating with Mary Jo and her son, as she'd expected to, she'd embarrassed them. Fortunately, they were gracious about it. She regretted causing them any discomfort, but maybe she'd given them something to think about. . . . She hoped so, anyway.

They stayed for another hour after dinner. Mary Jo helped her clean up, and they chatted in a companionable fashion about the letters and the diary. Corrie packed up the leftovers to send home with them.

It didn't escape her notice that Mack was deep in conversation with his father when she and Mary Jo joined them in the living room.

The young couple left soon afterward. Corrie watched as her son backed out of the driveway and headed down Harbor Street.

"So?" Corrie asked, turning away from the window to look at her husband. "What did Mack tell you?"

"What makes you think he told me anything?"

"Roy McAfee, don't you dare do this to me! I have every right to know what's going on between Mack and Mary Jo."

"And you think *I* know?"

"Yes. I saw the way you and Mack had your heads together, so tell me what he said."

Roy sighed. "He loves Mary Jo."

"Of course he does! I think he fell in love with her the night she had Noelle."

"And he loves the baby."

"That goes without saying. He's practically her dad."

Roy nodded. "But Mary Jo has a few issues she needs to work out and until she does Mack doesn't feel he can propose."

She recalled that Mack made some remark along these same lines. "Issues? What kind of issues?" she asked.

Roy picked up the television remote. "I'm afraid they have to do with David Rhodes."

"That jerk has a lot to answer for," Corrie muttered, crossing her arms. Every time she heard the man's name she felt irritated. How anyone as decent and honest as Ben Rhodes could have fathered such a . . . a *creep* was beyond her.

"Mary Jo's afraid of what might happen if David gets involved in Noelle's life."

"She has reason to be."

"So she's doing nothing, which only perpetuates the problem."

"What does Mack suggest?" Corrie asked, then answered her own question. "Mary Jo has to find the courage to stand up to David."

"Yes," Roy agreed, "and until she does, their lives aren't going to move forward."

"Oh, dear," Corrie whispered. "I *am* right, though. He does love her."

"He does." Roy gave her a reassuring

smile. "Don't worry, it'll all resolve itself in time."

Corrie's fear was that this process might take much longer than it should.

## EIGHTEEN

"Da-ad, I need your help." Holding her math book, Jolene sat on the sofa arm.

"Algebra? You think I know this stuff?" Bruce asked with a short laugh.

"I would hope so," Jolene said. "You're the adult."

"Yes, but it's been a lot of years since I was in school."

"Just look, okay?"

Rachel had finished the dinner dishes — by herself, since it was easier that way — and was enjoying the exchange between Bruce and his daughter. If Jolene was counting on his mathematical skills, then the girl was in trouble.

"I don't understand why I have to do this," she lamented.

"You're going to need it in life," Bruce argued, not sounding convinced.

"Why? You don't," Jolene said.

Bruce ignored that. He reached for his

glasses, a recent acquisition, and opened the textbook she'd handed him to the page she'd marked. Next, he appeared to be studying the problem as if staring at it long enough would miraculously produce the answer.

"Get me a pencil and paper," he commanded with the urgency of a surgeon requesting a scalpel.

"Just a minute." Jolene hurried back to her room.

As soon as she was gone, Bruce turned to Rachel, who hovered in the doorway. "You'd be much better at helping her than me."

"She asked *you.*"

"I'm going to look like a dope when I can't figure this out."

Rachel snickered softly. "Well, you know what they say about the shoe fitting."

He scowled but didn't get a chance to comment before Jolene returned with a pencil and yellow pad.

"I still don't get why this stuff is so important," she muttered.

"You need to solve for $x$," Bruce said.

"I know that, but why?"

"Not $y$, $x$."

"Daddy, you're confusing me."

"Good, because I'm confused, too." He sent Rachel a look that pleaded for mercy.

As much as she wanted to step in, Rachel didn't dare. The request had to come from Jolene; otherwise, the girl would reject Rachel's offer and resent her for having made it.

After several minutes, Bruce threw in the towel. "Sorry, kiddo, I can't do this."

"I have the final at the end of the week and I'm going to *flunk,*" Jolene cried, as if leaving this one problem unsolved would ruin her entire academic career. "I'll never get into college if I can't pass Algebra I."

"You've got years and years before you need to worry about college," Bruce said, but if he hoped to reassure his daughter, his words fell flat.

"How can you *say* that?" Jolene wailed. "I *have* to get this right, I have to."

"Ask Rachel," Bruce suggested.

Jolene glanced in her direction. Pretending not to notice, Rachel began to wipe down the kitchen counters, which she'd already done once.

"Rachel," Jolene said hesitantly, "do you think you could figure this out?"

"Would you like me to try?"

"Please." This was not a word she was used to hearing from Jolene — and it gave her hope.

Pulling out a kitchen chair Rachel motioned for Jolene to join her at the table. "Let's look at this together." She had no intention of doing the work for Rachel. Her goal was to help the girl understand the concept so she'd be able to solve algebra problems logically.

"The teacher said we'd learn the quadratic formula next year. Do you know what they use it for?"

Rachel remembered learning it, but not its purpose. "Sorry, no."

"I know," Bruce said, sounding superior.

"Really?" Rachel was impressed — but wary.

"Sure," Bruce said. Standing, he swaggered over to them. "The quadratic formula is used to solve for $x$."

"Daddy!"

Rachel tried to conceal a smile but with little success. "You should go back to your online game," she advised.

Glancing at the textbook, Bruce winced and said, "Gladly."

Rachel read over the problem, then wrote it down on the pad Jolene had brought.

"Do you get this stuff?" Jolene asked.

Rachel nodded. "I do. I've always had an ability with numbers."

"How come you work in a salon, then?"

"I use my mathematical skills there every

single day, Jolene. Not everyone who's good with math works in a bank or an accounting office. For example, I need to calculate how much coloring to put into the mix when I'm doing a dye job."

"Oh." This appeared to be a revelation.

They worked together for the next forty minutes, until Rachel thought Jolene had grasped the concept and could finish a series of problems without help.

Jolene stood and gave Rachel a tentative smile. "Thanks."

"You're welcome."

The girl returned to her bedroom, and Rachel moved into the living room, just in time for her favorite cop drama on TV. Bruce came in a few minutes later. "That went well, don't you think?" he said enthusiastically.

Rachel nodded. This was almost the way it'd been between her and Jolene before the wedding.

"School is out next Wednesday," she said. She dreaded summer vacation and the changes it would bring into their lives. Jolene was too old for day care and too young to be left alone all day without supervision.

"I've got her signed up for that drama camp for the first two weeks," Bruce reminded her.

Yes, but the expense would be a real challenge to their budget, especially if they had to continue this through the rest of the summer. What Bruce didn't know was that in a few months she'd need to stop working, which would take a big bite out of their income.

"It's expensive. And if we have to cover this cost all summer . . ."

"Yeah, but we don't have any option, do we?" Bruce put his arm around her shoulders.

In previous summers Jolene had spent one or two days a week with Rachel, the rest of the time at municipal or church programs. But these days, the girl wasn't interested in attending any summer camp that also catered to "little kids."

"I . . . might have a solution."

"What?" Bruce asked eagerly.

"I could do half days." She'd been making excuses lately to explain why she was so often tired and lacking in energy. She also worried that it wasn't good for the baby if she spent too much time around the chemicals in the salon.

If she was at home half days, she could at least keep an eye on Jolene. . . .

He considered that. "But you keep saying

Jolene would rather not be around you."

"She wouldn't."

"Then you staying home with her might not be such a great idea."

"In other circumstances I'd agree with you. But I'm making this suggestion as much for me as Jolene."

Bruce studied her as if he had difficulty following her line of thought.

"Haven't you noticed how tired I've been these past few months?" she asked.

"Well, yes, but I blame myself for that." He slid his hand between her thighs.

"That's *not* why I need to cut back to half days."

"You're tired because of all the extra hours you had to put in after Teri quit," he guessed.

"Well, yes, and . . . for other reasons."

"Other reasons? Like what?"

"Bruce," she said, exhaling softly. "I'm trying to tell you something important here."

"I'm listening, I really am."

"I know you are." She took his hand. "But you're not hearing me, are you?"

"I'm trying."

The best way to say this was straight out, Rachel decided. "I'm pregnant," she told him quietly.

Bruce blinked. When he apparently realized what she'd said, he leaped off the sofa
and started pacing. He shoved his hands
through his hair. "Did you just tell me
you're . . . *pregnant?*"

"Yes."

"You're sure? This isn't a false alarm?"

"I'm sure."

"Have you been to the doctor?"

"Yes."

"When?"

"Last month."

"Last month?" He spewed out the words.
"You've known this for a *month?*"

"I found out the night Teri had the triplets."

Bruce stared at her. "But how —"

"This might be news to you," she broke
in, "but guess what? I didn't get pregnant
all by myself. This baby has a father."

"Me."

"No kidding!"

"I'm . . . not sure what to say."

"How about — oh, I don't know — 'Wow,'
or 'That's great,' or 'I couldn't be happier,'
or —"

He knelt down in front of her and grabbed
both her hands, smiling the goofiest, happiest smile she'd ever seen. "How about
'Thank you'?"

Rachel swallowed back tears. "That works."

He placed his hands on either side of her face and kissed her. Rachel flung her arms around his neck and reveled in his love.

"Why didn't you tell me sooner?" he asked.

"I was afraid," she whispered.

"Afraid," he repeated. "Of what? We both want a baby. We've talked about it. Okay, we'd planned to wait, but it happened — and frankly, I think it's wonderful."

She slipped her fingers through his hair. "I hoped you'd feel that way. The pregnancy came as a shock to me, a total surprise, and I was afraid it would to you, too."

"This is the best kind of surprise. I can't believe you kept it to yourself for so long."

She looked away. "I had to. Because of Jolene."

The instant she spoke, she saw doubt pass over his face.

"It was the one thing she asked us to do. To wait. Not to have a baby yet."

"We can't live by her dictates," Bruce argued. He kissed her again with an adoration that made Rachel go weak in his arms.

"I know and I agree, but Jolene has had to deal with a number of significant changes this year. Adding my pregnancy to the mix complicates everything."

Bruce frowned. "I still think we should tell her right away."

"No," Rachel pleaded. "Not yet. Let's give it a few weeks. Once school's out, I'll start working half days. I'm hoping that the time I spend with her one-on-one will allow us to repair our relationship." Maybe just being together, without Bruce, would make a difference. Maybe Jolene would stop competing for her father's affection. Maybe she and Rachel could regain the love and trust they'd once shared.

"Well . . . today was good. She asked you to help her with math."

Rachel nodded.

"Maybe it'll work."

"Well, I want to make the effort."

He continued to look a bit uncertain.

"Let me tell her about the baby," Rachel said. "I want her to know what an important role she'll play as the baby's big sister. My goal is for Jolene to be as excited about this addition to our family as we are. To welcome this child, prepare for her —"

"Or him."

"Or him," she added, smiling, "with joy and anticipation."

Bruce exhaled slowly. "Fine. I'll leave it up to you. Tell her when you feel it's right."

"Thank you," she whispered.

He sat back down beside her and they watched the rest of the police drama together. Twice she caught him staring at her.

"Bruce," she muttered the second time.

"What?"

"Try to wipe that silly grin off your face."

"I can't."

"Try harder."

"Don't want to."

Rachel groaned. "You're going to make this impossible."

"No, I won't."

The credits rolled across the screen. "Are you tired yet?" Bruce asked.

"It's only nine o'clock."

He stretched out his arms and gave a loud yawn.

"Bruce," she chided. If Jolene walked in on them now, she'd be horrified.

"I can't help it, woman, I'm crazy about you." Then he chuckled and placed his hand over her stomach. "As *this* proves right here."

"Shhh," she warned.

"My lips are sealed," Bruce said.

Rachel sighed and snuggled close to her husband. He'd promised not to tell Jolene and she prayed he would keep his word. That he *could* keep his word and not let it slip before she was ready to tell Jolene. And Jolene was ready to hear.

# NINETEEN

Gloria parked outside the McAfees' house and sat in her car for ten minutes before she found the courage to approach the door. She badly needed a mother's advice, and although she wanted to speak honestly with Corrie, she wasn't sure she could.

Chad had left ten messages on her phone. She hadn't answered even one. His final message was that this was the last time he'd contact her. He'd obviously meant it. Gloria hadn't heard from him in the two weeks since.

That was what she wanted. Wasn't it?

Yes, she insisted to herself again. It was!

Then why, oh, why, couldn't she stop thinking about him? She'd spent so many sleepless nights pounding her pillows, fighting to get his image out of her mind, that she was about to go mad.

Yes, he was attractive, but so were lots of other men. The simple truth was: No man had ever affected her as powerfully as Dr. Chad Timmons.

All her life Gloria had been a reserved and private person. She didn't freely share her thoughts or feelings with others. Yet an hour after meeting Chad, she'd practically spilled out her entire life story. She'd shared her emotions, her doubts and fears. At that time, that first night, she'd even told him why she'd moved to Cedar Cove. No one else knew. Only Chad. That he could so easily strip away her defenses alarmed her. Terrified her.

Now, after two weeks of silence, she still couldn't get him off her mind. She had to do something, but she was helpless to know what.

Holding her breath, she rang the doorbell and waited for her birth mother to answer. Roy was gone; Gloria had seen him drive away as she turned onto Harbor Street. She remembered that Corrie sometimes took Tuesdays and Thursdays off and hoped she'd be at home.

She was.

"Gloria! What a pleasant surprise. Come in, come in."

Gloria stepped into the family home and glanced at the photos lining the mantel. The one of her, in her sheriff's uniform, stood next to Linnette's and Mack's high school graduation pictures. The professional family photograph on the wall above the fireplace showed Roy and Corrie maybe fifteen years earlier with their two children and a dog, who must have passed into doggy heaven. She didn't even know that dog's name.

"I was just emailing Linnette," Corrie said.

"How's she doing?"

"Terrific," Corrie told her. She walked into the kitchen and over to the coffeepot and refilled her mug. "Would you like some?"

Gloria shook her head. "Would it be all right if I had a glass of water instead?"

"Of course." Corrie immediately opened the cupboard above the coffeepot and took down a glass, which she filled with ice and water and brought to Gloria.

She sat on the stool and drank half the water before setting the glass on the counter. Her throat felt dry, her skin clammy. "I . . . I need some advice."

Corrie dragged a stool to the other side of the counter. "I'm happy to help in any way I can," she said, sitting down.

"I . . . met someone a few years back."

"Male?"

Gloria avoided eye contact and nodded. "I barely knew him and we . . ." Admitting

282

what she'd done was more difficult than she would've guessed.

"You went to bed with him," Corrie said matter-of-factly.

Gloria nodded again. "I was embarrassed and shocked by my behavior and chose not to see him again." Her hand tightened around the water glass. "He made numerous efforts to contact me. . . . I rebuffed each one until he finally gave up."

"Why, exactly, did you refuse to see him?"

"First, like I said, I was embarrassed. Second, I felt vulnerable around him. Emotionally vulnerable." She paused. "There was another . . . complication. Another woman, someone I cared — care — about was interested in him. So even if I'd been willing to risk a relationship with this man, I felt I had to step back."

Her mother seemed to understand. "Do you still have strong feelings for him?"

Gloria shrugged. "I must, because I can't stop thinking about him — but there's more to the story."

"The other woman?"

"No, she's out of the picture." She had to hope Corrie wouldn't guess that she was talking about Linnette.

"Okay, fill me in on what happened next."

Gloria could hardly believe the water glass

didn't shatter in her hand from the pressure. She made a concerted but unsuccessful effort to relax.

"About a month ago, this man . . . he let me know he was moving away and . . ." She closed her eyes and inhaled. "I asked him to stay. He agreed and we went on a second date." The lump in her throat felt huge and she tried to swallow it. "The same thing happened all over again." She said this last part in a harsh whisper.

"You spent the night with him?"

Gloria hung her head. "Yes. I woke up embarrassed and . . . and furious with myself. I don't think either of us planned it but . . . it just . . . happened. Again."

"Have you seen him since?"

Her birth mother seemed to intuitively ask the right questions. "No, and I don't want to."

Corrie smiled knowingly. "Because you're afraid."

"Yes, and can you blame me? The only thing we have in common that I can see is our . . . our sexual interest in each other. He also knows too much about me. I don't talk about myself with other people — it makes me uncomfortable."

"But you do with him?"

"Yes."

"Are you in love with this man?"

If Gloria had the answer to that, she wouldn't be sitting in Corrie's kitchen seeking advice. "I . . . I don't really know. I think I might be, but I don't know my own heart. I feel so confused. I'm not sure of myself anymore or how to react." She shook her head and her hair fell forward. Tucking it behind her ears, she realized her hands were trembling.

"What would you like me to tell you?" Corrie asked.

"I . . . I don't know."

Corrie reached across the counter and took one of Gloria's hands in her own. "I think you owe it to this young man and to yourself to talk to him."

"What should I say?"

"I can't tell you that. But it seems to me that you're running away from him and, more importantly, from yourself. You tried that once and it didn't work, did it?"

"No," she said miserably.

"When you thought you were about to lose him, you asked him to stay. That tells me you do have feelings for him."

"He left ten messages for me. In the tenth message he said he was finished and that I wouldn't hear from him again — and I haven't."

"You need to talk to him," Corrie said a second time. "Even if you agree never to see each other again, you need some closure. Some way of acknowledging what happened so you can both move on."

Gloria knew her birth mother was right. She'd recognized all along that this was what she needed to do, but she'd wanted confirmation from someone she trusted. Corrie wasn't her real mother; Gloria's mother had died in a plane crash. But she was certain the woman who'd nurtured and raised her would have said the same thing.

"Thank you," she whispered.

Corrie squeezed her hand. "Anytime. Will you let me know how it goes?"

Gloria promised she would and left soon after.

That afternoon, she waited outside the medical clinic for Chad. She wore her uniform, since she had to report for duty in thirty minutes. She was on swing shift and, through a quick phone call, had learned that he was on the early rotation. That gave them twenty minutes together at most. The time limitation suited her fine; she'd say what needed to be said, then leave with a clear conscience.

Chad saw her the moment he stepped out the clinic door. He hesitated briefly before heading in her direction.

Her own reaction to seeing him caught her by surprise. She hadn't expected to feel anything. But she did. Her heart seemed to trip into double time and her throat closed. This wasn't going to be easy and Chad would probably go out of his way to make it as awkward as possible.

"Took you long enough" was his only greeting.

"I thought we should . . . acknowledge what happened," she said, consciously quoting Corrie. She kept her hands on her hips, feet spread, the stance she used when pulling over speeders.

"Yes, I suppose we should. Do you want to meet me somewhere so we can talk in private?"

Gloria shook her head. "Here is fine."

"In the parking lot?"

"I have to be at work soon."

"The parking lot?" he reiterated.

"Yes."

"So this'll be short and sweet."

"Well, yes."

He raised his eyebrows. "I guess that tells me everything I need to know."

Rather than ask what he meant, she started in on her prepared speech. "Clearly there's a strong physical attraction between us."

"You think?"

She ignored his sarcasm, although it irritated her. "I can't explain why you affect me the way you do."

"But you don't like it."

"I don't think we're right for each other," she finally told him.

"Yeah, sure."

"There's no need for sarcasm, Chad," she returned pointedly. She'd been correct about one thing; he intended to punish her, make this as hard as he could.

"You might not think so, but it's either that or . . ."

"Or what?"

He started to walk away from her. "You drive me crazy, Gloria. I've never met anyone like you. You're hot one minute, and when I say *hot,* we both know what I mean. Then the next minute, you can't get away from me fast enough."

Gloria couldn't very well deny his accusations.

"The night we had dinner, things got out of control. I hadn't intended to bring you back to my apartment. I told you what would happen if we went inside and if I remember correctly you didn't voice any objections."

She swallowed and looked away, embarrassed because what he'd said was true.

"I woke up the next morning happier than I could remember being in a long time — only to discover you were gone."

She couldn't meet his eyes.

"Then I found your note. What a shock. 'Don't call me again. Last night was a mistake.' "

Gloria stared down at her shoes.

"It might've been a mistake for you, Gloria, but I refused to think of it that way."

She had nothing to add.

"Hot one minute, cold the next. I tried to reason with you. I lost count of how many messages I left you."

"Ten," she said, then wished she'd kept her mouth shut.

"Ten," he repeated. "Ten messages, and how many weeks of silence?"

"Two." There, she'd done it again, letting him know she'd counted each and every one of those tortured days.

"And now you're telling me to take a flying leap into the nearest cow pasture, right?" His stance remained guarded, defiant.

"I think it's for the best not to see each other again."

"That figures. Well, go ahead, Gloria, run away and pretend there's nothing between us if that makes you feel better. Trust me, after this last episode, it doesn't come as a surprise."

She blinked at the vehemence in his voice, the hardness in his face.

"I'd rather we parted as friends," she said.

He went still, then shook his head. "Sorry. If you want to water this relationship down to 'friends' in order to make it palatable, then feel free to do so, but it doesn't work for me."

"How . . . what are you talking about?"

"Friends, you say? First, I don't know what *you're* talking about. Friends are people I trust. You've burned me twice, and I don't feel that friendly toward you. If this is the way you treat your so-called friends, I pity them. I pity you."

Gloria's stomach tensed. "I didn't mean it like that."

"Then what did you mean?"

"I . . . I thought, you know, that if we passed each other on the street we could . . . be polite. And if I ever came to the clinic, we could be cordial to each other."

He rolled his eyes. "That isn't going to happen, so don't worry about it. Fine, you want to be *friends,* we'll be friends."

He stepped away from her and started across the parking lot to his car. Every instinct demanded she follow him and make things right between them. Yet she remained rooted to the spot.

She stood frozen for several minutes, warring within herself. Chad climbed into his car and drove off, and still she stood there, not knowing what to do.

Corrie had said she needed to "acknowledge what happened" and move on. Chad had agreed. But if that was what she'd sought, she'd failed miserably. Instead of ending their affair on a friendly note, they were more at odds than ever.

Somehow she made it through her shift and, at eleven that night, went home. Although she was mentally and physically exhausted, she couldn't fall asleep. Many hours later, she downed two over-the-counter sleeping pills and pulled the sheet over her head. The sun had begun to rise, and morning light slithered into her bedroom through the gap between her curtains.

Gloria rolled onto her left side and bunched up the pillow. Ten minutes later she was on her right side and then she rolled onto her back.

She glanced at the clock and wondered how long it would take for the sleep aid to kick in. She closed her eyes, but when she did, all she could see was Chad standing defiantly before her. He didn't say a word, yet she felt his disappointment and his pain.

She felt her own.

All at once she threw aside the covers and sat up as his words echoed in her mind. She'd suggested that being friends meant that if they ran into each other again, they'd be cordial. Chad had said that wasn't going to happen. He hadn't meant he wouldn't greet her.

What he was telling her, she realized now, was that he wouldn't be around for her to greet. He was leaving town.

The Tacoma hospital had told him they'd hire him anytime he wanted the job.

Chad was leaving Cedar Cove. And her.

# TWENTY

Mack finished his five-mile run and walked the last block to the duplex to cool down. Cool down physically from the exertion of the run and emotionally from his churning thoughts.

He'd been upset with Mary Jo after their confrontation with David on the waterfront two weeks earlier. Twice since then he'd tried to talk to her about the situation, and both times she'd abruptly changed the subject. The only thing she wanted to talk about was their search for Jacob and Joan. And that interested him, too, but it wasn't about *their* lives. Clearly she wasn't comfortable discussing David. Not with him, anyway. And that hurt. He felt he had as much at stake as she did. Not to the same degree, perhaps, but he loved Noelle, too.

Their dinner with his parents hadn't helped. His mother — and even his father — thought they'd come to announce their engagement.

He wished.

Mary Jo wasn't ready, and frankly, Mack was growing frustrated. He'd recognized long ago that she was afraid. He understood that. But for the past six months he'd bent himself into a pretzel trying to prove how trustworthy he was. Okay, he'd stumbled once, when Mary Jo discovered he'd misled her regarding the ownership of the duplex. Even then he'd had her best interests at heart. If he had to do it over again, hindsight being what it was, he'd tell her the truth. How much that error in judgment had cost him remained to be seen.

He was tired of the brush-off she'd been giving him lately, and he wasn't sure how to handle it. Running helped him clear his mind, so he'd pounded the pavement for five miles while he mulled over the events of the past few weeks.

He loved her and Noelle, but it felt as though with every step forward, he immediately took two steps back. After six months he was beginning to think she might never feel as strongly about him as he did about her.

After his run, Mack showered, changed clothes, did a few errands and returned home midafternoon. As he brought groceries into the house, Mary Jo came out of her place.

"Hi," she said, sounding uncertain.

Good. He hoped she enjoyed the feeling because he'd been experiencing it for the past half year.

"Hi," he said back, and reached for another bag of groceries.

"I didn't see you this morning." He usually made himself available to Mary Jo and Noelle in case they needed anything. Maybe that was his problem — being too helpful, too eager to show he cared.

He brought the second load into the house and left the door open. A couple of minutes later, he was back to get his dry cleaning.

Mary Jo came farther into the yard, watching him. Mack pretended not to notice.

"Are you upset?" she asked.

He stopped and met her look head-on. "As a matter of fact, I am."

She blinked as though his honesty had taken her by surprise. "Do you want to talk about it?"

"I've tried twice, and Noelle and her future obviously isn't something you want to discuss with me."

"You're not her father," Mary Jo snapped.

She couldn't have said anything that

would have wounded him more. He considered himself Noelle's protector. He loved that baby as if he *were* her father. He'd brought her into this world and been the first to hold her in his arms. From that moment forward, Mack had felt a special bond with Noelle, warranted or not.

"Right," he said stiffly, and walked past her. Once inside, he closed the door. He hung up his clothes, put away his groceries and swallowed a groan of sheer frustration.

Not more than five minutes later, his doorbell rang. Assuming it was Mary Jo, Mack toyed with the idea of not answering. Instead, he walked to the front door and threw it open. He wanted to make sure she understood that he resented the intrusion.

Staring at him intently, she stood on the other side with Noelle in her arms. "I hate it when you're upset with me."

He left the screen door shut and waited for his heart to stop pounding. "Are you ready to talk?" he asked.

She nodded.

Mack held open the screen and let her in. He motioned for her to sit down on the sofa and went into the kitchen to make them coffee. He brought out two cups. She ignored hers. He ignored his. Mary Jo set Noelle on the rug, and the six-month-old immediately

296

began crawling toward the coffee table.

Despite his dour mood, Mack couldn't help smiling. He bent down and scooped the baby into his arms. Happy to see him, Noelle gurgled with delight. Then, remembering why Mary Jo was in his home, Mack sobered and set Noelle back on the carpet to crawl about as she pleased. As Mary Jo had so recently reminded him, he had no rights with regard to this child.

"You . . . aren't Noelle's father," she said again.

He glared at her. She'd already made her point and he could see no reason for her to say it again.

"But I wish you were," she added.

Those words removed the sting from her earlier comment. "I do, too," he admitted.

"It's obvious that you love Noelle."

He couldn't have made his feelings toward Mary Jo and her baby any plainer. He loved them both, although so far it'd done him little good.

"I . . . I spoke with Ben and Charlotte recently," she continued. "They talked to Olivia, who recommended that I file for child support. Apparently it doesn't matter whether David has a job or not. They said it was important that I register with the state."

He wondered if Mary Jo would accept that

advice. When they'd last spoken, she'd been dead set against taking any action, certain David would follow through on his threat.

"According to Charlotte, Olivia has lots of experience in these cases and she said David would be forced to own up to his responsibility."

"But you're afraid he'll ask for joint custody of Noelle once the support request goes through?" Mack believed that was a scare tactic.

"That's what people keep telling me, Linc included. I hate it when everyone seems to think they know what's best for me and Noelle." Her voice quavered slightly.

Mack found himself wrestling with indecision, but he'd done too much of that in the past. He had to hold fast to his convictions.

"You want what's best for Noelle, yet you're willing to let David terrorize you."

"I'm afraid he'll find some way of taking Noelle away from me," she said, sounding close to panic at the mere thought of it.

"Which is playing right into his hands, isn't it? David doesn't want to be part of Noelle's life. He couldn't care less about his daughter — or you, for that matter."

"I know," she whispered. She reached down and picked up Noelle, who squirmed in her arms, wanting to be put down again.

Mary Jo clung to her baby.

"Do you honestly think any judge in the land would consider giving Noelle to David?" Mack asked incredulously.

"I . . . don't think so, but it could happen. I can't risk that. I don't need David. I don't want anything to do with him. Basically he's saying he wants me to leave him alone, and I'm happy to do that."

"But then you aren't protecting Noelle."

"Yes, I am," she insisted.

Mack walked to the other side of the room. "Is he named as Noelle's father on the birth certificate?" He turned back and watched her nod reluctantly.

"What if something happened to you?" he asked. "What if, God forbid, you became ill or were seriously injured and unable to care for Noelle? Who would take her?"

"Linc and Lori . . . maybe. I hadn't thought of that."

He wanted to shout that these were the very scenarios that ran through his mind in the middle of the night.

"If you were . . . gone or incapable of caring for Noelle, the state would contact David, because he's Noelle's legal father. She would then become his responsibility."

Mary Jo looked horrified. Noelle slid out of her arms and plopped down on her thick diaper, sitting at her mother's feet.

"When Ben talked to me, he said he was afraid that if . . . sometime down the road I got married and my husband wanted to adopt Noelle, David would do everything he could to cause problems. He'd use Noelle for his own purposes."

Mack had thought of that himself. He didn't trust that jerk for a second.

Mary Jo glanced his way. "I'll never understand how I could've been so blind and stupid. One error in judgment, and look what happened." She swallowed visibly.

"Ben must have urged you to take action for another reason," he said.

Mary Jo nodded. "He told me that if I were to approach David with relinquishment papers now, he'd probably sign them, which would save us all a lot of trouble down the road. Ben also told me that Noelle will always be his granddaughter. He's already made provisions for her in his will."

"I wouldn't expect anything less of a man like Ben Rhodes."

Mary Jo bit her lip. "I'd want someone else to talk to David, though."

"Let me." Mack would get David to sign those papers without a problem, and it wouldn't take long, either.

"No . . . I was thinking I might hire Mr.

Harris to do it. He could deduct his fee from my paycheck."

It seemed she was still considering that action as she spoke. Mack took a moment to digest her words.

"So you're willing to approach David? Or have someone approach him on your behalf?"

She hesitated. "I . . . don't know yet."

He stiffened and wanted to tell her that she should inform him when she'd made her decision. Until then, he'd rather she didn't torment him with her wishy-washy attitude.

Again, Mary Jo sensed his irritation. "Can I change the subject for a moment?" she asked.

He wondered if this was just another delaying tactic, and then with a sigh of resignation nodded for her to continue.

"I had a wonderful time at your parents' house last week."

They'd barely spoken since then. Right afterward, Mack was on duty for four days straight. Once he got back home, he'd tried to talk to Mary Jo but she'd been unresponsive. He'd more or less ignored her ever since.

"I apologize if my mother embarrassed you," he muttered.

"She didn't," Mary Jo told him. "I was kind of amused that she assumed we were going to announce our engagement."

Mack shoved his hands in his pockets. *"Amused?"* This woman had him so twisted up in knots he didn't know if he was coming or going. He felt he'd done nothing but make a fool of himself over her.

"Why are you looking at me like I said something offensive?" Mary Jo asked. "Honestly, Mack, you're so prickly these days. . . ."

"The idea of marrying me is a big joke?" he said in a sullen voice.

"I didn't say that!"

"Sorry, maybe I need my hearing tested because that's exactly what it sounded like."

"Do you love me?" she asked.

Mack didn't answer because he didn't want her scoffing at him, didn't want her to disparage his feelings.

"Well, I guess that's that," she said after an awkward moment. She reached for Noelle.

Mack knew if he didn't say something fast, she'd leave. This might be his last opportunity and he didn't want to waste it on resentment or retaliation. "I couldn't have made my feelings for you and Noelle any more obvious if I tried. Yes, I love you, Mary

Jo. My thoughts haven't been my own from the second I answered your 9-1-1 call last Christmas."

Once again Mary Jo bit her lip. "I fell in love before, and I was so stupid and foolish. David —"

"I'm not David!" he flared. "I don't know how much longer it's going to take you to realize I'm nothing like him. What have I ever done to make you think I'd harm you or Noelle?"

He was just warming to his subject when Mary Jo put Noelle down and walked over to him.

"I —" He wasn't allowed to finish. Mary Jo placed her hands on his shoulders and practically forced him to look directly at her.

"I love you, Jerome McAfee," she said.

The air rushed from his lungs and Mack found himself unable to speak — and not just because she'd used his given name, which was known to very few people.

"Did you hear what I said?" she asked.

He couldn't respond, couldn't even manage a nod.

"Do you need me to repeat that?"

This time he bobbed his head.

She dropped her hands and gave him the most dazzling smile he'd ever seen. "I love you. Noelle loves you, too. We *both* love you."

Feeling completely out of control, it was all he could do to return her smile.

"You could kiss me now if you wanted," Mary Jo suggested.

Mack wanted, all right. He wanted to hold her and kiss her. He gathered her in his arms and his heart seemed about to take flight. Lowering his mouth to hers, he felt an incredible surge of emotion. Just then, with Noelle holding on to his pant leg and Mary Jo in his arms, he felt as if his whole world had been transformed.

Mary Jo tasted sweet and wonderful, and one kiss wasn't nearly enough. Soon they were kissing each other deeply, intensely. They might have continued kissing and discovering their newly declared feelings if Noelle hadn't let out a sudden cry.

Reluctantly Mary Jo broke away and picked up her daughter. "You made me forget about Noelle," she whispered as though she had trouble finding her voice.

*Me, too,* he thought, hard as that was to believe.

Mack slid his hands down her arms, because he needed to keep touching her.

"I'm glad we finally talked," she said. "I couldn't stand having you upset with me."

If he received this kind of reaction every time, he might consider getting upset with her more often. . . .

"I'll discuss the situation with Mr. Harris next week," she told him. "I'll get his opinion and make my decision then. Okay?"

"I'd appreciate it if you'd talk to me before you decide. Will you do that?"

She agreed with a quick nod. "I think that's fair."

"I'd like to adopt Noelle," he said. "When . . . when it's appropriate, I mean," he stammered.

Mary Jo smiled. "She does love you, you know."

As if on cue, Noelle squirmed in her mother's hold, thrusting both arms toward Mack.

He took the baby and Noelle pressed her head against his shoulder. He experienced the profound sense of making a promise to this woman, this child. "And I love her," he murmured. "My little girl."

# TWENTY-ONE

Linc Wyse parked his battered pickup truck outside their Cedar Cove apartment building. After the confrontation with Leonard, he'd wanted to move — but finances made that impossible for the moment. He found that it grated on him to feel beholden to a man who had no respect for him — or for his own daughter. Linc hoped that eventually their relationship with Leonard would improve, but he couldn't guess when or how that would happen.

Despite everything, he had no regrets about his marriage. Absolutely none. He'd never been happier in his personal life. His business life, however, was another matter. After his move to Cedar Cove, he'd hit one roadblock after another in getting his auto body shop up and running. He'd purchased the building and made the necessary renovations, spending a significant part of his savings. While the work was in progress, he'd applied for a business license, which shouldn't have been a problem. But his application had been delayed twice. It wasn't hard to figure out that Bellamy was somehow behind this. Linc wasn't sure how his father-in-law had done it, but Leonard clearly had friends in high places.

In the end Linc had been forced to hire an attorney and he'd eventually received his license. At any other time, the frustration would've infuriated him. Yet when he arrived home at the end of each day and saw Lori, every negative emotion he'd experienced drained away. All she had to do was smile and Linc's troubles seemed to disappear. He'd never told her about his legal problems and his suspicions about her father's role in them. No need to upset her further, so he'd dealt with it all quietly.

He anticipated one of Lori's smiles when he walked in the door. Instead, she rushed across the room and wrapped her arms around him, hugging tightly.

"To what do I owe *this* reception?" he asked.

Generally they were kissing by now or talking nonstop about their day. He usually helped with dinner, not that he was much good in the kitchen. To him it was an excuse to spend time with Lori; each minute with her was precious and to be treasured.

"My mother phoned," she said.

"And that's bad?"

Lori nodded.

"What did she want?"

"She invited us to dinner on Saturday night."

Now Linc was completely perplexed. The relationship between Lori and her family was strained, and an invitation from her mother should please her; instead she was distressed.

"Will your father be there?"

"Of course!" she cried.

That explained some of her anguish. Linc patted her back soothingly, although he didn't understand why a dinner invitation had unsettled her so much.

"What did you tell your mother?" he asked. If he came up with the right questions, he might discover what was so terrible about this invitation. Didn't it mean Lori's parents, or at least her mother, were trying to build a bridge? Maybe this was a hopeful sign, the possible beginning of a reconciliation.

"I said no."

"Flat-out no . . . ?"

She nodded, her hold around him tightening.

"You didn't think to ask me first?"

Tilting her head back, she looked up at him with wide brown eyes. "No."

"Because?" He felt offended that she hadn't even sought his response to this unexpected olive branch.

"Because I know why Mom invited us."

"And that is?"

Lori looked down and didn't answer.

Tucking his finger under her chin, he raised her head. "Lori?"

"My parents want to embarrass you."

He arched his brows. That wasn't a motive he'd considered. "And they would do that how?" he asked.

"I showed you a picture of my parents' home, remember?"

"I do and it's beautiful."

"It has a guesthouse and an Olympic-size pool and acres of landscaping."

"Ten acres, you said?"

"On the water."

Ten acres of waterfront property had to be worth more money than Linc could hope to earn in his lifetime. He remembered that Lori had mentioned a live-in housekeeper and cook, as well as groundskeepers.

"My father is wealthy and influential."

"As he let me know," Linc muttered. And well-connected, too. Still, Leonard Bellamy could erect all the roadblocks he wanted, but he couldn't stop Linc from setting up business, no matter how many friends he had.

"Mom will make sure dinner has three forks, two knives and four spoons just to confuse you."

He laughed. "After Mary Jo moved out, my brothers and I didn't have that much silverware between us."

"This isn't a laughing matter," Lori said. "I won't give my family an opportunity to embarrass my husband, and that's what they're hoping to do."

Linc wasn't the least bit intimidated. "I might have grease under my fingernails, Lori, but I'm not a country bumpkin. I'll hold my own. There's no need to protect me."

"Yes, there is," she insisted.

He kissed her forehead. "No," he said. "It's okay. Really."

"You don't have any idea how uncomfortable Dad will make you. He'll try to trap you. He'll act all friendly and then start asking for your opinion on stocks."

"I'll answer him truthfully. Other than my 401(k), I don't follow the market."

"That's exactly what he'll want you to say and then he'll make fun of you. Only he'll do it in this supposedly witty way that's demeaning and belittling. I won't have it, Linc. I refuse to stand for it."

Leaning down, Linc kissed the tip of her nose. "Phone your mother back and tell her you've changed your mind. We'll be happy to join them for dinner."

She stared up at him with shocked disbelief. "No!"

"Lori, sweetheart, you could be misreading the situation."

"I'm not," she said. "I know my parents — especially my father. He thinks I've made a terrible mistake marrying you and he's dying to prove what an idiot I am."

"You're not an idiot, Lori." The fact that Leonard thought this infuriated him. "And neither am I. In fact, your father's going to see that, and soon."

"Clearly you haven't spent much time with him."

Their single encounter had been unpleasant enough; still, Linc was willing to give it a second try. When the time came, Lori's parents would be his children's grandparents — their only grandparents. Linc knew the importance of family and longed to build a solid relationship with the Bellamys. He realized it might take months, even years, but he hoped that if Lori's parents had the chance to know him, they'd see how much he loved her. He'd wait them out if he had to and he'd endure Leonard's interference and wouldn't let it defeat him.

"This is an opportunity we shouldn't turn down," he said.

Lori held her ground. "We aren't going."

"Friday night, was it?" he asked.

Lori sighed and shook her head. "Saturday night, but it doesn't make any difference — we won't be there."

"Lori, we *should* go. I want to."

"Linc . . . you wonderful man. You don't have a clue."

Oh, but he did. "Call your mother back, Lori. Please. It's time I met her."

A frown puckered her brow. "I can't do it. I'm sorry, Linc, but I just can't." She broke free of his embrace and hurried into the kitchen.

Linc waited a couple of minutes, then followed her. "Are we having our first fight?" he asked.

Lori, who had her back to him, turned and then smiled. "You know, I think we are."

A smile broke out across his face.

"What are you so happy about?"

"Well," he drawled, "I've heard that make-up sex is the best there is."

"Lincoln Wyse, I can't believe you just

312

said that!"

"Wanna find out?"

He could see Lori struggling not to smile. "We haven't resolved this yet."

"Can't we do that later?"

"Linc, you're impossible."

"Can't help it." He motioned toward the bedroom. "Dinner can wait, too, can't it?"

Lori giggled.

Linc scooped her into his arms and carried her to the bedroom. Together they fell onto the bed.

A half hour later, sated and content, Linc lay gazing up at the underside of the pink canopy.

"Well," Lori murmured, stretching luxuriously, like a cat in a patch of sunshine. "You were right about the making-up part."

"Maybe that means we should argue more often." Rolling onto his side he leaned over her and kissed her. "Call your mother, sweetheart, okay? I promise not to embarrass you."

"Oh, Linc, I'm not worried that you'd embarrass me. I just don't want them making you feel uncomfortable. I love you for who you are, not the amount of money you make or anything else."

"Good." He kissed her again, his lips lingering on hers.

■ ■ ■ ■

Late Saturday afternoon, Linc dressed casually in slacks and a white polo shirt for dinner at the Bellamy family home. When they arrived, they had to stop at the iron gate and wait for admittance. Entering the circular driveway, Linc had to make an effort not to stare or look impressed. The photograph Lori had shown him didn't do justice to the stately home.

He'd just helped Lori out of the car when the front door opened and an elegant blonde woman stepped outside.

"Lori, darling, I'm so glad you're here." Lori's mother came forward with her arms extended.

Mother and daughter hugged before Lori turned back to Linc. She slipped her arm around his waist. "Mom, this is my husband, Lincoln Wyse."

"Mrs. Bellamy," he said, and extended his hand.

She smiled and shook it. He noticed that her palm was smooth and soft, her rings obviously expensive but understated. "Welcome to our home, Lincoln."

"Most folks call me Linc."

"Linc, then. My friends call me Kate."

"Kate." He hoped that he would, indeed, be considered a friend.

Lori's mother escorted them into the house. The foyer was massive. A round inlaid wood table dominated the area with a floral arrangement so huge it was like one he'd expect to find in a five-star hotel lobby.

"Where's Dad?" Lori asked, glancing around.

That was Linc's question, too. He intended to do his best to reach an understanding with his father-in-law over dinner — or at least make some progress toward that goal.

"Unfortunately, your father was called away at the last minute," Kate said with undisguised frustration.

Lori's hand tightened around his. Linc wasn't sure what she was attempting to tell him and looked down. His wife mouthed three words — *that's a lie.* He frowned as Kate led them into the living room.

The hors d'oeuvres had been arranged on a silver platter. Linc didn't recognize a single one — except for the caviar, which he'd never had before. This was no crackers-and-cheese plate. Nor was it stuffed mushrooms or Greek olives. Rather than admit he didn't know what he was eating, he leaned forward and helped himself. He scooped up some caviar with a small triangle of toast and shoved it in his mouth — not bad. He saw Lori glance pointedly to the right. That was when he noticed the delicate china plate and napkin.

"Can I offer you something to drink?" Kate asked.

"I'll have a beer," Linc said automatically.

"I will, too." Lori slid closer to Linc.

Her mother grinned. "Then so will I."

Linc saw his wife relax visibly. "I didn't know you drank beer, Mom."

"Well, the truth is, I never have before, but there's no reason I can't give it a try."

"I'll take mine in the bottle," Linc told her, fearing the housekeeper would feel obligated to serve it in a fancy crystal glass.

"Me, too," Kate said.

Dinner wasn't such a painful affair, after all. The beef Stroganoff was incredible and he went into the kitchen to personally thank the cook and praise her work. Dessert was homemade angel food cake, served with fresh strawberries and whipped cream. The real stuff. The last time Linc had tasted real whipped cream had been the Thanksgiving before his parents died.

The evening ended on a companionable note, with Kate suggesting they do it again. All controversial topics were avoided, which certainly made for a more comfortable visit. On the drive home, Lori leaned her head against Linc's shoulder. "You were right about Mom wanting to build a bridge."

He'd guessed that early on when Kate had insisted on having a beer with him. Although she'd never tasted one before, she'd liked it and had a second with dinner.

"I found out Mom didn't tell Dad we were coming to dinner until this afternoon," Lori said.

"I hope that didn't cause a problem between your parents." He couldn't help feeling guilty if that was the case.

"Mom didn't say, but I told her make-up sex is the best — and that I was speaking from experience."

Linc nearly drove off the road. "Tell me you didn't."

Giggling, Lori wrapped her arm around his. "You're right, I didn't, but I was tempted."

"Where did your father go?"

"I don't know, and neither did Mom."

"He refused to join his family for dinner because of me?" Linc almost felt sorry for the other man whose stubborn pride had prevented him from enjoying a wonderful meal and a good time. And Linc knew a little something about pride.

"It isn't about you," she said softly. "This is about me. Dad still hasn't forgiven me for what happened with Geoff."

Linc felt her cringe just saying the other man's name.

"He's convinced I have no judgment whatsoever. And then you and I married so quickly, it sent him over the edge."

Linc realized this was the crux of the problem. He hoped he'd reassured Kate and that she'd share what he'd said with Leonard.

"The fact that you apologized for excluding the family from our wedding went a long way toward winning over my mother."

Linc had broached the subject between courses. His own family hadn't been invited, either, he'd explained, and he'd said that in retrospect he regretted it. If at some point Lori's family wanted to throw a formal wedding, that was fine with him. From the smile Kate sent him, Linc knew he'd scored a few points.

"Remember what I said about make-up sex? Well, I heard there's an even better kind."

"Oh?" Lori straightened. "Is there really?"

"Yup, it's the I-told-you-so-and-I-was-right kind of lovemaking."

Lori's smile filled her entire face. "Are you

318

making that up?"

Linc grinned from ear to ear himself. "Tell you what, my wonderful wife, I'll let you be the judge."

# Twenty-Two

In the past six months, Shirley Bliss had had a few so-called dates. Spending time with a man other than her husband had felt wrong in the beginning, but she'd gradually begun to accept that Jim was gone and she needed to — as Miranda put it — "forge a new path in life."

Not that Miranda was a great example . . .

Shirley didn't count Will Jefferson as a real date. The only reason she'd accepted his invitations was out of gratitude, and in truth, she rather hoped Miranda would start seeing Will. In her opinion, her very forthright friend was perfect for the man who seemed to consider himself a gift for women to appreciate and admire.

This date with Larry Knight was in an entirely different category. For one thing, it *was* a real date. She felt as if she was in high school all over again, waiting to be picked up for the senior prom. That afternoon, before Larry arrived, she must have checked her reflection in the mirror a dozen times, as giddy as a schoolgirl. Thankfully Tanni had gone out with friends for the day.

She'd had several conversations with Larry in the past three weeks. She'd offered to drive into the city today but Larry had arranged for the car to show up at her place around two that afternoon. He'd told her he probably wouldn't see her until she got to Seattle. They'd attend his friend's show — Manny Willingham, an artist whose name recognition had increased substantially in the past year — have dinner and then the car would take her back to Cedar Cove.

While she was fussing with her hair one last time, the doorbell rang. The car was ten minutes early. Flustered, Shirley grabbed her purse and hurried to the front door. She opened it and, to her astonishment, Larry stood there on her porch. Just seeing him like this, so handsome and dynamic, just seeing his smile, left her breathless.

When she didn't immediately greet him, Larry said, "You weren't expecting me?"

"No," she blurted out. "I wasn't expecting you to arrive with the car."

"It worked out so I could. Are you ready, or do you need a few more minutes?"

"I'm ready." Or she would be, once her

heart settled down and she could breathe normally again.

He guided her to the car. The driver held open the rear passenger door for her while Larry walked around to the opposite side.

Because of her initial reaction, Shirley was convinced she wouldn't be able to utter an intelligent word during the entire eighty-minute drive into Seattle. But they talked constantly — about everything, from personal histories to what they were reading to preferences in art. When the driver pulled up in front of an elegant Bellevue gallery, Shirley couldn't believe so much time had passed.

She'd learned a great deal about Larry, and had confided much about herself. Like her, he'd lost his spouse, which she already knew. His two children were both married. He asked about Jim and her children, whom she discussed at length. Shirley thanked him again for helping Shaw and brought up her concerns about Tanni.

Manny Willingham was a sculptor. Larry introduced Shirley, and Manny took her hand in both of his, looked her directly in the eyes and said, "Go easy on my friend. This has been a long time coming."

Larry growled something under his breath, but Shirley didn't hear what he'd said, only that he was displeased with Manny's remark. Soon after, Manny was inundated by others with questions about his work and they didn't speak to him again.

They viewed Manny's work and Shirley could see why he commanded the prices he did. Several items already had red dots beside them, indicating a sale. Several others were for display only. One piece in particular struck Shirley, and she studied it for at least ten minutes. It was a bronze, a bouquet of roses just at their peak.

"This is one of my favorite pieces, as well," Larry said, standing behind her.

"It's not for sale," she noted. She would gladly have purchased it if the price had been one she could afford — which she doubted. But the decision had been taken away from her.

"Actually, I own that piece," Larry said.

Astonished, she turned to face him. "You do?"

"Manny made that for me shortly after Rosie died."

"Your wife's name was Rose?"

"Rosemarie. I called her Rosie."

Until that moment, Shirley hadn't realized that Larry had never mentioned his wife's name.

They left for an early dinner at about five.

Unlike Will, who'd taken her to one of the most expensive steak houses in town, Larry chose a quaint family-run seafood place along the Tacoma waterfront.

"I hope seafood's okay with you," he said when he told her about it. "I'm not much of a meat eater."

So this was something else they had in common. "I love seafood. This is perfect." And it was.

She wanted to remember every minute of their time together, everything they talked about. They had so many of the same likes and dislikes, from small things like favorite songs and movies to big ones like philosophies and beliefs. After a while, all the similarities between them seemed almost eerie — and yet wonderful.

As the limo driver took them back to Cedar Cove, Larry reached for her hand. Shirley gave it to him, acutely conscious of his nearness — his touch. It seemed as though her senses, long dormant, had suddenly sprung back to life.

She and Larry spent the rest of the drive just like that — holding hands, exchanging quiet comments, completely focused on each other.

When the car pulled up in front of her house, Shirley was sorry the day had ended.

Tanni wasn't home yet and Shirley couldn't decide whether she should worry or appreciate the privacy.

"Would you like to see the dungeon?" she asked him. The invitation was a way to keep Larry with her for a little while. Her art studio was nothing special, certainly not compared to what his must look like.

"Very much." Larry asked the driver to wait and followed Shirley inside.

She led him down the stairs and once again felt her heart beating out of control. He was going to kiss her and she wanted that, more than anything she could remember wanting in a very long time.

At the bottom of the stairs, Larry rested his hand on her shoulder. Without thinking, Shirley turned into his embrace and slipped her arms around his neck. As she knew he would, as she'd hoped and prayed, Larry kissed her. This was the first time another man had touched her like this since she'd lost her husband. She'd avoided anything physical with the few men she'd dated, fearing the rush of guilt she knew she'd experience. She felt none of that when Larry kissed her. No guilt, no dread. Just peace. And happiness.

After several kisses, she buried her face against his throat.

"After we met, that night you came to my show, I had to see you again," he confessed in a husky whisper. "Manny's exhibit in Seattle was a convenient excuse."

"Can you make up more excuses?"

Larry's collarbone vibrated slightly against her cheek as he chuckled. "I think I'll have to."

"You felt it, too?" she asked, already knowing his answer. The attraction was there from the moment Will Jefferson had introduced them.

"Oh, yeah . . ."

Shirley heard the front door open and close. Tanni was home.

Larry dropped his arms and stepped away.

"Mom?"

It was unusual for Tanni to seek her out; generally her daughter retreated immediately to her bedroom.

"Down here," she called. "That's my daughter," she explained unnecessarily.

They started up the stairs, and when Tanni saw Larry with her mother, she raised questioning eyes to Shirley.

"Tanni, this is my friend Larry Knight."

Her daughter's face instantly warmed as she recognized the name. Tanni pumped his hand as if she expected it to spout water. "It is a real pleasure to make your acquaintance," she said in an oddly formal fashion, hardly sounding like herself. "I can't thank you enough for everything you've done for Shaw, and for me, too."

"Happy to," Larry said. When Tanni released his hand, he turned to Shirley. "I'd better get back to Seattle. I'm flying out early."

Shirley hated to see him go. She walked him to the door in silence.

"I'll call you," he promised.

"Please." She vowed she'd sit by the phone until she heard from him. Until they talked again she couldn't allow herself to believe any of this was real. She watched him return to the car, watched it leave, before she found the strength to face her daughter.

"He's nice, isn't he?" Tanni said reverently.

"He's *wonderful*." The word was inadequate to describe him and the way he made her feel.

Tanni gave her a speculative look and Shirley thought maybe she'd said too much.

"Are you falling for him, Mom?"

Shirley couldn't lie. "I think I might be. Truthfully, it's all a little soon . . . and a little scary."

"It is. I know how I felt when I fell in love

327

with Shaw. My stomach felt weird all the time and I didn't want to eat and all I could think about was him." As she spoke, Tanni's eyes filled with tears.

Instinctively Shirley opened her arms. Tanni walked into them and laid her head against her mother's shoulder.

"What's wrong, baby?" Shirley asked softly as she stroked her daughter's hair.

Tanni broke away. "I can't stand it when I cry," she muttered angrily. She scrubbed roughly at her face as though to punish herself for being so weak.

"It's Shaw, isn't it?"

Tanni nodded.

They went into the kitchen and sat on adjoining stools. Shirley waited for Tanni to get control of her emotions. After all these months of dealing with her daughter's contentious attitude, she was grateful that Tanni had confided in her.

"I hate myself," Tanni blurted out.

Shirley wanted to argue and demand Tanni never say anything like that again. Instead, she held back and composed herself before responding.

"Why?" she asked simply.

"I hate how I act when I don't hear from Shaw. I text him and if he doesn't immediately text me back, then I accuse him of seeing other girls and we argue. I knew everything would change when he went to San Francisco. He said it wouldn't, but it has."

"*Shaw* is changing."

Tanni bowed her head. "He makes me crazy. I hate the things I say and do. I want to believe he still loves me, but deep down I don't think he does."

"Has he met someone else?"

Again, she nodded, her head down, her chin almost against her neck.

Wanting to comfort her, Shirley leaned over and placed one arm around her daughter's shoulders. "It's hard to let go of the people we love. Even when we have to."

"I don't want to lose him!"

"Of course you don't."

"I see girls behave like this at school and I look at them with disgust."

"See them do what, exactly?" Shirley asked. "You mean the texting?"

"That's part of it. They hang on to their old boyfriends. They're so clingy and weak, and now I feel like one of them and I hate it. I hate myself," she said, choking back a sob.

"Oh, Tanni."

"I know I shouldn't text Shaw, but I can't make myself stop." She looked at her mother tearfully. "Take my cell phone away."

"Do you mean that?"

"No," she cried, and followed that with a tremulous smile.

They hugged, and then Tanni surprised her. "Thanks, Mom," she whispered as she slid off the stool.

By Monday evening Shirley understood her daughter's angst much more clearly. She hadn't heard from Larry since he'd dropped her off. All of Sunday night she'd waited for the phone to ring. Nothing. She considered calling him, but decided against it.

Early Tuesday afternoon, Tanni answered the door to a lovely floral arrangement that was being delivered.

She carried it into the kitchen, where Shirley was preparing a curried chicken salad.

"They're for you," her daughter announced.

Shirley wiped her hands down the front of her jeans and reached for the card. Tanni watched as Shirley tore open the envelope and silently read the message. "Thank you for a lovely day. Larry."

"They're from Larry, aren't they?" her daughter asked.

Shirley nodded and felt an overwhelming wave of sadness.

Tanni frowned. "You don't seem happy that he sent you flowers."

Shirley gave what she hoped was an indifferent shrug as she dropped the card on the kitchen counter. "He doesn't want to see me again. Flowers are a man's way of saying goodbye." All the ecstatic feelings she'd experienced after their time together had turned into mere fantasy. Because she'd been so attracted to Larry, she'd made the wrong assumptions about his feelings for her. She was just another in a long list of women who'd do anything to date him.

"He doesn't want to see you again?" Tanni asked incredulously. "And he let you know by sending you flowers? I don't get it."

Shirley nodded again as she struggled to deal with her disappointment. "Yes." She felt as if a thick fog had descended.

"That's ridiculous," Tanni insisted.

Shirley knew otherwise. Larry Knight was an important artist, a celebrity in constant demand. He lived and worked in California and with his busy promotion and travel schedule he must've realized how difficult maintaining a relationship would be. She'd wondered when she hadn't heard from him and now she had her answer. Not that she blamed him; a long-distance romance would be impossible. Besides, she'd probably just been a weekend's entertainment to him, not someone he'd taken seriously. . . .

Rather than let Tanni see how depressed she felt, Shirley managed to swallow a few bites of dinner. That evening she sat in front of the television, mindlessly watching a rerun of a reality show, too disheartened to do anything but stare at the screen.

Her head whirled with emotions she didn't want to confront. If Tanni had asked her about the program, Shirley wouldn't have been able to give her a single detail.

The phone rang, and she didn't even bother to look at caller ID. She couldn't see any reason to torture herself. Besides, Tanni would grab it fast enough.

Ten minutes later, her daughter wandered casually into the living room, arms swinging at her sides. "That man who wants to cut off his relationship with you is on the line."

Shocked to the very core of her being, Shirley nearly fell off the sofa. "Larry?"

Tanni grinned. "He's really nice, Mom. I like him. We talked."

Larry had spoken with her daughter for *ten minutes?*

"I asked him about Shaw, and he said he checked and Shaw's doing really well at the art institute." Her smile revealed her pain. "I'm glad for him. I mean that."

Shirley knew what it had cost her daughter to make that statement.

"Mom, answer the phone," Tanni teased. "You don't want to keep Larry waiting."

Tanni was right. Feeling better than she had in days, Shirley picked up the phone.

# TWENTY-THREE

Tanni Bliss parked in the lot adjacent to the library — and did a competent job of it, too. At least in her own opinion. Having her driver's license had made a big difference to her life. It meant freedom! Her mom had been pretty good about letting her take the car, too, especially if it involved her work at the library.

The Reading with Rover program had gotten off to an excellent start. The first few weeks were an experiment to figure out how it should work when school began again in September.

Grace had called a meeting for the volunteers on Thursday afternoon. Tanni was on her way there now. She liked working with the kids and dogs; what she didn't enjoy was being around Kristen Jamey. Tanni wasn't sure why she disliked Kristen so much, other than the fact that she was dumb. She didn't know how else to put it.

Kristen was about as empty-headed as anyone could get.

Her lack of intelligence didn't matter one iota because Kristen was beautiful. The boys at school stumbled all over themselves every time Kristen walked down the hall. She was popular with just about everyone — except Tanni. Already there was talk about Kristen being crowned homecoming queen next October when they were seniors.

Tanni suspected Grace thought she was jealous of Kristen but that wasn't the case. It *wasn't*. She simply didn't respect the other girl. The head librarian had asked Tanni to make an effort to get along with Kristen, and she'd tried. She really had, not that it'd done much good. Knowing that Kristen would be at the meeting today put Tanni on edge.

The library was busy, probably due to the upcoming Fourth of July weekend. Half a dozen people stood in line waiting to check out books. All the computers were in use, too.

One of the librarians recognized Tanni and greeted her with a smile. "Grace is in the conference room," she said, pointing in that direction.

"Thanks." Tanni headed toward the back of the library.

The conference room door was open, and she saw Grace sitting at the table with a pile of tissues in front of her. Tanni hesitated. Either Grace had come down with a wretched cold — or she'd been crying.

Not until she walked into the room did Tanni notice that Grace wasn't alone. Kristen Jamey sat across from her, and instinctively Tanni stiffened.

Grace glanced up. "Oh, hello, Tanni. I apologize for the tears. My dog, Buttercup . . ." She didn't finish.

"Grace found Buttercup dead this morning," Kristen explained. "She died in her sleep. Grace's husband, Cliff, is burying Buttercup in her favorite shady spot."

"Oh, Grace, I'm so sorry." Tanni felt terrible for her. She'd lost her own dog, Bingo, when she was ten and, until her father's death, it'd been the worst event of her life.

"I'd had Buttercup at the vet earlier in the week and everything seemed to be okay. She was getting on in years and sleeping a lot, but . . . this was unexpected."

"Maybe we should cancel the meeting," Kristen suggested, looking at Tanni.

"Sure. I can come another time."

"No." Grace dabbed at her eyes. "You're both here and the others are coming. I'll be fine. Just give me a few minutes."

Kristen reached across the table and squeezed her hand gently. Tanni wanted to say something but she didn't really know how to comfort Grace. She thought of telling her about Bingo and how sad she'd been when he died. Only it didn't seem like a good idea to share her own pain because it might make her weep, too.

"My dog's name was Bingo," Kristen whispered.

Tanni's head shot up.

"He was part cocker spaniel and part something else, although no one ever seemed to know what. Maybe poodle. My brother found him. The poor dog looked like he'd been lost a long time. Bingo didn't have any identification, and we put an ad in the paper but no one claimed him. The day my dad was going to take him to the shelter I cried and cried, so my parents let me keep him. He'd become my friend. He even slept on my bed."

Bingo had slept on Tanni's bed, too.

"I got Buttercup from a friend of Charlotte Rhodes. It was shortly after my first husband died. I was so lonely, and Buttercup seemed to know how much I needed her. She loved Cliff . . . and me." Grace grabbed another tissue and blew her nose. "Enough. I have to get a grip here."

"If it's any consolation, it does get easier with time," Kristen said in the same soothing voice. "I still think about Bingo and sometimes —" she glanced hesitantly at Tanni "— sometimes I feel as if he's still at the end of my bed asleep."

Tanni looked away. She felt the same thing about *her* Bingo.

The meeting lasted two hours. The four original volunteers showed up, plus three other adults who sat in to listen to the presentation. All three decided that they, too, wanted to be part of the program.

Tanni kept her eye on Kristen. The other girl had been so good with Grace. Kristen had said everything Tanni wished she'd been able to say. Kristen had expressed sympathy and understanding and done it in a compassionate, thoughtful way.

Tanni didn't know the airhead was even capable of that. While Kristen had been comforting Grace, Tanni had sat like a dope with her tongue glued to the roof of her mouth.

When the meeting ended, Tanni followed Kristen out of the building. She wanted to tell her about Bingo. Her Bingo.

Apparently Kristen saw that Tanni was behind her because once they'd left the building, she whirled around. "What do you want?" she snapped.

"Ah . . ."

"You've made it clear you don't like me, Tanni. I don't know what I ever did to you, but it must've been awful."

"Actually, I wanted to tell you something."

"So tell me."

She hated the way Kristen made her feel. Grace had asked Tanni to make an effort with the other girl, and so far nothing had worked. Well, okay, she could've tried harder. She took a deep breath.

"I had a dog named Bingo, too," she told her.

Kristen's gaze narrowed as though she didn't believe her.

"You can ask my mother if you want. It's true. He died six years ago."

For a long moment Kristen didn't say anything. "I still miss my Bingo."

Tanni stared down at the pavement. "I miss my Bingo, too."

The other girl hesitated. "Would you like to walk over to Mocha Mama's?"

Her suspicions immediately shot up. "Why?"

Kristen shrugged. "To get something to drink. If you've got other plans, it's no big deal."

Tanni made a show of looking at her

watch. "I've got a few minutes."

"Great." Kristen was all smiles now.

They walked across the street and down the next block to Mocha Mama's, where Shaw had once worked. His uncle owned the shop and had replaced Shaw with another manager. Adam was a college student who instantly perked up when Kristen and Tanni walked in. Tanni knew his sudden interest wasn't in her. Adam's eyes went straight to Kristen.

"What can I get you ladies?" Adam asked cheerfully.

Twice when she'd stopped by, Tanni had to wait while Adam talked on his cell phone. Seeing the way he reacted to Kristen confirmed everything Tanni knew about the other girl. It wasn't fair that this airhead would command such adoration. Shaw would probably want to draw Kristen's portrait, too, she thought cynically.

Thinking about him made her tense. Without being too obvious about it, she got out her cell phone to see if there was a text message from Shaw, desperately hoping he'd answered her while she was in the meeting at the library.

He hadn't.

No surprise there. She hadn't heard from him since the night before, when she'd practically begged him to reply. Then his answer had been short and had basically said he was studying and she should leave him alone. She'd tossed and turned half the night.

"What would you like?" Kristen asked, breaking into Tanni's thoughts.

It took her a moment to respond. "I'll have a chai tea."

"Me, too," Kristen said,

Tanni rummaged in her purse for money.

"It's on the house," Adam said.

Kristen thanked Adam and when they'd been served she led the way to a table by the window. It was the same one where Tanni often used to sit with Shaw.

"That must happen to you a lot," Tanni said, unable to hide her sarcasm.

"You mean getting stuff for free?"

"Yeah."

She shrugged. "Sometimes."

Tanni's cell dinged, indicating she had a text message. In her effort to reach her cell, she nearly tumbled off the chair. When she saw that the message was from her brother, Nick, who'd stayed in Seattle for the summer, she wanted to weep with frustration. She became aware of Kristen watching her and quickly shoved the phone back in her purse.

"I wanted to tell you something," Kristen said. "I know you don't like me. I'm not sure why, but I can guess."

Tanni doubted Kristen would understand her feelings, but she wasn't going to argue. "Let me ask *you* something, okay?"

"Sure." Kristen sounded eager to clear the air.

"Why did you volunteer? Are you doing it because your GPA stinks and you figure having this on your college application is going to help?"

"No." Her denial was instantaneous and vehement.

"Then why?"

Kristen's hand tightened around her drink. "I had trouble learning to read, too. I'm dyslexic, but when I first started school we lived in this really small town and they didn't test me for it. I struggled for a long time before I caught on to the concept of reading. I wanted to help another child learn because if a volunteer hadn't stepped in to help *me*, I might've turned out to be one of those functional illiterates Grace talked about in the meeting this afternoon."

"You're dyslexic?" Tanni found it hard to believe.

"I know you think I'm an airhead. But I'm not stupid. It's just that I have a different way of learning than most people."

"Oh." Tanni felt immediately guilty. "I assumed your heart wasn't really in this."

"It is," Kristen said with such conviction that Tanni would never doubt her again.

"What about you?" Kristen asked, then sipped at her creamy chai tea.

Tanni hesitated. The other girl had been honest with her. The least she could do was repay her in kind. "I need to get my mind off Shaw."

"Shaw used to work here, didn't he?"

She answered with a nod. "He's attending the San Francisco Art Institute now."

"Wow, that's great."

"For him it is." Tanni, on the other hand, was stuck in Cedar Cove and would be for another year, if not longer. Before Shaw left, they'd promised never to let anything or anyone come between them. He hadn't even been away three months and he was giving her the brush-off.

When he'd first gone to San Francisco, they'd been in constant communication. Now she was lucky if she heard from him three times a week. Whenever she did she was so happy; her behavior was downright pitiful. She hated her own reaction to his lack of contact as much as she hated what had happened between them.

"Not so good for you, right?" Kristen asked.

"You could say that." Tanni was unable to hide the pain in her voice. "We used to text every hour. . . . Now I hardly hear from him. I just wish he'd say he wants to break up, you know. Instead, he's killing me with this silence."

"Guys usually don't."

"Don't what?"

"Initiate the breakup."

Kristen was the one with the experience in the dating world. Shaw was Tanni's first real boyfriend. He'd also become her best friend. They'd shared their love of art and each other, and everything had been perfect. Well, not completely, because Shaw was stuck here at Mocha Mama's brewing coffee and dying on the inside because he wanted to be an artist.

"Do you think Shaw wants to break up with me?" Tanni asked. Maybe Kristen could help her understand what was going on.

"Tell me how he's been acting."

Tanni talked for thirty minutes, rattling off a litany of slights Shaw had committed since he'd moved to California.

"You say he never would've gotten into the art institute if it hadn't been for some friends of your mother's?" Kristen asked.

Eagerly Tanni nodded. "He owes me."

"He knows it, too, which complicates his feelings."

"All he has to do is say the word and I'm out of his life." She made it sound cut and dried, although it would be one of the hardest things she'd ever had to go through. Not as hard as losing her dad.

Kristen's laugh poured salt into Tanni's already wounded heart.

"This isn't funny!" she flared.

"I don't think it is," Kristen said quickly. "It's just that Shaw is so typical of guys I know."

"He is?"

"Sure. He's being a total jerk to you — and getting away with it."

"What did I do to him?" Tanni wanted to cry at the unfairness of it all. The only thing she'd ever done was encourage, love and support Shaw. Now he couldn't even take two minutes to send her a message.

"Probably nothing," Kristen told her.

"Then why's he doing this?" Even as she asked the question, Tanni had the answer. "He's met someone else, hasn't he?"

Kristen didn't even try to soften the truth. "Probably."

"Then why doesn't he just say so?" It

would hurt a lot less if he was honest with her. Yes, it'd still hurt, but the pain would be easier to deal with than being left hanging the way she was now.

"That's what guys are like," Kristen said confidently. "Especially guys who've been going out with you for a while. He's ignoring you, hoping *you'll* break up with *him*."

"That's what he wants?" Tanni asked with a catch in her throat.

"From everything you've told me, yes, that's what Shaw's waiting for you to do."

Instinctively Tanni knew Kristen was right.

"You need to get out more, see other guys," Kristen advised. "Do you know Jeremy Reynolds?"

The name seemed familiar to Tanni but she couldn't visualize a face to go with it. "I don't think so . . . maybe."

"He's interested in you."

"Jeremy Reynolds," Tanni repeated out loud. "I'm not sure I've even met him."

"He graduated this year. He lives next door to me, and when I mentioned that you and I had volunteered for the Reading with Rover program he asked a whole bunch of questions about you."

Tanni planned to dig out her yearbook the minute she got home and look him up.

"Jeremy's kind of shy," Kristen went on.

"Besides, everyone knows about you and Shaw. Would you like me to tell him you're not going out with Shaw anymore?"

Tanni shrugged, biting her lip.

"Give it some time," Kristen said kindly. She finished her tea and set down the empty plastic cup. "I'm glad we talked, Tanni."

"I am, too." And she meant it. If they hadn't, Tanni would never have guessed why Kristen had volunteered to work with kids at risk. "Thanks for the advice about Shaw. Would it be okay if I called you and let you know how things go?"

"Definitely." She paused. "I'd like it if we could be friends."

Kristen wanted to be friends with her? This was another twist Tanni hadn't expected. "Yeah, I'd like that, too," Tanni said a bit shyly.

They stood, waved goodbye to Adam and walked slowly toward the library parking lot, chatting as they went.

When Tanni got home, she found her mother in a happy mood, which meant she'd heard from Larry. They were on the phone practically every day, often two or three times.

"You seem happy," her mother said, watching Tanni in a way that would once have irritated her.

"I'm going to be okay, Mom," she said. She went into her room and got out her Junior Annual to look for a photo of Jeremy Reynolds.

# TWENTY-FOUR

On the Fourth of July, Mack and Mary Jo gathered down at the Cedar Cove waterfront with dozens of other families for the fireworks display. It was almost dark, and there was a buzz of anticipation in the crowd.

Linc and Lori sat on lawn chairs beside them. Noelle was already asleep, limp in Mack's arms, unaware of what was about to take place. Mary Jo doubted she'd stay asleep once the fireworks began.

Mack had been on duty four days straight, but had the holiday itself free. The fire station was on high alert this week, due to the hazards caused by fireworks.

Being able to spend the entire day with Mack and her brother made this Fourth of July special. Because Mary Jo's relationship with Linc had changed — more than changed, *improved* — since her brother's marriage, she'd discovered that he was a good friend. Lori was fast becoming one, too. The more she got to know Linc's wife, the more Mary Jo liked her. Lori was a gifted seamstress who'd recently made an adorable summer outfit for Noelle.

Earlier in the day, the two couples had taken a picnic lunch to Point Defiance Zoo. While Noelle might be too young to appreciate the experience, she'd loved seeing the animals. Even Linc seemed to have fun. Her brother had always been so serious; seeing him relaxed and enjoying himself revealed a side of him she barely remembered.

"Isn't it time?" Lori asked impatiently. "I thought the paper said ten o'clock."

That was when they heard the whine of fireworks being set off. "There they go," Linc said, just as the rocket burst into a cluster, spraying red, white and blue sparks across the clear night sky.

At the explosion, Noelle woke with a start and began crying. Mack held the infant against his shoulder, gently rubbing her back. Noelle was content until the next explosion. She let out another startled cry.

"Oh, dear," Mary Jo said. "This is scaring her."

"Should we take her home?" Mack asked, his face marked with concern.

"I don't know," Mary Jo said uncertainly. She didn't want the evening to end, but Noelle's comfort came first.

Noelle began to whimper. "Look," Mack told her, and pointed up at the sky.

Mary Jo wanted to tell him he couldn't reason with a six-month-old infant.

But somehow, Mack was able to calm her and eventually Noelle returned to sleep, despite the noise and excitement. When Mary Jo glanced over at her sleeping daughter, she noticed Linc and Lori holding hands. Lori's head rested on Linc's shoulder.

She looked at Mack again and saw him watching Noelle, his expression vigilant. He must have felt her scrutiny because he turned to smile at her. She smiled back and reached for his hand.

Mack held it for a few minutes before releasing it in order to shift Noelle in his arms.

By the time they arrived at the duplex, it was almost midnight. While she put Noelle in her crib, Mack brought in the blanket, the diaper bag and the remains of their picnic. She'd made potato salad, which he'd raved about. She resisted telling him that the recipe had actually come from his mother.

In fact, Mary Jo had talked to Corrie McAfee twice in the past week. She liked

Mack's mother; his father, too, although Roy was more difficult to know. Maybe because he was a detective and ex-cop and therefore used to keeping his reactions to himself.

When she came into the kitchen Mack was standing there, hands in his back pockets. He didn't say anything, as if gauging how best to broach whatever subject he had in mind.

Mary Jo waited for him to speak. "What's up?" she finally asked.

"Something's bothering you," he said bluntly.

Her feelings, her dissatisfaction, were still vague and unformed, and she was surprised by his perceptiveness. She tried to put her unease into words but that was harder than she'd realized. She didn't want to say the wrong thing.

After another minute or so, Mack exhaled. "You'd better tell me what it is."

Mary Jo felt awkward. "Tonight, with . . . Noelle."

"Yes?" he urged.

They stood and faced each other, and both seemed tentative, as though frightened of where this conversation might lead them.

"You want to be a dad."

He nodded. "Very much."

She stared down at the floor. "You love Noelle."

"You can't doubt that, can you?"

"Never." His love for the baby was apparent in everything he'd said and done ever since he'd helped deliver her on Christmas Eve. When she raised her eyes she saw his smile.

She met his look. "What about me?"

"What?" He blinked in confusion. "Are you asking if I love *you*? Mary Jo? You can't be serious! I'm crazy about you. I've told you that more than once."

"You're crazy about Noelle. I'm just sort of . . . attached." She didn't like feeling so insecure and yet . . . she had to wonder. Furthermore, she'd prefer the truth. She wanted to believe he cared, but she'd been misled by David and could no longer trust her own instincts. She shouldn't ever forget that.

"I love you," he said, without hesitation or embellishment. "As soon as this mess with David is straightened out, I'd like us to become engaged. I want to spend the rest of my life with you."

His words warmed her heart, but she refused to allow those warm feelings to sidetrack her. "After this mess with David is settled," she echoed.

"Yes?"

She swallowed hard and found she couldn't speak. The proposal was the reward he dangled in front of her to resolve the situation with Noelle's father. *She* was the one who was supposed to take the risk of pressing forward on the very issue David had warned her against. No one except Mary Jo seemed to see David as a credible threat. She had to take him at his word in this, if nothing else. His intentions were clear — if she filed for child support, he'd make her life miserable.

"Have you talked to Allan Harris like you said?" Mack asked.

"No," she admitted. "Not yet." Mack had been at the fire station most of the past two weeks; otherwise, she knew he would've hounded her about this.

"And the reason for that is . . . ?"

"I don't trust David," she said, although that didn't really answer his question.

"You shouldn't, because he can't be trusted."

She moved away and walked over to the picture window, crossing her arms. "Why are you waiting for me to deal with David? If you love me and Noelle and we love you, then why can't we become engaged now?"

Mack took his time answering. He took so

354

long that Mary Jo turned around to look at him.

"I have a good reason, Mary Jo."

"I'd like to hear it." She tensed, afraid she was going to have a problem with what he had to say.

"If David gets wind of the fact that I want to adopt Noelle, it might be all the justification he needs to refuse to sign the relinquishment papers. He isn't willing to support his daughter, but as soon as he discovers I want to adopt her, you can bet he'll do whatever he can to thwart that. Ben agrees with me."

"You've talked to Ben about this?"

"And my father, too. They both said the same thing, and I respect their opinions."

"What happens if David doesn't sign away his rights as Noelle's father?" she asked slowly. "Then what?"

"We'll deal with that when the time comes. Why are you assuming the worst?"

Funny question. "With David I've learned that's what I need to do."

She couldn't look at Mack, so she turned away again and walked into the kitchen. Needing to occupy her hands, she unpacked the picnic basket, setting the empty potato salad container in the kitchen sink and filling it with soapy water.

"Mary Jo, we're in the middle of an important decision. I think cleaning up can wait, don't you?"

She leaned against the counter. "If David refuses to sign the papers, would you still want to marry me?"

"Yes." He didn't pause for an instant.

"You're sure about that?"

"Yes." He sighed, obviously exasperated. "Let's go back for a moment."

"To what?"

"You haven't talked to Mr. Harris."

She should've guessed this was coming. "No. He's been in court."

"Has he gone into the office at all?"

"Occasionally," she told him. "But he's had other things on his mind. The trial only wrapped up on Friday, and I didn't want to distract him before that." This was true, but more than that it was an excuse, and as she offered it, Mary Jo realized Mack saw it for what it was.

"O . . . kay," he said, dragging out the word. "What about next week?"

"Mr. Harris is on vacation." Her relief tumbled out with her answer.

Mack walked into the living room, picked up a few toys scattered about, then returned to the kitchen. "You don't want to deal with this, do you?"

She could lie, but Mack was right. "No."

"Because?" Again, he waited for her to explain.

"Because of all the reasons I've already brought up. Nothing has changed, Mack. David will do whatever he can to ruin my life. He doesn't want me or Noelle, doesn't want the responsibility of a child, but he'll do everything in his power to make sure no one else can have us."

"Let me talk to him," Mack said through gritted teeth.

"No." She couldn't, wouldn't, allow him to get into a physical confrontation with David.

"Why not?" he argued. "I'll tell him I'm marrying you and that I want to adopt Noelle."

"Do you really think that would help?" she cried. "You just told me how important it was that David *not* know our plans."

Mack groaned, sounding frustrated and tired.

"Listen, Mack, it's really late and we're both upset. We should've waited for another time to talk about this."

"No," he countered. "Let's discuss it right now, tonight. This whole thing started because you're afraid I'm more interested in adopting Noelle than I am in marrying

357

you. Correct?"

Reluctantly, Mary Jo nodded. It seemed so frivolous when he put it like that. Looking at him now, his eyes soft with tenderness, she wondered how she could have doubted his feelings for her.

"You do love me."

His smile widened. "You've got it."

"Okay, then let's call it a night. Forget I said anything."

"Okay." Mack headed for the door, opening it forcefully before turning back. "Would you mind waiting just a moment?"

"Oh . . . Okay, I'll wait."

Mack tore out of the house and she heard him enter his own. Three or four minutes passed before he came back. She'd used that time to finish cleaning up.

Mary Jo looked at him expectantly as he hovered in the kitchen doorway.

"I want you to know I didn't plan it like this, but I think the timing is right."

"Timing? For what?"

"Maybe you should sit down."

Puzzled, she sank into a kitchen chair.

Mack frowned and gestured at the living room. "Maybe the sofa would be better."

"The sofa," she repeated. Fine, she'd sit on the sofa.

As soon as she was seated, Mack paced in

front of her. "I love you, Mary Jo."

She smiled. "I believe we've established that."

"Have we? Are you sure? I don't want there to be a single doubt. Ever."

"You've reassured me, Mack. Honestly, you have."

"I wanted to talk to your brother first."

"My brother?"

"To let him know my intentions — that I'm asking his sister to be my wife."

Mary Jo blinked back tears as she understood exactly what Mack was doing. He was about to formally propose to her. Her hand flew to her mouth in shock — and yet she shouldn't have been surprised.

"Mary Jo." She stood, and when she did, Mack took her free hand in his. "Will you marry me?"

Not trusting her voice, she simply nodded.

Mack fumbled for something in his back pocket and brought out a diamond solitaire ring. "I realize most women like to choose their own engagement bands. I picked it out myself, but if you don't like it I'll exchange it."

"It's beautiful." In truth she couldn't tell what the ring looked like because her eyes had filled with tears that blurred everything around her. Mack's sweet, wonderful face swam before her.

Mack slipped the diamond onto her ring finger. "Okay, now we're officially engaged. Come what may, Mary Jo, no matter what happens with David and with custody of Noelle, you and I will face it together. As husband and wife."

Unable to hold back her tears, Mary Jo threw her arms around Mack and clung to him.

He drew her into his embrace. "I didn't expect you to cry."

"I can't help it," she wailed.

That was when Mack started to laugh, and the only way she could stop him was to take his face in both hands and kiss him.

# TWENTY-FIVE

Leonard Bellamy stood behind his massive desk as Roy McAfee was escorted into his office. He walked toward Roy, extending his hand.

As they shook, Roy scanned his surroundings.

The office was impeccably furnished. Pieces of modern art were prominently displayed and Roy guessed that none of them were reproductions.

"I appreciate your coming here," he said, gesturing for Roy to take a seat. Prior business had always been done at the McAfee office, and Roy was well aware that this time Bellamy wanted the advantage of being in his own territory.

"That's part of the service." Roy sat in the leather chair, letting his body language convey self-assurance. Bellamy's assistant brought him a cup of coffee. He thanked her with a smile and took a sip.

Bellamy reclaimed his seat. "I hope you did a thorough search on that freeloader."

"I did," Roy said. He put the coffee on the edge of Leonard's desk and balanced his briefcase on his legs.

"Glad to hear it. I want to pin him to the wall. He thinks he can move into Cedar Cove, set up business and marry my daughter? I've got news for him. Wyse is going to learn that I'm not letting him ride on my good name."

Roy wondered what Leonard meant. He'd seen no evidence of Linc exploiting Bellamy's name or influence. Could the other man have information he didn't? Roy doubted it.

As for a bad report on Wyse . . . he suspected Bellamy would be disappointed. He withdrew a folder and handed it to him.

Bellamy eagerly took it and started flipping through the pages. He frowned, and his frown darkened as he read.

"There's nothing here," he said.

"On the contrary, I've given you a six-page report. I took extra time to do an exhaustive background check and found that Lincoln Wyse has no police record. He pays his bills on time. No problems with the IRS. He attends church —"

"That doesn't mean anything! I go to

362

church, too."

Roy continued to outline his findings. "From everything I've gathered," he concluded, "your daughter made a good choice in the man she married."

"I don't get it," Bellamy said angrily. He tossed the report aside, his look sour with disappointment. "First, my wife takes up his cause and now you."

"Then your wife's met Wyse?"

He nodded. "Without my knowledge she invited our daughter and that gold digger to dinner at the family home — keeping it from me until the last moment. I refused to have any part of it. Later, she told me how much she enjoyed meeting him. I thought Kate had more sense than that, but apparently I was wrong."

Roy had assumed Bellamy was capable of recognizing when he'd made a mistake; he'd obviously misjudged the other man. Bellamy was committed to the idea that Lincoln Wyse had married Lori for his own selfish reasons. Nothing would change his mind, not even the truth — that Linc was a decent man and that he was in love with Lori.

"Dig deeper this time," Leonard bellowed, slamming his fist on the desk. "There's got to be something. Find it!"

Roy had hoped the report would reassure

Bellamy; however, that wasn't happening. Obviously the man's agenda was more complicated than he'd realized. Roy had initially wondered if Bellamy believed *no* man was good enough for his daughter. Now he discounted that assumption. For whatever reason, Bellamy wanted to prove he was right and Lori was wrong.

To be fair, Roy could understand Bellamy's concerns. Lori and Linc hadn't known each other long before they were married. Not inviting family to the wedding exacerbated the situation, and Roy could appreciate that, since his own daughter had done basically the same thing. He reminded himself that he had the advantage of having spent some time with Pete Mason. Bellamy knew next to nothing about Lincoln Wyse.

"Go back, and bring me some facts I can use," Bellamy said. He stood as though to dismiss Roy.

Slightly amused and yet irritated, Roy remained seated. "Do you think I didn't do a thorough report?"

"I don't like that man and I don't trust him. I haven't gotten this far in business without being a decent judge of character. I'd hoped you'd be able to uncover what my gut told me when I met Wyse."

"As I explained, I did a complete background check. In addition to all the normal sources, I interviewed business associates and friends and investigated his finances. I found no evidence of gambling, excessive drinking or any other vice. He has good, solid values. If it were me, I'd welcome him into my family."

"I'm not you," Bellamy informed him, still standing. "I'm telling you right now, Lincoln Wyse is not to be trusted. He's taken advantage of my daughter. Lori's not only easy to fool, she's rebellious. She's defied me from the time she was five years old. Well, with this, she went too far."

It seemed to Roy that the real issue here wasn't Linc Wyse but Bellamy's relationship with his daughter. His apparent contempt for Lori, for her decisions in matters of work, love and who knew what else, rankled him. This was more about control than caring, more about pride than truth. He recalled how Bellamy had berated Lori because she'd been engaged to Geoff Duncan. Roy felt like pointing out that Duncan had fooled nearly everyone. He'd managed to deceive his employer, attorney Allan Harris, and that was no small thing. Duncan was smart, although thankfully not smart enough to get away with his crimes. It was grossly unfair to criticize Lori for being taken in by Duncan when he'd misled almost everyone else in town. Ironically, Duncan had resorted to theft because he'd been in over his head — all in an effort to impress Lori's demanding father.

"You mentioned that you had a connection with Wyse when I hired you," Bellamy said disparagingly. "I relied on you to be objective. Knowing what I do now, I can see that was a mistake."

For Bellamy to question Wyse's integrity was one thing, but to raise doubts about Roy's went over the line. He jumped to his feet and glared at the other man. Neither spoke.

"I completed the job you hired me to do," Roy finally said. "This report will stand up, despite what you want to believe. Wyse is a decent man." He would defy anyone to come up with anything different.

"That remains to be seen."

Roy opened his briefcase and removed the envelope that contained his bill. Bellamy thrust his hand out to take it. Instead, Roy tore it in two. "In the future I'd prefer if you took your business elsewhere." He didn't wait for Bellamy to respond, just grabbed his briefcase and walked out the door.

In a ten-minute conversation, Leonard Bellamy had insulted and infuriated him, to the point that Roy had actually thrown away money and lucrative future jobs — and felt good about it.

Rather than return to the office, Roy drove straight home. Corrie, as she often did, had taken Tuesday off to run errands. Checking his watch, he guessed she'd be home by now. His wife always had a calming effect on him. He decided he wouldn't mention his meeting with Bellamy; that would only rile him up again and solve nothing. Roy applauded Lori for defying her tyrant of a father.

When he walked in, Corrie was sitting in the kitchen with several bags of groceries lined up on the counter. She appeared to be deep in thought. In fact, she didn't seem to notice he was home.

Roy waved his hand playfully in front of her nose. Her face melted into a smile, and she automatically turned to him so he could kiss her, which he did. His wife's smile brought him peace and smoothed the sharp edges of his confrontation with Bellamy.

"You're home early," she commented as she slid off the stool. "How'd it go with Bellamy?"

She'd remembered. Well, no need to hide the events of the afternoon, then. He shrugged. "I won't bore you with the details, but I won't work for the man again."

She arched her brows, but if she was tempted to say *I told you so,* she didn't. "Oh? Why?"

"We have opposing points of view," he said simply. He gestured at the groceries. "Any reason you haven't put the milk away?"

"I was waiting for you to get home and do it for me," she teased.

Grinning, he reached for the half gallon of milk and set it inside the refrigerator. "Anything else that needs attention?"

"Ice cream," Corrie cried, and searched hurriedly through the bags until she found the carton, which she shoved in the freezer.

This scattered behavior was odd for his practical, even-keeled wife. Roy walked over to the sink and turned on the faucet to pour them each a glass of cold water. "Okay, what's wrong?"

She didn't deny that she was upset. "I ran into Gloria at the grocery store." She paused as though to collect her thoughts.

Roy knew better than to prod her. She'd tell him when she was ready.

"I know Linnette so well," she said, although Roy had no idea what Linnette had to do with this. "I would've realized in a heartbeat that she was pregnant the moment I looked at her."

"It's a bit more difficult over the phone," he agreed, although he didn't know what that had to do with meeting Gloria in the Safeway store.

"She's upset about something and —"

"Linnette is?"

"No, Gloria."

Roy was beginning to get her drift now. Corrie had talked to Gloria and couldn't read her the way she could their daughter. Except that Gloria was their daughter, too. Their first daughter.

"I asked her to dinner on Sunday."

"Good." Spending time together was the key. There were wounds to heal and relationships to build. He wanted Gloria to feel part of their family because she *was* family.

"She can't."

"She's working?" Roy knew that as the most recent addition to the sheriff's department, Gloria pulled the less desirable shifts. She'd been on duty over the Fourth of July, and was probably working weekends, as well.

"She didn't give me a reason." Corrie was putting away the groceries. "I suggested a weekday as an alternative and she said she'd get back to me, but I'm afraid she won't." Corrie shook her head. "She's avoiding us."

That was one possibility but his wife could

be exaggerating, making unwarranted assumptions. He didn't want to say that, though. Gloria was still a sensitive subject for them.

"Do you know if she's seeing anyone?" Corrie asked him out of the blue.

"Dating, you mean?"

"Yes, dating."

"Not really. She hasn't said. Did she mention anyone to you?"

Corrie nodded. "But not his name."

"So you think this might be about relationship troubles?"

"Well, isn't it always?" she challenged.

That seemed to be the end of the conversation.

Roy spread the *Cedar Cove Chronicle* out on the kitchen table and opened it to the crossword puzzle.

Suddenly Corrie exclaimed, "It's that doctor!"

Roy glanced up.

"What doctor?"

"The one Linnette was so keen on. At the clinic. I remember that he seemed more interested in Gloria, and that really bothered Linnette."

Roy managed to conjure up a hazy memory of this. Linnette had liked some doctor but then given up on him and fallen for that horseman, instead. Cal Washburn, his name was.

Roy returned to his crossword as his wife washed fresh herbs and rolled them in a paper towel to store in a refrigerator bag. He had one corner of the puzzle completed when Corrie interrupted him again.

"Todd," she announced triumphantly. "No, not Todd. Tim."

"Tim?"

"Timmons," she said with a snap of her fingers. "Chad Timmons. Dr. Chad Timmons."

He looked up and saw her watching him intently. Apparently something else was required of him, although he couldn't figure out what. "You think Gloria's seeing this doctor and having problems with him?"

Corrie nodded. "I'm afraid she's having major problems."

"But Gloria doesn't want to talk about it."

Abruptly Corrie turned away, then plucked a tissue from the nearby box and held it to her eyes. Corrie was crying? He got up from the table and stood behind her, clasping her shoulders.

"It hurts that our daughter can't talk to us, doesn't it?" he said quietly.

She sniffled, then turned and slid her arms

around his middle, burying her face in his chest.

"Everything will work out," Roy murmured, hoping he sounded reassuring. Corrie's feelings had been hurt, and while he wanted to comfort his wife, it was understandable that Gloria would choose not to share her emotions with them. If she'd had a falling-out with Dr. Timmons, then either the two of them would resolve the issue or they'd go their separate ways.

He would've commented on this if not for the fact that Corrie started to weep in earnest. Huge sobs racked her shoulders. Then, shocking him completely, she broke away and ran down the hallway.

For an instant Roy was too stunned to react. He found her standing on the tips of her toes in front of the hall closet, reaching for a new box of tissues.

"What's going on?"

"She wouldn't tell me. I was right there. I saw it, Roy. I saw it and she could barely look me in the eye. I tried to talk to her and she . . ." The rest was muffled as Corrie tore open the box and pressed a large wad of tissues to her face.

"What did you see?" Roy asked gently. He was growing concerned. This behavior of hers wasn't like any he'd seen in more than thirty years of marriage.

Corrie lowered her hand, crumpling the tissues. "I didn't tell you earlier, but I saw what was in Gloria's cart," she whispered.

Roy couldn't imagine what their daughter might have purchased to cause this kind of reaction. Had Gloria taken to eating weird food? Like what? Or —

"Roy," Corrie said, grabbing his sleeve. "Gloria had a pregnancy test kit in her cart."

"She's pregnant?"

Corrie started weeping again. "I think she must be."

# TWENTY-SIX

Christie patted little Christopher's back in the hopes of coaxing a burp from the squirming infant. Teri sat across from her holding Robbie. Thankfully Jimmy was sound asleep in the nursery. Bobby was busy elsewhere, doing whatever it was Bobby did.

Although Christie continued to come over on Wednesdays to help her sister with the babies, she hadn't seen James yet. Their disagreement had gone on far longer than she'd ever expected. He hadn't budged, nor had she. Christie hated to think their relationship was over, but maybe it was, since obviously neither one was willing to make the first move.

"I haven't seen James around lately," she told her sister cautiously. Christie didn't want to ask and didn't want to put up with an inquisition from Teri, but curiosity had gotten the better of her. Always before,

James had sought her out. Not this time. She had the distinct impression he was away — traveling or perhaps simply gone.

Or . . . another possibility. Maybe he was keeping out of sight, waiting for her to apologize. Perhaps she should; she didn't know anymore. Pride and stubbornness had carried her this far, but they'd worn thin.

"James has been doing a lot of traveling lately," Teri said.

"Oh." Christie remembered one occasion, back in May, when Bobby and James had gone on some kind of business trip. Other than that, Bobby hadn't been gone much; when he did travel, James accompanied him. He was more than Bobby's driver, he was his confidant, best friend and — although no one had ever said as much — his bodyguard.

" 'Oh'?" Teri echoed. "Is that all you have to say?"

Christie considered the question. "All right, if you must know, James and I had a falling-out."

Her sister laughed, startling Christopher. "You think I don't know this? You've been in a bad mood for weeks."

"That is a gross exaggeration." Christie had done her utmost to be bright and cheerful whenever she spent time with Teri, pretending nothing was amiss. To all outward appearances, she was doing just fine, busy with work and school.

Given that she was at the house every Wednesday, James could easily have spoken to her, if he had any interest. However, he hadn't taken advantage of the opportunity, and now she was wondering if he planned to end the relationship. That possibility was a painful one, but she had to admit it was what she'd started to believe.

Christie stared down her sister. "I have made every effort to be as congenial as possible." Apparently Teri had little appreciation of how difficult that had been.

Her sister rolled her eyes. "Yeah, right."

"I have so."

Teri released an exaggerated sigh. "It's taken you long enough, but thank goodness you're coming to your senses."

"What do you mean?" Christie asked, defensive now but still curious.

"You finally got up the nerve to ask about James," Teri said, smiling down at the baby as she spoke.

"Has he asked about me?"

Teri nodded.

"Tell me," Christie urged, and edged slightly forward, eager for the tiniest bit of information.

"This might come as a surprise but James can be stubborn, too," Teri said.

No kidding.

A hundred questions flashed into her head. Did James miss her half as much as she missed him? Did he love her? She desperately wanted to believe he did. But if so, why hadn't he made the slightest attempt to patch up their differences? For that matter, why hadn't she? Why did she always sabotage herself like this?

Instead of approaching James with the goal of reconciliation, she'd plowed ahead with her studies, getting A's on several tests, working long hours and doing everything she could not to think about him. She'd even cleaned her oven, which gave her a sense of accomplishment and a feeling of righteousness.

"What did he ask about me?" Christie inquired, unwilling to pretend disinterest for another minute.

"Oh, nothing much. He wanted to know how you were — that sort of thing."

"Oh." Disappointment fell heavily on her shoulders.

"He's been traveling a lot," Teri reiterated, placing emphasis on the *he*.

"Traveling with Bobby?" Her sister was trying to tell her something important, although Christie had never been much good at reading between the lines.

"Traveling with and without Bobby," Teri clarified.

Christie frowned. "Whatever you want to say, would you just *say* it?"

"I would've told you a whole lot sooner if you'd asked," Teri said, and pressed her lips primly together.

"Okay, fine. I'm asking now."

Teri's face lit up and she grew excited. "James invented an online game that he and Bobby have been working on day and night for weeks."

"Online game?" Christie repeated. "A chess game?"

"Sort of," her sister explained. "It starts out with a chessboard and two players."

That didn't seem to warrant the enthusiasm Teri displayed. "Okay, but what's the big deal? I'm sure there are plenty of those."

"This one's different. When a player makes a particular move on the chessboard, he or she enters a parallel universe, which is set in medieval times. The player is confronted with knights and beasts and can end up in the same world or in different worlds at different times. It's complicated. The game's been compared to World of Warcraft. There are sixty levels and James has been asked to create more."

"Is Bobby involved?"

"Yes, but minimally. This has been great for Bobby *and* James. The idea came from James and he did most of the work. It sold, Christie, and it sold big."

"Big?"

"*Really* big."

"Oh." James hadn't shared any of this success with her. No wonder he hadn't been in touch. He had lots of things on his mind — and they didn't include her.

"Is that all you have to say?" Teri looked dumbfounded by her lack of reaction.

"I'm . . . happy for him."

"You don't act very happy."

She made a genuine attempt to smile. A moment later she noticed that Teri was staring at the entrance to the kitchen; Christie glanced up to see James standing there, looking healthy and vital and just so . . . good.

Her sister immediately stood. "I'm putting Robbie in his crib," she whispered, blatantly an excuse to leave Christie and James alone.

Christie waited until her sister had left. "I . . . I understand congratulations are in order."

"Thank you." He moved slowly into the

family room, hands buried in his pockets. "It's nice to see you."

"You, too," she returned cheerfully, wondering if the intense effort that required was as obvious as it felt.

"I've missed you." So he was the first to admit it. . . .

Gazing down at the baby, she whispered, "I've missed you, too."

"I guess Teri told you about Polgar World?"

"That's the name?" she asked, looking up.

James took the seat across from her that Teri had vacated. "Bobby was kind enough to lend his name. We got word of the sale yesterday. . . ."

"Just yesterday?"

James leaned back. "My agent's been in negotiations with two companies."

"You have an agent?" That made her question how many other secrets he'd kept from her.

He didn't respond. "I've been waiting, Christie."

She looked up, struggling to hide how hurt she was. "Waiting?"

"You said you'd come to me when you were ready to forgive and forget."

"Didn't I say the same thing to you? It doesn't do any good for me to forgive and forget if *you* can't, does it?"

"No, I don't suppose it does."

He didn't say anything else for another lengthy moment. Christie almost wished Christopher would wake up and wail to distract her from this anguish — and to give voice to her own discontent.

"Where do we stand, then?" he finally asked.

"I . . . don't know. I . . . I'd give anything to be able to wipe the slate clean and be the woman you deserve." Her mouth was so dry she could hardly speak. "I can't do that, but I can't live with the threat of you throwing it in my face every time we disagree, either."

"And I can't live with you constantly bringing up the fact that I let you down when I . . . left."

"I . . ."

"Yes?" James urged when she hesitated.

"Why didn't you tell me about Polgar World?" she blurted out.

The question seemed to hang in the air. Before he answered, James exhaled deeply. "I feel that I've failed at almost everything I've tried to do in my life. The idea for the game came to me two years ago. I've been developing it for the past year and a half. I didn't even tell Bobby until six months ago. I could live with failing, but I couldn't live with disappointing you."

"Oh." An inadequate response, but the best she could manage.

"I figured if and when it was a success, I'd come to you."

"You didn't, though."

"I'm here now. I didn't just happen to stop by the house. I saw your car outside and I couldn't stay away."

Christie stared up at him, eyes wide.

"The thing is, I thought I'd be the happiest man alive when this game sold."

"Aren't you?" He had every reason to celebrate.

"Not if I can't share it with you." A tentative smile came and went.

She smiled back.

"I love you, Christie. I'm tired of being alone, tired of my pride."

"Pride doesn't really keep you warm at night, does it?" She was speaking for herself as well as him.

He stood then and moved toward her with his usual long strides, taking the seat beside her. "I want us to get married."

"Okay." Not the most elegant answer, perhaps, but it got the point across.

"It's not like we're kids who don't know what they want."

"I want *you*," she said, her voice cracking.

"Bobby and Teri were married in Vegas. . . ."

"We could make it a family tradition," she suggested.

James grinned. "I couldn't agree with you more. Hey, are you doing anything this weekend?" he asked.

"Yeah, I am," she said, then sent him a huge smile. "I'm getting married."

"Good, because so am I."

He reached for her and she went willingly into his arms, almost forgetting Christopher.

Between kisses James murmured, "No more arguments."

"Well, that's unlikely, but at least we know we can get past them." Her lips lingered on his. "Oh, James, I'm so happy for you."

He gave her a loving kiss. "I'm marrying you and that makes me happier than anything."

"Should we tell Teri and Bobby?" she asked.

"We heard," Bobby said from the kitchen.

James straightened and looked over at them. "I'm going to need a best man."

"He'll be there and so will I," Teri said, standing next to her husband. Bobby had his arm around Teri's shoulders. "I'll be the matron of honor," Teri added.

Christie wouldn't have had it any other way.

# TWENTY-SEVEN

Gloria needed to tell Chad that their night together had consequences. She was pregnant. He had a right to know. It'd been more than a month since he'd moved away. When she'd called his old phone number, she was given a number with a Tacoma area code. So she'd guessed correctly. Chad had taken the job with Tacoma General to work in their E.R.

What surprised Gloria was how much she missed him since he'd left. That wasn't even logical. They weren't a couple; in fact, she'd refused to see him again. The only thing to which she could attribute this sense of loss was the comfort she'd found in knowing he was close at hand. If she'd wished to, she could've sought him out. She hadn't, though. Instead, she'd made every effort to banish him from her thoughts. But nothing had worked.

And now . . . now she was pregnant with

his child. This baby was the result of their irresponsible behavior, yes, but . . . she'd never been happier. While this new life was about to turn her own upside down, she felt the most incredible sensation of joy. She wanted Chad's baby, and she was sure that when she told him, Chad would be happy, too.

Because of the baby, she had no choice but to confront her fears about her relationship with Chad. He'd knocked down all the protective barriers she'd so carefully set up. Because of the baby she couldn't rebuild them. The baby made her vulnerable. She had to admit she did love Chad. She needed him.

Her parents' deaths had forever shaped her future. When she'd found her birth family, Gloria had expected these strangers to fill the empty places in her heart. That was unreasonable; she saw that now.

It was while she was struggling to reinvent her life, to find a new family, that Gloria had met Chad. A few weeks ago, when she suspected she might be carrying his child, she'd nearly panicked. This *couldn't* be happening. But despite her fears, she'd gradually come to accept that this baby was her new family. Hers and Chad's. Once she saw the pregnancy in this light, she began to feel a sense of peace.

After she'd done the home pregnancy test, she made a doctor's appointment. The next step was to tell Chad. She realized the news would come as a shock; it had to her. She assumed his reaction would be similar. She'd give him time to adjust, and then they could make their decisions about the future. Decisions and plans . . .

She knew it would be a future together. Chad loved her. He'd said so. And while she'd been hesitant to admit it, she loved him, too.

The drive into Tacoma took thirty minutes. Gloria used that time to rehearse how she planned to break the news to Chad. She had his new address, which was close to the hospital. The reverse telephone directory had even included his apartment number.

She didn't see his car in the parking area, but she rang his doorbell and waited. As she'd feared, he wasn't home. She should probably have phoned ahead, but she hadn't, primarily because she was afraid she'd blurt out everything then and there. And that would've been unfair. No, a face-to-face meeting was better.

Her other option was to go to the hospital. She'd see him, however briefly, and they could arrange a time to talk. As luck would have it, she arrived just as the shift changed, so she decided to wait. Her news would be shocking enough without adding to the drama by asking to speak to him privately while he was on duty.

She located his car in the staff parking lot and steered into a space two rows over, where she could keep his car in view. Ten minutes later she saw him.

Except he wasn't alone. An attractive blonde woman walked with him. They were deeply involved in conversation, his head leaning close to hers. Chad laughed frequently as they talked; clearly they enjoyed each other's company.

Gloria watched him escort the blonde to her car. Her heart plummeted when he bent to kiss her passionately. Then he stepped back and waited as she pulled out of her parking space and drove off.

When Chad started toward his car, Gloria sat, unmoving, in her own. He opened his door, then looked up and paused. He'd caught sight of her.

With no choice now, she climbed out of her car.

Chad walked over, and judging by the frown that darkened his face, he wasn't happy to see her. "What are you doing here?" he asked bluntly.

The answer should be obvious. "I came to see you."

"Why?"

This was her opportunity to explain the reason for her visit. And yet . . . she couldn't.

"I thought I made myself clear in our last conversation," he said stiffly. He thrust his hands in his pockets. "I'm through with our hot-and-cold relationship, Gloria. I hung around Cedar Cove far longer than I should have, wanting to give us a chance. I honestly hoped we could make a go of it, but you let me know you weren't interested."

She had no defense. That was exactly what she'd done.

"When I left, I told you I was finished and I meant it. You aren't good for me."

"No, I don't suppose I am," she agreed sadly.

"I'm starting over here in Tacoma and you know what? I like my life."

"I see you have a . . . friend."

"I do." He didn't embellish but simply confirmed the fact.

"I can't argue with anything you said. I wish you well, Chad, I really do. I apologize for —"

"No need," he said, cutting her off. "You taught me some valuable lessons."

She merely nodded, unable to speak. With

the pregnancy, her emotions had become volatile; she didn't want to risk embarrassing herself or him, so she offered him a smile. What she wanted was to tell him about the baby, but she couldn't do it. He'd begun a new life, a new relationship. Some might argue that it wasn't ethical to keep the baby a secret, but that was what she intended to do. Wasn't it fairer to him that way? She could see to it that one night of his previous life, one night in an ill-fated relationship, wouldn't return to damage his future hopes and dreams. With the decision made, she turned away, got back in her car and sped out of the parking lot.

The tears came as she headed home to Cedar Cove. By the time she exited the freeway she was a mess. Her eyes were puffy and red and the seat next to her was piled with crumpled tissues.

Hardly aware of what she was doing, Gloria was mildly surprised to find herself in front of the McAfee home on Harbor Street.

She needed her mother. At one point in her own life, Corrie had been in the same situation as Gloria. She'd know what to do, how to guide her.

She wiped her face and walked up the steps to the door. If Roy answered, Gloria had no idea what she'd say.

He did. Taking one look at Gloria, he whirled around and called out, "Corrie!"

There was an urgency in his voice, and Corrie appeared almost immediately. Roy stepped aside and Corrie took Gloria by the hand and led her into the house, straight to the kitchen. Pulling a chair out from the table, she sat Gloria down and then sat beside her, still holding her hand.

Gloria discovered she couldn't say a word. Not a solitary word. Every time she opened her mouth, nothing came out. After several futile attempts, she stopped trying. Instead, she held a clump of tissues to her eyes and wept loudly.

Corrie moved away from the table long enough to make two mugs of decaffeinated tea.

Roy briefly entered the kitchen and promptly left. "I'll be in the other room if you need me," he said on his way out the door. He seemed grateful that nothing was expected of him.

"Here," Corrie said soothingly. "Drink this."

Gloria did. The hot liquid eased the ache in her throat. The mug held in both hands spread warmth through her chilled body.

When her vision cleared, Gloria saw that

Corrie's eyes were brimming with tears.

"I'm pregnant," Gloria whispered.

"I suspected it." Corrie patted her hand gently. "I saw the pregnancy kit when I ran into you at the grocery store."

"I wasn't sure. You . . . you didn't say anything."

"No, I didn't," she said. "I wanted you to trust me enough to come to me. I'm so glad you did." Leaning over, she wrapped Gloria in her loving embrace.

A number of times in the past Corrie had hugged her and Gloria had responded, although it had all seemed rather forced. Not this time. They clung to each other in mutual understanding.

"When I first learned I was pregnant with you, it felt as if the world had come to an end," Corrie said in a low voice as they moved apart.

Gloria made a sound that was half tearful, half amused. "I felt like that, too."

"Roy and I weren't seeing each other anymore and he was dating some cheer-leader."

Gloria lowered her head. "Did you tell him when you found out?"

"No. What good would it've done for him to know? We were so young . . . I was still in my teens. He was out of my life, and I was too stubborn and too hurt to go to him. Right or wrong, I believed this was my problem and I'd deal with it myself."

"You went home?"

"Yes, I dropped out of college for the rest of the school year and returned to Oregon to live with my parents. They were wonderful, helping me decide what was best for you — and for me." Tears slipped down Corrie's face. "I loved you so much. . . . You'll never know how hard it was to give you up for adoption."

Now it was Gloria who comforted her mother; she drew her close and murmured words of love and reassurance. They held each other for several minutes.

When they reached for tissues at the same time, they both laughed, soft, embarrassed laughter.

Gloria sipped her tea and took a moment to compose her thoughts.

"When . . . when did you tell . . . Dad?" These were all questions Gloria had wanted to ask; she'd never found the courage. Facing her own pregnancy without the baby's father gave her an entirely different perspective on her mother's situation. The rejection she'd felt, the feelings of resentment she'd experienced at being denied the joy of growing up with her brother and sister, evaporated. Her mother had loved her and had done the best she could under the circumstances.

"Roy didn't know about you until you were over a year old."

He hadn't known about her until she'd already taken her first steps. "What made you decide to tell him?"

Corrie hung her head. "I went back to school and we met on campus at the library. It was all rather awkward, as you can imagine. I didn't want to see him, and at the same time I did, if that makes any sense?"

"It does."

"We started dating again. I'd never stopped loving him, but I wasn't willing to let him break my heart a second time. When he asked me to marry him, I felt he needed to know about you." She exhaled shakily and reached for her tea with a trembling hand. "He was upset with me, Gloria, terribly, terribly upset. I've never seen Roy like that, before or since. He was so . . . angry."

Gloria peered into the other room and saw that Roy was working on the computer, his back to her.

"We agreed that we wouldn't discuss it again and we both accepted that we had a daughter we'd never know, but would always love." She paused to get control of her emotions before she continued. "Then you came back into our lives and I can't tell you how happy that's made us."

"Thank you, Mom," Gloria whispered. It was the first time she'd ever addressed Corrie as her mother. It had always been Corrie and Roy, but from this point forward they'd be Mom and Dad.

"Okay," Corrie said, slowly releasing her breath. "How can I help you?"

"I . . . I don't know yet. It's still pretty new."

"Does . . . does the father know?"

Gloria shook her head. "No. And I'm not going to tell him." She'd already made that decision and it was one she meant to keep.

Corrie studied her for several seconds before she spoke. "I just told you how upset your father was that I withheld the information from him."

"I know. But in my case I feel this is the right thing to do."

"At the time I did, too," her mother said.

"Mom, please support me in this."

Again, Corrie hesitated and then nodded. "If you're sure that's what you want, then that's what I'll do."

"I want to raise my baby — at least, that's my thought for now. I might have a change of heart later, but for right now that's my plan."

"Your father and I will support whatever decision you make," Corrie said solemnly.

"Thank you." She'd been certain her mother would say that but was grateful to hear it.

"Linnette's pregnant, too, so Roy and I are going to become grandparents twice within a twelve-month period." Corrie's face beamed with joy and anticipation.

"I should tell . . . Dad." Gloria drank the rest of her tea, then went into the other room.

Roy's computer was set up in a small alcove there, and Gloria saw that he was checking stock prices. When he sensed her presence, he turned to look up at her. "Did you and your mother have a good talk?"

Gloria nodded, swallowing hard. Telling her father about the baby was even more difficult than she'd expected. "I'm going to make you a grandfather."

"So I understand," Roy said. He cleared his throat. "Is there anything you need me to do?"

At first, his meaning wasn't clear, and then Gloria understood that he was asking if she wanted him to confront the baby's father. "Everything's fine."

He frowned. "Are you sure about that?"

"Very sure."

He returned to the computer screen. "It's been a lot of years since we've had babies in this family," she heard him say. "High time we did again."

# TWENTY-EIGHT

"I think taking your parents to dinner is a lovely idea," Mary Jo said as she slid into the booth across from Mack at D.D.'s on the Cove. They'd arrived first and been seated.

Linc and Lori had agreed to watch Noelle for the evening. The baby, familiar with her aunt and uncle, had gone to them without a fuss.

"Aren't *you* the one who said we should tell them about the engagement over dinner?" Mack smiled. He picked up the wine list and began to study it while Mary Jo read over the menu.

"When I suggested dinner, I assumed I'd cook."

"This is a celebration," Mack said. He reached for her left hand, and she flexed her fingers, showing off her diamond ring. "I didn't want you to have to do all that extra work."

This man who would soon be her husband was considerate, thoughtful, loving. As it stood now, Mary Jo wasn't sure what they were going to do regarding David. His presence in their lives hung over them like a storm cloud. Either it would eventually blow past or it would rain down upon them in torrents. Mary Jo was braced for whatever happened, whatever the future held. One thing was certain; she wouldn't allow David to take Noelle away from her. Mack wouldn't, either. They'd stand side by side and face any threat from David together.

"Here's Mom now," Mack said. He stood to greet his mother as the hostess escorted her to their booth.

Corrie kissed her son's cheek and smiled down at Mary Jo, who held her left hand under the table, in her lap. "Roy's parking the car. We got caught in traffic."

"Traffic?" Mack repeated with a laugh. "You could walk to the restaurant." The McAfee family home was up the hill, only five or six blocks from the waterfront.

"True," Corrie admitted, "however, we did drive and we had to wait at the stoplight."

Mack shook his head. "You've been away from Seattle too long."

Mack's mother smiled as she pulled a

menu toward her.

Mary Jo had already chosen her meal. The fresh Alaskan halibut, steamed and then topped with shrimp, cheese and a dollop of sour cream sounded delicious. Her brothers had always been meat-and-potatoes people and she rarely cooked fish. Now that she was living on her own, she took every opportunity to sample the bounty of the Pacific Northwest.

Roy joined them, sitting in the booth next to Mack. "Sorry we're late," he said.

They weren't, not really. Well, maybe a minute or two. Mack got his promptness from his family, Mary Jo thought. This was another admirable trait he shared with his parents.

"Roy," Corrie said, glancing up from her menu, "on your way in, did you notice that the special of the day is oysters?"

"Fresh from Hood Canal," Mack added. "That's what I'm having."

Roy didn't bother to pick up his menu. "Sounds good to me, too."

Corrie continued to study the offerings. "Everything looks so wonderful, it's hard to decide."

"While you're thinking," Roy said, "I'd like to say this dinner invitation is a pleasant surprise. It isn't every day one of our

400

children treats us to a meal out."

"There's a very good reason," Mack said, smiling tenderly at Mary Jo.

"I suspected as much." Roy leaned back in his seat and crossed his arms. "You want my help, right?"

"Help?" Mary Jo asked in confusion.

"With Jacob Dennison's letters. I talked to Mack about it the other day and he said the two of you have hit a dead end."

"Well, yes," Mary Jo began, "but that's —"

"Actually, Dad," Mack said, gently cutting off Mary Jo's response. "We could definitely use some help with that if you have the time."

"I like nothing better than solving a good mystery." He sent his wife a smug glance as he spoke.

Corrie sighed and directed her question to Mack. "That's the reason you asked us to dinner?"

"Well, no." He was about to explain when the waiter came for their drink order.

"I believe we're all having fish," Roy said. "So I suggest a white wine."

"We'll take a bottle of your best champagne," Mack told the waiter, ignoring his father's advice. "It isn't every day a man gets engaged."

At his announcement, Corrie nearly flew out of her seat. "I knew it! I just knew it." Grinning, Mary Jo raised her left hand, and Corrie shrieked with delight. "Oh, Mack, I'm thrilled. And the ring's beautiful." She took Mary Jo by the shoulders and hugged her close. "This is absolutely *perfect*. One day we're longing to be grandparents and then suddenly we discover we're going to have three."

"Three?" Mack said, looking bewildered. "Is Linnette having twins?"

Roy, as usual, got straight to the point. "It's Gloria," he said.

"Gloria," Mack repeated, frowning. "I didn't even know she was seeing anyone."

"We didn't, either," Corrie told him. "We only just heard the news ourselves. . . . I probably should've let her tell you herself."

"I'm glad you said something," Mack said, concern in his voice.

"Let's get back to you and Mary Jo," Corrie said eagerly. "Have you set a date?"

"Not yet," Mary Jo said.

"But soon," Mack insisted.

She nodded as they locked eyes.

"I'm thinking August," Mack said next.

"*August?*" Mary Jo and Corrie chimed in simultaneously.

"Mack," Corrie said, pressing her hand

over her heart. "That's next month!"

Mack looked from his mother to Mary Jo. "Is that a problem?"

Mary Jo didn't know how to answer. "I . . . We haven't discussed what kind of wedding we're going to have." Between Mack's schedule and her own, they hadn't had time to go over the details of their engagement. Nor had they given any thought at all to the wedding itself or a honeymoon or anything else.

"Do you want a church wedding?" Roy asked.

"I do," Mary Jo answered.

"I guess," was Mack's reply.

"You guess?" Mary Jo muttered, and rolled her eyes.

"Okay, okay," Mack said, recovering quickly, "I definitely want a church wedding."

"What about a reception?"

Mary Jo and Mack both nodded.

"Would you two want a dinner with the reception?" Corrie asked.

Mary Jo hadn't considered that. It sounded more expensive than they'd be able to afford. "Would a cake, maybe some mixed nuts and those colorful mints be enough?"

"That's fine," Corrie assured her.

"If Mary Jo wants a dinner, that's okay by me," Mack said decisively.

Corrie smiled at her son. "Serving a dinner might mean postponing the wedding by a month or two," she explained. "These things take time and planning."

Mack shook his head. "Then we can do without the meal."

Mary Jo couldn't hold back a laugh. Mack's eagerness to marry her was endearing — and it also sent a chill of excitement through her. Excitement about the days and nights ahead. . . .

The champagne arrived and they ordered their meals. Once their flutes were filled, Roy offered a lovely toast. Mack's normally succinct father was downright lyrical and his kind words brought tears to her eyes.

For most of the meal they discussed wedding plans, to the point that Mary Jo's head started to spin. She'd only drunk half a glass of champagne or she might've thought the alcohol was affecting her.

Watching Mack with his parents, seeing how close he was to Linnette, she recognized once again that this was a man she could trust. Mack had been brought up with the same values she had. Knowing Ben, she realized David had been raised that way, too, but at some point, years before, he'd abandoned those values for his own selfish purposes.

Their dinners were served and Mary Jo's halibut was every bit as good as she'd imagined. Better. Perhaps it was because of the occasion; she couldn't tell. Mack's family had welcomed her, accepting her and Noelle without question, without voicing a single doubt. How fortunate she was to marry into a family like this!

As they ordered coffee, Mack returned to the subject of the letters. "Dad, you mentioned Jacob Dennison when you first got here."

"I did. Your mother and I had a small wager going."

"And I won," Corrie said, looking pleased with herself. "Your father assumed your dinner invitation had to do with those letters."

"And your mother assumed it was because you two had something important to tell us."

"Which they did," Corrie stated gleefully.

"I would like to remind you," Roy said with a comical scowl, "that you made the same assumption once before and you were totally off base."

"Yes." Corrie nodded. "I was then, but I'm not now."

Mack held up his hand. "The thing is,

405

Mary Jo and I ran into a problem in our research. So we kind of dropped it for a while."

"It's been fascinating, learning about World War II," she told them. "Mack and I rented the movie *The Longest Day* and we found out even more about the Normandy invasion."

"Jacob was part of the 101st Airborne unit that dropped in behind enemy lines," Mack reminded them.

"One group missed their target and landed right inside Sainte-Mère-Eglise, only to be mowed down by the Germans," Mary Jo said. "It was horrible." She'd hardly been able to watch the scene, especially since the man who'd written those beautiful letters might well have been one of the young soldiers who'd lost his life there.

"I believe the group you mean was the 82nd Airborne," Mack inserted.

"I saw that movie, too," Roy said. "Years ago." He rubbed the side of his face. "Didn't the men who parachuted in have a clicking device?"

"Yes," Mack confirmed, "the clickers were handed out so the men could find one another. They were to click once and those replying were to click twice."

"They dropped dummies in parachutes,

too," Roy said. "They exploded on impact and confused the enemy."

"Getting back to the letters . . . What stumps us is the fact that they stop after that one in early June 1944," Mary Jo said. For her own satisfaction if nothing else, she wanted to learn his fate, even if he'd been killed. All they knew was that he hadn't been listed among those buried in France or among the known dead.

"Are you sure Jacob's his actual first name?"

"That's how he signs all his letters," Mack said. "He —"

"Mack," Mary Jo broke in softly.

He glanced at her.

"If you wrote me, you'd sign your letters 'Mack,' right?"

"Right."

"But your given name is Jerome."

Mack's eyes widened. "I hadn't thought of that. There were other Dennisons included on the website."

"Let's go back and check," Mary Jo said excitedly.

"There's another possibility," Roy murmured.

"What?" Mary Jo wished now that they'd taken this to Roy earlier. Talking to him had given them a new approach. If they found

Jacob, if he was still alive or even if he wasn't but had family, they might also be able to learn Joan's fate.

"What's your idea?" Mack asked his father.

"You said he isn't listed among those who were killed?"

"That we know of," Mack said.

Mary Jo felt it was important to add, "We couldn't find a list of the wounded, though — so he might've been injured and shipped home."

"But we discounted that," Mack said. "If he was injured, he still would've had a way of getting in touch."

"Yes." Mary Jo nodded. "If he was injured, he could've written eventually or had someone write for him." Mary Jo was convinced that if Jacob had been capable of it, he would've found a way to tell Joan he'd survived.

"He might have been captured," Roy suggested.

"Captured," Mack echoed. "You mean taken as a prisoner of war? We didn't even consider that."

Mary Jo stared at Roy, stunned. How could they have overlooked such an obvious possibility?

"Well, I guess we'll be doing some more

research. You've certainly given us something to think about," Mack said. "Thanks, Dad."

"No, thank *you*," Corrie told him. "It'll be a long time before I let your father live down the fact that I was right." She gleefully rubbed her palms together. "We're going to love having you and Noelle as part of our family, Mary Jo."

And Mary Jo was going to love being a McAfee, too.

# TWENTY-NINE

Bellamy Towers. Linc stared up at the four-story building in Bremerton, feeling his mouth go dry. He'd got the address of his father-in-law's office out of the telephone directory but he'd only had the street name and number. He was shocked to discover that Bellamy obviously owned the whole complex. He knew from visiting the family home that Lori came from money; what astonished him was how much.

He needed to speak to his father-in-law. Pacing back and forth in the parking lot, Linc realized that in his present frame of mind he'd make a mess of this. He was too angry to think logically or speak calmly. Linc had a temper, which he tended to fire off quickly; with enough provocation he'd say something he couldn't take back. This conversation was too important to be ruled by emotion. He needed a clear head and cool reason.

Just as he was finally ready to enter the building, out came Leonard Bellamy. The other man frowned when he saw Linc. "What are you doing here?" Bellamy demanded.

Linc bit back a sarcastic reply. He felt like telling Lori's father that he was in the area and thought they could go for a beer together. Instead, he spoke in as polite a tone as he could manage. "I'd like to talk to you for a couple of minutes."

"I'm busy." Bellamy attempted to step around him.

Linc blocked his move. "Unfortunately, I have a lot of time on my hands and my guess is you know why." The man had set out to ruin his business and had just about succeeded. Linc couldn't hang on much longer. He'd been able to find out that Bellamy had told certain influential people in Cedar Cove and adjoining communities that Linc was a gold digger who'd married his daughter for her money. Bellamy had also tried to thwart him by delaying his license application. When that didn't shut Linc down, he'd apparently spread false rumors. Not that Linc could prove it, but there'd been hints. Mack McAfee had made a point of telling him that he'd heard Bellamy was "out to get" him.

Linc had spoken to his attorney, who said there was basically nothing to be done. He could file a suit for slander or for restraint of trade but Linc would rather end this than take his father-in-law to court — especially with a weak, hearsay case.

Long before he'd set up his shop he'd done extensive research on the area. Only because he felt he could make a go of it had he decided to branch out into Cedar Cove; otherwise, he would've continued his commute into Seattle. Based on his findings, he'd obtained a loan from a local bank to cover his start-up costs and he'd drawn on his savings, sinking most of the money into remodeling the garage.

As part of his research, Linc had gone to visit various local insurance claim adjusters. These were the people who generally sent work his way. He'd talked to a number of them before he'd made his decision to move. Every one of them had assured him there was a need for his business.

When the promised work didn't come, Linc went to see them all again. On his second series of visits Linc found his reception much cooler. The adjusters had no work to send him and weren't interested in receiving his bids. When he dug deeper, Linc learned that Bellamy was good friends with someone high up in the state insurance commissioner's office. Linc couldn't *prove* that Bellamy had used their friendship to influence the adjusters but it all added up.

He'd purchased a garage that had sat in disrepair for several years, cleaned it up and remodeled it. Then he'd hired two employees. Now these employees were twiddling their thumbs while Linc paid their wages from his dwindling reserves. Another month like the last one, and he'd have no choice but to close his doors.

"I said I don't have time, nor do I have the desire to speak with you," Bellamy said in a tone few would question. "Now kindly step aside."

"You're spreading lies about me in the community." Bellamy's attitude made Linc reconsider the advisability of taking him to court. But the idea went in and out of his mind in seconds. Much as he disliked Bellamy, the man was Lori's father. Linc refused to jeopardize that relationship — or at least jeopardize it any more than Bellamy already had himself.

"We can make this all go away," Bellamy said, his mood suddenly more affable. "With a snap of my fingers, I can set things straight for you."

Linc hesitated. The man had essentially confirmed everything he'd suspected. "What do you mean?"

"Leave my daughter."

"Leave Lori?" Linc couldn't believe what he was hearing.

"I'll buy you out, make all the trouble you went to in getting that garage set up worth your while. All I ask is that you walk away from my daughter and don't look back."

How friendly he sounded. How cordial. Linc's financial difficulties would disappear if he abandoned his wife.

Linc stared at him, still unable to believe that even Bellamy would suggest such a thing.

"I hear you're late with last month's payment to the bank."

The only way Bellamy would know that was if someone from the bank had fed him the information.

"You made a mistake when you married my daughter." His tone grew threatening again. "You saw her as an easy target."

"I saw her as the most incredible woman I've ever known," Linc countered. He meant it — meant it with everything in him.

Bellamy snickered. "And that's why you married her . . . what, two weeks after you met?"

"Something like that." After meeting Lori's mother, Linc felt he should have insisted to Lori that they wait. In their haste to get married, Linc had planted the seeds of suspicion within her family. In retrospect he would've preferred to meet her parents first and give them the opportunity to know him. Bellamy might still have objected, but at least Linc would've made the effort. At least he would've created the beginnings of a relationship.

"There's still time to fix this," Bellamy said.

"You want me to leave Lori?" He shook his head as he said the words.

"Divorce her."

The words hit him with such force, Linc stumbled back two steps. "I realize I was wrong. I should've come and talked to you first before marrying Lori. I should have —"

Red-faced, Bellamy leaned closer and when he spoke it was through gritted teeth. "Where you were wrong, young man, was in thinking you could get to me through my daughter."

"Get to *you?*" The man seemed to assume the entire world revolved around him and his bank account. "I didn't even know who you were." Bellamy started to scoff but Linc talked right over him. "I married Lori because I'm in love with her. As for leaving her, I'd rather die first."

Bellamy laughed in his face. "We both know my daughter's incapable of making a decent decision. She's an empty-headed —"

Linc had heard enough. He grabbed Bellamy by his fancy suit lapels and jerked him forward. "Don't *ever* speak about my wife like that again," he snapped. "Lori has brains and integrity, and if you don't see that in her, I pity you." He abruptly released the other man.

Bellamy straightened his sleeves and glared at Linc. "I could have you arrested for assault."

"Go ahead." If the man was determined to ruin him, he might as well do a thorough job.

"You stay married to my daughter and I'm cutting her out of my will. I swear to you that you won't get a penny."

"I doubt you'll believe me, but I have no interest in your money."

"You're right. I don't believe you."

"Then that's your problem." Linc figured he might as well leave now, while his dignity was relatively intact.

When he returned to the garage, he saw that both employees were lounging around, idly entertaining themselves. One was working on a sudoku puzzle and the other was tossing cards into an empty coffee tin. Linc sent them both home.

An hour later, after he'd sorted through the bills that were stacked on his desk, he hung his head in abject frustration. He wouldn't be able to make this month's payment to the bank, either.

Unless something changed fast, Linc was about to go belly-up. He knew he had the option of filing for bankruptcy, but he refused to consider it. No matter what happened, he wouldn't take the easy way out, wouldn't walk away from his debts. He was the one who'd taken the financial gamble; he'd pay the price.

With his elbows propped on his desk, he shoved the hair away from his face. It was time to go home to Lori. At five-thirty, he posted the closed sign on the door.

Shoring up his resolve, Linc sat in his truck for several minutes before he headed into the ground-floor apartment. As much as possible he tried not to inflict his worries on Lori.

When he walked in, the aroma of simmering barbecue sauce tickled his nostrils.

"Lori?"

"Hi, honey, I'm out back."

Linc followed her voice and found her dressed in shorts and a T-shirt, standing over their barbecue grill on the small patio. He kissed her the way he always did, and the instant his mouth settled over hers, Linc's worries fled. He held her tight against him, enjoying the feel of her body so close to his. Give up Lori? Walk away from the most precious gift he'd ever received? Bellamy was out of his mind, and if Linc had the chance, he'd tell him that.

# THIRTY

Tanni knew from the nervous, excited way her mother was acting that Larry Knight must be arriving any minute. They had a Friday-afternoon date, and Shirley had spent the past hour getting ready.

Watching the changes in her mother since she'd met Larry had been interesting. Tanni used to wonder how she'd feel if her mother became involved with another man. It seemed weird to think of Shirley falling in love with someone other than Tanni's dad. What surprised her was that she was all right with it. That might not have been the case if it was anyone other than Larry. He was special, and Tanni understood why her mother had fallen for him. Besides being a fabulous artist, Larry was thoughtful, generous and just plain nice. Not only was he responsible for helping Shaw get into art school, but he'd brought the spark back to her mother's eyes.

In the past few weeks, her mother and Larry had been on the phone practically every day, and these weren't short conversations. One night they talked for three hours straight. Tanni knew because she kept track of the time. She'd taken delight in teasing her mother. Even more fun was seeing the flush that crept over her cheekbones. Shirley had it bad. This Tanni recognized because she'd once had those same intense feelings for Shaw. Not anymore, though.

"Do I look okay?" Shirley asked. She wore pale linen pants and a white top with a teal-and-lime-green scarf. She'd thrown a linen jacket over the whole ensemble.

"You look great." Tanni wasn't just saying that. Her mother had been paying far more attention to her hair and makeup since she'd started dating Larry. Even when all they did was talk on the phone, her mother's hair was brushed, her makeup applied and she was neatly dressed. She'd stopped wearing old jeans and her father's too-large sweatshirts around the house. It was as if she thought Larry might drop in unannounced at any second. Tanni found that amusing but remembered she'd been the same way when she first met Shaw, too.

Shaw . . . She didn't want to think about him. It was over. She hadn't heard from him in more than two weeks, but the choice had been hers. She'd decided to cut off the relationship. That had been painful, but as Kristen had assured her, it was the right thing to do. Tanni had taken control. Rather than let him ignore her, she'd quit playing the game.

Shirley tugged at her jacket sleeves. "Miranda insisted I wear this."

"It's nice, Mom."

"Miranda has such a good eye for color."

"So do you," Tanni said, surprised her mother lacked confidence in her own sense of style. Shirley worked with fabric and color all the time, so no one, in Tanni's opinion, had a better eye than she did.

Shirley thanked her with a brief smile, then glanced at her watch.

"When's Larry due?" Tanni asked.

"Around one." She set her purse by the front door.

"Where's he taking you for lunch?"

"I . . . I didn't ask." She grew flustered. "How silly of me."

Tanni couldn't resist rolling her eyes. "Was I this dopey after I met Shaw?" she asked.

"Worse," her mother said wryly.

"That's hard to believe."

They exchanged a smile. She felt relieved to be on good terms with her mother again.

The change had come about gradually over the past few months, ever since Shaw had moved to San Francisco. They used to be at odds with each other all the time, and now they weren't. "Do you have plans this afternoon?" Shirley asked.

Tanni shrugged. "Jeremy might come over. Kristen, too." If anyone had told Tanni she'd become friends with the girl she despised most, she would've fallen down laughing.

As little as a month ago, Tanni could barely stand to be in the same room with her. These days they hung around, went places together and talked nearly every day.

Kristen had been such a help with the whole Shaw situation. She'd broken off a number of relationships herself and said it was best just to be done with it. If Shaw was sending Tanni all the signals that he wanted their relationship to end — and he was — then Kristen said she should make it easy on him. So Tanni had.

It hadn't been easy on her, though. When she called Shaw to tell him, he seemed shocked. Kristen said that was to be expected, too. Guys might want to end the relationship, but then they had a change of heart as soon as the girl took the initiative. At first, Tanni had thought her friend was exaggerating, but everything Kristen had said would happen did.

Almost immediately after she broke up with him, Shaw started texting her five or six times a day. After weeks of driving Tanni insane by disregarding her messages, he suddenly wanted to be in contact. She gained a perverse satisfaction from ignoring him. But that only encouraged him to text more often. He'd even tried to phone. She'd had to force herself not to answer, but managed to hold firm. Kristen praised her for being in control. It felt good, she felt good, and she was determined never to let anyone treat her emotions so lightly again.

As a bonus Kristen had introduced Tanni to her neighbor Jeremy Reynolds and they'd met several times. He was very different from Shaw. Knowing that Jeremy was interested in her made the fact that Shaw was out of her life a lot more tolerable.

The doorbell rang and her mother rushed into the living room. Tanni followed her, wanting to greet Larry and hear about their plans so she'd know when her mother would be home. *That* was a role reversal if ever there was one.

Halfway into the room, Tanni froze. Larry Knight was at the door, but he wasn't alone. Shaw was with him.

"Hi, Tanni," Shaw said as he sauntered

into the house.

"What are you doing here?" She made it clear that she didn't appreciate his unexpected arrival. If she'd known Shaw was coming, she could have mentally prepared herself for the confrontation. She would've liked to discuss this with Kristen first and gotten her advice.

"Tanni." Her mother said her name softly, reminding her of her manners.

"Hello, Shaw," she said with less of an edge.

Larry had his arm around her mother's waist. "Tanni, I brought Shaw along as a surprise." He gave Shaw a skeptical look. "I was led to believe you'd welcome a visit."

"You are so thoughtful," Shirley said, smiling at him.

Larry's expression indicated he was no longer so sure of that. "Would you rather I dropped Shaw off at his family's place?" He spoke directly to Tanni.

"Come on, Tanni," Shaw pleaded. "I just want to talk."

Larry regarded each one in turn. "Is that what *you* want, Tanni?" he asked.

He didn't seem any too pleased with Shaw, which was all right with her.

"Fine. I'll talk to him," she said.

Still, Larry hesitated. "I'd like to take your

mother to lunch here in Cedar Cove, and then we thought we'd stop off at the art gallery," he explained. "We shouldn't be gone more than a couple of hours. Would that suit you?" Again, he looked at Tanni.

She shrugged, letting that be her response. She wanted Shaw to realize that her feelings about him were lukewarm at best.

Larry and her mother left and then Tanni was alone with Shaw. At one time she would have welcomed the privacy. That wasn't true anymore.

"How's it going?" he asked. He made himself at home on the sofa, crossing his legs and stretching his arm across the back.

Tanni sat on the other side of the living room, as far from him as possible. He looked different, but then so did she. With subtle suggestions from Kristen, Tanni had changed her wardrobe. She'd stopped wearing all black and added color here and there. Today she had on regular jeans and a pink T-shirt. She'd changed her hairstyle, too; now she wore it shorter and parted on the side. Again, she had Kristen to thank for that. Kristen had good instincts about style and together they'd found a new, more flattering look for Tanni.

Her mother liked her new hairstyle, too, although she seemed reluctant to say much.

That was understandable.

For a long time after her father died, Tanni didn't want her mother to comment on anything to do with what she wore or how she looked. That wasn't the case now; their relationship was a lot more comfortable these days, a lot closer. Tanni wasn't sure what, exactly, was different but she suspected it had more to do with her than with her mother.

"It's going," she said flippantly, answering his question.

Shaw shifted his position and leaned forward. "You look great."

"You, too," she said curtly. When they'd first started going out, Shaw used to wear dark clothes, the same as her. He had on blue jeans and an artsy T-shirt now.

"School's going really well," he said, and seemed to want her to comment.

She didn't.

"Come on, Tanni, if you're mad, fine, but get over it."

"I'm not angry." Okay, so that wasn't entirely true. But Kristen had helped her cope with those negative feelings. They'd talked at length about how to end a relationship properly, and Tanni had absorbed every word.

"If you're not mad, then why aren't you

talking to me?"

"I really don't have anything to say."

"Sure you do," he said. "I know I do. I've missed you."

That wasn't the impression he'd given her after he got to San Francisco. He'd made it seem as if he was far too busy to bother with her. She could remind him of the grief and frustration he'd caused her, but then decided that was exactly what she *shouldn't* do.

"How long will you be in town?" she asked instead.

"I'm here over the weekend."

"That'll give you time to see your friends," she said, folding her arms.

"The only person I want to see is you."

Yeah, right.

"And Will Jefferson," Shaw added. "I want to thank him. I owe him big-time."

"What about my mother?" she asked, unable to disguise her irritation. Shirley had been just as instrumental in getting Shaw into art school as Will Jefferson and Larry Knight. Her mother was the one who'd put everything in motion.

"Of course." Shaw was quick to make amends. "I'd never have made it into art school if it hadn't been for your mom."

"How are things with your family?" she

asked after an awkward pause. From the very beginning, Shaw's father had been against his becoming an artist. He'd wanted Shaw to attend law school. It'd taken real courage for Shaw to stand up to his father and live his own life.

"Much better," Shaw said. He seemed pleased to be able to say it. "Mom's proud of the fact that I'm attending on a full scholarship, and Dad's actually coming around. I've emailed them some of my work and I keep in touch. I'll be with the family tonight for this big dinner Mom's cooking."

Tanni thought that was a good idea.

"Would you like to drop by Will Jefferson's place with me?" he asked.

Apparently Shaw could tell that she wouldn't be having any cozy chats with him.

"I don't have any other plans for a while," Tanni said, keeping her voice casual. "I can drive."

His eyes widened. "When did you get your license?"

She'd texted him the day she'd passed her driver's test. Obviously he hadn't taken the trouble to read it. Rather than berate him, or remind him that he should know, she shrugged. "A while back."

"Hey, it's great that you've got wheels," he said enthusiastically.

Again, she pretended it was no big deal, but in actuality her whole life had undergone a transformation. Now that she had her license, she felt a new sense of freedom and independence. She felt like an *adult.*

They left the house, and during the short drive to the gallery, Shaw dominated the conversation, acting as if hardly anything had changed between them. He was animated, telling her tale after tale of friends he'd made in art school. He didn't seem to notice that she said almost nothing.

He avoided mentioning any of the girls he'd met, although Tanni knew he hung around with several. One name in particular stood out — Mallory, Marcie . . . something like that. Tanni briefly considered bringing up Jeremy, but decided against it.

Tanni parked down the street from the gallery. The place looked attractive; Will Jefferson had done some work recently, refreshing the outside with a coat of white paint and arranging large baskets of red geraniums in front. He'd redesigned the inside earlier, with new display cases and glass enclosures. Will had put a lot of money into the renovation, and it showed.

When they walked into the gallery, Shaw's eyes went immediately to the wall where her mother's dragon quilt was displayed.

There was no denying that "Death" was a masterful piece of work.

She hadn't fully appreciated the skill involved in the creation of fabric art, and this piece in particular, until Will Jefferson had hung it on his wall. To Tanni, that dragon breathed life — and death — and spoke of grief, love, passion. It captivated the attention of all who saw it. She knew there'd been numerous offers to buy it but the work wasn't for sale.

Will stepped out from his office, and when he saw them, he smiled. "Shaw," he said, holding out his hand as he advanced toward them. "Good to see you."

"Hi, Mr. Jefferson."

They shook hands and then Will turned to Tanni. "Great to see you, too." He looked around as though he expected her mother to be with them.

Tanni smiled and out of the corner of her eye she caught a movement. Someone else was in the gallery.

"Hello, Tanni," Miranda Sullivan greeted her, emerging from the back room a moment later. "What's your mother up to this afternoon?"

"She's with Larry."

Will Jefferson stiffened noticeably. "Larry Knight's in town?" he asked, and he didn't sound pleased to hear it.

"I flew in with him," Shaw told them. "It was a chance to reconnect with friends," he said pointedly, glancing in Tanni's direction. "I wanted to see you, too, so you'd know your faith in me was justified. If you speak to Larry, he'll tell you I've done well in each of my classes so far."

Will hardly seemed to hear him. "Has your mother been seeing a lot of Larry?" he asked Tanni.

"Well . . ." She wasn't sure how to respond and looked to Miranda for help. As her mother's friend, Miranda had encouraged the relationship with Larry — not that her mother needed much encouragement.

"Larry and Shirley are grateful for your introduction, Will," Miranda said smoothly, coming toward them. "They have a great deal in common, you know."

Will frowned. "Really." The comment was more sarcasm than affirmation.

"I believe they might be stopping in later," Miranda added.

Tanni recalled that Larry had said something about that.

"Here?"

"Yes," Miranda said. "Larry wants to see the red dragon piece."

Tanni hadn't heard that, but it made

sense. Larry had only seen photographs of the massive fabric hanging, which had been featured in several newspaper and magazine articles. "That's not a problem, is it?" she asked Will.

"Not for me, it isn't," Will muttered. He turned to Miranda as though he thought she could supply more information.

Shaw had apparently become aware of the tension in the room. Moving closer to Will, he said, "I want to let you know again how much I appreciate what you've done for me."

Will nodded absently.

"Will," Miranda said. "Shaw just thanked you."

He broke out of his stupor. "Right. My pleasure," he said without emotion. "Stop in anytime."

"I will," Shaw returned, looking puzzled.

It seemed they were being dismissed; Will Jefferson all but hustled them out the door. Tanni met Miranda's eye and the other woman shrugged as if to say she didn't understand it, either.

One thing *was* clear. Will Jefferson didn't like the fact that Tanni's mother was seeing Larry Knight.

Tanni smiled inwardly as she headed toward the parked car, with Shaw behind her. If Mr. Jefferson needed help getting over her mother, maybe Tanni would suggest he talk to Kristen.

"Well . . . nice seeing you again," she told Shaw when they reached the car.

"We . . . we aren't going back to the house?"

"No, sorry. I'm meeting up with a friend."

"Oh." The word was weighted with disappointment.

"Jeremy and I have plans."

"Jeremy?" Shock reverberated in his voice as he repeated the other boy's name.

Tanni grinned. "Oh, honestly, Shaw, you didn't think you were the only guy in my life, did you?"

## THIRTY-ONE

"Can you talk?" Mack asked urgently.

Placing one hand over the receiver, Mary Jo glanced toward her boss's office. Allan was with a client, and the meeting would probably go on for a while.

"I guess," she said. "For a few minutes." She rarely took personal calls at work. The fact that Mack had phoned her meant it was important. "Is anything wrong?"

"No, not at all." He paused. "I just finished talking to my dad and he wants to see us right after work."

Mary Jo waited. "Did he find out anything?" she prodded. "About Jacob?"

"He must have."

Mary Jo was too excited to sit still. "I *knew* we made the right decision when we asked him for help." They'd tried to track down Jacob Dennison on their own. Roy, however, was the one with experience. People hired him to do this; he was the expert and they were amateurs.

"I'll pick you up at the house after work, okay?"

"I'll have to get Noelle before we go over to your father's."

"Can I get her? That'll save time."

"Okay, I'll phone Kelly and let her know."

"Thanks."

The rest of the afternoon dragged by. Mary Jo didn't think she'd ever been more anxious for a workday to end. At precisely five, she leaped out of her seat like a jack-in-the-box and reached for her purse.

"See you in the morning, Mr. Harris," she called out.

Her boss came to the doorway between their two offices. "You seem to be in a hurry this evening."

"I am," she said. "I think Mack's father might have some information about that World War II soldier I mentioned a while back. Roy offered to help us."

"Interesting. Update me when you can."

"Will do," she promised. True, it might be another dead end, but she had a feeling there was more.

Mack was in his truck, waiting for her, as she pulled into the driveway at home.

"Where's Noelle?" she asked immediately.

"Mom has her. She claims she needs

grandma practice. You don't mind, do you?"

"Not at all." Actually, she was touched that Corrie wanted to spend time with Noelle.

They rode in silence for a couple of blocks. "Aren't you excited?" she asked.

Mack grinned. "Yes, what about you?"

"Oh, Mack, I can hardly stand it. Did your father tell you *anything*?"

"No, he just said he'd uncovered some information he thought we'd want to hear."

"How did he sound?"

"Sound?"

"Was he happy? Sad? Did his tone of voice give anything away?"

"Not really. But that's my dad. Always keeps his cards close to his chest." Mack parked in front of the office. Mary Jo jumped out, not waiting for him to open her door or give her his hand. He met her on the sidewalk. "You ready?"

"O-o-oh, yes. You?"

"Ready," he said, and held open the door.

Mary Jo entered the investigator's office and glanced curiously around. She'd never been inside before. The reception area had a sofa and a chair, with magazines neatly fanned out on the adjoining end tables. The door leading to Roy's private office was ajar and he waved them in.

"What've you got, Dad?" Mack slipped into a visitor's chair and Mary Jo took the one next to him.

Roy tipped back his own chair. "The other night Mary Jo pointed out that Jacob might not be Dennison's given name."

"So he had another name?" Mary Jo asked breathlessly, leaning forward in her eagerness.

"No. His name's Jacob. That was an excellent theory but it didn't go anywhere."

"Dad!" Mack warned. "Just tell us what you found."

Roy grinned sheepishly. "I was right. He was taken captive by the Germans."

"He was a POW?"

Roy nodded. "Apparently Jacob was captured in the first few days after the invasion and sent by train into the heart of Germany."

Mack was leaning forward now, too. "Did he survive the war?"

Roy nodded again. "Amazingly, he did."

Mack and Mary Jo exchanged glances. Next came the question that burned inside them both.

"Is it possible that . . . he's still alive?" she whispered.

The wide grin that broke out across Roy's face was answer enough. "He is — alive and kicking."

"Wow," Mack said. He reached for Mary Jo's hand and squeezed it hard.

"Where's he living? Is there any chance we can meet him? I'd love to ask him about Joan. Can we talk to him?" Mary Jo stopped to take a breath.

She wouldn't have thought Roy's smile could grow any wider, but it did. "That's the best part. I don't know how to describe this. Call it luck. Call it coincidence. Call it whatever you like, but I think it's pretty darn close to divine intervention."

Mack's eyebrows gathered. "What do you mean?"

"Jacob Dennison is living here. In Cedar Cove."

Mary Jo gasped.

"Get out of here!" Mack said exultantly.

Mary Jo couldn't believe their luck. "He must be . . . how old now?" she asked.

"Mid-eighties for sure, maybe older," Mack said.

"Where is he?"

"Reveille," Roy told them.

"The veterans' home on the hill?" All this time Jacob Dennison had been practically under their noses!

"He'd like to meet you."

Mary Jo nearly fell out of her chair. "You

mean you've already talked to him?"

"No," Roy said. "I called their office to be sure I had the right Jacob Dennison. The manager confirmed it and she gave me some useful information. From what she said, he's only been at Reveille House since March. Before that he lived in Seattle and his three children are still there." Roy shook his head. "I learned that he's a widower but I don't have any details."

"Oh, no . . ." Mary Jo was saddened by that. "I'm so sorry." It felt as if she'd just learned that a close friend had died.

"He doesn't know about the letters?" Mack asked.

"No, no," Roy assured them. "I told the manager, a Ms. Roberts, but she promised not to say a word about that to him. Besides, you two found those letters and the diary. You should be the ones to tell him."

"Do you think we should bring them with us?"

"I do," Mack said, answering for his father. "It's what we've wanted to do from the moment we read them."

Mary Jo agreed.

"We'll get them and head up to Reveille now," Mack told his father.

"Roy," Mary Jo said, coming to her feet. "Thank you, thank you very, very much."

She walked around the big desk and hugged her soon-to-be father-in-law. He'd managed what she'd thought was impossible — and with apparent ease.

They stopped at the duplex first, then drove toward Reveille House, a few miles away. The winding road to the facility went up a steep hill that overlooked the cove. The view of Bremerton and the naval shipyard against the backdrop of the Olympic Mountains was breathtaking, but for once Mary Jo barely noticed.

The receptionist met them, and Mack explained that they were there to see Jacob Dennison. They were asked to wait and paced anxiously in the reception room until the woman reappeared ten long minutes later. "Mr. Dennison will be with you shortly," she said. She led them down the hall to a cozy lounge, fortunately not in use at the moment.

There were bookshelves and a fireplace that looked inviting. A piano stood in one corner, while a number of upholstered chairs and a sofa in matching fabric occupied the middle of the room.

They sat down, Mary Jo perched on the edge of her chair, with the cigar box resting in her lap. It held the diary as well as the letters.

About five minutes later, a young male attendant wheeled in a white-haired man. "Here we go, Mr. Dennison," he said cheerfully as he settled the wheelchair between Mack and Mary Jo, then left the room. The elderly man regarded them both with faded blue eyes.

He looked from Mack to Mary Jo and smiled. "Do I know you?" he asked shakily.

"No," Mack answered. "But we know you."

"How's that, young man?"

"We've read your letters," he explained.

"Your letters to Joan Manry," Mary Jo added. "From the war years."

Jacob frowned. "Where did you find those?"

Mack moved closer to the end of the sofa. "We're getting ahead of ourselves," he said. "I'm Mack McAfee and this is my fiancée, Mary Jo Wyse. We're thrilled to meet you, by the way."

"Thank you," Jacob said. "It isn't often I have a beautiful young woman come to visit." He clasped her hand between both of his. "That is, unless it's one of my granddaughters." He chuckled softly. "Now tell me about those letters. I have to admit you've piqued my curiosity. You say they were written during the war years? By me?"

Mary Jo nodded. "Mack and I live in a duplex on Evergreen Place in Cedar Cove," she said.

"Evergreen Place," he repeated.

"I believe that's the house where Joan once lived with her sister."

"You wrote Joan letters at that address," Mack told him. "Only it isn't a single house anymore, but a duplex."

"Evergreen Place," Jacob said again, and it seemed that the address had disappeared from his memory.

Mary Jo didn't know where to start, there was so much to tell. "I noticed a loose board in the closet one day. When I went to investigate, I discovered a cigar box full of letters hidden under the floorboards."

"My letters?" Jacob hardly seemed able to take it in. "From the war?"

"Yes." With infinite pleasure Mary Jo gave Jacob the box. She placed it on his lap and, as she started to move away, the old man reached for her hand and kissed it. Tears spilled from his eyes; embarrassed, he wiped them away, but his emotion brought tears to her eyes, too.

"I always wondered where these ended up. Joan never said. She wasn't close to her sister, and the two of them shared that house. Elaine was jealous of her, I think. At any rate they were estranged until near the end of Elaine's life, and then Joan went to her and they made their peace."

Mary Jo was interested to hear this and relieved that the two sisters had finally settled their differences.

"Joan's diary was hidden in there, too," Mack told him.

"What happened to Joan?" Mary Jo asked, anxious now for more of the details. "We know she died, but . . ."

Jacob opened the box and reverently pulled out the diary. "After the liberation of Europe, Joan and I were married." Jacob looked up from the treasure in his hands and shook his head sadly. "She died far too young. She was seventy-one. We had three children, a boy and two girls. Mark, Margaret and Marianne. . . ." He paused as the reminiscence, the grief, overcame him. He withdrew a handkerchief from his shirt pocket and dabbed at his eyes again.

"Would you tell us about your experiences on D-day?" Mack asked.

"There's not much to tell. I was one of the fortunate ones. I was herded, along with other Americans, onto a train. It took us to a POW camp in central Germany, where I spent the rest of the war."

"That couldn't have been an easy time."

Jacob sighed. "War is never easy, young man."

"When were you released?" Mary Jo asked. His imprisonment was clearly a painful memory he'd rather not discuss.

"May 1945. American paratroopers dropped onto the field outside the prison camp," he said with a far-off look. "Those of us who'd survived were afraid the German soldiers would kill us rather than expose the conditions under which we'd been held."

"They didn't, thank God," Mary Jo whispered.

"No. Instead, they threw down their weapons and ran. Many of them were just boys, fighting a war they didn't want to fight. Like me, all they wanted was to go home to their families."

His attitude was one of forgiveness and generosity, which impressed Mary Jo and moved her deeply. "Did Joan know you'd been taken prisoner?"

Jacob nodded. "Not for several weeks, though. She assumed I was dead. She'd moved back to the family home in Spokane to help with her younger brothers and sisters. Apparently her mother had taken ill and she was needed there."

"How long before you saw her again?"

Jacob sat up a bit straighter. "Far longer than I wanted. When I was rescued I weighed less than ninety pounds. The army sent me home in a hospital ship." He chuckled hoarsely. "I would've gotten well much faster if they'd just flown me back to my family. My mother was the best cook in the world."

Mack exchanged a smile with Mary Jo.

"At nights, back in the camp, I used to go to sleep thinking about my mother's apple pie. The first meal she cooked for me was fried chicken. I ate almost an entire bowl of mashed potatoes by myself." Again, tears filled his eyes. "That was one of the happiest days of my life."

Mary Jo could well imagine. "Do you know why Joan hid the letters?" She asked the question that had haunted her all these weeks. Now she might finally learn the answer.

"Not really, other than the fact that Joan and her sister never got along."

Mary Jo was disappointed that this part of the mystery would probably never be solved. For whatever reason, Joan's relationship with her sister was difficult and that was as much of an explanation as they were likely to get.

"Not only that," Jacob said, "she wasn't

445

keen on me, either."

"Why?"

"Don't know. She just wasn't. Felt it was up to her to say what Joan should do and who she could see."

"Tell me more about Joan," Mary Jo said.

Jacob leaned back in his wheelchair. "She was a beauty. We met at a soda fountain here in Cedar Cove. I came over from Fort Lewis for a USO dance and stopped at the drugstore. She was working behind the counter and caught my eye. I had a soda and asked if she'd be at the dance. At the time, her sister worked there, too. It was later that they got jobs at the shipyard. Her sister told me to stay away from Joan."

"Clearly you didn't heed her advice," Mack said.

"Wild horses wouldn't have kept me away. I was smitten the first time I laid eyes on her."

Mack looked at Mary Jo as if to say he understood the feeling.

"We met up at the dance and then again the following day. Joan had to sneak away from her sister and they had words afterward. It was too bad that Elaine and I started off on the wrong foot, but honestly, I don't think it would've mattered. Elaine wasn't a happy person. She tried to control

Joan and to thwart our romance, not that it did much good."

It occurred to Mary Jo that maybe Joan hadn't hidden the letters all at one time but had kept them — and her diary — in the closet to prevent her sister from finding them.

"How did Joan die?" Mack asked.

"Cancer. I don't think I'll ever recover from losing her." He paused. "But we had almost fifty years together. And my children are good to me. They visit when they can and the grandchildren, as well."

Mary Jo could see that the old man was tiring. "We should go," she said. "I'll get someone to take you back to your room."

"Would it be okay if we stopped by and visited every now and then?" Mack asked.

"I'd be very pleased to see you again." He clutched the cigar box and the small diary. "I can't thank you enough for going to the effort of finding me so you could return these letters." He inhaled softly. "They'll mean the world to my children — and to me."

Mack stood and so did Mary Jo. Impulsively she bent down and kissed the leathery cheek. "Thank you," she whispered.

"Why are you thanking me?" he asked. "You're the ones who found me and brought me back my letters."

"Thank you for writing them, and for showing Mack and me how much we owe the heroes of your generation."

He dismissed her comment with a wave of his hand. "Nonsense, I'm no hero."

"I disagree," Mack said. "I can understand why you're called the 'Greatest Generation' — because you are."

The old man looked up at them and smiled. Then, raising his hand to his forehead, he saluted them.

# THIRTY-TWO

Olivia slipped into the row of seats behind Grace Harding. The wedding of Faith Beckwith and Troy Davis was about to start. The large gazebo outside Justine's Victorian Tea Room was filled to capacity as so many well-wishers had come to share this special day.

No sooner had she sat down than the music swelled and Pastor Flemming came forward. Faith and Troy stood, with their families and friends gathered in a semicircle around them. After a few words from the clergyman, Faith and Troy quietly exchanged their vows. The ceremony, while short, touched Olivia's heart.

Jack was obviously moved, too. Her husband clasped her hand and she squeezed back. They'd both come to a fuller appreciation of each other in the past eight months, while she'd battled cancer. Just as Jack's heart attack several years earlier had showed Olivia how much she loved this man, her cancer had brought him the same realization. These illnesses had made the prospect of loss very real, and they'd both learned to treasure each day together.

Jack Griffin, the town paper's new editor, had stormed into Olivia's life twenty years after her divorce. Now she wondered how she'd lived all those years without him.

Like Faith and Troy, she and Jack had hit more than a few snags in their relationship. But their marriage was worth every hard lesson in compromise and tolerance. She knew the same would be true for Faith and Troy.

They'd all attended high school around the same time, and Olivia remembered that Faith and Troy had dated. After graduation they'd gone their separate ways, only to meet again almost forty years later, both widowed by this time. They'd quickly renewed their relationship.

Now, seeing them look at each other with such love, Olivia couldn't help feeling this marriage would be as happy as hers and Jack's.

The reception was inside the recently opened restaurant. Troy and Faith stood at the entrance and greeted each of their guests. Faith was beautiful in her soft pink suit, with a bouquet of white rosebuds. Troy had never looked handsomer, wearing a dark suit and pink tie. A white rosebud boutonniere was pinned to his lapel.

"I'm so glad you could make it," Faith told Olivia, hugging her. Justine and her staff bustled about, carrying trays of food to the buffet table.

"I wouldn't miss this for anything," Olivia said, and it was true.

Grace and Cliff followed Olivia and Jack as they entered the restaurant. A number of round tables, covered in white linen, were artfully arranged about the room. Each had a pink floral arrangement at its center. A buffet table, set up against the wall, held a tiered wedding cake, with a large silver punch bowl beside it.

Holding Olivia's hand, Jack led the way to a centrally located table. Grace and Cliff joined them.

"How long do you think it'll be before they cut the cake?" Jack asked, leaning toward Olivia.

"Jack!" Pretending to be scandalized, she elbowed her husband. "You're worse than a kid!"

"I can't help it, I'm hungry," her husband protested. "And I'm *especially* hungry for cake."

Olivia laughed. "Okay, it shouldn't be long."

"There's lots of nice-looking food over there," Cliff said, pointing at the buffet table. "If you get some, bring extras for me."

"Cliff," Grace chastised. "We just had lunch."

"That was *hours* ago."

"No one else is going up for food yet."

"Hey, somebody has to be the first."

Grace exchanged a look with Olivia and rolled her eyes.

Jack suddenly turned to Olivia. "Is that your brother?" he asked in a low voice.

Olivia craned her neck to see. Sure enough, it was Will. She hadn't even realized he'd been invited to the wedding. With the art gallery to run, it was unusual for him to take time off in the middle of a Saturday, which was the most profitable day of the week, particularly during the summer. "I didn't notice him in church earlier, did you?"

"Can't say I did," Jack commented. "He looks a bit lost to me."

Olivia glanced over at Grace and Cliff. "Would you mind if I invited Will to join us?"

Grace deferred to her husband.

"Fine with me," Cliff said. He stretched

his arm across the back of Grace's chair in what Olivia recognized as a possessive gesture.

She approached her brother, who stood just inside the restaurant. Although past sixty, Will was still an attractive man. In some ways his natural good looks and charismatic personality had been a detriment. Everything had come too easily to Will. He'd been a star football player, the high school's homecoming king and an equally big success in college. He'd done well as an engineer and risen steadily up the ranks of his company, retiring early after his divorce. Personally, Olivia was pleased to have Will living in Cedar Cove. Despite his irresponsible behavior toward his ex-wife, Georgia — and toward Grace — she valued his wit, his intelligence and his friendship with her and Jack. She couldn't fault his emotional and practical support when she'd been so ill. Besides, their mother was getting on in years, although Charlotte would be the first to insist she didn't want her children looking after her. Regardless, Olivia welcomed her brother's presence in town and was grateful she wouldn't have to make any decisions concerning Charlotte on her own.

"Will, come and sit with us," she said,

impulsively touching his arm.

Will turned around. "Oh, hi, Liv. Thanks, but I've got Mom with me. She's in the ladies' room at the moment."

"You brought Mom?"

He answered with a sigh. "She phoned at the last minute and said she needed a ride to the wedding and asked if I could take her. As it was, we missed most of the ceremony."

"Where's Ben?"

Will shook his head. "She didn't say, but something's up."

Olivia wasn't sure what to make of this. She'd talk privately with her mother when she had the chance. "It was good of you to drop everything and bring her here."

"No big deal," Will said, shrugging off her thanks. "I wasn't that busy and Miranda Sullivan's filling in for me."

"Miranda Sullivan," Olivia repeated. "I don't believe I know her."

"You probably don't. She lives in Gig Harbor but she's in town quite often. She's friends with Shirley Bliss."

"Oh." Olivia would make a point of seeking Miranda out and introducing herself. She wanted to thank the other woman for taking Will's place at the gallery so he could escort Charlotte to the wedding.

Olivia touched her brother's arm again. "Will, is everything all right?" She'd rarely seen him so disheartened.

"Everything's fine." His answer was quick. Too quick. He must have realized it because he gave her a chagrined look. "Okay, if you must know, I had a bit of a surprise last week."

"What kind of surprise?"

"Not a good one." He sighed. "I made a point of letting Shirley Bliss know I was interested in her."

Olivia was well aware of it; her brother had set his sights on Shirley and actively pursued her.

"You might recall that she and I went out a few times."

After each outing Will had talked endlessly about Shirley. He'd asked Olivia to suggest a restaurant in Seattle, and then followed her advice and made a reservation. The next week he reported what a wonderful dinner they'd had.

"How is Shirley?" Olivia asked.

"According to Miranda, she's in love," he said despairingly. "And it isn't with me."

"Oh, Will, I'm so sorry."

"There's nothing to be sorry about. It's my own fault. I introduced her to an artist friend of mine and then, next thing I know, the two of them are head over heels for each other, which Miranda was happy to share. A week ago they came to the gallery — and they *thanked* me," he said sardonically. "Trust me, I can read the writing on the wall." He stared down at his feet and shrugged again, trying to pretend it really didn't matter.

Clearly this rejection had come as a shock to her brother. Women had always been interested in Will, and he'd been interested in them. It seemed that, in the past, Will could've had almost any woman he wanted. Grace was an exception, but that was a whole other story.

"The thing is," her brother said. "I'm getting old."

"Older, Will, not old."

"Same difference."

"Oh, come on. You're as attractive as ever."

He raised his eyebrows but didn't respond.

Olivia was surprised by the fragility of her brother's ego. She wanted to laugh off his concern, but she could see that he took this seriously. She supposed his inability to cope with rejection made sense, considering he'd received very little of it over the years.

"I'm afraid," he said.

"Of what?"

He looked away. "Of growing old alone."

She searched for the words to reassure him and would have spoken if not for the fact that their mother stepped out of the ladies' room just then. Olivia knew immediately that Will was right; Charlotte was distressed about something.

"Mom," Olivia said, meeting her halfway. She slipped an arm around her mother. "Come and sit with us."

"You don't mind, dear?"

"Of course not." She steered Charlotte toward the table where Jack and her friends were waiting with their champagne flutes. Will followed two steps behind.

Charlotte sat next to Olivia and set her small handbag in her lap. Olivia noticed that her mother hadn't brought her knitting, which was unusual. Charlotte never allowed a spare moment — even at a formal event like this — to pass without knitting.

Moving a little closer to her mother, Olivia asked, "Where's Ben?"

Her mother stared at her blankly.

"Ben, Mom," she repeated. "Where's Ben?"

"He went to talk to David."

This wasn't welcome information. Anything to do with Ben's son was generally bad news. "David's in town?"

Charlotte worried her lip. "I wouldn't

know, dear. Ben took a phone call and then said he had to leave for a while. I completely forgot about Troy and Faith's wedding. Thank goodness Will could bring me."

Her mother was obviously distraught. "You know David's living in Seattle now?"

Olivia nodded; Ben had mentioned it the day they'd come for lunch.

Charlotte lowered her head. "That's not all." She paused and exhaled slowly. "David was let go from his job. He's unemployed."

Olivia had already heard about that, too, and wondered why her mother was repeating it. She sounded as if it was news to her.

"He's living with a woman and . . . oh, dear, Olivia, I don't think I've ever seen Ben this upset. He thought David had lost the power to hurt him, but he was wrong. Ben can't believe his son would stoop to letting a woman support him. It's bad enough that David seems to enjoy terrorizing Mary Jo over that precious baby."

Olivia reached for her mother's hand. "Don't worry, Mom," she said in a soothing voice. "Ben knows how to deal with David."

"What David needs is someone who'll talk to him without taking any of his garbage," Will interjected. "If he won't listen to his father, maybe he'll listen to me."

"Will," Olivia muttered, silencing her

458

brother. He was only throwing gasoline on the fire.

"Like I said," she told her mother again, "Ben knows how to handle his son."

"Oh, Olivia, I do hope you're right. I can't tell you how worried I am."

Will scowled, clearly angry at what this business with David was doing to their mother. Good thing David Rhodes wasn't anywhere close to her brother, who had little tolerance for that kind of behavior. One look at him told her Will would love to straighten David out.

"Ben knew Faith and Troy's wedding was this afternoon. We planned to attend together. I bought a new dress and Ben got a new tie and we'd been looking forward to it. He must have forgotten."

"I'm sure that's not the case, Mom," Olivia murmured.

"It's just that I'm afraid of what David might do. He doesn't know that Ben's found out where he's living. If Ben shows up unexpectedly, everything might blow up in his face."

"Who told Ben all this about David?" she asked, hoping to keep Charlotte from dwelling on the negative possibilities.

"I don't know for sure. Somebody . . . And then a woman phoned the house early this afternoon and asked to speak to Mr. Rhodes. When he finished with the call, Ben didn't tell me who she was or why she phoned. I have to assume this is another young lady David has hurt in one way or another. All Ben said after he hung up was what I told you."

Charlotte paused and seemed to need a moment to collect her thoughts. "Ben was *so* upset. He said it was time he paid his son a visit." She glanced up. "I'm so worried. . . ."

"You don't seriously think David would hurt his father, do you?" Olivia tried to hide her alarm but wasn't sure she'd succeeded.

"With David, it's hard to tell." Her hands opened and closed the clasp of her purse.

Olivia placed an arm protectively around her mother's shoulders.

Faith and Troy were walking toward the cake, and Olivia watched as Jack sat up and took notice. He'd finished a plateful of crab salad, broccoli quiche and smoked salmon canapés, but he was ready, as usual, to indulge his sweet tooth. She nudged him with her foot as a warning to behave. Honestly! Anyone would think Cliff and Jack hadn't eaten in a week.

"Ben!" Charlotte cried out, raising her arm and giving an anxious wave.

Olivia looked toward the front of the restaurant and saw Ben Rhodes enter the dining area. Charlotte stood and hurried toward him. He smiled down at her and slid his arm about her waist. The two of them talked intensely before Olivia's mother brought Ben back to the table.

Both Jack and Cliff stood to greet the other man. Will did, too, but his dour, thoughtful mood hadn't improved.

Although Olivia sympathized with her brother's disappointment, she felt a bit of rejection might be good for him. He did seem genuinely hurt that Shirley Bliss had fallen in love with someone else. But then, most people had learned by this age that life had its share of disappointments.

Ben leaned close to Charlotte, whispering a few words in her ear. Almost immediately, Charlotte relaxed.

Olivia didn't want to seem too inquisitive, but she couldn't help being curious. "Is everything all right, Ben?" she asked.

Ben's hand rested on his wife's back. "Never better," he assured her, although his face was expressionless.

Olivia wondered what had taken place between David Rhodes and his father. Obviously Ben wasn't about to divulge what had happened, nor was he willing to feed anyone's speculation. But she guessed that whatever had been said would eventually come out.

An hour later it was time to go. Olivia had visited with various friends she hadn't seen since she'd taken a leave of absence from court. As they filed out of the restaurant, Olivia felt that Faith and Troy's wedding had been lovely in every way, exactly what she'd wanted for them. Earlier, she'd learned from Grace that they'd booked a honeymoon trip to Alaska. The couple planned to fly out the next morning.

As Jack escorted her to the parking lot, Charlotte called out to them. Olivia walked back to meet her mother.

"Olivia, I can't seem to find my knitting. You didn't see it when I arrived, did you?"

"No, Mom, sorry. Are you sure you brought it?"

"Olivia, sweetheart, you know me well enough to realize I never go anywhere without my knitting."

Yes, which was why Olivia had wondered about it. "Could it be in Will's car?"

Charlotte smiled in relief. "Of course! How silly of me. That's where it must be." Will was ready to pull out of the parking lot when Ben stopped him.

Will lowered his window as the two men

had a quick exchange. Will reached over to the passenger seat and handed Ben the quilted bag. Ben turned, holding it up so Charlotte would know he had her precious knitting.

"Oh, thank goodness," Charlotte breathed.

"Everything's going to be fine, Mom," Olivia said more confidently than she felt. "I'm sure of it."

Jack came up then, and the two of them saw Ben and her mother off. "Poor Mom," she said to her husband.

"She was worried about Ben, that's all," Jack said. "We all get confused when we're concerned about someone we love. And when you're dealing with someone like David, someone who seems to have no conscience at all, everything's that much harder."

Olivia had to agree. In her opinion, David Rhodes had already done untold damage. She could only hope this was the end.

# THIRTY-THREE

Rachel was convinced that telling Jolene about the baby this soon was a mistake. Bruce, however, disagreed. He seemed to think that the longer they could give his daughter to adjust to the news, the better it would be.

However, Rachel couldn't see Jolene accepting this gracefully. Certainly not with joy or excitement.

Bruce decided the best way to make the announcement was to take his "girls" for a night out. He planned every detail, starting with reservations at D.D.'s on the Cove.

As Rachel dressed for dinner she felt sick, but her queasiness had nothing to do with the pregnancy. She'd managed to hide her morning sickness from her stepdaughter all these weeks and doubted Jolene even suspected she might be pregnant.

"Are you ready?" Bruce called from the living room.

"Give me a minute," she called back. Then, sitting on the edge of the bed, Rachel closed her eyes and offered up a silent prayer that her stepdaughter would welcome her half brother or sister into their family. A cold sweat broke out across her forehead as apprehension settled over her.

"Hey, Rachel," Bruce said, crashing into the bedroom. "What's the holdup? If we don't leave now, we won't make our reservation."

She gave him a weak smile. Bruce didn't appear to notice her uneasiness as she reached for her purse.

Jolene was waiting in the living room and eyed Rachel curiously when she appeared. "You aren't sick, are you?" The question wasn't one of concern. She asked it as if she expected Rachel to do something to ruin this evening her father had planned for them.

"I'm fine," she lied.

Bruce pulled the car out of the garage and Rachel got into the front seat beside her husband.

Jolene slammed the rear door as a reminder that until Bruce had married Rachel, *she'd* always sat in front. Bruce had yet to comment on the abuse his daughter gave the rear door. Rachel let it go. That door was the least of her problems.

Bruce located a convenient parking spot at D.D.'s and the three of them walked to the restaurant. Rachel saw that Jolene stayed close to Bruce's side, preventing her from walking next to her husband. Bruce seemed unaware of the girl's maneuvering and Rachel wasn't about to get into a shoving match over whose right it was to be next to Bruce. She followed quietly a couple of steps behind, desperately hoping she'd make it through the evening.

The hostess seated them and Jolene instantly slid into the booth beside Bruce.

"The last time we were here we split a bowl of steamed clams," Jolene told him. "Can we do that again?"

"Sure," Bruce said, without looking up from his menu.

Jolene knew that Rachel disliked clams. She hated to be paranoid but her stepdaughter seemed to be going out of her way once again to prove that Rachel was an intruder on their happy family.

This was all the more reason, in Rachel's view, to delay telling Jolene about the pregnancy. Unfortunately, Bruce didn't agree. He also disagreed that counseling might help. Rachel had tentatively brought it up, but he insisted that they could work out their own problems — and that Jolene would refuse to go anyway.

Bruce and Jolene had steamed clams as an appetizer, while Rachel sipped herbal tea. She did her best not to watch for fear that looking at them eating clams would upset her stomach even more. Jolene made slurping sounds as she ate, suggesting that she was thoroughly enjoying herself.

"Let's order dinner," Bruce said as the waitress removed the bowl of clam shells. "Do you know what you want?" he asked Rachel.

"Can I have steak?" Jolene cut in, not allowing Rachel to respond.

Bruce smiled indulgently at his daughter. "You can order anything you like, sweetheart." He looked at Rachel again.

"Dad, what are you going to eat?" Again, Jolene cut Rachel off before she had an opportunity to answer.

"I believe I'll have a T-bone. This is a celebration, after all." He smiled at Rachel, clearly pleased with himself.

He didn't seem to share any of her concerns about Jolene's reaction to their news. Rachel wondered how her husband could be this oblivious. After helping Jolene with her algebra, she thought her relationship with the girl had improved. That peace, however, was short-lived. Within a matter of days, everything returned to the way it was from the moment Rachel had married Jolene's father.

Instead of the family friend Rachel had been, starting when Jolene was in first grade, she became an interloper, the woman who'd trespassed on the girl's territory. It'd been just Jolene and her father for so long that no one, no matter how close, would fit into the family picture.

When the waitress came for their dinner order, Rachel was finally able to announce her choice. She asked for crab cakes with rice pilaf and a green salad. Both Bruce and Jolene chose the full steak dinner, complete with baked potato, soup and salad.

Bruce, at least, was in high spirits. Rachel tried to catch his mood; she ignored every slight Jolene threw at her, smiled sweetly and pretended it didn't hurt that her own husband hadn't noticed the way his daughter treated her.

To be fair, Rachel didn't know if she was being oversensitive, since the pregnancy had played havoc with her emotions. The best she could do was disregard the verbal jabs and refrain from countering even the nastiest ones.

Father and daughter spoke animatedly

through dinner. Rachel swallowed a few bites and then asked for a take-out container. By contrast Bruce and Jolene both ate their entire meals.

"How about dessert?" Bruce said when the last of their dishes had been removed from the table.

Rachel placed her hand on her stomach. "I'm full. I couldn't eat a single bite," she protested.

"I could," Jolene said eagerly. "What would you like, Dad?"

Bruce read over the dessert menu and then looked at his daughter. "I suppose you want the ice cream sundae with chocolate sauce."

"Dad," she moaned playfully. "That's for kids."

"You're still a kid," Bruce said.

"No, I'm not." Jolene giggled.

The girl was happier than she'd been in all the months since Rachel had married Bruce. It was easy to see why. Jolene was in her element. She had her father's full attention and she'd managed to shut Rachel out.

What Jolene didn't know was that her father was about to deliver a devastating blow that would disrupt her entire world.

They each ordered a different dessert. Bruce got the apple tart warmed and with vanilla ice cream and Jolene chose a slice of chocolate cake.

Bruce waited until their dessert was served, then stretched his hand across the table to reach for Rachel's. His fingers curled around hers.

Jolene stared at Rachel and narrowed her eyes menacingly.

"I mentioned that tonight's a celebration," Bruce began, turning to his daughter.

Jolene slowly nodded.

"Do you know what we're celebrating?" he asked.

For a moment, Jolene looked confused. "I passed my algebra test and advanced to intermediate in swimming, remember?"

"I do," Bruce commented.

Jolene had been forced to take the swimming test three times before advancing. In addition, she'd gotten a B- on her algebra final. Both tests had been hard for her. Rachel was proud of Jolene, although the girl had scorned her praise.

"This isn't about making it into the intermediate swimming class or doing well on your algebra final," Rachel told her.

Jolene looked blankly at her father. "Then what are we celebrating?"

Bruce glanced at Rachel and offered her a soft, reassuring smile. "Rachel told me some

470

exciting news recently."

"*Rachel* did?" This was asked as if she had difficulty believing Rachel was capable of saying anything of interest.

"Jolene, tonight we're celebrating the fact that you're going to become a big sister."

The girl looked from her father to Rachel, and then back at Bruce before the light dawned. She turned to face Rachel. "You're having a *baby?*" The question was an accusation more than an inquiry.

Gazing down at the table, Rachel nodded and then, reminding herself that she had nothing to be ashamed of, boldly met Jolene's eyes.

"Daddy?" The girl turned to her father. Her face crumpled as if she was begging him to tell her it wasn't true.

"Didn't you hear me?" Bruce asked in the same animated way he'd announced her pregnancy. "We're having a baby."

"I heard," Jolene muttered.

"Aren't you happy?"

Reluctantly she nodded.

"You can name the baby if you want," Bruce said next.

He hadn't discussed this with Rachel. However, if it helped Jolene adjust, she was more than willing to let the girl make suggestions.

"Is it a boy or a girl?" she asked sullenly.

"It's too early to tell," Rachel said. "I won't have an ultrasound for several weeks." Personally, she'd rather not know the sex of their baby. However, it seemed important to Jolene. Rachel took longer than she should have to realize why. Jolene was afraid a baby girl would be competition for her father's affection.

"I thought you'd show more enthusiasm than this," Bruce complained.

"Give her time," Rachel said, hoping a gentle approach would soothe Jolene's feelings. She directed her subsequent remark to Jolene. "I understand this is a shock and I apologize if it upsets you."

"Jolene's not upset," Bruce said. "You aren't, are you?"

She didn't respond. Instead, she glared straight ahead, avoiding eye contact with both her father and Rachel.

The waitress brought the bill and Bruce reached for his wallet. "How about a movie?" he suggested as he slid his credit card into the holder.

Rachel couldn't imagine Jolene agreeing to spend any more time with her than necessary.

"Can we just go home?" the girl asked.

"Sure." Bruce was more than eager to appease his daughter in any way he could.

They left the restaurant and drove back to the house. Bruce stopped to set the garbage cans by the curb while Rachel and Jolene went inside. Jolene immediately raced to her bedroom.

Rachel slumped down in a living room chair. This had gone exactly as she'd expected.

"Where's Jolene?" Bruce asked as he threw his car keys on the kitchen counter.

"Her room." Rachel guessed she was on her cell, talking to her friends, spilling the disastrous news to anyone and everyone who'd listen. And once Bruce was out of the house, the silent treatment would start. It was either that or a tirade against Rachel because of how she'd single-handedly ruined the girl's life.

Bruce stood in the middle of the room, hands on his hips. "Why's everyone so miserable?" he asked. "I couldn't be happier about the baby. I'm thrilled to death. Okay, I know we agreed to wait for Jolene's sake, but the deed is done. She'll get used to it."

Rachel feared that was simply wishful thinking on his part. "I hope so," she whispered.

"Give the kid some credit," Bruce said.

"Jolene is flexible. It might take her a while to come to terms with the fact that we're adding to the family, but eventually she'll be as happy as we are."

"Eventually," Rachel echoed. She wasn't a pessimist by nature, but she didn't share his optimism about Jolene.

He studied her for a moment. "You look tired."

"I am," she said. It was a mild exaggeration, but she needed time alone to think. "Would you mind if I went to bed?"

Glancing at his watch, he arched his brows. "It's only seven-thirty."

"I know."

He smiled slowly. "Interested in company?"

She smiled back. "Sorry, not tonight."

His face fell. "Is it going to be like this during the whole pregnancy?" He sounded like a little boy who'd been deprived of dessert.

"Bruce," she snapped, in no mood to deal with this.

"All right, all right, I apologize. It's just that it's been a while."

"Three days," she reminded him.

"Are you keeping track?" he asked. "Isn't that like closing the barn door after the cow gets out?"

"It's a horse."

"Whatever."

"I suppose you're right. We should've paid more attention before now." She stood and started toward their bedroom.

Reaching out, Bruce grabbed her hand. His eyes were dark. "Are you saying you'd rather you weren't pregnant?"

"Oh, honestly, Bruce. You have to know the timing's all wrong. Jolene is upset and —"

He released her hand. "Fine. If having my baby is such a hardship, then I won't trouble you again. I'll move into the spare bedroom and you can rest assured I won't interrupt your precious sleep."

So it had come to this. The two of them were at odds, attacking each other. This should be the happiest time of her life and it was all Rachel could do not to break into tears.

"Did you hear me?" Bruce demanded.

"If moving into the spare bedroom is what you want, then don't let me stop you."

# THIRTY-FOUR

Roy McAfee wasn't a man who got involved in other people's affairs. In his line of work, he'd seen enough to make any man skeptical of the human heart. Because of that, he tried to stay away from divorce cases, especially those that included child custody disputes. Most of his work concerned background checks and insurance investigations. In his opinion, people had a right to live the way they wanted, unless they hurt or swindled others.

The reason he was making an exception now had to do with his daughter Gloria. She'd made her decision not to tell Chad Timmons she was pregnant. Corrie had given Gloria her word that she'd abide by that decision. Roy, however, saw his own situation reflected in Chad's — a situation that hadn't been righted for more than three decades. He refused to let that happen again.

"Where are you off to?" Corrie asked as he headed out the front door on Wednesday afternoon.

In an instance such as this, it was best to be vague. "There's something I need to do."

"Is this something I know about?" Corrie eyed him speculatively, as if she'd guessed exactly who he intended to see and what he intended to do.

Roy swore his wife had some sort of psychic ability. She seemed to instinctively know this had to do with Gloria and Chad. He hedged, reluctant to lie, and at the same time unwilling to admit he was a man on a mission — or to tell her what that mission entailed.

She raised her eyebrows. "Why don't you want me to know what this is about?"

He muttered a few words he'd rather she didn't hear and opened the door.

"Roy?"

"Like I said, this is something I need to do."

She slipped in front of him, blocking his exit. "You're going to talk to Chad Timmons, aren't you?"

He didn't confirm or deny the statement.

"Roy, don't. Please reconsider," Corrie whispered with an urgency that gave him pause.

He clutched the car keys so tightly they dug into his hands. "That young man has a right to know about his baby."

Corrie closed her eyes and he knew she was thinking back to the time she'd found herself pregnant and alone. The same memory had haunted him from the moment their daughter came to tell them she was pregnant and the father was out of her life.

"This is the first time Gloria has ever come to us with a problem," Corrie argued. "It's been a breakthrough in our relationship. If you say anything to Chad, it could destroy her trust. It could destroy everything. I'm begging you, Roy, don't do this."

Roy's eyes bored into hers and he stood his ground. They so rarely disagreed that it made this standoff even more difficult. Still, Roy was determined. "The young man has a right to know," he repeated.

Corrie gave him a sad smile. "What you're saying is that *you* had a right to know and I didn't tell you."

"Yes!" he all but shouted. When he'd discovered he had a daughter he would never meet, it had nearly broken his spirit. He loved Corrie and had asked her to be his wife, and yet she'd kept this secret for months. The anger and anguish had nearly consumed him. What she'd done had the power to tear them apart. Roy hadn't let that happen; instead, he'd buried his feelings. But he understood now that this unresolved matter could still undermine their marriage, their relationship.

"I've never begged you for anything," his wife said. "Don't do this. Please, Roy, don't do this."

Unsure now, he walked over to his recliner and sagged into it. His car keys dangled from his hand as he leaned forward, gripped by indecision. He believed that contacting Chad Timmons was the right thing to do for Gloria and her baby. Yet everything Corrie said was true. Their daughter, the very one he'd thought forever lost, was back in their lives. Corrie feared, as he did, that going against her will would destroy their fragile bond.

Corrie remained where she stood.

"I need to think," he murmured.

"Okay," she agreed after a prolonged moment.

He heard the reluctance in her voice.

"Think of Gloria — this is what she wants," Corrie said. "Right or wrong, these are her wishes."

Feeling the full weight of his years, Roy wiped a hand down his face. "Have you ever wondered what would've happened if I'd found out you were pregnant?" he asked.

Corrie didn't answer him.

"You'll never know because you made the decision not to tell me." He tried hard to keep the bitterness out of his voice.

"You were seeing someone else." Her words rang with painful accusation. "What did you expect me to do?"

"I expected you to tell me," he barked. Corrie had taken the choice away from him. He'd been young and stupid, and even now he couldn't be completely sure how he would've handled the situation. He liked to think he would have stepped up and been a man, but again that was something he'd never know.

"Let me give it more thought," he said when he'd regained control of his emotions. What had happened had happened; they couldn't go back and undo the past. Reviving these dead emotions could only hurt them.

Corrie sat down on the sofa and pressed her hands between her knees. When she spoke she lowered her head, her words barely audible. "I know what Gloria feels."

"Tell me," he urged, wanting to understand how she'd rationalized her silence all those years ago.

"She's afraid."

"Of what?" he challenged.

Corrie glanced up. "Rejection. Blame."

"Blame?" Roy stared at her. "Why would I blame you? The responsibility for birth control should be shared."

"It was more than that."

"Explain it to me."

"I . . . had an important decision to make and I wanted to make it myself, without pressure from you."

Her reasoning irritated him. "Don't you think that was rather selfish?"

"No." Corrie would not back down. "I was young and immature," she said. "I had all I could deal with already. I couldn't handle you being in the center of the situation. Gloria feels the same way. Chad is out of her life. He, too, is involved with someone else. Gloria feels as I did — that she'd rather deal with this on her own."

Hearing her so coldly cut out Chad, just as Corrie had eliminated him from the equation, made the decision easy for Roy. He came to his feet and stalked out of the house.

"Roy!" his wife called after him. "Don't do this. Please . . . don't do this," she wailed.

Roy ignored her, climbed into his car and drove off. He couldn't say he looked forward to meeting Chad Timmons. The task of

481

informing the other man that he was about to become a father wouldn't be pleasant.

He drove into Tacoma and parked at the hospital. His visit was brief. He left a message for Chad with the receptionist, asking the doctor to meet him at a tavern close to the hospital. Whether or not Chad decided to show up was his choice. If he didn't arrive within half an hour of the end of his shift — which the receptionist had told him was 4:00 p.m. — Roy would take that to mean Chad wasn't interested in talking to him. In that case, he wouldn't pursue the issue. Corrie and Gloria would get their wish. But, by the same token, Roy would feel he'd done what he had to do.

He sat at a table in the darkened room and ordered a beer. He wasn't much of a drinking man. Never had been, but there were occasions that seemed to call for it. This was one of them.

He'd drunk about half his beer when the door opened and Dr. Chad Timmons entered. They'd met briefly at the opening of the medical clinic, and Roy recognized him immediately. The younger man paused near the entrance and looked around.

Roy raised his chin just enough for Timmons to spot him.

Chad walked the length of the room and

stood in front of him. "You wanted to speak to me?" he asked defensively.

Roy gestured toward the chair.

Chad ignored the silent invitation to join him. "What's this about?"

"Sit down, son."

With obvious reluctance he pulled out a chair and sat.

"You know my daughter," Roy said without emotion.

"I know both your daughters," Chad returned.

For a moment Roy had forgotten that at one time Linnette had been infatuated with Chad.

"Has something happened to Gloria?" Chad asked. A look of concern passed over his face.

Roy managed to disguise a smile. "That's one way of putting it." He caught the bartender's eye, lifted his nearly empty glass and held up two fingers. A minute later, two pints were delivered to their table.

"I didn't ask for this," Chad said, still sounding defensive.

Roy resisted the urge to suggest he was going to need it. Instead, he offered the other man a few words of advice. "Don't turn down a free beer."

Chad cracked a smile.

"Would you mind if I told you a story about me?" Roy asked.

Chad motioned for him to proceed.

"Corrie and I were college sweethearts. I was playing for the football team and became a bit of a campus celebrity. I'm afraid I let that attention go to my head."

"It can happen easily enough," Chad said. He leaned forward and put his elbows on the table.

"Especially when one of the sexiest cheerleaders on the squad made a play for me."

"Hey, you're only human."

"Yeah, only human." Roy wasn't proud of this next part. "I broke up with Corrie. As they say, I had bigger fish to fry. I knew I'd hurt her and I felt bad about that, but Alicia — the cheerleader — made it clear she didn't like competition."

Chad grinned as if he understood Roy's quandary. "It was either one or the other, right?"

"You've got the picture." Roy paused and sipped his beer. "Corrie left school and I have to tell you I was relieved not to see her around campus. Especially after Alicia dumped me."

"Any particular reason you lost the cheerleader?"

Roy nodded. "I got hurt, put on injured

reserved. My star had fallen. Alicia moved on."

"Bigger fish?"

"You bet." Roy's hand tightened around the beer mug. "I decided that if I was going into law enforcement, I couldn't risk another injury. So I gave up sports and concentrated on my studies."

"You joined the Seattle police force, didn't you?"

Roy nodded. "I made detective."

Chad arched his brows.

"That injury returned to haunt me years later, when I hurt my back during a chase, and it led to my taking early retirement. But that's another story."

"Is there a point to *this* story?" Chad asked.

"Oh, yes, there's a point. I'll get to it in a minute."

Chad lifted his mug. "If you're buying the beer, take as long as you want."

Roy chuckled, relaxing against the back of the captain's chair. "I ran into Corrie on campus a short while later. That was the following year. We met at the library. When I saw her again, I was stunned by how beautiful she was. How genuine. I couldn't believe I'd left her for someone as superficial as Alicia."

"I'm surprised Corrie would have anything to do with you."

Roy had to agree. "She didn't make it easy. I sort of accidentally on purpose showed up at the library every night, about the same time I knew she'd be there."

"Smart man."

"I didn't make detective on looks alone."

Chad grinned.

"Eventually Corrie realized I was serious and agreed to go out with me again. I didn't make the same mistake twice, and just before I graduated I asked her to be my wife."

"Now that was a good move."

"I couldn't agree with you more." Roy straightened and stared down at his beer. "The night before we were married, Corrie told me that when she'd gone home to live with her family she'd given birth to my baby." He made eye contact with Chad.

"Gloria."

"Yes, Gloria. I didn't know I had a daughter until after she'd been given up for adoption."

Chad frowned.

"Like her mother, Gloria tends to be . . . cautious with what she shares. Private."

"Yes, she does," Chad said.

Uncertain how to lead into the purpose of

his visit, Roy met Chad's eyes again. "She says you're seeing someone else now."

Chad held his look. "If you don't mind, I'd rather not discuss my personal life."

"That's fine with me. However, before I say anything more, I want to tell you that I'm taking a huge risk seeing you this afternoon."

"How so?"

"My wife is dead set against it, and when Gloria finds out she'll probably never speak to me again."

"She came to see me." Chad took a sip of his beer. "About three weeks ago."

"So she said. Did you ever ask her why?"

"I know why. She changed her mind again. Frankly, she's done this to me twice and I'm through playing her games. If she sent you to talk to me, then you've wasted your money on good beer." He paused, as though everything was beginning to add up. "But you said she might not appreciate the fact that you came to see me, so what's up?"

Roy ignored the question. "I came because I wasn't going to sit idly by and let history repeat itself."

Chad stared at him.

"Are you that obtuse, young man?" Roy asked.

Chad's mouth fell open. It seemed to hit

him all at once. His chest expanded and then as quickly deflated. He stood, thrust his hands in his pockets and walked around the table.

"Another beer?" the bartender called out.

Roy shook his head.

"Bring me a shot of whiskey," Chad told him, and then, looking at Roy, he said, "Never mind. Just bring the bottle."

# THIRTY-FIVE

Mack had always assumed it was the bride who'd be nervous, not the groom. He certainly didn't expect to be the one pacing back and forth an hour before the wedding. Everything had come together so quickly that his mind was spinning. Once Mary Jo had agreed to marry him — and once they'd told his mother — the wedding seemed to take on a momentum of its own. But the best news was that Ben Rhodes had gotten David to agree to sign relinquishment papers, although he hadn't told anyone how he'd managed it or what he'd said. It had happened the day of another wedding — Troy and Faith's. Some people, like his father, thought Ben had offered David an incentive; others, like Jack Griffin, believed he'd used some kind of leverage. All Mack cared about, however, was the fact that he could now adopt Noelle.

Linnette and Pete's plan to visit Cedar

Cove in early August made the choice of a wedding date easier. If his sister and new brother-in-law were going to be in Cedar Cove, he and Mary Jo should take advantage of it.

Once the date was set, the details all seemed to fall into place. A whirlwind of events followed. His mother had arranged the reception and hired a photographer, while Mary Jo and Linc's wife, Lori, worked on the wedding dress. Lori had designed it and had seen to its completion in record time. According to Mary Jo, Lori was immensely talented, not that Mack knew anything about women's clothing. Although he hadn't actually seen this work-of-art wedding creation, he'd certainly heard enough about it from Mary Jo.

In getting all the arrangements made for the wedding, they'd also attended premarriage classes with Pastor Dave Flemming for two weeks. The sessions had seemed like a waste of time and effort when the pastor first mentioned them. Now that they were over, Mack was happy Dave had urged them to attend. Of the many things they'd discussed, the one that stuck in his mind was the way that assumptions could be detrimental to relationships. Assumptions about themselves and each other.

The six hour-long meetings with the pastor had made him aware of various issues between him and Mary Jo. Issues that could lead to contentious problems later on. Like his tendency to be overprotective and Mary Jo's to withhold her feelings. He was grateful to have had this opportunity to prepare for marriage and felt confident that they had a good chance of making their life together work.

"You okay?" His father stepped into the small vestibule behind the altar where Mack waited. Waited and paced. He'd sit down and then vault to his feet and resume pacing.

"I'm fine." He heard the hesitation in his own voice.

Roy chuckled and slapped him on the back. "Linc will be here in less than ten minutes, so you can stop worrying."

Linc Wyse would serve as Mack's best man, and Lori was standing up as Mary Jo's matron of honor.

"You mean to say he's not here yet?" Mack stopped abruptly. He'd been so consumed with his own nervousness that he hadn't realized his best man hadn't shown up.

"Everything's going to be just fine," Roy assured him, grinning widely.

Mack scowled at his father. "I don't know why you think this is so funny."

"Sorry, I can't help it. This wedding business brings up a lot of memories. I was a nervous wreck before I married your mother, too. In fact, I nearly fainted at the altar."

Mack could hardly believe that his highly competent, unflappable father had ever been nervous about anything, let alone his own wedding.

"Your mother was so beautiful I couldn't keep my eyes off her and when it came time to repeat my vows I was so tongue-tied —"

"Dad, stop it," Mack said. He was already having enough difficulties; he didn't need his father regaling him with horror stories just before his wedding.

"Sorry, son." Roy did have the good grace to look guilty.

"Where's Mom?" Mack asked, hoping a change of subject would settle his mind.

Appearing cool and relaxed, his father sat on the chair so recently vacated by Mack and crossed his legs. "She's with Charlotte Rhodes, getting everything set up for the reception."

The church had agreed to let Mack and Mary Jo use the Fellowship Hall following the wedding for their reception. Mack would have liked the waterfront gazebo, but that had been reserved months earlier by another couple, as was nearly every other facility in town. When Pastor Flemming had offered them the Fellowship Hall, it had been a big relief to his mother, who'd been working diligently on the problem.

"Why is Charlotte Rhodes helping Mom with the reception?" he asked.

His father gave him an odd look. "She baked the wedding cakes."

Mack remembered that now — or at least the part about Charlotte doing the baking. She was justly famous for her culinary skills. "Cakes, as in more than one?" If he distracted himself with details, he might actually get through this wedding without making an idiot of himself.

"Apparently you and Mary Jo are going to have one big cake and three smaller ones."

"We are?" Mack didn't recall that. "Why?"

"Don't know. That's what your mother told me."

Mack had only a vague recollection of their long discussions about the flowers and cake and a dozen other matters. Mack had left most of it to his mother, Mary Jo and Lori. He didn't have the patience for that sort of thing. He guessed few men did.

As it was, he found wearing this tuxedo

downright uncomfortable. The last time he'd worn a suit had been for his grandfather's funeral and that was . . . He'd lost count of the years.

A tuxedo. Him? Mary Jo and Lori had said he should rent one. He'd gone along with it, thinking he didn't really have a choice. Only when he and Linc had gone for the fitting had he figured out otherwise. His brother-in-law had complained at great length, but by then it was too late for them to take a stand. In Mack's opinion, an opinion seconded by Linc, formal wear was an instrument of torture.

"I understand Ben Rhodes is bringing a special guest," Roy said.

Mack didn't have a chance to respond or ask who it was before the door flew open and a breathless Linc shot into the room. "Sorry, sorry," he said. "I got a flat tire. Have you ever tried to change a tire in one of these getups?" he demanded. He straightened his sleeves and exhaled heavily.

Mack leaned against the wall.

Linc stared hard at him. "You're looking pale. You're not going to faint on me, are you?"

"I'm not planning on it." Now that Linc mentioned it, Mack did feel light-headed. His father's admission of his own wedding-day troubles hadn't helped. Feeling a sudden need to sit down, Mack sank into a chair and leaned forward, bracing his elbows on his knees.

Roy placed a comforting hand on his shoulder. "The wedding will go off without a hitch, don't you worry. You'll do fine."

Mack hoped so. Before he could think of anything else to worry about, Pastor Flemming came in. It was time.

His father left. Then Linc and Mack came through the vestibule door to stand beside the altar. He watched as his parents were seated in the front row next to Linnette and Pete. Gloria sat with them, on his parents' other side. Noelle slept in her arms.

Ned and Mel Wyse sat in the pew across from them, together with some of Mary Jo's Seattle friends.

As Mack looked at his family he saw his mother reach for a tissue. Trying not to be obvious, Corrie dabbed at her eyes. The music hadn't even started and already his mother was getting emotional.

This was supposed to be a happy occasion! Strangely, seeing his mother so affected by this wedding seemed to relax him. He found he was smiling. As he glanced at his father, Roy winked in his direction.

The church was nearly full. Mack and

Mary Jo had mailed out invitations; he couldn't keep track of the number of people his mother had added to the list. His parents' friends had made a point of attending, along with half the fire station. Their support touched him. He'd become close friends with these men in a short period of time. He wasn't surprised by the number of guests as much as he was honored.

Then the organ music began. Everyone stood as Mary Jo appeared at the back of the church. Mack straightened his shoulders and turned to face the woman who was about to become his wife.

One glance at her, and his breath caught in his throat. He must have taken a small step forward because Linc placed a restraining hand on his arm.

Mary Jo had never looked more beautiful. The dress, lace and pearls over silk, was everything she'd promised. Their eyes met, happiness radiating from hers. He felt her joy and experienced his own profound sense of rightness. For a moment he forgot to breathe. He stood transfixed, unable to move. Not until Pastor Flemming spoke did Mack realize it was time to stand by Mary Jo's side and repeat his vows.

The rest of the ceremony was lost in a whirl of words. Somehow he managed to say and do all that was required of him. While he'd been nervous earlier, now he felt calm and confident. Deep in his heart, his soul, he recognized that he'd made the best decision of his life when he'd asked Mary Jo to be his wife.

Organ music soared through the church as they walked down the aisle together as husband and wife. Several guys from the station high-fived him as he walked past. Mack's smile was so big it hurt his face.

Everyone followed them from the church to the Fellowship Hall, where the tables were set up. The area had been transformed with flowers, decorations and balloons. Mack had no idea who was responsible for all this but he guessed his mother, Linnette and Gloria had played a large role.

Together with his parents, Mack and Mary Jo formed a short reception line and greeted their guests as they came through the door.

"You might remember that I mentioned Ben Rhodes was bringing a special guest," Roy said to him in a low voice.

"Oh, yeah. Who is it?"

His father pointed at the other side of the room, where Jacob Dennison sat in his wheelchair.

"Mary Jo, look," he said, and nodded

toward Dennison.

"Oh, Mack."

When their last guest had entered the hall, Mack took Mary Jo by the hand and led her across the room. Dennison smiled up at them. "What a fine young couple you make."

"It's such an honor to have you at our wedding," Mary Jo told the old man in a tremulous voice.

"I wouldn't want to miss this. You two gave me a priceless gift by returning the letters I wrote Joan. Reading them brought back memories I'd long forgotten, memories I want to pass on to my children and grandchildren. This is a piece of my history — of their history, too. I will be forever grateful to you."

Mary Jo bent down to kiss Jacob's cheek.

"Now," he went on to say, "I wish for you the same happiness Joan and I had together. May your life be filled with love and may you always be as happy as you are this day."

Mary Jo smiled tearfully and looked at Mack. He tightened his hand on hers.

Dennison glanced at the wedding cakes. "I don't suppose you'd mind cutting me a piece of cake, would you?"

"I would love to," Mary Jo told him.

They made their way through the crowd

toward the wedding cakes. When they were almost there, Mary Jo paused and placed her hand over her heart. "What Jacob said? I *am* happy, Mack, so happy."

"I am, too." This was no exaggeration. Mack wasn't even sure how to describe the emotion that suffused every part of him. He felt both calm, supremely calm, and ecstatic, surrounded by his family and friends, surrounded by happiness.

He and his father exchanged a smile. Roy wasn't a man who smiled often or freely, but he did now. Mack felt his approval, his support. His mother was mingling with guests, completely in her element. His two sisters sat at a table, their heads close together, chatting about heaven knew what. Gloria continued to hold the sleeping Noelle.

Linnette was obviously pregnant now and due in another six weeks. Pete seemed content, talking to one of Mack's firefighter buddies.

Mary Jo cut the large, tiered cake and after they'd posed for pictures they delivered the first slice to Jacob Dennison. Ben and Charlotte sat with him and had been joined by Olivia and her husband, Jack Griffin. Grace and Cliff Harding were at the same table.

Corrie and Charlotte took over cake duty,

much to Mack's relief, with the assistance of Emily Flemming, the pastor's wife.

Noelle woke then and wanted to be held, so Mack took the baby in his arms and carried her around the room. Then he and Mary Jo went to sit with her brothers for a few minutes. Mel, Linc and Ned were all enjoying wedding cake, tasting and comparing the different varieties.

"I can hardly believe my baby sister's married," Linc said to no one in particular.

"Isn't it time for us to go?" Mary Jo whispered to Mack. "Before my brothers start crying in their cake?"

"We aren't crying," Mel insisted.

"Well, I'm not giving you a chance to get started," Mary Jo informed them. "Besides," she said, smiling up at Mack, "we need to leave for our honeymoon."

## THIRTY-SIX

"I don't want her here!" Jolene shouted loudly enough to be heard on the opposite side of the house.

"Jolene," Bruce snapped. He knew Jolene wanted Rachel to hear every word, which she probably had. The tension between them was driving him to the point of madness. He was trapped in a seemingly hopeless situation, and anything he said or did only made matters worse.

"I don't want her living here," his daughter continued.

"Rachel is your stepmother and my wife," he said with barely restrained anger. "That's not going to change, so you'd better adjust your attitude." Bruce had tried to let the two of them work this out themselves. Unfortunately, that hadn't happened. He didn't understand how all this crazy, competitive jealousy had gotten so out of hand, although he was well aware that Jolene had played the major role.

At one time she'd loved Rachel almost to the point of idol worship. They'd been close from the day they'd met, when he'd taken Jolene to Get Nailed for a haircut. It was through his daughter that Bruce had gotten to know Rachel.

Bruce slumped onto his recliner in the living room and wished this senseless bickering would end. Rachel had told him before they were married that Jolene needed more time. He hadn't listened. He'd wanted the three of them together as a family, so he'd rushed things and brushed aside Jolene's doubts and Rachel's fears. Now they were all paying the price.

No one was happy, least of all Bruce. Since their argument the night of the dinner, he'd been sleeping in the spare bedroom. That was a week ago. A week without Rachel in his bed. He missed her and wanted her back where she belonged. With him. He'd made overtures to that effect, but Rachel had ignored them.

"Dad," Jolene demanded. "You've got to do something."

Slowly he raised his head. "About what?"

"Rachel."

"Rachel is my wife." He wasn't going to argue with his teenage daughter.

Jolene's eyes narrowed. "She isn't even sleeping with you. The two of you hardly talk anymore."

Bruce couldn't deny the truth. "Every couple goes through an adjustment period. Rachel and I will sort this out." He certainly wasn't prepared to call it quits, and he didn't think Rachel wanted that, either. They'd come a long way in the past few years. It wasn't as if they were kids who'd rushed into the relationship. The marriage, yes, you could say that, but not the relationship. When they'd first met, Bruce was determined he'd never fall in love or marry again after Stephanie's death. Then gradually, through the years, he'd come to appreciate Rachel. More than once he thought he'd lost her. More than once he'd been sure she'd marry Nate Townsend, that navy guy. But she hadn't. No, Rachel was meant to be with him — and with Jolene, too.

"We don't need her," Jolene insisted, unwilling to drop the subject.

"But she's pregnant . . ."

"So? She doesn't have to be part of our lives, does she? Everything changed after she moved in with us, and I —" Jolene stopped abruptly when Rachel entered the room.

"I hope you don't mind if I join this

conversation," his wife said calmly.

Jolene crossed her arms, looking venomously at Rachel.

"Jolene has a point," Rachel said, again in the same low voice, a voice completely devoid of emotion.

"How?"

"She told us she was uneasy about us getting married, remember?"

"I *tried* to tell you, but you wouldn't listen," his daughter accused him, righteous indignation in every word.

"We'd already made the decision," Bruce countered. "Okay, so we rushed the wedding a bit, but I wanted you with me and you said you felt the same way."

"I did at the time."

He frowned at the implications of her remark. "Are you saying you regret it now?"

To his dismay Rachel nodded.

Jolene thrust a triumphant finger at her stepmother. "See? See, she doesn't want to be here."

Rachel ignored her. "Jolene has never accepted me as her stepmother."

Bruce didn't like the way this conversation — like so many of their conversations — revolved around his daughter's likes and dislikes. He and Rachel were the adults in the room; he wasn't about to let a thirteen-year-old girl dictate his life or his marriage. He realized now that stepping aside and leaving his daughter and his wife to work out their differences had contributed to the problem. "Jolene," he said pointedly, "will learn to accept you." And if it took a counseling session with some stranger to make that happen, so be it.

"Daddy!" the girl screeched.

"Maybe she will." Rachel shook her head. "And maybe she won't."

"All she needs is time," Bruce muttered.

Jolene marched up to Bruce. "Stop talking about me like I'm not even here." Whirling around, she confronted Rachel. "I hate you. I never wanted you to marry my dad. Look what you've done! You ruined my life."

"Jolene!" Bruce had taken all he could from his daughter. Rising to his feet, he clasped the girl's shoulders and turned her to face him. "You will apologize to Rachel. I won't have you speaking to her that way."

Jolene glared back at him, her eyes flashing with defiance. His own anger simmered just below the surface. He'd been stupid and blind. Jolene and her malicious jealousy had driven a wedge between Rachel and him.

"What Jolene said is true." Rachel surprised him by siding with the girl. "I *am*

505

pregnant and now there's another person to consider in this equation. Jolene doesn't want this baby any more than she wants me in her life."

"Now just a minute." Bruce needed to make it clear that despite his daughter's attitude *he* wanted this baby.

"It's fine. I understand —"

"You understand what?" he asked.

"To paraphrase you, when Jolene said you don't need me, you basically told her you're stuck with me because I'm pregnant."

How she'd arrived at that conclusion, Bruce would never know. "I didn't say anything like that!"

"I heard you, and frankly, neither one of you made any effort to hide your conversation from me."

"Does that mean you're going to leave?" Jolene asked, eyes wide with feigned innocence.

Bruce was quick to answer. "Definitely not. Rachel's staying here, where she belongs."

Jolene's shoulders slumped forward. "Daddy, let her go. We *don't* need her."

"Jolene's right," Rachel confirmed. "And as she's said more times than I can count, I've come between the two of you and ruined everything."

Jolene's eyes blazed with triumph. "See! Even Rachel admits it."

"*I* need you," Bruce argued, ignoring his daughter's outburst. "Our baby needs you."

"I agree," Rachel said far too easily. "Our baby does need me. He or she needs me to live in a stress-free environment. This child also has to know he or she is loved and wanted by this family."

"I love our baby," Bruce insisted.

"I think it would be best if I left," Rachel said firmly, as if anything he said, any opinions he held, shouldn't be taken into account.

"No." Again, Bruce's response was quick and automatic. This wasn't what he wanted. Rachel was actually suggesting she move out. None of this seemed real . . . or right.

"I think it would be best if you left, too," Jolene chimed in, sounding gleeful at the prospect of getting rid of her stepmother.

"That's not going to happen," Bruce said heatedly.

Rachel just smiled. "Do you plan to hold me captive?"

"No." Bruce couldn't believe it had come to this. "You don't mean it. Rachel, tell me you aren't really going to walk away."

A sad, defeated look came over her. "I can't continue like this. All the fighting and stress isn't good for the baby and it isn't good for me. Jolene is anxious to be rid of me and I don't have the energy to fight her anymore — not when I have to do it alone."

"Okay, you're right. I made a mistake," he said. "Maybe I should've taken a more active role in this . . . this conflict between you, but I was afraid if I intervened it would only aggravate the situation. I don't know . . ."

"Well, *I* know," Jolene yelled. "Get Rachel and that baby out of here."

Bruce's patience had reached its limit. He pointed to the hallway. "Go to your room. Rachel and I need privacy to talk this out."

"No." Jolene stamped her foot. "You can't keep me out of this. I have a right to my say, too."

"Go to your room! Now."

His daughter seemed about to argue, but then shrugged and marched out of the room.

Bruce waited until Jolene had disappeared before he spoke again. "Let's talk about this."

Rachel's eyes revealed pain and disappointment. "I'm not sure what there is to talk about. I can't live like this, Bruce. I love you and Jolene, but I think we can both say we made a mistake."

"No." Bruce refused to see their marriage that way. Okay, he'd admit it; he'd made more than his share of blunders. He should've done more to reassure his daughter and to support his wife. Perhaps he'd been naive to assume that Jolene would be as thrilled about Rachel's pregnancy as he was. He'd hoped she'd be excited. That seemed a vain, foolish hope now. . . .

"What if we went to family counseling?" he said desperately. "We could see someone at the clinic or . . . or Pastor Flemming or —"

"It's too late. And as you told me before, Jolene won't go anyway."

"But . . ."

"I'm leaving, Bruce," Rachel said simply. "Please don't try to persuade me otherwise."

That had been his intention, but seeing the determination in her eyes, he knew it would do no good. "Where will you go?" he asked, feeling defeated.

"A friend offered me a place to live until I can make other arrangements."

"Teri?"

"A friend," she repeated.

"For how long?" he asked. "How long will you be gone?"

She took her time answering. "I don't

know yet."

"One week?"

"Longer."

"Two weeks?"

She shook her head.

"A month?" She couldn't possibly intend to stay away an entire month. He couldn't bear it.

"I . . . I can't answer that."

It hit him then that she might not ever come back. The realization stunned him. "This . . . this is what you want?" he asked.

Tears filled her eyes. "I never dreamed it would end like this."

"Me, neither." He sat up straighter. "Will you keep in touch, let me know how you are, where you are?"

She didn't immediately agree. "Okay," she finally said. "I'll phone you."

In other words, she wasn't willing to give him her contact information. Still, if that was all she'd offer him, he'd take it. The alternative was too harsh to even think about.

"I'll leave in the morning," she said, and started to walk away.

Bruce caught her hand. "Give Jolene time. Please. She'll come around."

"No, I won't." His daughter's voice rang down the hallway.

Despite the seriousness of the moment, Rachel smiled. "She's always had the best hearing of anyone I've ever known."

Bruce smiled, too, remembering the early days of their marriage when they'd self-consciously tried to hide the fact that they were lovers from his daughter. In retrospect it had been ridiculous. They weren't fooling anyone, certainly not Jolene.

"I'm sorry, Bruce," she whispered.

"I am, too." It occurred to him that she might need help. "You'll call if you need anything, right? You'll keep in touch?" he asked again. He'd go mad if she didn't. He couldn't believe he was actually letting her walk out the door, not knowing where she intended to live or how long she'd stay away. This wasn't supposed to happen. Not to Rachel and him.

"I'll be in touch," she promised.

"Can I hold you?"

She considered his request, tears brightening her eyes, then slowly nodded.

Wrapping his arms around her, Bruce held her close, savoring the feel of her in his arms. "I don't know if I can let you go," he whispered into her hair. "Don't," he said again. "Please don't do this."

Her shoulders buckled in a sob. "This isn't what I want, either, but I don't see any other alternative."

"We'll make it work," he said urgently. "We *can*."

"I thought we could, too, but I was wrong." She disentangled her arms and stepped away from him. "Like I told you earlier, I'm afraid all this stress is hurting the baby. . . . This is something I need to do for me and for our child."

"But —"

"Please don't make this any harder than it already is."

Although it felt as if his chest was about to cave in, Bruce nodded. "All right, go if you have to, but know that I'll be here waiting when you're ready to come back." Reaching out, he stroked her cheek and a tear ran down her face onto his hand.

Leaning toward her, Bruce kissed Rachel goodbye. His heart pounded with fear that this might be the last time he ever kissed his wife.

# ABOUT THE AUTHOR

**Debbie Macomber,** author of the number one *New York Times* bestsellers *74 Seaside Avenue, 8 Sandpiper Way,* and *92 Pacific Boulevard,* as well as *A Cedar Cove Christmas, Summer on Blossom Street,* and *Twenty Wishes,* has become a leading voice in women's fiction worldwide. Her work has appeared on every major bestseller list, including those of the *New York Times, USA TODAY,* and *Publishers Weekly.* She is a multiple award winner, and she won the 2005 Quill Award for Best Romance. More than one hundred million of her books have been sold worldwide. For more information on Debbie and her books, visit her Web site, www.DebbieMacomber.com.

The employees of Thorndike Press hope you have enjoyed this Large Print book. All our Thorndike, Wheeler, and Kennebec Large Print titles are designed for easy reading, and all our books are made to last. Other Thorndike Press Large Print books are available at your library, through selected bookstores, or directly from us.

For information about titles, please call:
   (800) 223-1244

or visit our Web site at:
   http://gale.cengage.com/thorndike

To share your comments, please write:
   Publisher
   Thorndike Press
   295 Kennedy Memorial Drive
   Waterville, ME 04901